DAUGHTER
OF THE
SALT KING

DAUGHTER

OF THE

SALT KING

A. S. THORNTON

CamCat
Books

CamCat Publishing, LLC
Brentwood, Tennessee 37027
camcatpublishing.com

This is a work of fiction. Names, characters, places, and incidents are either products of the author's imagination or are used fictitiously.

Hardcover ISBN 9780744303919
Paperback 9780744300499
Large-print Paperback 9780744303537
Ebook 9780744300505
Audiobook 9780744300512

Library of Congress Control Number: 2020949407

Cover and book design by Maryann Appel
Map illustration by Rebecca Farrin
Audiobook narrated by Vaneh Assadourian

5   3   1   2   4

For C,

Whether my first or my last,

it will always be for you.

1

KHALAD
—◆—
CREATION

There was an immense tree that gave strong wood and sweet fruit. The goddess Masira thought, This tree makes life too easy. Man grows weak. She tore it from the ground and shook out its roots, spilling grains of sand and drops of water. From the sand, Eiqab was born. From the water, Wahir.

She was fascinated by her Sons and grew so possessive over them, she desired that none else should have Sons of their own.

From this point forward, Masira said, there shall be no more trees that give life. And so, the desert was born.

The Sons were exhausted by the world's bleakness and angered by the weak people who caused it.

Mother is right, Eiqab said, People must be made hard from a hard life. So Eiqab crafted a great light above his head, so hot the ground desiccated beneath his feet. Now, Eiqab said, the people will suffer as they deserve.

Seeing his brother's searing light and dried earth, Wahir was repulsed. He said, Mother, Brother, man cannot live in the world you have made, and cruelty will not lead to strength. He stepped through the sand, and in his footsteps, people found cool water and a respite from the sun under the small trees that grew there. Seeing how man swaddled his body in cloth to protect himself from Eiqab's light, Wahir fashioned a dark sky and pale light that split the world so that they would have cool nights to break from the day.

Masira watched her Sons and saw that they were both right. She was satisfied, for her Sons were of her spirit, and she proclaimed all living things, but man most of all, shall likewise be of both light and dark.

—Excerpt from the *Litab Almuq*

1

T HESE CARDS WERE WORN to fatigue like everything we had, and I cradled them with my fingers, the better to keep them secret from my sisters. Three cards lay on the ground between us, awaiting mine—the last. The images had long ago begun to fade, so I surveyed them carefully before making my next move: a spider in a glistening web, a buzzard above its carrion, a vessel of fire.

I looked back to the cards in my hand, and a greedy smile spread across my face. Next to the others, I placed a golden eagle soaring beside a blue moon. My sisters groaned.

I had won, again.

"Praise Eiqab for this embarrassment of riches!" I held out my hand, and they dropped their chipped glass beads and cowries into my palm. The cards were collected and shuffled while I added the tokens to my pile, now the largest. My smile widened as I picked up my new hand.

There was a rush of air and shock of sunlight as the tent's entrance was pulled open. Our attendant, arriving just as I won, of course. I huffed and turned to her, waiting to see whom she would call so we could return to our game.

"Emel, come." She did not look at me. She tossed my name at the twenty-six of us who sat inside—daughters of the Salt King, my full and half-sisters—and disappeared behind the fabric that sealed the entrance.

Sons, I was not prepared to hear my name. My heart quickened, and like the sand of an hourglass, dread filled me. I had hoped the suitor would choose one of my sisters so I would not have to endure another failed courting—to face lengthy preparation before an evening of pretense, only to conclude in a morning soaked with failure. Then again, a suitor was the only answer to my wish for escape. Sighing, I set down the limp cards.

"Open that tent back up, eh?" Pinar called to the guards outside. "We could provide drink for the gods if you collected our sweat!" She wiped at her hair, a wet lattice on her forehead.

"Store it in silver bottles and perhaps Father could sell that for dha, too," Tavi muttered under her breath.

The request would go unanswered. We were not allowed to draw open the tent, lest palace visitors glimpse us in our home. We were the Salt King's most protected jewels. The mythical ahiran, whom powerful men from across the desert came to bed and, if satisfied, carry home astride their camels. Each daughter married was another jackal leashed. Father's reign strengthened every time he transformed a would-be contender into a son.

I pushed my winnings to the center of our circle with shaking hands, the pile spilling.

"Better to end when the sun is high. Let's all remember that I was the winner, eh?" I stood slowly.

"Good luck tonight," Raheemah said as she divided my prize among the remaining players. My sisters watched me go. Some mumbled under their breath, wishing they had been chosen in my stead.

"If you aren't choking on his dagger, you aren't doing it right," Pinar said. The girls giggled from their sand-strewn mats. My lips twitched.

"If he talks too much, just shove those udders in his face," Kadri added, "Or your kuz."

Riotous laughter now. Even I succumbed. "Quiet!" I hissed. "You'll get us all in trouble." My sisters fanned themselves with the corners of thin blankets as they bantered about the best bedding techniques, ignoring me.

I lifted a dark wool abaya from the basket and patted sweat from my brow with its embroidered edge. The intricate designs marked us as belonging to the King, but the tattered and fraying hems revealed, to the keen observer, our worth.

I shook my head at my sisters' ribaldry, but I was grateful for their distractions.

"Maybe this time you can get him to request you for a second night?"

My smile disappeared at Sabra's bitter words. She always found a place to sink her stinger. I did not acknowledge her and pulled the cloth quickly over my head so that my amber-dyed fustan was completely covered. I tied a threadbare black veil over my hair. The setting sun sizzled outside of the tents. Though our walk would be short, the sun punished those who did not protect themselves from its glare.

My attendant waited for me outside. The veil covering her face did not conceal her disapproval as she listened to the advice my sisters were still hollering through the fabric walls.

An adolescent boy, as swathed as the attendant beside him, was more discomfited by the obscenities. He shifted his weight from side to side, absently brushing his fingers against the hilt of his rusted scimitar. He was one of my many half-brothers. He was also my guard. Our eyes met. His shoulders tensed, and I quickly looked away. Make no mistake, he was not there to protect me from others.

I nodded to the pair. "Hadiyah. Bahir. Shall we?"

Hadiyah strode away with a huff, her robes billowing like clouds behind her. Indecent shrieks and groans emerged from behind me now. I looked back to my tent. Beside the entrance, two guards' eyes watered and shoulders shook with mirth.

WE WALKED briskly through the narrow path between rows of palace tents. Bahir trailed close behind me, his chest puffed and chin raised high.

The servants' homes were held open with thick camel's hair rope, in hopes that the wind would find ingress to carry away the heat. Goats were spun over fires, milk poured into big vats for cheese, and pots set out to harden in the sun. Servants called to one another, shoving reels of fabric into each other's arms or dousing the flames of the smelting fires with sand. The flurry and sounds of the palace collided around us. All for the Salt King.

My stomach turned on itself as we walked, my nerves a pestle to my insides as I prepared for my role in the King's court. I envied the servants in that moment—how simple their lives must be, to roast or weave or hew, then be done for the day. Sure, there was no great glory, but too, there was no great risk. And security, a clear future, was favorable to my unknown.

The servants looked up from their work as I passed, carefully positioned between my attendant and guard. This procession, the embroidered clothes on my back, revealed what I was, and they knew what awaited me. Did they watch me, thinking of my past failures? I'm sure they laughed behind my back—a waste of time for the King. I was to be a "forever ahira," until I was twenty-three and thrown into the streets as used and useless as the playing cards.

A little girl ran from her home into the path, shrieking with laughter, chased by two boys not much older. A red birthmark trailed from her eyebrow to the edge of her lip. I remembered when she was born, how I had thanked Eiqab I was not cursed with the same mark upon my skin. But now, I saw that it was she who was lucky. The trio whipped past Hadiyah, who grunted in disapproval, before they flew past me and further down the lane. A laughing woman emerged from the tent behind them, and upon seeing us, fell to her knees.

"Forgive me, forgive them," she mumbled over and over, brow pressed to her clasped hands.

Bahir barked at her, his boy's voice suddenly harsh like a man's. A bird cried out as it soared above us in the purpling sky. Oh to be that bird.

Finally, we arrived at a large tent the color of sunrise—the zafif—where I was to be prepared. I followed Hadiyah in, leaving Bahir to stand guard outside. It was time.

Scents of crushed roses and warm honey met my nose. Attendants in flowing, colorful fustan stood from cushions and thick mattresses at my arrival. They rushed to greet us as Hadiyah whisked off her coverings, revealing braided graying hair and a camel-colored dress, which I eyed enviously. Because she was a servant, her clothes were simpler than mine— no bright patterns nor embellishments that signified she belonged only in the palace. She could go anywhere in those.

Hadiyah's eyes softened when she smiled—the stern charade had been cast off with her abaya and veil.

"Beauty." She smoothed the hair from my face. "It's been too long." Her hand moved down my back. She tapped my bottom and winked. "You should listen to your sisters; they give good advice." She walked off and began fussing with the various jars and vessels they would need to ready me that evening, calling over her shoulder. "This will be your husband, I just know it. Eiqab has given many signs today."

"Did you see the clouds on the horizon this morning? They were so dark, perhaps promising rain," Adilah said.

"And the vultures that circled the bazaar," another attendant added. "There were three. One who searched for his mate." The women trailed off, discussing the good omens bestowed on us that day. Of course, I had seen none—ahiran were forbidden from leaving the palace.

Their hope smoothed my unease, but still, the pressure of the evening was too great to smile, the knot in my chest too tight to speak. I had met the suitor that afternoon at the courting where he surveyed my sisters and me like a meal to be savored. He was stiff and proud, and when he finally spoke to me, even his curious accent was not intriguing enough for me to take interest. Evidently, I had played my role well. He'd chosen me tonight.

Hadiyah saw my face and banged her open hand against the copper basin, a loud ringing startling us all.

"Well, come on then! The prince needs more than a hand to keep him company."

I slipped off my sandals and flexed my toes into the soft, woven rug before I went to the jasmine-scented water.

The water's surface rose to my neck as I lowered myself into the bath. The pain in my chest eased as I relaxed against the basin wall, my shoulders falling back. I listened to the attendants' gossip, their words a calming cadence as I closed my eyes.

Then, "A runner arrived today."

My eyes flew open.

"The caravan arrives tomorrow," the attendant continued excitedly.

"From where?" I asked.

"Emel," Hadiyah warned as she scrubbed my skin.

The woman pursed her lips. "North, I think."

North! Hoping she was right, I mused about what and who the caravan might be bringing. Hadiyah dunked a bowl full of water over my head. I sat forward, sucking in a startled breath.

"Look at you. A woman of the court." She emphasized the last words. "I remember when you were just a girl." She took my hand to clean under my nails. "You were so excited when you were requested the first time."

"Must you remind me?" My free hand covered my eyes.

"You talked and talked about what kind of wife you would be for him and how you would please him. Where has that girl gone? Now you want to talk of salt trade and politics." She tutted disapprovingly and pulled my hand from my face to clean that one, too.

"I was naive. Not such a fool now."

"You weren't a fool," Hadiyah said. "You were smart, focusing only on that which affected you." She narrowed her eyes at me. I bit my tongue as she continued. "And you were hopeful, too. As you should be still."

It was true. I was not yet finished as an ahira, with over a year left before my father would cast me out. There was still a chance a man would choose me for a wife, still a chance I would finally leave the palace. But finding hope was difficult when it was buried beneath the rejections of dozens of suitors who had come before. Perhaps I'd have better luck if I doused flame with salt.

What was it they saw to make them turn from me every time? I looked at my knuckles. Too boney? My palms. Too many lines? Or did they see that I did not want them? That I only wanted what they could offer me, that I only wanted to be free from the palace?

When my bath finished, my skin dry, Hadiyah brought me a large goblet of wine. I consumed it dutifully, barely tasting it.

An attendant waved a fan of palm fronds toward me as I lay back onto the feather-stuffed mattress. I shivered beneath the breeze.

"Thank you," I sighed. I wanted to stay there forever, never feeling heat again.

The wine hit me swiftly, and the world began to shimmer and spin. I closed my eyes and smiled lazily as my worries began to recede. A sharp burn splashed against my thigh and my eyes flew open. Hot honey wax. With a terrible rip, it was removed. I clenched my teeth and my eyes watered. It was repeated again and again and again.

"You need a stronger drink," Hadiyah grunted when the women finished. She mixed two liquids in a curving vessel and decanted it into a small goblet. Arak. It smelled of anise and looked like camel's milk. My father's favorite spirit could unsteady even the strongest carouser. I sipped it slowly, disliking its bitter taste but needing it to soothe me. I knew with it, I would perform better. The world twisted and tilted.

"Stay still," Hadiyah put her hands on my shoulders to stop my swaying. Hadn't the world been moving under my feet? My hair was braided as she held me, kohl was lined around my eyes.

"He will want to devour you whole," Adilah said as rose-scented oil was smoothed into my skin.

"And I will let him," I purred, touching a droplet of the oil and pressing it to the bow of my upper lip.

I stumbled when I stood, Hadiyah's quick hands holding me up. "Careful."

An unblemished, diamond-studded garment of shining green silk was taken from a copper box. Besides the jewels that decorated our necks and wrists, it was the nicest thing an ahira would wear. All loans from our father for courtings only. Strings pulled at my back, tightening the clothes onto my breasts and hips until I could take deep breaths no longer.

Soft slippers cocooned my feet. Hadiyah placed my headpiece, from which hung delicate chains that veiled my mouth and jawline and tickled my skin.

"Everything sparkles, and I sparkle, too," I slurred as I gazed at my reflection on the basin-water's surface. The attendants sighed in admiration.

Hadiyah said, "How can he say no to a beauty like you?" Then whispered into my ear, "Don't spoil anything by talking of that which doesn't concern you, and you will be sealed into marriage."

There it was again. Marriage. Like a hook, it pulled back all of my dread, my fear of failure.

"The Buraq?" I searched around the room for that which I knew would help.

Adilah rushed to a table to collect a tarnished silver tray. Hadiyah worked efficiently with the metal instruments there—igniting, scooping, adjusting. I watched, entranced by the deftness of her hands. She held out a curved pipe, and I slipped it between the strands of my veil, seating it between my lips. Tasting the tang of metal, I leaned over the lamp until the dried petals burned. Hungrily, I inhaled.

Charred honey filled my mouth, filled my lungs. The burning desert rose was named after Buraq, the winged steed of legends, for its effects on the mind. The one who inhaled the rose would feel light enough to fly. I gulped in the smoke, eyes closed, clutching the pipe like it was my only tether to the world.

"Take me to him," I said when I was finished.

"Good girl," Hadiyah said, her hand rubbing my back. "Can't take your pride into those halls. Best to leave it here with us."

Alcohol swirled in my blood; smoke spun in my chest. I floated inches above the ground. This suitor was my only chance out. I could not let my fears and worries of failure tarnish my performance. Tipping up my chin, I left the zafif and strode into the palace.

I was an emerald goddess and ahira of the Salt King.

And I would find my freedom.

MY STEPS were silent in the hallway. Only the chink, chink of the chains hanging from my clothes could be heard as I staggered through the narrow corridors, trailing the guard.

Mesmerized by the torch flames that danced in the air, the patterned carpets that covered the sand, and the pristine fabric walls that towered above me, I took slow, unsteady steps. I was within the opulent heart of the palace, the King's tents. It was the most heavily guarded, entered only by wealthy visitors and royalty.

Holding my arms out to the side, I spun in the hallway, pretending to be a bird flying through the sky. I was a kite with green feathers soaring above the tall, white peaks of Father's tents. Circles of servants' quarters and workrooms surrounded Father's private chambers.

I imagined how it would appear on a map. How *did* maps get made if people could not fly? I stopped to consider this seriously. Birds were somehow involved. I strutted around like a walking bird, a map-making bird. I giggled.

The guard whipped his head around. "Sons be damned," he muttered. "Stop that!" He stopped and reached his hand toward me. I backed away from his grasp.

The drunken fantasies fell away. "Forgive me," I mumbled. I took measured steps forward, now using my arms only for balance.

We entered a soaring room that glowed golden from its glinting metal lanterns. Servants waved palm fronds toward the center. The softly moving air sent the fires into violent fits that demanded my attention.

"Not bad!" boomed the King. I jumped at the sound and tore my gaze from the flames. My father sat upon an immense gilded throne, peering at the goblet in his hand as he licked his lips. "They said they'd be bringing more?"

"Twenty bottles, and if you found this to your liking, you get first pick before they're sent to the bazaar," Nassar, my father's vizier, said from his seat at a small table nearby.

My father took another long drink. He was not a large man, but in that chair, he was tremendous. Heaps of white crystalline granules and stacked gray slabs surrounded him.

Salt. His wealth displayed so all who visited could see the worth of their ruler. It was why the caravans came, and what the rest of the desert needed so desperately. The Salt King was the only one who had it.

Neither he nor Nassar acknowledged me, though I now stood before them. They continued their conversation about the runner that Nassar met earlier in the day and what the caravan promised to supply. Father nodded absently, tapping his goblet until Nassar filled it again. Finally, as if an afterthought, he turned to me. I stared at his feet, willing the world to stop its revolutions, and knelt before the Salt King.

"My King," I said, sweetening my voice. I pressed my forehead to the rug, my palms flat on the ground. Tightly closing my eyes, I stretched my arms in front of me, slowly reaching until I felt it: the edge of a salt pile.

Moving slowly so I wouldn't be seen, I pushed my fingertips into the heap until the coarse salt swallowed them.

"Very good. Up," Father said, bored.

I curled my fingers and scooped the fine crystals into my palm. Standing, I raised my eyes to him slowly. His white, silk-lined boots had rubies that sparkled at the end of curling toes. The folds of his red and ivory robes cascaded around his large belly. A long beard draped from his face of deep, waxy creases. His black eyes—the eyes we shared—were yellowed from life at a decanter. He stared at me with furrowed brow.

Cold panic swept through me, washing away the liquor, and I dropped my gaze to the ground, chewing my cheek behind the veil. Had he seen my theft?

"Aashiq will be pleased with her." The vizier's voice dripped with honey. I nodded toward Nassar, but Sons, I wanted to spit on his silk slippers.

The King set the goblet on the table and dabbed sweat from his face with his handkerchief. "They are never pleased," he said. His thick bejeweled fingers twirled the fabric, his long nails snagging the threads as he leaned back in his chair. The accusation in his gaze was quickly replaced with apathy.

So he did not see me steal his salt, he simply wanted to remind me of my inadequacy. Of course. I stopped grinding my cheek between my teeth.

"Aashiq's time has begun," the King said, gesturing to the tall hourglass whose narrow stream of sand was just beginning to fill the base. "But your own time is short, Emel. If he is not satisfied when I speak to him tomorrow, I will urge him to request one of your sisters and not waste further time with you. No doubt with another, he will find his wife."

One night? My heart sank. If the suitor desired it, I could have three nights to show how I would be a suitable wife. If my father convinced him to choose someone else after the first night, there would be no hope for me.

Nassar butted in, flailing his hands. "When you have had such successes with your other daughters, we must ask if perhaps it is not the sire, but the dam."

Anger burned through the rest of my high. I collected bloodied spit in my mouth, rolling it between my cheeks, imagining a life where I could really do it. Where I could reach his feet from where I stood, damn all the consequences.

"It is no flaw of mine, of that I am sure." The King waved his hand toward his vizier, keeping his gaze on me. "Emel, let me remind you that these men are threats to our home. Weak ones, sure. I could destroy their settlements if I wanted. But what good would that do me? Your mother will be so ashamed if two of her daughters fail. Sabra? Well." He shrugged, dismissing her so casually, even I felt stung. "You're almost what, two and twenty? I cannot bear the thought of throwing such a beautiful bird out to the foxes." He pouted and looked down at his sash, from which several blades and trinkets hung. Carefully, he detached a glass vessel wrapped in golden bands.

I said, "I will try harder. I will not disappoint you or Mother." I pressed my hands together and took a step toward my father.

He paid me no more attention, distracted by the vessel he held in his palm. Inside, tarnished gold smoke churned lazily with nowhere to escape. His eyes followed the billows and swirls of the smoke possessively. I followed his gaze. I could not deny its allure as I, too, was entranced by its beautiful movement. Even Nassar peered at it curiously. My father was never without the thing, and I did not let myself linger on the thought that my father found wine and a trinket more worthy of his attention than his own daughter.

Tearing his gaze from the vessel, he said, "Aashiq is from a strong family. He would be an asset to me, and it is your duty to secure him. Eiqab has blessed you by allowing you to share his bed tonight. Do not squander this gift." He waved his hand to dismiss me and rose, unsteadily. Nassar jumped up to support him.

"Isra!" My father shouted, and with Nassar at his side, left the tent, a train of slaves at his heels. His absence sent a ripple of relief through me, and my shoulders fell forward as I waited.

A woman entered the room, and I turned eagerly toward her. Her flowing dress, fastidiously decorated with bright stripes and zig-zagging lines, barely concealed the curves she had acquired as a mother and a wife. She held her head high, the coins and colored beads on her beautiful veil—the veil of a king's wife—glinting as she approached. I mirrored her strong posture. The kohl lining her eyes swept up to her temples. The corners of her mouth pulled up into a tight smile, as if secrets were waiting to tumble from her lips.

"Mama!" I ran to her.

She stepped forward, arms stretched wide, and we collided. Frankincense clung to her hair and clothes.

"You're lovely." Her fingers pressed the jewels on my head, my hips, passed over the skin of my arms, my shoulders. Her touch lingered on the metallic veil that covered my mouth. "And, how are you?" She asked with eyebrows raised. A test.

"I am much better now—"

"You do not sound sincere," she interrupted. "Try harder."

"Mama . . ."

"I am trying to help. Don't get mad at your mother."

"This is pointless," I spat. "It isn't my fault they don't choose—"

"I don't want to fight. I just want . . ." She hesitated and closed the distance between us. "For you to be wed—to get out of here." She said it quickly and quietly into my ear. To any guard it would have seemed as though she had simply pressed her cheek to mine. She stepped back, "Are you ready to meet him?"

"Of course." I squeezed the salt in my left fist more tightly.

She put her arms around my shoulders and pulled me close, her scent surrounding me.

"Be your very best tonight, Emel." I did not understand the plea I heard in her words. Why did she seem a touch more desperate to see me gone than before? Had she heard that Father was allowing me only one night with Aashiq?

I pulled away, not wanting to hear more when I seemed destined to fail. Unable to meet her eyes, I dropped my gaze to the golden medallion she always wore around her neck.

She grasped my shoulders one last time, taking in every detail, then she said, "Show him why he must take you home."

POURING THE salt into a leather pouch I hid beneath the beaded fabric on my hips, I followed the guard. He led me through the palace until we came upon the private courting tent.

"He waits," the guard said and parted the entrance.

I pushed out my chest, lifted my chin, and stepped into the dimly lit space.

"You're here," Aashiq said, stepping on his robe as he stood in a rush. I maintained my composure. Most suitors did not feel the need to acknowledge our arrival with such fuss.

He continued with an apologetic shrug, "I have been waiting so long, I am afraid I've drunk almost all the wine." His accent had been notable at the courting, but now, slurred with drink, it was enchanting. I wondered what life was like where he was from, but I promised Hadiyah I would not ask of such things.

I bowed. "My apologies for keeping you waiting. It takes time to prepare for a muhami such as yourself." I spread compliments like oil.

"Let me pour you a drink," he said. Maybe it was the wine, or maybe it was being away from the piercing stare of the King, but now, Aashiq seemed more at ease, less proud. He turned back to the table where two goblets sat by a silver decanter, but I grabbed his arm. I trailed my fingertips down the sleeve of his robes to his hand where he held his pipe.

"I would rather put my mouth on this," I whispered, taking his pipe and placing it between my lips. I inhaled the sweet honey smoke, feeling a rush of warm air beneath my feet.

"Ah, well . . ." He watched me warily. "May I remove that?" He asked of the metal veil.

"Aashiq, you may do whatever you please."

He reached over with clumsy fingers and removed it. I closed my eyes while he did, the world swirling slightly as I leaned forward. The veil tangled in my hair and pulled sharply as it was detached. He tossed it onto a cushion. The sounds of the chains and jewels clattering against each other muted the instant they landed on the carpets.

"You are much more beautiful than your sisters," he said, "I could see as much this afternoon, and I see it again now."

"Is that why you chose me?" I asked.

"No. It was the way you watched your sisters and the servants. They held your attention so much better than I did. I had to know why." He smirked. "It is no wonder you have not been wed, if that was how you act around all of the suitors."

I pressed my lips together, wondering if he was right. Was that my problem all along? Could they all see that they were only a means to an end? Finally, I said, "Perhaps I have not found the right man."

"Perhaps it is me." He shrugged, and I saw that in his hesitance, he was as nervous as I.

Taking my hand, he guided me to the large bed in the center of the room. It was so soft, it took great effort to keep my eyes from drooping closed. We leaned against the pillows, and I faced him, eager to prove him wrong, to show him that I cared for him.

"Tell me of your family."

"I have two wives, Fadwa and Amani. They are older than you and have given me five children. Four sons and a daughter." As he told me of his family, he spoke so kindly, I found it was easy to listen, to watch his mouth move and face soften. "My daughter's eyes are like yours, black as night. She is a child of Eiqab." He seemed to stare at nothing, but certainly he saw her there beside him. "Always running without shoes, uncaring of the sand's heat." He smiled as he talked, laughing as he described his wild children. He loved his family tenderly. I imagined what it would be like to count myself among them. Would he love me as he loved his other wives? Would we have children who danced in the desert? A little girl who looked like me and ran across the ground with feet bare. Soon, I smiled with him, warming to his words. And to him.

"Are you comfortable?" I fingered the edges of his robes as I curled into him, wanting him to see he had my full attention.

He shrugged out of the robes. I helped, pushing them from his shoulders, deliberately sweeping my fingers over his chest and neck. I dropped my gaze to his mouth as I placed my hand on his thigh. I moved up to his hip.

He pitched forward and pressed his lips to mine.

His heat and scent of dusty, sweaty skin surrounded me. I closed my eyes and moved my mouth to match his as I was taught. His tongue was greedy, and I responded in kind. I hummed softly and reached for the bulge between his legs. He caressed my breast through the beading. I felt little at his touch, but moaned as I knew men liked. He broke free of my mouth and twisted his body so that he lay beneath me. His hands explored me in a clumsy effort, and I was reminded of the young muhamis I had bedded.

I pressed into him rhythmically, faster and harder, harder and faster.

"Perhaps you should . . . ?" He gestured to my clothes, breathing heavily.

I rose. With my back to him, I undressed methodically, seductively. When I turned to face him, he was already naked. I studied the man who would share my bed that night. His chest sagged and his belly bulged forward.

It mattered not how he appeared, only where he might take me. And if he treated me well, too, then I could not let him slip through my fingers.

I pulled him with me back onto the cushioned bed.

He clambered over me. His body was atop mine, elbows digging into the mattress beside my chest, his breath blowing in my face at quick bursts. I was grateful for the rose oil on my lip. He stabbed between my legs, attempting to find where he fit, and I tilted my hips to guide him.

When he found his place, he thrust firmly. I gasped and tossed my head back. Welcome, fresh air met my nose and mouth. He continued, grunting. Drops of sweat fell off of him and onto me. His pace quickened and his groans increased in frequency. I knew I performed my role satisfactorily when he found release. He cried out, I cried out. And it was done.

Aashiq said nothing and rolled to his side, scooting away until we no longer touched. My stomach turned and my mind spun. So that was it then? I counted my exhales, letting out my drunken, stupid hopes. Of course this man would be no different than the others. He would choose one of my sisters. They all would.

"It's all a bit awkward, isn't it?" Aashiq said after a long time passed.

I said nothing, unsure of what he wanted to hear. The bed shifted, and Aashiq rose, retrieving his clothes.

"Care for a walk?"

"We can't. I can't leave the palace." I sat up, watching him curiously.

"Through the palace then." He bent down and picked up my clothes, peering at the tangled chains and ties with alarm. He set them on the bed beside me. "Please, come."

I would follow because I had to, but I did so without hesitation, because something about this man was different than the others.

2

WHEN AASHIQ SAID HE WANTED to leave the tent with his ahira at his side, the guard's face creased with disapproval. It was an unconventional request. My suitor was again the man I saw at the courting—haughty and uncompromising. With a show of reluctance, the guard let us go, and he did not follow.

I stayed silent as I led us through the palace, waiting for Aashiq to explain his strange behavior. Wrapped in his robe that smelled of Buraq smoke, I imagined I was his wife and we were walking through our own home. He wanted to breathe the night air, he had said, so I led him to the edge of the palace where there was a gap in the surrounding date-palm fence. It was where we could slip through so that we could see the sky as it fell to the ground.

Silent, I sat beside Aashiq. He stared at the desert, nearly invisible in the moonless night, and I was comforted by his slow breaths. Though I was

exhausted, my mind spun with worries of how he felt about me. Had I not been enough? But he had wanted to walk with me. Surely that meant something?

Hadiyah's recollection of my first suitor slid through my thoughts, how different I had been then. In my fourteenth year, my hopes were sky-high. Everyone told me I would wed quickly. I would not be long in my father's court. Mama especially told me with glistening eyes how she couldn't wait for me to see the desert. My first muhami took me quickly. What man could resist a virgin girl? He did not request me again. Another sister, superior in every way—smaller hands, quieter steps, softer hair—left with him. I cried and cried to Hadiyah, vowing I would not fail again. I told Mama I would not disappoint my family once more. Aloud, I never said how unclean he made me feel. How it felt like a part of me left with him.

Dozens of suitors later I was an expert lover, but even so, I splintered with each bedding, each rejection. Though questions and self-doubt plagued me, still, I wished for them to come and take me away. Because after all, this was my fate, and whatever waited for me after marriage had to be better than this. Perhaps love was in my future, or at least a life of choices I could own.

I was an ahira and slave to my King. I would carry on until I bedded expertly and was wed or I was discarded by my father to live in squalor as a forsaken ahira. They were the only cards I held in my hand, so I had to choose the one that, at least, held hope.

"Emel?" From the light of the palace tents behind us, I could see him looking at me.

"Hmm?"

"What's this?" He pressed his finger against my cheek, against a tear.

He was again the hesitant, kind man who loved his family and home.

I wiped at my cheeks with my palms and shook my head. "Nothing. Drink makes me emotional, that's all."

"A distraction is what you need then." He took my hand in his, concern in his eyes. Without his turban, he appeared much younger. "My children say I am an excellent storyteller." He raised his eyebrows like a merchant selling spice for twice its value.

"I am no child who needs a story."

"You'll be sorry you missed it. It was a good one about a jinni and the child who found him." He threw his hands into the air, gesturing offense, and leaned back.

I scoffed playfully, eased by his light-heartedness despite myself. "I've heard all the stories of jinn."

"Ah, if you've heard them all, tell me one I don't know." He was teasing me now.

I narrowed my eyes. "I don't understand you."

"No, you don't." He took my hand in his and kissed my knuckles very seriously. His beard tickled my skin. "I am a complicated and mysterious man."

I couldn't help it. I laughed. Had I ever laughed with a suitor before? My hopes fluttered dangerously close to the fire.

He said, "Tell me a story of your home. Is there anything better to take from travels than a story? It can be shared again and again and won't weigh down my camel's back."

"The story of the Salt King then."

A large grin spread across his face, and his eager attention locked on me.

"The Salt King was born along the northeast trading route in a large settlement that traded ivory and gold for bricks of salt. He learned quickly that the greatest rulers were not dependent on the salt trade, and he knew the tales of the city where salt was not mined but found glistening on rocks."

"Bah!" Aashiq swung his hand through the air. "You mean the desert's edge?"

I nodded excitedly. "You've heard of it?"

"It's all legend. Fantasy. My people have spent our entire lives on camel-back. The desert doesn't end."

I shrugged. "Shall I continue, or will you tell me more about my story?" The words came out like they would have with my sisters. I bit my lip, fearing I'd been too harsh.

Aashiq waved me on, smirking. I relaxed.

"He set out to find what he knew must exist. Gradually, others joined him, also eager to find wealth. The people packed and unpacked their lives—hitching and unhitching their camels, moving their livestock, assembling and disassembling their homes—over and over again in search of salt."

"So your father started as a salt chaser. I didn't know that," Aashiq said, shaking his head.

"I hate that epithet. Isn't everyone, until they find it?" I lifted my chin, and he had the decency to look scolded. I softened my voice. "Their journeying stopped when they came upon an oasis."

"I can't wait to hear more of this oasis."

I shushed him.

"My apologies, princess."

"They came upon an oasis. It seemed like all others with the small patch of swaying trees that beckoned. An island of green amongst the sand." I spread my fingers and, in the air, painted the oasis with my hands. "My father went in to be the first to drink from the water—was it life-giving or life-taking? The people watched him disappear, praying that he would return.

"They waited through two sunrises, sure he had not survived the drink. At last, he was seen leaving. The King spoke with the guards who protected his path. Then, the guards turned toward the people, raised their swords high over their heads and pressed their blades into the sand. The journey had ended."

Aashiq cackled loudly. "That is very dramatic. Is that really how your father would end his travels? With a sword show?"

Pressing my hand to his lips, I turned to the palace tents behind us, ensuring no guards were nearby.

"Quiet! No opinions are secret behind cloth walls," I whispered. When he had settled, I continued. "The people reconstructed their homes, restarted their lives, and began anew, awaiting notice from their king of when they would travel again. When the nights grew longer and still the

King kept them there, questions were asked about why. What of the desert's edge? Did he care no longer?

"But the questions stopped when the King's wealth exploded. He had found it—salt. No one understood how he acquired it. There are no salt mines here, and salt can't be found from the sand. Where did it come from?" I paused, then whispered, "It must have been magic. Hidden in the watery heart of the oasis."

"Have you been there?" Aashiq asked.

I shook my head.

"Then I will tell you what lies in the oasis."

I leaned in close, keen to hear. He took a deep breath and looked over his shoulders before he said, "A salt mine." Laughing again, he planted his lips against my forehead. "What else could it be? Magic is not real, Emel! If your father has seemingly unlimited salt, it is from a mine. And if none are allowed in the oasis, surely that is what he hides."

I replied, "People have visited." Though indignant at his rejection of magic, my brow was still warm from his kiss. "They talk of palm fronds that collide, branches with thick leaves that brush together in the wind, a pool that sits in the shade. But I've heard no account of white burrows and trenches, nor of salt stacked in bricks."

"I saw the oasis when I arrived. Soldiers ensured I did not visit."

"Yes, only the King, his vizier, runners, and the villagers who collect our water are allowed."

"What do you think he protects if not a mine?"

I turned to him. "Am I to finish?"

He lay in the sand and laced his fingers behind his head. "I suppose."

"With my father's wealth came power, and the Salt King, as he quickly became known, attracted traders from across the desert. In the footsteps of traders came foreign aristocrats who sought political alliances and protection that only the Salt King's wealth could buy. Royals brought their sisters and cousins and daughters, hoping to secure valuable connections. Soon, the

King had seven, ten, eighteen wives, and the King was deemed the greatest and most formidable ruler the desert had ever seen. The thread from which legends are woven.

"Daughters and sons were born and born again. With his sons, the Salt King created an army. With his daughters, the Salt King created a court."

Our eyes met, and he turned away.

I said, "In the dawn of his rule, brave nomads attacked the village. Ambitious men who challenged the King, hoping to win his throne. No match for his scimitar, they were slain. Soon, the desert learned to fear the King's soldiers and his mythic power. The last challenger was almost ten years ago. I barely remember it." I only remembered my fear as my father faced the stranger—the man whom Mama had warned me I must accept as ruler should the King fall.

I continued. "Princes, nobles, and even kings began flocking to the Salt King's court looking to wed his daughters. The reputation of his power soon took second to that of his court, and more men sought to align themselves with the King whose might brought armed men to his side and women to their knees. The man who from the sand of the desert found the salt of tears."

"Very impressive." He stacked his bare feet and wiggled his toes.

"Aashiq!"

He laughed quietly. "Ah, forgive me, but I must admit, it pleases me to tease you." He leaned in. "Plus, the story is quite theatrical, is it not? You tell it like a wizened elder."

I harrumphed and leaned back as he did. "Can I ask you something?" The question burning in my mind the entire evening fought to pour from my lips, but Hadiyah's warning to mind only ahira matters echoed. "Where exactly are you from? My father said east, but your accent, I have not heard . . ."

"Very far east of here. Our settlement is much smaller than yours, but our oasis is much larger." Smug, he ran his fingers down his short beard. "And anyone can visit any time they please. The hottest days, half the village is in its water, I swear it."

Pulling his robe tight around me, I spun and found a place on the ground lit softly by the filtered torchlight.

"What are you doing?" Aashiq asked.

I held my finger to my lips and beckoned to him. He came dutifully, sitting beside me.

Whispering as I drew, I dragged my finger through the sand until I created the map I knew so well: the desert's salt trade, my home at the center of the routes. I pointed at the eastern lines and circles. "Where?"

"How do you know all this?" He said it quietly, but I heard the surprise in his voice. Worry clenched in my gut. Had I gone too far, revealed too much?

He leaned over and with his finger, drew a cross far along the eastern route, almost off my map. I asked him question after question, and he answered them all.

"Gold grows out the earth, it seems. We see so much, it's more plentiful than water. Yes, spices, too. The sand is painted yellow and orange after caravans come through. The winds are stronger, though, and we often have to move our settlement from the paths of shifting dunes." He drew smaller crosses on and off the routes, telling me of oases near him. Despite his proclamation that his people had been all over the desert, he knew little other than the east, but it enthralled me all the same.

"Emel," he said, tentatively, "how does my home sound to you?"

"It sounds much like mine, but smaller, as you said. Your oasis sounds nice."

"I mean, does my home sound like somewhere you would like to live?"

Fluttering erupted in my chest. "It does."

He smiled. "Because I think I would like to take you there."

"To visit?"

"No, not to visit. I have come to the Salt King's court to form an alliance with the King. I wanted more security for my family, my settlers, and our village. I hoped I would find a woman that would fit in well with my wives. I did not expect I would . . ." He stopped for a breath. "This is unorthodox—I know I should seek permission first from your father—but I would like to take you home with me. As my wife."

I stared at him, disbelieving what I heard. Triumph swelled in my chest, and my hopes flew to the flames. No, I realized, not to fire. To a promise of something good. To sanctuary—a cool hollow filled with water underneath shady trees.

"I would like that very much." A wide smile stretched across my face.

He took my hand into his again and looking into my eyes, he said, "Let me take you home to your sisters. Find sleep at their side. On my third evening, I will call you to me once again. Only that time, if your father allows it, it will be forever."

I did not walk home, I floated. And it was not because of the Buraq.

"BACK ALREADY?" Raheemah whispered groggily.

"Emah, it's almost morning. Go back to sleep," I said beaming, my cheeks aching.

Silently, I reached under my mat and collected my preciously guarded jar of ink and hollow reed and unrolled an equally well-protected parchment. In the gray dawn light, I could see just enough. I dipped the reed into the ink. Along the eastern trade route, I drew a tree with small waves beside it. Nestled beside the tree, I wrote a curving **Å**. I stared down at the map, following the trade routes that led to my home at the center. I looked at the marks where I had drawn the homes of other suitors—where an **ſ** was drawn in with a younger girl's hand. The settlement of my mother.

My gaze traveled to the edges of my map, and I frowned at the blank spaces. What else was there? Was it endless, as Aashiq said? His people had spent their entire lives on camelback. Maybe I would travel with them, too.

The ink dried, and I tucked everything under my mat again along with the small leather sack filled with salt. I stuffed a twisted blanket beneath my head. Raheemah's hand reached for me in her sleep. I clasped it in my own, knowing that it would be one of the last times I held it. Bringing her soft knuckles to my lips, I thought of saying goodbye to my sisters, to Hadiyah, to Mama. Tears stung my eyes.

But then I imagined my hand clasped around Aashiq's as we traveled back to his home, and the tears fell in relief. Finally, my time had come.

I AWOKE to murmuring sisters and the buzz of the palace—roosters singing at the sun, servants sending their children off to the market and greeting each other in the lanes, the clang of metal against metal as iron was forged. A ceramic jug of sweetened sage tea sat beside my mat along with a plate with a large piece of flatbread. Sitting up, I pulled the food and drink to my lap.

Raheemah saw me rise and came over.

"Tell me," she said eagerly.

I did not want them to know, not yet. So I sipped the tea to hide my joy. "He was quite kind." I gestured to the food and drink. "Thank you."

Raheemah stared expectantly.

"He did not hurt me, since I know you will ask. We talked at length. He told me of his home, and I told him of ours."

"Other wives?"

"Two." I added, conspiratorially. "Though you wouldn't know." Raheemah giggled, and I warmed at the sound.

"Do you think he will request you again?" Her eyebrows soared up her forehead. The suitor could use his three nights in the court how he pleased: with the same ahira, a different one, or sleep alone.

I looked down at my hands, remembering both my father's threat and Aashiq's promise. "I don't know . . ."

"You liked him."

"I did." I picked at my bread. He seemed a good man, and more importantly, he was going to be my escape from the palace.

"Then, we can have hope." Just as I was at her age, she was optimistic, seeing only the glistening promise of love.

Though Raheemah was born six years after me to a different mother, I was fiercely protective of her. She dreamed of becoming a wife and making our father proud. She would spend afternoons describing the embroidery and embellishments of her wedding veil, how she would dance for her husband the first night in his home, how she would oblige him—they were not my same dreams, but they were what made her happy. I knew that Raheemah's sincerity and innocence would soon get her married, and I feared not being here to see the man who chose her.

"How is Mama?" Tavi sat beside me, immediately taking my hair in her hands, brushing it through with her fingers until it was soft. Sabra lingered, watching, wanting to hear about our mother, too.

"She was worried about me, about all of us." I looked at my sisters. "She wants us to be wed, of course."

Sabra scoffed. "Doubt she thought of me once."

Tavi and Sabra were my full sisters. We had one full brother, a soldier now, who we saw infrequently. Sabra had the misfortune of inheriting most of her features—and personality—from our father. Very few suitors requested her, and those who did had not found that which they sought. If she received no proposal by the first day of her twenty-third year, she would be banished. With each day that passed, she grew more bitter, angrier, and as desperate as the desert before rain. Tavi was the only one who could stand to be around her.

"Don't say that," Tavi said, dropping my hair and turning to Sabra. "Mama wants the same for you that she wants for all of us."

"She's given up on me. But not Emel, no. Never the beautiful Emel. When is the last time she came to see me?" Sabra said it as if that proved everything.

I picked at my nails. This happened every time Mama was mentioned—I was the favorite because I was the most beautiful, and Mama loved Tavi because she was the youngest and still had promise, but oh, how Mama didn't care about Sabra.

"When is the last time you went to see her?" I said, unable to resist. "Sons, Sabra, I go to her all the time. She does not love me more; I just see her more often. If you want to wait around for whatever your impossible expectation is, then do it. But don't complain."

Tavi said, a little too brightly, "Why don't we go to her together? Later today, after midday meal, eh?"

There was silence as Sabra and I glared at each other. Spending my limited time with Sabra was the last thing I wanted to do, but my older sister nodded and said, "Mama would like that."

My shoulders dropped. If she agreed, then I had no choice. "The sounds nice, Tavi."

Tavi combed through my hair again, happiness weaving through her words like her fingers through my hair. "This will be great. Mama will love seeing all of us together."

I began picking at my fingers again. Raheemah reached over and used her hand to separate mine. "So tell me," Raheemah pressed quietly, "what did you wear?"

Grateful for the change in direction, I told my sisters, whose dewy faces had turned toward me. "Oh, that one is my favorite!" one exclaimed as I shared details of the outfit Hadiyah had chosen for me.

"Emerald pales you," Sabra said from across the room. She pretended to fuss with her weaving threads, but her eyes kept flicking up to mine, and her mouth murmured words I could not hear.

Tavi exhaled.

"Well, I certainly think Aashiq will propose," Raheemah announced, clapping her hands together.

"We will see," I said, still scowling at Sabra.

I took a long drink of the sage tea, trying to rekindle the excitement I had felt moments before. It did not take much, as I realized that by leaving the palace, I would also be leaving Sabra. Bless Eiqab for the gift of Aashiq.

3

THE MIDDAY HORN'S LOW BLARE sounded through the settlement. Some of my sisters rose to go to the rama—sun-scorched sand in the palace where they could pray to Eiqab. The longer they held their palms and brow to the ground, the more likely the god would hear their prayers.

"How about praying," Tavi said loudly to the backs of the ahiran that exited the tent, "for our damn meal. I hope whoever's bringing our food doesn't stop to gossip on the way. She should know I'm starved after someone," she peered pointedly at one of the girls' backs, "ate more than her share this morning."

"I hope Aashiq requests you again tonight," Raheemah said as she splashed her face with the browned basin water.

It needed to be thrown out, but we would keep that basin until the air had sucked it dry. Then, maybe, we'd get another bowl of fresh water to

clean. Our father's small charity for being an ahira was the luxurious baths we received before the suitor.

"He said he might wait until the third night before he makes a decision," I said. Raheemah appeared so stricken by the notion, I changed the subject. "A caravan arrives today, so maybe the attendant will tell us of a new muhami, eh? You could have your chance."

Raheemah gazed dreamily at nothing, a lazy smile playing on her lips.

Tavi groaned. "Hope not. I want to eat until I look like I'm with child." She held her hands before her belly. "No chains are fitting around my waist tonight if we're to go to court."

The tent entrance was peeled open. A young woman peered in. "Nothing, girls."

"Eiqab answered my prayers!" Tavi rubbed her palms together. "Let there be stacks of bread so tall, they're charred by the sun." She turned to me. "Wait, Emel. Let's eat first. Then we can go see Mama."

Already standing, I had retrieved my sack of salt and was moving to get dressed, having forgotten my promise to Tavi and Sabra. "Oh . . ." I hesitated. So eager to please Tavi, I wasn't thinking when I agreed earlier. "See, I forgot about the caravan."

Tavi narrowed her eyes. "It won't take long," she lowered her voice, "and it's a chance to mend things. For all of us." She did not need to say *before Sabra is gone forever.*

Holding the leather sack firmly in my hand, I grimaced. "Caravan, Tavi. You know I can't miss it." A caravan's arrival was one of the biggest events in the settlement, and I loved seeing the people and the things they carried from other parts of the desert.

"Yes, just a caravan," Tavi said. She understood nothing about it. She did not have the courage to leave the palace. "There will be more."

She did not know that Aashiq had promised to propose, and I did not want to tell her. I did not want any of them to know until we had my father's approval. So how did I tell her there wouldn't be more?

It would be one of the last times I saw our settlement, that I saw Firoz.

Shaking my head, I pleaded with Tavi, "I have to go. I'm sorry. We'll go when I get back, eh?"

"What kind of example do you think you're setting for our sisters?" Sabra said from behind me. "They look up to you, and you run off at every opportunity. What are you teaching them? To run from their problems? From their family?"

I pressed my fingers against my temples. "Does everything have to be a fight?"

Sabra leaned in so Tavi wouldn't hear. "When I am gone, you are the only thing she will have." Tavi couldn't bear hearing about Sabra's impending banishment.

"Mama isn't dead," I spat. "She'll have her, too."

"Don't forget about Tavi when you're chasing whatever it is you seek."

Tavi interrupted, a little too brightly. "It's actually fine. Today probably wasn't the best day. We'll go tomorrow."

When an attendant brought our midday meal, Sabra left me to join Tavi, who eagerly grasped a handful of dried dates, babbling about how she would want to nap after the meal anyway and really, there just wasn't enough time to see Mama that afternoon. I swallowed my guilt.

At the bottom of a basket I shared with Raheemah, I found my servant's abaya and veil. They were plain, no fancy embellishments nor rich colors, and would allow me to sneak from the palace without suspicion.

"Don't you want to eat first?" Tavi asked as she spat a date seed into her palm.

Raheemah grasped my ankle. "Stay for a bit. We can finish our game." She and a few other sisters had begun a new game of cards, and though I wanted to revisit my win, market day was far too alluring.

"Can't miss anything," I said, shaking the sand out of my clothes, already thrilling at the prospect of the bazaar. My fustan was too long for me, so I used my leather belt to hold it up from the ground so none of the bright edges could be seen beneath the abaya's hem. I dressed until I was covered from my hair to the tops of my feet, taking care that I tied my scarf to adequately protect me from the sun and to conceal my face.

"See if you can find me a handsome and rich merchant while you're out. These noblemen are overvalued," Pinar said, staring down at her cards, then put her finger on her chin as she considered something. "I think I'd prefer rich . . . over handsome, you see. Just in case you've a few to choose from."

My worn sandals slid easily onto my feet. "I will tell him of your erotic prowess and he will come bursting through our tent to steal you away." I clasped the salt tightly in my palm.

"Tell him I'm a virgin; he'll come sooner."

IT WAS almost always the same two men who guarded our home during the day, and the same two who were there at night. Stepping out of the tent, I glanced at Jael and Alim.

"Blessings of Eiqab, brothers." It was our signal. Perhaps it was because they actually knew us—standing by our tent for years, hearing our hopes and sufferings—but aside from my full brother, they were the only two of the King's men who were kind to us.

"And of Wahir," Jael replied, nodding his head and holding out his hand.

To anyone who saw, it looked like a simple greeting, but quickly, I pressed my leather pouch into his palm. The salt was a small bribe when split between the two, but it was enough for each to bring home several decent meals to their families. It was worth it.

Fussing with my sleeves, I let Jael stride ahead of me, then I followed. He walked quickly, and I felt my tucked dress slipping from beneath my belt. I clasped the fabric at my waist tightly, praying it would hold until I found somewhere to better secure it.

We walked along the sandy lanes, then through the rings of tents. The less vital the person or task, the further they'd be on the periphery. Finally, we reached one of the two entries into the palace: the servant's access. It was heavily guarded, the men fervently questioning those entering and leaving, inspecting the wares they were bringing to and from. But it was also congested on caravan days, so I would slip through easily. Especially with the help of Jael.

He approached a cluster of the soldiers—all identifiable as King's men with palace-white ghutras tucked around their faces and camel wool secured around their crown—and pointed at me. He muttered something about King's business, and they waved me through. All the servants were similar in their plain coverings—arms curved forward, eyes downcast. I mirrored them and followed four men carrying baskets of goods to sell at the market.

Suddenly, the basket slipped from one man's arms, spilling glass beads all over the sand. The camel being led into the palace startled at the commotion, and the people clamored, moving to get out of its way. Distracted by the chaos, and eager to slip through, I ran into the man in front of me, stumbling backward. And then I felt my fustan slip from the belt. Glancing down, I saw the green sparkling with golden thread from beneath my abaya, drawing the attention of any who was looking at the ground. Which was everyone as they stepped over the spilled goods.

"Stop!" A guard shouted.

I didn't turn, taking quicker steps through the people. *Just let me get through.*

"Stop slave!" he yelled again.

Glancing back, I saw him approaching me quickly, his hand outstretched. My breath was hot against my cheeks, sweat dripped down my neck. No, no, no.

Abruptly, Jael stumbled into the guard.

"Forgive me, brother," he said, wiping at the guard's pristine tunic. He moved swiftly so that he stood between me and the approaching man. "This is much too chaotic. Help me get this cleared up. Everyone stay calm!" Jael shouted, spreading his arms wide so that one was on the guard's chest and the other was shooing me toward the village. "Those leaving, go now so that we can clear this space."

I did not waste the opportunity. I fled.

The first time I decided to leave the palace was four years ago. I learned a banished ahira had died, and the news came at the heels of another rejection by a muhami. My mind spun with my fate, and I was nauseous with its lack of promise. Would I follow in the footsteps of my dead half-sister? I could not stay another moment idling with the other ahiran or wandering through the kitchens or praying to a deaf god at the rama. That leaving the palace was forbidden by our father mattered little to me. The prospect of change was alluring, and the freedom became addicting. The consequences of being caught became more immaterial with each uneventful outing.

Whenever I had the salt, I would leave the palace on caravan day. There was nothing that thrilled me more than seeing the rest of the world brought to our home. Traders from across the desert traveled far to reach our settlement with their hundreds of camels, brimming bags, and stuffed vats hanging from the animals' strong backs. The people would heave them to the bazaar, and the whole settlement would flock to hear impossible stories, savor delicious food, and collect magical treasures. After a day or two, the traders left with heavy pockets that clinked from coin—dha and fid and nab—and more importantly, slabs of salt teetering on their camels' humps.

Since the Salt King's rise to power, my settlement was the only place people came for salt. Old salt mines were lost to the wind that filled them with sand, so the movement of the desert, the routes of trade, all were oriented around my home. It had to be; people needed salt to live.

The sun blistered against my back, and I delighted in it. Outside of the palace, I was grounded, like a clay doll cut from strings. I found a secluded niche between two tents and adjusted my fustan until it was better secured. Then, I went to the bazaar. In my excitement to reach the marketplace, I nearly ran, weaving through villagers, anonymous in my plain clothes.

Imagining that this would be what life was like with Aashiq, I giggled, ecstatic with the freedom that was soon to be mine forever.

Twangy strums of the oud and the percussion of the bendir reached me before I saw the bazaar. When I turned into the marketplace—the winding labyrinth of tents—I stopped and stared, giddy with its pulsing energy.

People pushed past me, rushing to their favorite shops, finding the rare spice or treasured gift or even relative from afar. I fell in line behind them, joining the swarm of the market. The chaotic chatter of shop-goers rang in my ears. From the tents, men and women yelled to the shoppers, calling for their attention. Those who did not arrive early enough to snag a tent stood in the middle of the lanes, rushing to people to shove exorbitantly priced jewels onto their wrists or a shining reflecting glass before their eyes. A woman sang a heartbreaking love song down the lane from a man who sang of Masira's capriciousness—street performers competing for coin. Barterers clamored as goods were exchanged, and wafting through the lanes was the aroma of roasted meats, spices, and scented waxes and oils.

Hurriedly, I navigated through the market until finally, I found the shop for which I searched. Sitting on a large blanket under a threadbare tent was a man not much older than me. His gaze flicked through the people passing by, following each for a few steps before looking to the next. I tutted at his dishevelment—could he not even dress up for market day? Cloak on the ground behind him, tunic untucked from his sash, turban unwound beside his bare feet. His mother would be horrified. Thank Eiqab she stayed home to take care of her young children.

"Spare a drink for a poor girl?" I said as I approached, nodding to the nearly empty drum of opaque, milky liquid.

He placed his hand protectively over his goods as he surveyed me with a skeptical frown. Then the tension eased in his face. "Emel?"

"Of course, you fool."

He broke into a wide grin, his joy at seeing me mirroring mine. Firoz was my best friend. My only friend.

"Come and sit." He scooted aside and ladled the liquid into a small bowl for me.

I sat beside him. "Thank you." I carefully lifted my veil and took a swift drink of coconut juice. It was almost cool, and deliciously sweet. I closed my eyes as it ran down my throat. "You're almost out?"

He nodded. "It's been a good day. I just need to sell a bit more for Ma, then we can go. They're from the north." He grinned knowingly at me.

"I know! Have you seen Rafal yet?"

"Not yet, but people are already talking." He filled a man's goatskin for a handful of copper nab. "So, the rumors you met with the prince Aashiq last night true then?"

"How you hear of these things so quickly baffles me."

"Those in the palace like to talk."

I swirled the drink in my hand, watching white flecks spin.

"What was he like? Was his snake long—"

"You brute!" I met Firoz a few years ago when Jael walked with me into the village. He worried about my safety outside the palace, so he introduced me to his friend. If trouble found me, I was to seek out Firoz. We had been friends since, and there was nothing in my heart that he did not know.

"Tell me he lasted longer than that other guy." Firoz's shoulders shook with silent laughter.

"Firo!" I said sharply, my face hot. "I am not talking about this with . . ."

Two guards, with bright white uniforms gleaming in the afternoon sun, turned down the lane. I scooted back and discreetly adjusted my scarf so it hung lower over my eyes. Firoz saw them too and shifted so that he was close to my side. He took my hand in his.

They stopped in front of Firoz's shop. I stared at their feet, clutching Firoz's hand tightly. My heart pounded against my chest, and I worried they could hear my terror.

"Eiqab has blessed us!" Firoz exclaimed at their arrival, his voice brightening as he transformed from my friend into a salesman. He pulled my hand up to his mouth to kiss my knuckles. "My love, the King's men desire our goods!" He turned back to the guards. "These coconuts were from a settlement afar and saturated by Eiqab's blazing sun. I cut the fruit myself at dawn, and my wife here poured them while singing Eiqab's prayers." I bowed my head more deeply, further hiding my face.

"Fill two," one said as he handed Firoz their goatskins. I did not recognize his voice.

"How will you pay, my fearless soldiers? You bravely protect my wife and our magnificent King, so I will only find ease if I give you a deal—no one will beat my price." Though blood roared in my ears, my lips quirked at his ridiculous exclamations.

The men pulled their pouches from their belts, coins jingling.

"We've salt and coin," the other guard said. Few paid in salt. Though my father's palace contained piles of it, the rest of the settlement was poor. Through the guard's spending, salt was dispersed through the settlement in small quantities, most people choosing to use it in their meals or to preserve their meat. For some, acquiring salt was an obsession—they were the salt chasers.

Firoz lowered his voice and leaned into them, never letting go of my hand.

"For both—now, tell no one I've given you this deal—I will take one palmful of salt or ten fid."

I nearly choked. Either price was outrageous.

"I will not hear your thanks," Firoz carried on, shaking his head gravely.

The guards grunted in agreement. There was an exchange, and they walked away.

Firoz chuckled, cupping the silver coins in his hand. "Ma will be happy with this." I scooted away from him. "Can you imagine me as a husband?" Firoz said, suddenly concerned by the prospect.

"Not for a moment, but you played your part well. You are a skilled peddler, though. 'Saturated by Eiqab's blazing sun'? Where do you come up with this?" We declared more and more ridiculous things Eiqab did to the coconuts prior to them being cracked for juice. Some more salacious than others.

Firoz grew serious. "Will he propose?" There was worry in his voice.

"Maybe." I did not hide the hope from my voice well. I stared fixedly at the people who passed.

He whipped his head to me. "Do you think?"

I nodded, and when I saw Firoz's face, I wished I had said nothing.

"Oh . . . that will be great. If you liked him. Was he alright?"

Nodding, I could only think of leaving Firoz, and the ache in my chest was much too great.

He glanced at me and shook his head.

"Don't, Emel. This is great news. You deserve it. Really, you do. I am very happy for you." It sounded more and more as if he were trying to convince himself. "Good." He clapped his hands together. "Well, I've sold enough." He poured what remained in the large bowl into his goatskin and then into the small bowl I'd emptied earlier. I finished that one, too. He rolled up the blanket we had been sitting on. He would leave his empty tent behind and claim it again once the traders had left. Using well-worn rope, he slung his entire shop onto his back. Already, a woman with a small basket of iron spearheads, finely honed, was shuffling in to take his place.

The crowd was densely packed when we arrived, and excited gulps of air filled my stomach when I saw Rafal standing at the center of it all. Firoz grabbed my hand and we pushed through the people to get closer.

Atop a large basin turned on its head, Rafal stood in all his enchanting splendor—a bright green tunic over red and white sirwal, golden chains from his neck, and an indigo turban upon his head. With sparkling eyes wide, he surveyed the spectators and danced his fingers through the air, telling his story. Beside him, sitting on a sun-dulled cushion, was his friend. I did not know his name, but he was always there, tapping his darbuka to dramatize Rafal's stories.

His stories. That was why people went to Rafal. None knew the desert like he did.

"And there were trees as high as the Salt King's palace! With tiny animals that swung through them eating from their branches. One picked up my bawsal," he held up his dulled, silver way-finder, and I squinted, trying to see where its spinning hands pointed right then. "And banged it on my head!" The crowd gasped and laughed. The friend happily percussed along with the laughter. I had heard this story, of his travels to the south, but still, I felt as though every word was new.

He barely finished his tale before people began calling for their favorites again. Request after request shouted at him: The oasis with no water! The dunes that shifted only in the night! The salt mine guarded by jinn! I remembered last night with Aashiq and my map, empty to the north.

"But what about you?" I called. "What of where you come?" He never told stories of the north.

"It is like here." He shrugged.

"How far north have you been?" I said over the muttering voices that grew bored.

He pivoted on his heel and swirled to face me, eyes fixing on mine. He smiled slowly, teeth opalescent behind his mustache.

"You wouldn't believe it if I told you," he said.

The people disputed, the excitement growing again, and they begged that he share.

"Okay, okay!" He held up his heads in defeat. "But you must listen close, for I will tell this only once."

Everyone hushed. The friend rolled his fingers along the drum.

"It is an inhospitable place." He looked into the swarm of tent peaks. "I have been once and will never return." He leaned over the crowd that stood beneath his hands. "I am referring, of course, of the desert's edge."

My mouth dropped open, and Rafal looked right at me with an eyebrow raised, daring me to believe.

A man standing in front shouted, "Lies!"

Another called, "It isn't real!"

Rafal shook his head. "It is." He pointed behind him with his bawsal, the little arm directing north. "Travel for forty days that way, but be careful that you navigate closely." He draped the bawsal over our heads. "If you miss one oasis, Masira's death birds will feast upon your flesh.

"Go as far as your camel will take you, until you hit the rocks—sharp cliffs, navigable only with foot and rope and faith." He paused, and the friend pattered away. "It takes the length of the day to descend the rock cliffs, and then after two days on foot, you'll reach it."

"You've not been!" a woman shouted. "It's impossible."

Another woman chimed in. "No man can carry enough water on his back for a foot-journey like that."

Rafal's lip twitched in amusement, but he ignored them. "There, the rocks sparkle like they're encrusted with diamonds, salt shining in the sun. And there, too, is the grave of a city. Buildings colored like beautifully feathered birds have been torn apart by the hands of Eiqab. They lie in pieces, half buried in the sand."

I said, "But where does the sand end? What is at the edge? Is there magic like the stories say?"

"Magic? Maybe. But I found none. At the edge, I found water so angry it roared. It was as wide as the horizon's mouth."

His eyes grew misty before he blinked it away. I believed none of it.

He stepped off of his stage. "That is all for today. If I tell you more, I will never see you again. If the price is right . . ." His eyes darted down to his stage toward the basin his friend was turning over, "tomorrow I will be back to share more."

I nudged Firoz, and he grudgingly tossed two fid into the basin.

Others followed.

"You have to come tomorrow," I told him as we dispersed with the rest of the crowd. "Remember everything he says, that way I can—"

"Yes, yes, your map," Firoz said. "I know. Why don't you run off and ask Rafal to fill in the rest, eh?"

The bright green of Rafal's tunic grew distant as he walked away. Even if I had the courage to ask him more, I feared mentioning my map. What if he wanted it back?

Years ago, after the first time I saw him tell his tales, Rafal had dropped his sack as he was packing to leave, spilling rolls of parchment onto the ground. All was returned to its place, except the one that had fallen just beside my foot, hidden beneath the hem of my abaya. It was the first map I had ever seen, and though it was more parchment than ink, I treasured it. He had not finished it, empty as it was, so I decided that I would take on the task. It was my obsession.

"Rumor is that a prince arrived with the caravan today. Likely seeking an alliance with the King," Firoz said as we walked through the congested paths. Firoz's business with traders provided him ample opportunity for discussion with travelers on the road. "It's strange, though. They don't usually arrive with the caravan. They're wealthy enough to come privately escorted. Hire their own runners."

Runners went ahead of the caravans to scout the oases, retrieve water to bring back to their crew, and receive approval to come into the settlement. Nassar met the runners at the oasis to see if they were bringing goods worthy enough to trade and to grant them allowance to access the oasis for water. If it was a muhami, he'd send word that the palace need prepare for a guest.

"Yes . . ." I said distantly, staring at my reflection in a polished copper vase.

"One of the nomads said he and his men kept to themselves for the journey, paying handsomely but speaking to none. Seems strange."

Silk adorned with thick bronze thread sat in waves upon a smooth wooden table. "A challenger to the throne, surely," I said absently, fingering the soft material, cold in the shade of the tent.

"It's what I fear."

"Firo!" I said incredulously, the allure of the goods vanishing like an ahira's frown. "There hasn't been one in years. It is probably two dozen princes coming to snatch up every one of my sisters. I will be the only one left, and I will lay around in my tent by my lonesome. Withered and pale like a sick goat. Muhamis will poke sticks at me to see if I stir."

He grunted, indignant, and waved his finger at me. "You'll see, I've got a feeling about this."

A platter of shining desserts with sticky red filling caught my eye. My stomach grumbled, and I rubbed my hand across my middle. We exited the bazaar, still surging with feverish frenzy, and Firoz set down his things to adjust the sash around his hips and tie his turban.

"You'll join me for a meal, then?" Firoz asked. The sun began to sink behind the tents.

"Only if you're paying." I smirked as I helped him with his turban, smoothing the folds. Firoz knew I gave all of my salt to bribe my way out of the palace.

"Today, I'm wealthier than Aashiq!" He bounced on his sandy toes, and the many coins in his pockets clinked together.

I bowed. "Then, Your Highness, I accept your proposal."

We walked toward Firoz's home, the lanterns and cooking fires brightening the lanes at twilight. He called out to his mother when we arrived that he would not be home for dinner. She hustled out of the tent, clucking disapprovingly until she saw me standing beside him. She stopped and smiled before she hugged him, then slapped his shoulder.

"Who is your friend? Invite her in, you disgusting brute."

Though I had met her several times, I knew Firoz had many friends. She would not remember me.

"Ma," he said, rubbing his shoulder. "She is in a rush, and we must get going. I will be back before the stars are bright." He kissed her cheek before depositing the basket at her feet and dropping three-quarters of the days' earnings into her waiting palms, taking extra care with the salt.

Firoz grabbed my hand and we walked away. His mother watched us go, affectionate hope in her eyes.

"You are cruel," I whispered to him.

"No, no. It is a kindness. She wants me to wed, but we know that will never happen." He squeezed my hand. "Let her have these few moments of hope. They give her happiness."

"She will only be disappointed."

When out of his mother's sight, our hands fell back to our sides.

"Perhaps you should leave with the caravan, find a Si'la out in the desert."

Firoz laughed uneasily. "I've already found one."

Gasping, I smacked him like his mother had. "I am no demon! Though, truthfully, I wouldn't mind the shape-shifting powers, eh? I'd turn into a guard and strut out of the palace with my chest puffed, yelling for no reason at all."

We turned into a small tent. A placard strung beside the entry read, "Food." The cramped space had three low tables with cushions scattered near. We were the only two inside. Firoz called out, and soon, a woman as wide as she was tall stepped in from the back. The smell of smoked lamb streamed in behind her.

"Two meals?" she asked, stepping toward us with a cheery face framed by wild hair.

Firoz nodded.

She grabbed two chipped ceramic cups and roughly placed them on the table we stood beside. She filled them each with tepid tea before stepping out, rattling off instructions to a poor soul working the fire.

"This is pleasant." I looked around the small space.

"It is. They're very discreet." He nodded toward the closed entrance providing privacy for the patrons. "We can stay here to eat if you like, but I figured you'd want to go to our usual."

"How'd you find this place?"

Before he could respond, the woman returned with two small sacks that Firoz would return when emptied in exchange for a few extra nab.

Oil dripped through the fabric. Firoz set a single golden dha on the table and collected our dinner. The scent of roasted meat and flatbread made my mouth water.

We walked up to the village edge, squeezing between two homes, until we faced the open desert. Well away from the ears of the people in their homes, we sat in the sand, still warm from the day. My eyes traveled along the dunes that never shifted. Like Aashiq's, most settlements had to move their homes regularly to avoid the dunes swallowing their tents, the wind pushing the sandy hills on their ravenous path. But the dunes never came close to us. We were lucky.

The caravan's camels—dozens and dozens of them—were off in the distance, specks of humped black. Their water was already filled, waiting to carry on their journey in the coming days.

There was a huddle of trees not far in the distance. One of the King's men led a small group of camels to it, each carrying enormous barrels between their humps. They would return to the village after filling them with water from its pool that never emptied.

"The oasis," I whispered, remembering how Aashiq described his oasis when we watched the horizon as Firoz and I did now. I couldn't wait to see the pool that was so large, half his people could sit inside.

"I'll race you to there," Firoz said as I sat beside him. He handed me my food and reached into his own bag using a piece of the bread. He pulled out roasted lamb with globs of yellow millet stuck to it.

"I would run like the wind," I said. Sons, it would be a dream to sprint through the sand. If guards weren't lining the perimeter of the settlement, I might have.

"What do you think it's like?" Firoz asked through a mouthful of food.

I untied my veil. The air touching my sweaty face felt cold. I closed my eyes.

"Cool. Quiet."

"Sounds perfect," he murmured, then hesitated before asking, "Would you run away? If you could?" There was pity in the depths of his eyes.

I took a bite of food. Once, I might have said yes. But now, with Aashiq, the answer was no. I would wait for him, for my future, to take me away.

"Of course not." I tried to laugh, but the sound was wrong. The bread turned into mush between my fingers. Firoz wouldn't understand Aashiq. He wouldn't understand how different he was, nor how he was the best thing for me. "I couldn't run away. Where would I go? How would I survive? And anyway, why would I run away? My family is here, you are here . . ." My voice was flat, emotionless.

My family was here. Firoz was here. And I would be leaving. The twisted ache in my chest cinched down.

"I would," he said quietly.

"Can't you?" I said after a pause. "Can't you go with the caravan?"

"I have asked already," he said.

My stomach dropped. No. I did not want to lose Firoz to the north. I would never see him again.

Selfish, I knew it was, but I wanted him where I knew I could find him, where I could return happy and soft in the middle, with beautiful children and a husband who said yes, we will travel to your home together to see your family and your friends.

Firoz continued. "But they want a quarter brick of salt, or eighty dha! An impossible price." I thought of the salt bricks that lay stacked in my father's palace. Firoz let out a long breath. When he looked back at the horizon, I turned to him. His brow was furrowed, his shoulders hunched forward. I wanted to ask him if everything was okay, if he was happy at home. But I didn't dare. If there was something wrong, knowledge of it was a load I could not bear.

I leaned over to him, my shoulder touching his, and whispered, "His snake was long, but he didn't have the stamina."

A loud guffaw burst from him, breaking the melancholy silence. We ate our food quickly. Rarely did I eat meals as delicious and abundant. I consumed everything with fervor, Firoz making fun of my eagerness.

"Thank you for this," I said as I gestured to the empty food sack and the desert.

"You are always welcome." He reached over and clasped my shoulder. "Since you've decided not to race me, I suppose I should take you home."

The sun dipped out of sight, and only its muddy trails of orange remained in the sky. I looked at the desert once more before we turned into the village. Was north that way? I squinted, trying to see if there was angry water where the sky met the land. I saw nothing.

Walking toward the palace, the smoke from fires wafted in the air as meals were cooked. Laughter and chatter of villagers mixed with the brays and neighs of animals. Near the palace, we found a small, secluded space. A stray chicken pecking through the sand ran away at our arrival, clucking and spreading its wings in indignation at the interruption.

"Take care these next few days," Firoz said.

"There is no threat, you know that. I will be fine." I waved him off, but he was so intent that I grew uneasy. "If it will make you feel better, I promise I will be careful."

We grasped each other in a long hug.

"Oh, and Emel?" He said as he pulled away. "If he . . . if you . . . come see me once more before you leave."

"I promise." I squeezed his hands in mine. "Find peace in the shadow of Eiqab's sun."

Discreetly, I waited by the servants' access, leaning against the sturdy date-palm fence. I was growing impatient as one or two servants approached at a time, worried that I would not have the opportunity to sneak in. It was the risk I took when I returned home late. Finally, a cluster of empty-handed servants strode up, having sold all their goods at the market. I fell in with them, and after questioning the few at the front of the group, the guards waved us in.

When I approached my home, I was surprised to find a third guard standing with the night watch.

"Jael?" I asked, reaching out my hand. "What are you doing here? You should be home." I could just as easily collect my leather sack from him tomorrow.

Swiftly, he took my hand in his, returning the sack to my palm, and mumbled, "It was growing late, so I almost left, but I wanted you to know a new suitor comes soon. Even if the ahiran aren't requested tomorrow, it's best to stay here the coming days."

It was a strange warning, and Firoz's caution echoed in my mind.

4

THE KING SUMMONED US to midday court two days later. The ominous words of Jael and Firoz had at first worried me, but the days that followed were ordinary, and the summons was typical for a muhami. We were prepared in the zafif, and the guards escorted us to the King smelling like crushed roses and looking like freshly plucked petals.

The courtings took place in the smaller receiving tents where ample plush seating was scattered throughout the room for the ahiran to drape ourselves. When we were instead directed to our father's tents, to where he sat upon his throne, a ripple of bewilderment passed through us—my sisters mumbling about who was so important, we'd meet them in such a formal setting.

"Aashiq isn't going to propose then," Sabra said coolly as we walked.

The teeth sank, and her poison spread through me. Though I told myself he was a man of his word, that there was no reason Father would dissent, that we would surely be wed, her words fueled my doubt. She was

right, and I hated it. It was nearly the third evening, and his time was almost at an end. If he had not done it already, there was no chance to ask my father to have me if a new suitor was here. There would be no proposal.

"You'll be like me," Sabra continued, falsely bright. "We can live in squalor together."

Fingers slid through mine. Raheemah had dropped back to walk beside me.

"Don't listen," she mouthed, squeezing my hand.

The guard held open the entrance to the throne room, and we filed into the room one by one. Each sister who entered before turned back to me with a wide smile on her face. My heart frenzied in my chest. What was I walking into? Did I dare hope? No, it was impossible. Proposals did not happen before all of the ahiran, and they certainly did not occur in the throne room. It was a transaction, not a ceremony.

But when I saw Aashiq standing beside my father's throne, resplendent in saffron robes, the ground seemed to shift from under me. His eyes met mine, and he nodded just once before his face split into an enormous smile, like the tipping of a goblet of sun between clouds. It was happening, it was really happening. My time as an ahira was done.

My vision hazed with tears, and I raised a shaking hand to my mouth to hide my disbelieving smile. Sabra stormed past me to join my sisters bowing before the King. I hurried to mirror their movements, finding it impossible to tear my gaze from Aashiq's. Forehead to the ground, my mind raced with colliding thoughts of self-doubt and excitement. When would I leave with him? Why were we all summoned? This was unusual. What if he was choosing a different sister? But no, he smiled at me. Would I have time to say goodbye to Mama, to Emah, to Tavi? Firoz?

"Daughters, stand," the King said sloppily. "I've joyous news." I stared at the carpet beneath my feet, following the path of a pale, brown spider as it disappeared between two of the rugs. *Little spider, I will be as free as you.*

"The prince Aashiq has chosen a bride."

Raheemah's hand pressed soothingly against my back, and I leaned against her. Small, constricted spasms ached my neck as I fought a deluge of tears. My breath caught on the knot in my throat.

"Breathe," she whispered.

The King continued. "Aashiq, my friend, my soon son. Step forward and claim your wife."

My sisters and I were unmoving, like stones in the sand. I did not raise my eyes from the carpet.

Soon, yellow-slippered feet emerged into my line of sight. They went still in front of me. I counted: one, two, three, four . . . waiting to see if they would move on to someone else. They did not move, and I nearly fell to the ground in relief. Aashiq's finger lightly traced my jawline. He caught my chin and pulled my face up to meet his gaze. His brown eyes burned into mine. The smallest smile, meant only for me, rested on his lips.

"Emel," Aashiq whispered, "I will take you as my bride." He reached down and clasped my hand. A hysterical laugh fell from my lips as the dimming world suddenly was reignited as if in flames—it was golden and beautiful.

He chose me.

He chose *me*.

His hand was warm, and I held it tightly as a battle of emotions waged inside of me. Excitement, hope, pride, relief. All of the things I had been taught to feel, the things that I now truly felt, were like horses galloping through my chest. I was chosen. My mother would be joyous. My father, finally, would be proud.

My life was like a newly woven carpet rolled out before me, and I saw it there with stunning detail: sharing wine with him as we ate, going to the market with his wives as we gossiped about the servants, visiting the oasis and submerging in the pooling water, walking through the desert with a camel's reins in my hand. Seeing the world, the entire world.

I bowed my head slowly, corralling the ecstatic dreams that launched up into the sky like birds taking flight. "Masira has allowed me a great honor."

But then I did it. I stumbled, thinking of everything I would leave behind—thinking only of the good, as always seems to happen when a goodbye looms near. My mother and sisters and Firoz. Was being an ahira so bad? Was life in my father's palace truly so terrible? I shook my head, sending away the traitorous thoughts. Sons, what was I thinking?

Aashiq was who Masira chose for me. After seven years an ahira, this was my husband. For the rest of my life, this was my husband.

My husband, my fate, my fortune.

My freedom.

I stared into his eyes, tugging back all the cloudy memories of the night I had lain with him. I did not linger on our drunken sex. Instead, I thought of when we had talked staring into the night, when he had been caring, sincere. He was a good man. He had chosen to be kind when he could have been anything else.

So I let the fear go, and I clung to the pride.

I was an ahira no longer. I was to be a wife and princess. My smile stretched wide across my face. The torch light glittered in Aashiq's eyes.

"Let us be wed," he said and led me to my father.

My chin lifted as we walked. I moved like a royal, like I had been trained. My sisters smiled around us, Raheemah and Tavi and the others wiping their cheeks. In my excitement, I had forgotten their presence. Why had my sisters been called to witness his proposal? Though I could not make sense of it, I was so glad they were there to share in my happiness.

My father slouched in his throne when he addressed us.

"May Eiqab bestow blessings unto you both. Aashiq, as part of this exchange, I give the strength of my army and the power of my renown to you. From your marriage to my daughter, your family will prosper, and your people will thrive. Your union to my family will raise you up closer to the Sons."

His glassy eyes were unfocused, his tongue lolled in his mouth, lazy and fat with liquor. His words were thick, his pronouncements absurd. He was drunker than I had seen him in a long time.

"And I know that I can expect your loyalty and army's strength in return." My father set his glass trinket and goblet onto the table, stood slowly, and grasped Aashiq's shoulder. Then he turned to me, his eyes almost glistening. "My dove, Eiqab has been kind and gifted you with a great fortune. Aashiq has been generous and gifted you with his kin, his home. Your union to this prince gives us pride and honors our gods." He reached out and caressed my knuckles with the pad of his thumb. I could not resist his words. Forgiveness and love and warmth for my father poured from my chest.

I tasted salty tears on my lips.

"You will be wed tomorrow at the sun's peak. Eiqab will oversee the ceremony from his blazing throne."

The King turned from us to my sisters. "Now daughters, you have not been summoned here only to witness Aashiq choose his bride."

It was surreal, gazing at the ahiran as I stood beside Aashiq. I was separate from them, no longer one of them. Raheemah beamed at me. Her face wet, smile brilliant.

"Matin, come and see!" The King spoke loudly, calling through the tents to someone far away.

I tore my gaze from my sisters and searched the room, waiting for someone to appear. Was this the man Firoz and Jael spoke of?

He continued. "See how my daughters are the jewels of the desert, the gems of the sand. They are beautiful and obedient, and you will earn great honor if you claim one as your own!

"My daughters, I am pleased to tell you we have another suitor to welcome to our home. He has traveled from the deep north in search of a wife."

I wondered how far north—the edge? If that were true and if Rafal could be believed, he might be one of the most powerful men in the desert—perhaps wealthier than even my father. That would certainly explain why we had been called to the throne room to meet him.

"Matin, join us!" The King clapped his hands wildly as we swiveled our heads from side to side. Aashiq pulled me close, tracing his fingers up and down the curve of my waist, making it clear to the new guest over whom he maintained ownership. I leaned into him, uncaring of his display, and he pressed his lips to my temple.

Finally, there was a swishing of fabric, and my gaze fell on a man being escorted in by Nassar. His age surprised me; suitors were generally younger. This man had more years than my father. He wore a dark blue ghutra around his face and had loose gold and navy robes. Two long scimitars were fastened at his waist. His beard, more silver than black, was long, and his face held a look of cold cunning. His eyes pivoted from the King to all of us around him.

The King rambled on, oblivious. "Welcome, welcome! Nassar has told me much of your home, and I think you'll find my daughters will suit you nicely."

Aashiq tensed, and so did I. There was something amiss with Matin. He walked stiffly with his arms curled forward, head bent low. He scanned the room rapidly, as if searching or preparing.

Nassar was oblivious, distracted by a torch whose fire had deadened. He went to a servant, pointing at the offense, so he failed to notice Matin reaching for his belt. The Salt King was so drunk on arak and pride that he babbled on, equally unaware.

Matin spun as he unsheathed his scimitars, the sound of slicing metal ringing in the room. A garbled cry sounded, and the guard standing near Matin clutched his throat, eyes wide, mouth agape. Blood poured through his fingers. He fell to the ground.

And then everything seemed to happen in the span of a heartbeat.

Chaos exploded. Screams ripped from the center of the room as my sisters saw the guard fall. They fled, disappearing from the room like snuffed flames. I turned into Aashiq, trying to pull him away as I stared at the horror before us. His eyes were wide as he took everything in, his hand reaching for his own scimitar. He shoved his arm in front of me and yelled, "Run!"

Sons, I wanted to, but I was fixed with fear.

The King bellowed for his guards with manic fervor, but he moved as though wading through honey. He dazedly spun around, pawing at his waist.

Finally, he pulled his sword from his belt and waved it unthreateningly at Matin, who turned toward the King.

"Where is it?!" Matin screamed.

Desperation was heavy in his voice. He strode toward the King, blades raised before him.

A rush of foreign men dressed in blue and black joined the melee, attacking my father's soldiers. Swords clanged, men hollered and screamed. My father moved to retreat. Unsteady, he knocked his table as he turned, everything falling upon the rugs, clattering loudly.

The sound broke my terror. "We should leave! Come with me!" I shrieked at Aashiq, pulling roughly at his hand.

"I can't! My duty is to your father! Go hide." I stared at him, horrified. "Go!" He screamed, pushing me away so that I fell onto my knees. Heart pounding, I scrambled behind the throne. I would not leave him. As if right next to me, another peal of swords rang out in the room. Peeking from behind the throne, I saw Aashiq parry Matin's attacks.

No. I could barely breathe. I was horrified, stunned, and fascinated all at once. They were fighting right in front of the throne now. I could not flee, as Matin was too close. With Aashiq's every stroke, I saw my future flicker. Now there, now gone. I turned away. I would not watch the fight. My spine was pressed to the back of my father's chair, my knees curled to my chest, my fingers clutched tightly around my shins.

Where had my sisters gone? Were they running to safety, or had Matin's men found them, too? Pressing my forehead to my knees, I prayed to Eiqab. Had I the salt, I would have given it all to smother flames if it meant Masira might listen and would protect Aashiq, my family.

The King's guards streamed in with scimitars brandished and joined the fight. They cried and shouted as the battle swelled from two to nearly two dozen.

Unable to resist the growing din, I glimpsed around the throne again and saw more men from Matin's army. They slashed their swords through the air at my father's soldiers—my brothers and neighbors. Matin had moved into the fray. He swirled his dual swords like a dancer, blades slicing into soft flesh. I did not see Aashiq.

My father stood on the periphery, swinging his scimitar uselessly above him, shouting until he was purple in the face with sweat dripping down his temples. He scanned the room, panicked. He seemed irritated with the men clustered tightly before him, shielding him from the fray with their beating hearts and soft flesh.

A soldier now guarded my father's throne, preventing any of the invaders from getting to his fallen treasures and the salt that sat behind it. He did not know he also guarded an ahira.

Red bloomed beneath robes. Men fell, and swords entered sacred places: slithering between ribs, carving into abdomens, slicing pulsing vessels that coursed through cores.

Fear and revulsion choked me. I wanted to run and find a real place to hide, but I knew these men would slay me as soon as they saw me. I was the daughter of the King they wanted dead. I was their enemy.

There was no sense to what was happening. A man did not take the throne by catching the King off guard. It was against all honor, all tradition. This was the whole purpose for the ritual that allowed men to challenge the King, so that such shameful betrayals need not happen. No one would respect a king who broke his opponent's trust as Matin had done. So what did he want?

Firoz's warning emerged through my muddled thoughts, and suddenly hysterical, I covered my mouth to stop from laughing aloud. *Here I am, Firo! Like I promised you, perfectly safe behind this royal chair!*

The tears of hysteria revived my fear, and I hugged my knees into my chest harder. I sat clenched like a fist until the sounds began to diminish. When my father's drunken cries were gone, I peered around the throne to see if I could find him.

I held my breath, fear and hope waging their own war, but then I saw him being pulled from the tent by several of his guards. Though drunk and weak, Father tried resisting the men that tugged at him. He reached out toward the center of the room, toward his throne, but the young guards' sober strength outweighed their ruler's, and they soon disappeared.

There was little left of the battle. Men had fallen to the floor, daggers jutting from chests, abdomens. Entrails spilled onto navy robes, and piles of salt were stained with the blood and ingesta of family and foe. I watched as one of my brothers thrust his sword into the neck of an enemy. The man's eyes bulged before his life was lost. He fell to the floor with a dull thud.

None of Matin's soldiers remained. I did not know if they fled or if they were all slain. The remaining guards sprinted from the room either in pursuit or to secure the perimeter of the palace.

A bell clanged. It was loud, frantic. More bells joined. Soon, they rang through the settlement, creating a cacophony that rattled my spine: a warning for villagers to arm themselves and prepare for battle. My breaths came in quick bursts, my heart thudded wildly. Were more men coming? Were the fleeing soldiers running free in the village, killing needlessly? I sat still, my hands covering my ears. Scared to move, scared to stay.

After a moment—or days, I knew not which—the ringing ceased. A heavy silence swallowed me.

Alone, I stood slowly, the muscles in my legs coiled and ready to spring should anyone come into the room. Dead men lay in piles atop the floor. Matin's men, my father's men. I gripped the throne tightly as I stared. Some might be my brothers, and now they lay dead, undignified and splayed. No prayer for deliverance spoken over their corpses. No keening cry from their mothers as their bloodied heads were cradled by the hands that raised them. Would they even be taken to the sands to be buried by the sky?

I stepped soundlessly toward the slain. Their wounds demanded to be seen, and my eyes kept falling on the mangled flesh. The metallic twang of blood and fetid smell of vacated bowels was strong. Bile rose. I covered my nose, averted my gaze, looking instead to the men's—the boys'—faces. Who were they? Their lifeless eyes told me nothing.

Matin was sprawled atop others, unmoving, heart beating no longer. I sat upon the ground, relief coursing through me, and stared at the man who had caused so much pain. A large sword was pinned to his abdomen, his muscles still twitching in final protest. His small eyes were open and vacant, a dull sheen to them.

I looked down at his robes, the navy stained a purplish-brown from his wounds. On the collar of his robe was the image of a crescent moon, stitched with glittering golden thread. On the opposite collar was a sun with thick rays, stitched with the same thread but muddied by blood.

Did any of his soldiers remain? Where would they go now?

Edges of bright yellow robes, stained with blood, puddled under Matin. A pit opened up in my stomach, filling with fear. I followed the fabric and lifted the heavy arm of the assailant to peer beneath.

Aashiq's lifeless face stared at me. His mouth slack and open, dark blood dripping from his lips onto the ground. Matin's arm fell with a thud and I scooted away, tears blurring my vision.

No, no, no. My life, my future, pulled from under my feet. A crushing weight collapsed onto me, onto my chest. I couldn't breathe. His beautiful robes, bright like the sun, marred by the monster. What of his wives? Of his children? What of me?

It couldn't be true. Not now. Not when I was so close. Everything within my grasp suddenly turned to water, and I could hold none of it. I had nothing. So quickly, I was again an ahira.

Heavy, retching sobs tore from my chest. I crawled away, messy in grief, disrupting piles of salt, desperate to get away from the death, uncaring that my knees and hands pressed into blood-soaked rugs. I threw my head back against my father's throne and cried—snot spilling down my nose and tears flooding my face. Choking and sobbing. I couldn't do it—go back to my father, go to the harem to tell my mother, go back to my sisters. I dropped my face into my hands as I attempted to reconcile my fate. As I attempted to understand why Masira could allow me so much joy only to snatch it away.

Could I return to what I was moments ago, when my mind had already drawn the map of my future? What would I do now?

My hands fell to my side, and my fingers brushed something small and metallic sending it spinning slowly beside me.

My father's vessel.

Golden smoke twisted and billowed within the glass walls, agitated like steam with no place to go. I looked around the room, seeing if someone, if my father, had suddenly arrived to retrieve it. Swallowing my tears and feeling cavalier in my grief, I reached for it. I was the disobedient child again, one who knows flames burn but yearns to touch them because they dance.

Lifting the vessel slowly from the ground, I was surprised both at its lightness and its warmth. I studied the intricate carvings in the thin gold bands wrapping around the glass. A chain arose from one band and connected to one of its ends. The end was almost flower-like with petals that closed down over the glass. I pushed against the golden petals, and they shifted. It was some kind of lid.

Tentatively, I placed my fingers over the lid, seating them so that I could pull it off. What was I doing? What was the smoke, and what would it do to me? It could hurt me. My father could hurt me. Or, Sons, what if the smoke did nothing and simply floated into the air and left the jar empty forever? If my father discovered that I had been the one to ruin his prized treasure . . . I did not want to think what he would do to me.

But, I realized, I did not care. What more was there for me? Aashiq was the only suitor of dozens who had wanted me. Surely, he was the only suitor who would ever want me. I would either be cast out by my father or I would die in the marauding of what now seemed an imminent war with Matin's men.

With a deep breath, I pulled the lid from the vessel.

As if it had a will of its own, the golden top shifted in my hand. I yelped and nearly threw the vessel across the room, but I held it at arm's length as I watched, fascinated, as the petals on the lid opened up like a flower at the sun. Horror quickly consumed the appeal as I realized the iridescent gold smoke leaked from its glass container. I continuously slammed the lid back onto the vessel as the smoke escaped beneath my hand, but it was transformed, and it no longer seated onto the top.

Whimpering, I tossed the vessel on the ground and began to stand. Golden smoke continued to fill the room, and soon I could smell it—dust with a hint of jasmine oil and something completely unrecognizable, like life and wetness.

I fell back into the throne, sitting paralyzed and staring at the impossible amount of smoke that flowed out of the vessel. Far more than could have fit inside.

Soon, the cloud of golden smoke was so thick, I could see nothing through it. I looked around the room. Someone would walk in at any moment, see the billowing gold, and know I had meddled with my father's things. I would be punished, perhaps sentenced to death, because I had been the one to lose his treasured . . . smoke?

The smoke was coalescing in front of me now. It did not behave as smoke should, spreading throughout the tent and disappearing up through its fine mesh. Instead, it collapsed down onto itself like falling motes of dust.

I frowned as a large, box-shaped form appeared. The tendrils of vapor dispersed, and I understood I was not looking at an object. It was a kneeling man. His back was turned, and his head bent low. My eyes widened, and a new terror gripped me. I was alone in a tent with an unknown man when only moments ago, unknown men had tried to kill my father, had killed his soldiers, had killed Aashiq.

But *this* man—he seemed to have arrived through the very thing Aashiq had denied was possible when I told him my tale of the Salt King . . . magic.

I stood, staying crouched low as I calculated the safest escape.

"Yes, master?" His voice was deep and smooth. He stood and began to turn toward me.

I dropped down to my hands and knees, cowering as I tucked my head behind my hands, my eyes squeezed tight. Let me die quickly.

There was a long pause.

"Master?" he said uncertainly.

His words were unexpected. He did not sound as if he had come any closer. I carefully raised my head to look at him. A soundless gasp rushed from my lips.

This man was not of my world. His skin was the color of tarnished gold, and his body almost appeared to be forged of the same metal. He seemed ancient, as though crafted one thousand years ago, yet also ageless. He had an intimidatingly large frame, and the curves of his arms and broad back undulated as he breathed.

Was this a god, one of the Sons?

I was immobilized with fear, with wonder. His hair slightly darker than his skin, was pulled back into a long tail, contained within thick golden rings. His face was bearded and appeared hewn from stone.

Below his hands, familiar golden petals encircled both wrists. I glanced to the glass jar beside me. The cuffs resembled its petaled golden lid, still attached to the vessel by the fine chain. Staring more closely, I saw that the edges of the cuffs seemed to melt into his hands, transforming into the faintest golden roots—veins?—that tapered off at his fingers. My attention moved from his hands to his hips, where a dark indigo sash was tied—the only color on his monochromatic figure.

For all his elegance and beauty, something was not right. Despite his immensity, he seemed very small. His eyes shadowed, his mouth held tight. His body was curled forward as if in surrender. Every piece of him conveyed powerlessness. He could not be a slave; there were no dark scars on his bare chest. So then, what was he?

His gaze was trained on the ground as I surveyed him. He did not approach. I watched him, curious.

"Who are you?" I asked.

At the sound of my voice, his eyes flashed up and met mine. I flinched. They were even more golden than his body. They almost shimmered as he stared. His shoulders fell back, his face softened, his eyes widened almost imperceptibly. He appeared relieved, intrigued. I tensed, regretting that I had spoken at all.

"My name is Saalim." He bowed his head forward. "Where is your father?"

"My—my father? I don't know . . ." It was a strange question. "What are you?" I finally asked.

"Do you not believe me to be a man?" A small smirk crept onto his lips. When I did not respond, he continued. "I am a jinni."

Jinn. My skin tingled. We had all heard the stories, legends of such creatures. They were rogues with volatile magic, not to be trusted.

He continued to stare at me until concern distorted his features. He stepped forward, his hand outstretched as if to touch me. I leaned back, flinching, but could not retreat further, as I sat pressed against the front of the throne. Heat radiated off of him, hot waves that crashed into me.

He paused when he saw me cower and pulled his hand back to his side.

"There is blood on your face. Are you hurt?"

I gestured to the dead men that surrounded us. The jinni looked around the room with surprise. How he had not noticed them before, I did not know. With his attention on the corpses, I roughly wiped my face with my fingers to remove the stains, realizing too late that the blood on my face had come from my own bloodied hands.

"Your father is safe," he said after a moment. It was not a question. Did he sound disappointed?

"How do you know?"

He looked back at me, as though considering an answer, but said nothing.

I asked, "Do you belong to him?"

"Some would say I do. Masira would disapprove of the idea that he had ownership over me. I serve whoever releases me, you see. I served your father. Now, you."

My brow knitted, and I cocked my head. This jinni belonged to the King. He could be his ally, his friend. Or, he might tell of my disobedience purely for his own amusement. My stomach lurched, and I sat straight up.

"He will be returning soon," I said quickly. "You should go back." I gestured to the empty glass jar on the ground. "I—I am sorry, I did not know what would happen when . . . If I had known . . . it was a mistake . . . I didn't mean to release you . . ." The words tumbled out. The last thing I wanted now was to face the Salt King's fury.

"Emel, stop," He said this soothingly, raising his palms to me. "I will speak nothing of this to your father, if that is what you fear."

He knew my name. I had not told him my name. I had to get out of there.

Fear flashed across his face as he watched me, but his words were level. "Wait. I am not yet ready to return home."

He flicked his fingers into the air, and suddenly, the room was absent of all sound. Even the torches blazing around the perimeter of the room were silent. Astonishingly, they had frozen in place and flickered no longer—their tapered flames like glowing stone. There was a stillness in the air around me that felt surreal, magical. I turned back to the jinni.

"What happened? What did you do?" I backed around the throne, my hands in front of me, preparing for I knew not what.

"Stilled time. No one will come now. No one can bother us." He seemed satisfied, pleased with what he had done. The edges of his mouth lifted into a small smile, though they scarcely reached his cheeks before he saw my face. His smile faltered.

"I don't want to hurt you," he said as he stepped forward, slowly closing the space between us. "I *can't* hurt you." His words were so earnest, I stopped moving. "Please," he said, and reached a hand toward my face. He moved slowly, as though approaching a wild bird. He touched my temple. I winced, closing my eyes. The heat of him rushed at me like a gust of wind, but his touch was soft. He ran his index finger across my forehead and down my cheeks, the tip of his finger leaving a muted burn.

His caress was soft, careful. And though it was not like Aashiq's, it reminded me of that which I had lost.

When he pulled his hand away, I opened my eyes. He continued to move slowly, his gaze repeatedly flicking to my face as if to check that I was alright. When he noted my trembling hands, I saw his shoulders fall.

"You can trust me," he whispered again. "Watch." He took my hands one by one and ran his finger along my palms. My mouth fell open. The blood disappeared beneath his touch.

"It is better this way. You won't draw attention when you return to your sisters."

Speechless, I touched my clean palms.

"Now," he continued. "You have released me from my vessel, so I am bound to fulfill your wishes."

"Wishes . . . ?" I was reeling.

"You are my master. I serve you." He dropped to his knees and began to bow. I was reminded of the palace servants, of my sisters.

"No. Stop it. Stand up." I touched his shoulder. His skin was hot, and I pulled my hand away as if I had been burned.

He looked up from his kneel, but he did not rise.

His offer was mesmerizing as endless possibilities flooded me. Oh, the things I could wish for: freedom, my sisters' freedom, a brick of salt for Firo, my mother's freedom, my father's death, one thousand dha, a cold bath, a large meal. But in that moment, I could think of only one thing that I wanted most, and I cared not that legends said to be careful with the jinn.

"Now? Can I wish for something right now?"

He nodded and smiled. "Anything."

"Bring back Aashiq." My voice shook when I said his name. I pressed my hands together and said it strongly. "I wish for you to bring Aashiq back to life." I dropped to my knees in front of him, growing hopeful again. Perhaps all was not lost! I smiled. "Please. It's all I will ask of you." The slave begged the slave.

He dropped his head. "That I cannot give."

My smile fell. "What?" I asked, the aching sorrow beginning anew.

"Once Masira takes, she will not return." His voice was quiet, and he looked at me sadly. "I cannot bring him back to you."

"Then what can you do?" I said, standing, tears spilling again. "What good are you?"

My words hit him like lashes. "Emel . . ." He rose to his feet. "There are limits to the magic. Your father had the same—"

My father. This jinni belonged to the Salt King, and jinn were dangerous. He was not someone, some *thing*, I could trust, regardless of what he said.

"My father?" I was incredulous. "I am not talking of your master," I huffed. "I need to return to my sisters. You must return to that." I pointed to the vessel. "And I want you to not speak of this to the King."

He nodded his head, his mouth turned down. "It will be as you want. Perhaps next time, you will have a desire that I can fulfill."

"I will never see you again. Let me go."

He sighed. "I will grant that for you. But know, if you need something, you need only to think of me. I will come, if I can."

With those words, the jinni moved close to me. He placed his hands tightly on my shoulders. I grimaced, trying to step away, fearful of a betrayal that proved he was loyal to my father, but before I could escape his grasp, the room shifted, and I found myself in front of my home.

I spun around. Jael and Alim beside the entrance, alert with hands on the hilts of their swords, were as frozen as the flames had been. I peered down the path behind me and saw nothing but a whisper of golden dust. There was no movement, and I heard nothing at all. Time did not move. Confusion throbbing in my skull, I pressed my fingers to my brow.

My sisters were arranged in a motionless cluster when I stepped into the tent, all still, draped in their sparkling ahira costumes. I saw tears and horror on their rigid faces, mouths hanging open, evidently in the middle of speaking. The large torch blazing at the center of the room reached toward the sky, desperate and still. I had only a moment to register all of this before everything changed, and the room was alive again.

"Emel! Thank Eiqab you are okay!" Raheemah cried.

Lamentations of concern for me, our father, and our brothers surrounded us. Seeing them, the pain of the afternoon stung me again. I could scarcely comprehend any of it, dizzy as I was by everything that happened. They asked where I had been, if I had seen anything. I shrugged and shook my head, not knowing how to explain that something else, something separate from them, had happened to me.

"What of Aashiq?" Tavi asked.

Our eyes met, and I shook my head. I did not want to talk about it now. She understood. Carefully, she wrapped her arms around me, and we embraced while my sisters talked and talked and talked.

When the guards informed us that we were safe for now, that the threat had been eliminated, I went to my mat. I wanted to sink into the deepest sleep. When I lay down, I felt a firm swelling beneath my back. Confused, I reached under and found a large indigo sack beside my map and ink. It was wide enough for me to fit both of my hands inside. This was not the small pouch I normally kept concealed. I pulled open the bag.

More salt than I had ever possessed in my life, more than all I had taken from the King, met my eyes. I looked to my sisters. None paid me any attention. A family could live comfortably for years with the amount I clutched in my palms. I had not stolen this, so who else would be so daring to steal and gift it to me—to put it where I hid all of my things? Who, besides my sisters, knew of that? It was almost as if it had appeared by magic.

Magic.

With a swift tug of the strings, I closed the bag and stuffed it beneath my bed. Who was this jinni, and what did he want with me?

I curled into myself and pulled the blanket over my eyes to sleep.

May Eiqab show me mercy and keep me forever in my dreams.

5

AFTER MATIN'S ATTACK, the settlement was secured, and the remainder of the invaders were chased and killed or captured and imprisoned. The entire perimeter of the palace was heavily guarded by the King's soldiers.

The days that followed, I wavered between crippling grief that Aashiq was gone and nauseous worry that my father would learn I released his jinni. When no one summoned me to the Salt King those first few days, I began to hope the jinni had been truthful after all. Either that or someone else was now master of the wish-granting legend.

One morning, I went to see my mother. She lounged in the harem on a thickly stuffed mattress, studying a long roll of parchment, her brow creased as she concentrated.

"Mama," I said, suddenly needing her to treat me like a child again despite the years of me demanding otherwise.

When the wound was deep, Mama could fill it fastest.

She sat up quickly, pushing the paper away. The loosely tied robe she was wearing fell off her shoulder, exposing her bright golden necklace. She covered herself and beckoned.

"Emel," she said my name as if she understood everything in the world. I went to her and curled into her lap. "I am sorry," she whispered. "I am sorry for so many things." She wrapped her arms around me and rocked me while I cried.

Even ungroomed, the wives in the harem glowed beautifully from their well-kept life, and seeing them was another searing reminder of what I had lost in Aashiq. They approached me, murmuring and cooing sympathetically, some nursing babes of their own, others perhaps wishing their own child would come in need of them too. The women pressed their warm fingers to my back and neck as they consoled me. To many, I was also theirs.

Since I was moved to the ahira tent at thirteen years, more than the others, I frequented the harem. I was never close with Mama, always feeling as though she had a wall of secrets between us. Some days she was soft embraces and warmth, others she was stiff shoulders and reticence. Still I loved to see her because she loved to tell me stories, and I loved to listen. Sometimes, a secret would slip through her tales, and I would understand her just a little better. Mama told me legends of the jinn that were as capricious as Masira, of the hatif that murmured across the dunes and confused travelers, of the Si'la who lured nomads and shifted her shape, of magic that sparked at the desert's edge. And some days, when we were alone, she'd tuck me under her arm and whisper tales that she made me promise not to share. The parts where she talked about her home. Of walking through her settlement alone, the excitement of visiting the marketplace. Of making friends with strangers and servants alike, teaching that kindness reaped fortune. And the most quietly, she'd tell me that I had to visit her home one day. That I had to promise her that I'd go and see it all. That I wouldn't let anything stop me.

I promised and promised and promised. Because I wanted to hear more. I understood later that those promises were like pipe smoke, weightless and gone with the slightest whisper of air. So in my quiet way, the only way I could, I made my map. If I wouldn't visit by foot, I would visit in my dreams.

When my tears slowed. When, finally, I felt the weight of my grief had lessened even just a little, Mama spoke. "Let's go to the rama, eh?" She helped me stand, then dressed to leave with the most stunning abaya and veil only a king's wife could wear—no villager could afford to decorate their veil with shining, golden dha.

We walked until we reached the wide, empty area surrounded by palace tents. Aside from the guards that stood at its entrance, it was empty. Most waited for prayers until the sun was at its highest—when the sand was hottest.

"Let us speak to the Sons," she said as she led me to the center of the rama.

I knelt next to her and pressed my hands and brow into the sand. It was warm, but I did not wince. My prayers would be quiet that morning.

We were silent for some time before, finally, Mama spoke.

"Your father will address the people today," she murmured beside me.

I opened my eyes, seeing each tiny grain piled to make the modest dunes.

"Tell me what he says," she continued.

"I—I don't understand," I said, tripping on my words.

"I know that you leave. I know what you do."

I tilted my head to look at her, my pulse quickening. What else did she know? Of the salt I stole? Of the jinni?

"Don't look at me," she hissed in warning. "They can't know we're speaking." I did as she said. "Your father has told us nothing about the attack, and I want to know more. Can you go?"

"I will." I swallowed hard, unsettled by what she knew. Who had told her? Who else would they tell?

BRIBING MY way out of the palace was not as easy this time. The guards were on edge as much as the villagers, and they stood with more to lose should they face the King's wrath. And though they would admit it to none, Alim and Jael worried about me, too.

"It's not safe for you," Alim said. But because of the jinni, I had deep pockets. There was no guard that could not be bribed, and after much persuasion, and a heavy payment, I headed toward the market to find Firoz.

The air crackled with nervous tension as I wound my way through the settlement. Passing villagers shot me uneasy glances before returning their eyes to the ground. People spoke quietly in tight circles, peering distrustfully around them. Nearly every face was covered, and the anonymity made me uneasy.

The people had grown complacent living under the Salt King's rule. Desert tribes attacked each other often, eager to absorb other tribes and grow more powerful. It was the life man knew, it was how nomads survived. But that unpredictable and violent life was abandoned when the settlement and the Salt King's reputation grew to such a stature that none dared strike. Most who came to live in our settlement did so for stability and safety. Matin and his soldiers ripped away that illusion and provided a stabbing reminder that nowhere was safe. We, too, were vulnerable.

With the caravan gone, and most of the villagers hiding away in their homes, the marketplace was a stark contrast to when I saw it last. It was eerily hushed with so few shops open, the lack of street performers, and only a handful of people making purchases.

Firoz sat with his arms propped behind him, indifferently watching the villagers pass. His basin of coconut juice was disconcertingly full.

"Firo," I said as I ducked into the tent. Our eyes met, and he jumped to his knees.

"Thank Eiqab!" he said, too loudly in the hushed market. In two kneeling steps, he had his arms wrapped around me, his fists clutching the robes at my back.

"Shhh!" I pushed him away. His affectionate display would draw attention.

"No one is looking at us," he said, gesturing at the empty lane. He did not take his eyes from me as we sat on the blanket. He was so relieved, I felt guilty I had not sent Jael to tell him I was okay. "The guards are probably assembling for the address. I haven't seen one in some time. That's why you're here, I assume?"

"Of course."

"Sons, Emel. I wanted to ask after you but didn't want to cause trouble." His fingers tore at his hair. "Were you there? I heard rumors . . ."

"Yes. I saw enough."

Despite his frown, his eyes sparked. "Come on. Business has been slow anyway. Let's go talk." We carefully carried the basin home to his disappointed mother.

We walked through the village until we arrived at the only area that seemed unaffected by the rising tension. Music floated through the air and met my ears as we approached, and when we turned down the lively byway, the sounds engulfed us completely. The baytahira—the part of the settlement where people were paid to do the same thing I did for suitors. Besides the loud music, the garish fabric suspended from shoddy tent framework declared we were amongst the village whores. Scantily clad women and men draped themselves on stools and blankets scattered outside open tents hoping for business. Some tents were closed, the sounds from within muffled by the music. Those who were unoccupied called seductively as we passed.

"I'll take two for the price of one."

"Handsome boy, I'll do whatever you ask."

The first time Firoz brought me here, I was horrified. It was the last place I wanted to be found if I were discovered outside the palace. I had stomped away, but Firoz had talked me down.

"There are no people better at keeping secrets than those that live here. There is also no better place to talk. We won't be overheard." The loud music was a testament to that. I never asked him why he was so familiar with the baytahira. I did not want to know.

"One private tent. Until the twilight horn," Firoz said to a formidable woman who owned an aggregate of tents. He handed her five bronze nab.

I felt a small prickle of guilt letting him pay for the tent when I had a brick's worth of salt attached to my hip, but I said nothing. Passing salt to palace guards was less of a risk because they were already paid in salt at times, but a servant woman paying in salt would lead to questions I was not ready to answer.

We were directed to a small tent covered in a zig-zagging red pattern on black fabric with its front tied open. The tents for hire were arranged so the entrances faced a small sandy passage. In the middle of the lane, two young men sat under a lean-to playing loudly a rhythmic melody with their oud and darbuka. I followed Firoz inside. Atop the thin, filthy sheet that covered the sand, a tan scorpion reveled in the darkness. I backed away swiftly, bleating like a goat. Firoz rushed in and chased it out.

"What is your problem?" he asked, laughing.

"Stung when I was a child," I said, tucking my legs beneath me once I was seated. I pointed at my foot as if the red mark was still there.

Once Firoz sealed the tent, the closed space grew unbearably hot. We unwrapped our faces, and I untangled myself from my abaya until I was only in my fustan.

"Tell me what happened?" Firoz took off his tunic and fanned himself with it.

I told him of the afternoon.

"So you were going to marry him," Firoz said in disbelief.

I nodded, feeling the pit open up in my stomach again. I wiped the sweat from my legs with my dress.

He exhaled. "I'm sorry."

Tears welled in my eyes. It seemed that one day soon, I would be dried of all my tears.

Firoz watched me closely. "There will be someone else."

"He was the first in seven years." That invisible fist again tightened on my throat, and I fussed with my nails.

"So? Another could arrive tomorrow."

I glared at him. "It does no good to give me hope, when we both know that I'll be out on the streets in a year." The pit in my stomach yawned wider, filling with sorrow and fear until it brimmed over the edge.

"I've been thinking I'll need a helper at the shop."

When I didn't smile, he softened. "You forget that with hope, we can be the most dangerous people here." Firoz took my hand and squeezed it. "Tell me what happened after," he said, and I told him of the attack. Of the swinging blades, the death and gore. Of my father's escape, of Nassar's oblivion.

That I remained by myself in the throne room. I did not mention the jinni. The secret too big to trouble him with.

"How'd you get home?"

I picked at a loose thread on my robe. "I found my way back."

"It wasn't so easy for some."

"What do you mean?"

"By the time the bells clanged, the streets were already swarmed with the Altamaruq—"

"The what?"

He sighed, exasperated by my ignorance. "The rebels, the soldiers. It's what the villagers call them. It was like the Altamaruq waited for something, and I assume it was like that in the palace. Of course, we didn't know what was happening with the King.

"I was in my shop when everything started. As more and more of those men arrived—lurking like jackals—I knew something was amiss. I went home. There were so many along the way. So many fools approached them. They seemed peaceful, really. They didn't attack unless a villager tried to fend them off . . ." He shook his head and pressed his fingers to his eyes as though trying to rub away the memories. "Eventually, more of their men came sprinting down the lanes, running away from the palace, hollering to flee. The King's guard chased them out."

"And I was worried about the few soldiers I saw . . ."

"So many more got away. Though I've heard there are still some hiding amongst us. I think they've got one in the prison. Ma said they are searching for something, but no one knows what."

"I know what they seek."

"You do?"

"My father's throne. Matin tried to kill him."

He shrugged.

"I suppose. Someone else said there's a spy among the King's men, so they'll surely be back."

"Spy?" I thought of what my mother knew of my leaving. Was she informed by this spy?

He shrugged.

"What else do you know about the Altamaruq?"

"Not much. They're suspected to be from the north since they arrived with the caravan, but we don't know where."

"My father said Matin was from far north. Do you think the desert's edge?"

Firoz looked at me skeptically.

I continued. "Do you believe the legends? The ones that talk of the magic there? Do you think they are true? Do you think Rafal is to be believed?"

"I don't know. If there is magic, it doesn't seem to have found us here. Besides Rafal, I have not met a traveler nor trader from the edge that claims to have seen it." Aashiq had said the same. "Rafal is a storyteller. I'm sure most of what he says is imagined."

I peered around the tent, then leaned close into Firoz. "Do you believe," I lowered my voice, "jinn are real?"

Firoz turned to me, confused. It was not something settlers often spoke of. Many of the elders cautioned against mentioning jinn, as though the word itself might summon one.

"Why ask that?"

I hesitated. "Since we're talking of dream-tales, you know."

"I remember those stories." He smiled sadly. "My favorites were the ones where they granted wishes. What would you wish for?"

"I wouldn't trust one enough to wish," I lied, realizing how foolish I had been with the jinni. I shouldn't even have spoken with him when I learned what he was. The salt grew heavy against my hip.

Firoz frowned. "That would be foolish. What would you have to lose?"

I stared at my feet, saying nothing.

He went on. "I would wish to be gone from here. Live somewhere I can be myself—where I don't have to act in this absurd charade." Firoz tossed his scarf across the tent, suddenly enraged.

I wanted to distract him from his ire.

"I'd wish for a bath to use every single day. Unlimited flatbread for Tavi. Rain." For Aashiq. To be free of my father's court. To be able to say no without consequence.

"This is childish," he spat. "Imagining what we would wish for. Living in some dream world, hoping for things that cannot be."

"Now where's that dangerous hope?" I said softly.

I saw a spark of a smile.

We were silent for a long time, enduring the heat to bask in the luxury of privacy. Then, the twilight horn sounded, so we left to watch our king address his people.

SHOULDERS PRESSED together in the great tent that sat adjacent to the King's palace. We stood huddled around an impromptu, wobbling, wooden stage where my father would make his speech. The tent felt cool, despite the number of people that squeezed in to see their king, because atop the platform, a swarm of slaves tirelessly swung palm fronds to circulate the air. Around the perimeter of the stage, the King's soldiers stood side by side, blades poised to strike.

A. S. Thornton

We tunneled our way through the people to stand toward the back of the tent. An excited murmur spread through the crowd, and I knew Father had arrived. Garbed in extravagant maroon robes studded with rubies, he was followed closely by Nassar, who carried with him a tightly wound scroll, a jar of ink, and a large, feather quill.

Nassar. How could a man who had arrived in our village unknown and alone climb the ranks of my father's sycophants so quickly? Three, maybe four, years ago, he come to our settlement with only the clothes he wore and a pack of things he had on his camel's back. My father was impressed, so much so that this past spring, Nassar had become the Salt King's partner and counselor, his first vizier. Nassar's ruthlessness and wicked cunning—and his saccharine flattery—certainly were attractive to my father, but Sons, where was that when Matin arrived? If he had been paying any attention at all, he may have saved some of the guards. He may have saved Aashiq. Anger sparked in me as I watched him.

Father climbed onto the stage holding up his bulbous turban with its heavy jasper stone as he bent forward. Nassar scurried up behind him. The room was silent, all held their breath as they awaited the address from their king.

His chest and belly jutted out, testing the strength of his shirt buttons, as he reveled in the praise. I watched him with disgust, remembering his sloppiness, his drunkenness when Matin attacked. There was no demonstration of his famed sword-skills that afternoon, and the same anger infused by Nassar's incompetence burned in me again.

Aashiq had died because they failed. My future had crumbled because of them.

"My loyal and beloved people! I hope Eiqab has seen to it that your days are warm and your olive trees generous!" the King bellowed. His oily face shined like polished silver, and his wide smile showed his stained teeth, glistening like wet stones. His people roared. Bile rose from the depths of my stomach, sour and acrid. Which god did these people cheer for: Eiqab or their king?

"I know you are afraid. I know that you have heard vile rumors of these people who challenged me—the Altamaruq."

Villagers hissed and heckled at the mention of Matin and his soldiers.

"Never fear," the King continued. "These people are nothing." He slammed his fist against an invisible barrier.

They cheered. Nassar wrote furiously on an unfurled scroll, the feather spinning along the parchment.

"They are no threat. They were a small army and were squashed like a mosquito between the tips of my fingers. They are a worthless tribe and launched their attack like children, unprepared and weak. My strong army—your army—chased them out of our settlement and killed every last one of them. The cowards who surrendered have been imprisoned."

My father continued on about his strength and his soldiers' bravery. I grew tired of listening. There was little I was going to glean from his speech suffused with lies.

My attention wandered to the people surrounding me, as I searched for the supposed spies.

Two dozen guards protected the King. None would be so foolish to attack him now. I scanned their faces, and my gaze snagged on a man, familiar yet strange. An uneasy tingling traveled down my neck. He stood close beside my father. I had not seen this guard before, yet something nagged at me, telling me I had. As if he felt my stare amongst the hundreds in the crowded room, the guard's eyes met mine, and the gentle tingling exploded into a fire that burned through me down to my toes. I gasped. His eyes were a flaming gold. His stare was unrelenting until, with the utmost subtlety, he gently dipped his head into a nod.

Firoz heard my gasp. "Are you okay?"

The jinni. Another who couldn't help, whom I couldn't trust, who failed to save Aashiq. My chest heaved with seething breath, my anger molten. I nodded to Firoz, but did not take my eyes from the masked soldier. He did not take his eyes away from me.

At first glance, he did not appear remarkable. He was just a man: gone was his golden skin and chestnut hair pulled back in golden bands. He was another one of the King's men: short, black hair, tanned skin, a pristine white uniform of the guard. But now that I knew who he was, I could almost see the radiating glow of his magic, the carved features of his deity-like face. I could even see the gold clasped to his wrists, seeping into his skin, peaking out beneath his sleeves.

The speech blurred by. I heard the King's words but could not make sense of them. I stared at the jinni, heart pounding in my chest, anger clouding my vision and every single thought.

I looked at the villagers who stood near. How did they miss this magical jinni standing beside their king? My eyes found his again. He still stared. Movement seemed impossible, his eyes pinning me down like a collector's moth. I trembled with fear, with fury. What was he doing to me? I wanted to scream at him, at all of them. But even more, I wanted to be free of them.

The jinni's mouth curved up to one side, a reluctant smile, almost a plea. No, I would not indulge. I tore my gaze from his and leaned into Firoz.

"I need to go."

Wedging my way through the hollering and heaving people, I thought I could feel the jinni's eyes on me and a warmth, like a hot wind, brushing against my neck.

When I stepped out into the open air, two partridges, with swirls of black on their wings, fluttered away. The sun was sinking behind the settlement tents. Their shadows were long, cast onto the sand, sharp like the teeth of a fox.

I ran rapidly back to my home. The warm wind at my back urging me on.

6

"YOU WILL GET US ALL beaten to death." Sabra stormed at me when I walked into the tent. Conversations were silenced as my sisters turned to watch us.

"I—what?" I stepped back from Sabra.

Her fury was palpable.

"Your little escapades," she hissed the words, speaking quietly so none outside would not hear. "Your selfish adventures. Going to the village—your forbidden life—while we are imprisoned in this infernal palace." She waved her hands wildly as she spoke.

"I don't understand." I looked from Sabra to my sisters who stared at us from around the room, waiting for someone to explain. Sabra could make the same choice to go into the settlement, she just never did. None of my sisters did.

Tavi crept over to Sabra. "Leave her. She didn't know. How could she?"

"Do you hear how she defends you? She doesn't even realize what you're doing could get you killed. Could get her killed." Sabra turned to Tavi. "Sit down. This is between me and Emel." Tavi did not move.

"Patrolling guards checked on us this afternoon," Sabra said. "They counted us. Imagine their surprise when they found one of us to be missing. Where were you? Oh, just out doing whatever it is you do out there." She fluttered her hand as though shaking off an insect.

"C–counted us?" I stammered. "But what about girls at the rama or harem?" My sisters came and went from our home frequently. It made no sense that they would suddenly expect all of us to be present in one afternoon.

"You were the only one missing."

Clutching the clothes on my chest, I steadied my breath. I thought of my mother. Had she set me up? I shook my head. That was ridiculous. So someone indeed knew one of us was leaving, someone that was not a friend. A traitorous guard—Alim, Jael? I would be punished, maybe even banished. Or worse.

"We lied for you. Said you felt ill and were occupied." Sabra tipped her head in the direction of the pots. "Had to save our own necks so we didn't get in trouble for not telling them you'd left. Didn't think of that, did you?"

She was right. I hadn't.

"They left without questions," Tavi said quietly.

I exhaled, grateful for their lies and for the large amount of salt I had given the guards as a bribe. Had they been asked, both men, I was sure, firmly denied the escape of an ahira.

Sensing my distress, Tavi added, "It's okay, Emel. There's no trouble."

"I'm sorry," I said quietly, and my eyes fell to the ground. I had been selfish.

Sabra said, speaking more loudly now, "You're caught up in your own world. You focus on only you. Father gives you extra attention, lavish clothes, more lenience. But what do you have to show for it?" Sabra laughed. "Nothing. Just like me. You aren't special, Emel."

I stared at Sabra, aghast at her words, at her callousness toward the death of Aashiq and my grief. The anger seemed to be years old, waiting for an opportunity to unleash.

The Salt King was shameless, as he was in all things, in his favoritism. He surveyed his ahiran periodically, deciding who was most beautiful, most worth his time. Those he chose would receive extra attention when being courted by a suitor, by gifts of gold-spun costumes and finely crafted chains and jewels. Sisters were always jealous of the chosen ahira, but the feelings vanished the moment the girl was wed.

I had been chosen quite young as a favorite of the King. My attendants said it was because of my beauty: the high bones of my cheeks; my slender neck; my long hair, dark as night; my strong frame that carried large breasts and wide hips. The only evidence I was of the King's blood was the charcoal black of my eyes. I had what men wanted to see, what they wanted to touch and hold.

My father was fascinated by me; touching me, fingering my hair when I was near him during courtings. Like the jinni's vessel, I was one of his favorite baubles. It took years for him to become discouraged by the lack of proposals I received. Even then, his obsession was apparent despite the heavy veil of frustration he pulled between us.

As the years passed, my sisters' jealousy toward me faded—I possessed nothing worth envying. Evidently, Sabra's did not. Our relationship frayed as we got older, and the time that remained for Sabra dwindled to months. I assumed it was her fear of being banished, cast out by her family. I remember watching the same tension snapping between the older ahiran those years ago when another was cast out.

I set my jaw and watched Sabra. I had apologized. There was nothing left for me to say.

"I won't risk my life lying for you," she said. "Don't leave the palace again. If not for your sisters' sake, then for your own. If you do, I'll tell Father." She turned from me.

The girls in the room gasped, and I stared at her retreating back, horrified. All the anger I had felt toward Nassar, the Salt King, the jinni, paled compared to what I felt for my sister—for someone I was supposed to be able to trust. It was cruel.

As I walked to my bed, my shadow jerked wildly from the torch-fire. I thought of Sabra's threat and whether or not it was to be believed. I began planning ways I could sneak out without her realizing. I dropped my veil and robe onto my mat and unfastened the sack full of salt from the leather belt around my dress. I dug a small hole in the sand into which I furiously stuffed the bag before sliding my mat over it.

Raheemah came to me, the stack of cards in one hand and the bowl of cowries and glass beads in her other. I picked up one of the beads, milky blue on the outside, a chip in its surface revealing it to be clear blue on the inside. Slave beads, we called them. As if slavery was something beneath us, as if it were something separate.

"I don't want to play," I said, setting down the bead.

"Okay," Raheemah said. She sat beside me and lowered her voice. "You should know that the guards were just patrolling. Seemed like maybe Father has them on high alert since . . ." She paused, chewing the words she did not want to say. Unlike Sabra, she did not want to remind me of what happened . . . of what I lost that day. "They didn't seem to care one way or the other that you were gone. I don't think anyone knows where you were."

Clasping her shoulder, I brought her to me and hugged her gratefully. She was wrong, though. People knew. Every guard I'd bribed, every hidden servant who peered through splits in tents, my mother. Who else? "It doesn't change Sabra's threat."

"She wouldn't. She's just angry." She picked up my servant's clothes, shaking out the sand before folding them, and hid them away at the bottom of our basket. There was no reason for an ahira to be in possession of clothes like that.

"I don't want to find out if you're right."

Exhaustion consumed me. I lay on my mat and pulled the thin blanket over my head to hide in its shadows. But the heat poured in, and sweat rolled off of me in large drops. I threw the blanket aside.

I was trapped. I had no hope of running and nowhere to run.

MAMA WAS distracted when I told her of the address.

"Did you see anything strange?" She said, interrupting my summary of the King's speech.

I shook my head, thinking of the jinni. "What do you mean?"

"Anyone out of the ordinary?"

I watched her, picking at her fingers just as I did when nervous. Then it hit me. Of course. She wanted to know about the Altamaruq. "No. I saw no one."

I pointed to the stacks of parchment, small looping handwriting scribbled across the pages. "What are you reading? A letter?" One looked to be signed by someone.

"These?" She picked them up and folded them. "Just stories." Reading letters was rare in the palace—the wives had none to correspond with—but reading for pleasure was equally baffling.

I reached for one. "Can I see?" My reading was not strong, and I had never read a story, but it seemed a good distraction.

My mother stood, tucking the parchment to her chest. "Oh, no," she said, a tremor in her voice. "Your father would frown upon it. They're only for children, he'd say. I should get rid of them. They're so silly." She spoke in a rush, smiled weakly, then raised the sheets up to the flames of a nearby torch.

The corners caught on fire, and she dropped them onto the sand and watched them burn, the frankincense in the room was swallowed by the smell of charred meat.

WITH SABRA'S threat at my heels, I did not stray from the palace, and each day that passed was a painful reminder of what I had lost in Aashiq. It was the life I was supposed to leave behind. I was never supposed to be in these tents again. Some days, I would cry. Sons, how often I cried. Others, I would sit and stare at the tent wall, watching to see if the fabric moved, if there was a wind outside I could not feel. I invoked the names of Eiqab and Wahir when gambling away beads in card games, gossiped of neighbors whenever tidbits of information slipped from our attendants, wove tapestries and blankets for palace trade.

In a moment of recklessness, I found the young girl with the marked face and showed her my map. I made her promise me that one day, she would see the world. She promised with wide, disbelieving eyes. Then, her father called to her and she ran from me into his arms. He lifted her from the ground and kissed the mark on her face it seemed one hundred times while she cackled and pushed away from him. He nodded to me before he took her inside their home. I heard her tell him about the world, and in his silence, I heard him listen.

The salt sat unused beneath my mat. As the moon waxed and waned again, the pain of Aashiq was dulled, leaving me in a haze of apathy. My sisters tried to help, telling vulgar jokes and pantomiming nights with suitors with ridiculous flair. Sometimes it did help but just for the moment. Sabra and I would sit across the room from each other, sharing our hatred for the world we lived in, but never daring to let that be something that brought us together. I would not be the first to yield. When servants chattered about the caravans that came and went, I found myself daydreaming of the things I would wish for in a world where the jinni could be trusted. Where he belonged to me and not my father. Always, it was freedom.

Summer was fading to autumn when still there was no sign of the Altamaruq. The King permitted suitors to court again. Some ahiran came back with hearts heavier than when they left, some with bruises, others with news of an impending engagement. I was not again requested by a prince but it was not for a lack of trying.

"I saw Basimah at the rama. She said the muhami may request me again tonight," Fatima said proudly. Rings of red bruises wrapped her forearms, a swelling in the hollow of her cheek. My sisters who sat weaving with us looked up from the tapestry, feigning joy. I stared down at the strands in front of me, pretending to focus on my task.

"Perhaps a wedding then." The false excitement in Kadri's voice provided comfort to none.

"I hope so," Fatima agreed. "I've prayed to Eiqab." The skin on her brow shone where the sand had burned it. "I doused Masira's flames with my tea."

This was the way of the ahiran: to eagerly embrace the life that was given to us, hoping enthusiasm would transform into happiness. Sometimes the men were too rough with us, sometimes intentionally violent. It was our burden as King's daughters, so we must endure it. Life as a thrashed wife was more honorable than life as a castoff, after all.

Fatima looked around the room conspiratorially before leaning in closely and whispering, "I let him kiss me. Down there."

"He wanted to?" The younger girls' eyes were wide with indecent curiosity. Fatima nodded and smiled, one eyebrow arching high.

"Next time he's down there, why don't you give him a heel to the head?" I murmured.

Fatima's lips quirked, and so quietly I almost did not hear the words, she said, "I can promise you that if I become his wife, he'll get more than that."

WHEN WE met the next muhami, I laughed with him, fluttering my eyelashes. When he was across the long room mingling with my sisters, I smiled seductively.

"Emel, come to me," my father said. He had watched me from his deep cushioned lounge. The midday sunlight soaked through the white fabric, heating the air despite the servants who fanned the room. I went to him, stepping around the slaves holding trays of flaky date pastries for only my father and his guests. I eyed the food.

"Sit down," he said, patting his knee. My stomach twisted. I did not want the suitor to see me as a child, destroying his visions of my legs around his waist in bed.

On my father's knee, I could smell the candied, bitter aroma of liquor and his unbathed body. His nostrils whistled in my ear with each breath in, the hot air touched my shoulder each breath out. From the corner of my eye, I could see the golden rings fastened to his nose gleaming.

The King's fingers trailed up and down my spine.

"You are beautiful tonight."

I stiffened. "Thank you, my King."

"Ah, Emel. King? I am your father." He snapped his fingers at one of the slaves holding a silver tray. The man came over dutifully carrying a bowl of small, red jewels. I had never seen anything like them. I stared as the King took one of the shining gems and placed it onto his tongue. He bit into it and tiny drops of liquid hit my cheek. I could smell its sweetness and was baffled. What magic was this?

He reached for another and held it before me. I reached for it.

"Not for you, my greedy minx." He placed it into his mouth. My cheeks grew hot.

He waved the slave and bowl of treasure away. I reached up to my cheek and wiped at the drops. On my fingertip was liquid the color of blood.

"Mmmm," his groan rumbled through me.

An exhibition just for me. A reminder of his power. It was always a show with him. The spark of shame that heated my face ignited into anger. I thought of the words my mother, my attendants told us: you are lucky to be the daughter of the King.

Show him your gratitude by being graceful, subservient. Still, the shame and anger lingered.

"Come, Qadir," the King called to the suitor, "and meet my beautiful daughter." His fingertips pressed into my shoulder, my hip, my back.

Why did I have to feel grateful when his sordid paws touched me like a prize he wanted to pawn? There was so little I could control in my life, why let someone else dictate how I felt about my father and his court? If I could not choose my love, at least I could choose my enmity.

I needed to get away from him and his wicked palace. I looked up to Qadir as he crossed the room. I attempted to smile, to show Qadir why he should choose me. *Take me from here.* My face cramped as I held my features in an eager expression despite the hand that now rested on my thigh.

My father discussed my prowess both intellectually and physically and my role in Qadir's home should he marry me. On and on, this and that. Talking of me like I was a goat to be raised on new land. Qadir listened more than he spoke, his narrowed eyes betraying his unease with my father's intimacy.

My father's hand traveled to my inner thigh. It was heavy and hot. I held my breath. I imagined myself to be a stone on his lap—unfeeling, uncaring. My eyes dropped to his hand, and I glimpsed gold and glass peeking from behind my father's robes: the jinni's vessel.

Qadir's eyes darted to my father's hand, too closely linked to his daughter, then to me, then back to my father. Almost imperceptibly he leaned back, the corners of his lips tugging downward. I turned away. Embarrassment, shame, and fury striking my temples like a hammer. I began to stand, to move away from my father, to get away from the monster, to save my pride, and show Qadir that I did not want it either. But my father's hand shoved me back onto his lap.

"My dove, where are you going? Stay." His words held an icy edge that terrified me.

Looking down, I saw again the glass vessel. Only this time, I noticed it was empty. Was the jinni there in that room? Quickly, I searched for him. Perhaps Firoz was right. What did I have to lose? The jinni could help me get out. I didn't have to wait until my father decided I was worthless. Maybe I could leave now.

My father's grip was tight on my leg now. I was shackled to him, under his control. Just like his slaves, just like my sisters. Just like the jinni.

When I met the jinni after Matin's attack, I had been too distressed by everything that had happened that I didn't see the jinni—how he had asked permission, had let me leave when I asked. What if he wasn't loyal to the Salt King? He had not told my father of our encounter. Could he be trusted after all? Maybe he was another unwilling slave, and I had let his offer slip through my grasp. I wanted to throw my head into my hands and kick my feet like an outraged child. What had I done?

Qadir and my father continued to talk, the muhami barely hiding his revulsion in his strained words. I did not pay attention to their conversation. I wanted to see the jinni again. Perhaps only to test his word. Did he truly intend no harm? Could he really grant wishes? Through him, could I be free? But there was also a part of me that wanted to see if he was real—had it all been a horrible dream?

"Go," the King said as he pushed me off his lap, his nails pinching my skin. "Speak with your muhami."

Qadir stiffly guided me to an unoccupied part of the room.

"You are the most appealing woman here," he said, his manner affected, just as Aashiq's had been when we met for the first time. Qadir's eyes raked me from top to bottom, seeing me as an ahira now that I was not sitting atop my father's lap. I looked behind him at the guards placed around the room. Hoping that the jinni lurked nearby, I peered at each face closely. But there were none like him, no unearthly shimmer in the air.

"Am I displeasing?" Qadir said, his voice sharp. The change in tone snapped my attention back to him.

"No, it is quite the opposite," I said in a rush, bowing forward. "You unsettle me by your presence. Your prosperous reputation precedes you. I am intimidated."

He seemed appeased, so we talked of frivolous things. Qadir found any excuse to lay his hands upon me—caressing my neck, touching the jewels on my bodice, the bangles on my wrists, feigning to brush a mosquito from my thigh or sand from my cheek.

"Emel," he said, taking my hand. "You fascinate me."

"You are generous with your flattery," I demurred. "I confess, I am the one who is enchanted."

"Let us go to your father." He began to lead me toward the King.

No.

I did not want to be chosen that day, to see the muhami that night. I wished desperately to see the jinni instead. If he could offer me another way out, one that didn't bind me in marriage . . .

At once, Qadir dropped my hand and walked toward Raheemah. I stood suddenly alone, nonplussed as I peered at my sisters, a few watching with expressions I am sure mirrored mine. What had just happened?

My father shot me a violent glance when Qadir informed him that he was choosing Raheemah in my stead.

I fell in line behind the rest of my sisters as we were escorted back home, still trying to understand Qadir's sudden decision, when I felt a hot wind rush at my back.

"Were you looking for me?" A quiet, deep voice rumbled behind me.

I jolted and whipped around. The jinni stood behind me, undisguised and wholly himself. He towered above me, the almost-golden skin of his chest gleaming in the filtered sun. His eyes twinkled with curiosity.

I turned back to my sisters, eager to see what they thought of the jinni who now stood amongst us. None of them had turned. They continued to walk away.

"What . . . ?" I pointed to my sisters' retreating backs.

"They won't notice me, not if I don't want them to." There was a thinly veiled conceit.

I looked back to them.

One by one, they went into another room until we were the only two standing in the hall. "What are you doing here?" I asked.

"They won't hear you, you don't have to whisper." He grasped the golden cuff on his wrist, his fingers absently moving over the place where the metal seemed to melt into his hand. "I have come for you. Unless I am mistaken, you were looking for me."

"How did you know?" I thought back to the courting. Had it been so obvious?

"When I am released, a vague connection is formed between me and my master. I can feel the tenor of all your desires, but I feel the most strongly when you desire my presence. It is how the jinni knows to come to his master should they be apart."

I widened my eyes, immediately uncomfortable. What else did he sense?

"I am not privy to your thoughts, Emel. I do not know what you are thinking."

I squinted at him, not sure if I trusted his answer.

"What I sense from you is indistinct at best. This afternoon, I felt you wish for me."

"You don't know what I'm thinking?"

"No. I am here because you sought me. Have you a wish?"

"I do." I knew what I wanted, and perhaps he did, too, but first, I had to make sure of one thing. "You said I do not have to fear you, that you are to be trusted."

He nodded.

"I wish for you to prove it."

The jinni cocked his head to the side. A smile slowly stretched across his face.

"Will that be your first wish, then?"

I shifted. Perhaps my wish was foolish. Was he laughing at me? But I thought of my father and all the men who took advantage of a sparkling, submissive ahira. I thought of the tales that told of guileful jinn. I needed to know that Saalim would not be the same.

"It is my wish."

Standing before me was the same man I had seen two moons ago, but in that moment, the jinni looked different. Eyes alight with flaming gold, shoulders back and chest up, instead of defeated, he looked hopeful.

Then, the ground slipped from beneath my feet.

7

THE UNMOVING, STIFLING HEAT of the palace tents was gone. The air felt open, and a breeze touched my face. It was hot but it did not cling like it did under the blanketed tents. The strained sunlight I had been walking under moments before had darkened. I was in a shaded place. I opened my eyes.

In the distance was a cluster of browns, reds, and blues distorted by the waves of heat rising up from the ground. It was isolated but massive, spilling into the surrounding expanse of sand as if it consumed it. Bright, white peaks emerged from the heart of the colors, and I understood. I stared at my settlement. So then, where was I?

Several dozen, tightly huddled trees—some palms, others broad and leafy—collided above me. The coos and chirps of birds streamed from branches that cast welcome shadows over a small, sandy area. At the center was a shining blue pool. The sand seeping into my slippers was cool.

"You are smart," the jinni said.

I turned to him.

"To ask me to reveal my intentions, to prove I am someone you can trust. It is a clever wish. You see, I am but a conduit for Masira's will. I do not have control over the outcome of a desire. She will fulfill wishes however She sees fit, so long as it honors the wish truthfully."

So he was not a god himself, but he was near to one. Watching the light glint off of the water, I thought of what it meant to be speaking with someone so close to the goddess. Did I want that closeness to a deity? It seemed it could bring great fortune or terrible destruction.

He continued, "She is fickle."

I knew this, so I did not understand why he was explaining it to me.

"If my intention were to hurt you or to reveal what you've done to the King, you would see that now, even if I did not want it to be shown. Masira will always honor a wish, but the more specific you are, the more clear your intention, the less creative She can be."

"Is it magic, what you do?"

"Some call it magic, but it is the providence of the goddess. If She wills it, then how can it be otherwise?"

His words came out as though he'd been waiting to tell them to me. I looked unhurriedly at his large, carved frame as he spoke. The jinni's skin seemed, unbelievably, to shine even brighter in the shade of the trees. My eyes lingered on his broad chest, narrow hips, and finally, his face. His eyes were set under a heavy brow that cast deep shadows. His nose was long and straight and led my eyes down to a wide mouth that was almost hidden within his beard. His sharp cheekbones reminded me of the royal men and women I saw woven in the tapestries hanging in my father's halls. He was beautiful in a divine sort of way, and upon realizing it, I felt absurdly self-conscious as one does when they hope they are, or fear they are not, regarded in kind.

Heat flooded my cheeks, and I ran my fingers through the leafy bushes as I examined them. "You have brought me to my father's oasis."

"I have."

"Why?"

"It is the safest place there is, without straying too far from your home."

The nervous flutter that started when the jinni had whisked me from the hallway now frenzied against my chest as I realized I really was away from the settlement. For the first time in my life. I briefly wondered if a guard standing at the perimeter would see my shadow amongst the trees, but I knew he could not. No one could see me, no one could hear me. None but the jinni.

It was an even greater freedom than being out in the village. I felt giddy, and a child-like smile spread across my face. I wanted to run around and jump from stone to stone and dive into the cool water. To frolic with the untethered feeling of being away from my home. But I also wanted to sit and comb through all of my questions that had tangled together since I'd first met the jinni.

"So I can trust you, really?" I asked, still not looking at him.

"My word is Masira's will, my promises unbreakable."

I raised an eyebrow and met his gaze. "Well, then I wish for one thousand wishes."

The corner of his lip lifted. "Granted."

A pleasant tingle crawled down my spine.

"Did my father find you here?"

"He did."

I nodded, unsurprised. So those rumors were true; that the oasis was a magical place was not wrong. I looked around the refuge, wondering where my father stood when he came upon the glass vessel filled with golden smoke. How did he feel when the jinni told him he would grant his desires?

"And you are the reason that he amassed so much wealth."

"I am." He watched me as I spun, looking at the trees and sand and water and rocks. He added, "The reason the dunes don't swallow the settlement. The reason no challenger can defeat your father . . ."

Yes, that all made sense now. I waited to hear what else he had done, but he did not continue. "Do others know about you?"

The jinni considered the question, then said, "I am sure they do not. Your father is very secret and very proud of his reputation. If people knew he had a jinni, it would destroy the illusion. It would also bring great conflict. People easily kill to possess something that grants wishes, something that promises fortune."

I thought of Matin and his soldiers. They killed without that knowledge, I could not imagine what would happen should the desert know of the jinni.

"But you can't grant every wish," I said, remembering Aashiq.

A shadow crossed his face. "No, I cannot." He did not elaborate, and I did not want to unbury the memories.

"What did my father wish for, to become what he is?"

"Why? Do you plan to wish for the same?" He sat on a smooth stone and did not wait for me to answer. "Your father is wise. Instead of asking to be the most powerful man or the wealthiest man, both of which can be interpreted as Masira sees fit, he wished to possess that which would make him the most formidable King in the desert."

"So She gave him salt."

The jinni nodded. "It changed everything."

Moving toward the pool at the heart of the trees, I thought of gods and jinn and my father's salt. I knelt and dipped my fingers in the pool. The water was cool, and I longed to bathe in it. I imagined lying in the water, my ivory clothes billowing up toward the surface around me, returning home soaking wet.

I spun. "Sons, I have to go back! Take me back!" In my awe at being in the oasis, I had forgotten about home. "Sabra! She will see me missing. She will tell my father!" I yelled the words at him, my heart slamming against my ribs. My fingers were clasped to his arms, attempting to drag him back to the village.

The jinni raised his hands, pulling his arms from my grasp.

"It is okay. Time does not move forward there. They won't know. They're frozen in their steps."

Confused, I looked at the trees above me, their quivering leaves. The ripples in the water traveling to the opposite shore.

"Time is stilled there?" I pointed to the village behind me.

"Just there. Here," he said and indicated around us, "time will seem to move forward, but to the world, we are the only two alive in the endless span between the beats of a heart."

That gave me pause. I took deep breaths, and my pulse slowed. I sat by the pool and stared into the bright blue water. I saw the jinni's reflection on its surface. His eyes found mine. I looked away and asked, "Do you come here often?"

"Not as often as I would like. But I must confess that this was my favorite resting place of all that I've had."

"Where else have you been?"

"Everywhere in this desert. Once in the open sand underneath the burning sun. Another time in the home of a dissatisfied man who made miserable those with whom he interacted."

"Are you aware of what happens around you when you're in your . . ."

"My home? My prison? Somewhat. I can feel the energy of the people or places around me. I felt uncomfortable and lethargic in the desert sands, sad and miserable in the man's home. Here," his hands fanned around him, "I was relaxed and as content as one could be living in a glass prison." His words hinted at the lingering sorrow I sensed was always with him, like smoke above a flame.

"Similar to how you can feel my thoughts, because I am your master?"

He nodded.

"I suppose, yes. But, Emel, you are no longer my master since you thought it wise to leave my vessel behind." He looked at me pointedly when he said this. "My master is whomever has last released me from my vessel, and your father soon became my master again."

"Oh." A prick of disappointment. "Then how did you feel my wishing for you earlier?"

"I can feel the desires of any master I've had—though only you and your father are the masters I've had who still live. Even if I were across the desert, I could feel your want, I just don't have to respond to it."

"When do you have to respond?"

"When a wish is spoken aloud, Masira hears it and will grant it. But if you think it, it does not have to be."

I asked, "My wish will be granted even if I am not your master?"

"I have promised you wishes, so that means that I—Masira—will grant them if you speak them."

So the power was in the words I said aloud.

Satisfied with my limited understanding of his magic, I turned to my more pressing question. "If you've been all over the desert, are you familiar with it? With the trade routes?"

"Trade routes? What do you care of caravans' paths?"

I told him about Rafal's map and proudly drew it for him in the sand, showing him the settlements I had already identified. Even more than Aashiq, he was amused by my fascination with the map. Too, he seemed almost impressed. Warmth slid down to my toes, and I bit my lip to hide my gratified smile.

He pointed to the paths and pursed his lips. "But these all point to your settlement."

I nodded saying of course they did, my father had all the salt. "Is it wrong?"

He was silent, staring sadly at the lines in the sand. "No."

I brushed the map away.

"Why do the legends of jinn say that you only grant three wishes?"

"It is what I—and maybe others—"

"Other jinn?" I blurted, wide-eyed.

He shrugged and stared at the swept ground, gaze clouded. "I assume there are others. By saying I only grant three wishes, I hope it will limit the time I spend with my master. So many are starved for power and wealth. Wicked people whose souls I cannot stand to be near. Sometimes I was lucky, and Masira would separate me from my master with their wish."

"What do you mean?"

"If their wish caused a big rift or sent them to a land far from where we were, my master would go and I would stay behind with the vessel."

My mouth dropped open. I had never heard of that happening in the legends. "They would lose you?"

He nodded, and I thought of how terrifying it would be to be sent far away without anyone or anything familiar. Without even magic to return home.

"What about my father?" Masira had not separated him from the jinni.

He winced. "Like all, I told him he had only three wishes."

"I assume he has already used them?"

"He has."

"But then, why do you stay with him? Can't you leave? Aren't you free?"

"Those questions are many, and their answers would take much time for me to tell. I am not free, no. I have already said that your father is a smart man. So many of the men before him assumed I was useless after the third wish. They endeavored to hide me, jealous of the next to find me and profit from their desires made real. So I would stay in my glass home, sometimes for several lifetimes, before another would find and free me. Your father did no such thing. After his third wish, he asked for a fourth."

"What did you do?"

"I granted it." Seeing my bewilderment, he continued. "You see, I offer people three wishes, but I am a slave to my master, and there is no end to what I do so long as my master desires it."

"But can't you walk away? Can't you leave?"

"No." Sadness was heavy in his voice. "I am bound to my home. If I am not contained within it, I can stray, but if my master calls me back, I must return."

"Why not freeze time in the village like you have done now and leave? Then he can't call you back."

"To live a life only to return to where it began when I grow tired? No, that would be impossible to endure. Even if my master is vile, he offers me change. I cannot endure a lifetime of sameness, of being alone." He looked from me to the village. "With change, at least, there is hope."

Yes, that was true.

I marveled at the ease with which I spoke with the jinni. Despite his being a stranger, he seemed safe. Perhaps it was his honesty. Or maybe it was our shared condition. After all, he was a jinni, bound to my father as I was. Or perhaps it was that in his words, I saw that he was more human than magic. Whatever the reason, I gravitated toward that feeling, toward him.

Our eyes met. "You didn't tell me I had three."

He looked away. "I did not."

"How did you know who I was? You knew my name, that the King was my father."

Saalim smiled and slid onto the sand on the other side of the pool. "I thought that was apparent the afternoon I saw you at the King's address."

I fussed with the silk fabric covering my legs, chagrined that he acknowledged my rule-breaking with Firoz.

"It is often your father's desire that I am disguised as his guard or slave. I have known you since you were born." That surprised me. I wondered how often our paths had crossed before. Had I bribed him with salt he did not need as I slipped by, unaware he could give me so much more than escape from the palace for an afternoon?

"How have I never seen you before?"

"You only see me if I allow it. As I allowed you to see me during the King's address."

"No one else could see you?"

"None but you."

"Were you there today? During the courting?"

He nodded. I was again embarrassed. By my coquettish behavior displayed so blatantly, that he saw my father handle me like one of his treasures, that he saw Qadir reject me.

"Qadir . . ."

"I sensed that you did not want him, just as I sensed you were looking for me. I redirected his attention."

I remembered the suddenness with which he had dropped my hand and nodded. My stomach rumbled. "What did my father eat today, do you know? They were little red jewels."

"The pomegranate?" the jinni asked, baffled.

"Pomegranate?"

"Yes, it's a fruit."

I thought of coconuts and dates. "It did not look like fruit to me."

"I will show you." The jinni brightened with a wide smile. He walked around the small pond and knelt down at my side, the heat of him fully surrounding me. He held his hand before my eyes and asked, "With your permission? It is more dramatic this way." Did I hear amusement?

I nodded. Carefully, his hand covered my eyes. I leaned into him ever so slightly. They rested lightly on my face for only a moment before they were gone. The gentleness with which he touched me left me with a deep longing for more, like when Hadiyah massaged my shoulders and back.

When I opened my eyes, I squealed and jumped up to my feet. Fruit, bright and shining, was piled high on tiered trays and platters. I scurried to them, the jinni trailing behind.

"Eiqab be praised," I whispered, as I picked up a slice of something orange and wet. I set it back down and picked up a small, red fruit connected to its twin. My eyes roved over the plethora. I did not know where to begin.

"This is a pomegranate. What your father had," the jinni said, coming up from behind me. He picked up a red, hard-sided fruit the size of his palm. I took it from him, and peered closely. It appeared much different than what I had seen earlier.

"No, this is not it."

The jinni took it from me. From the gentle pressure of his fingertips, there came a soft crack, and he split the red fruit in two. My mouth dropped open when I saw that at its core were glistening rubies identical to the ones my father had. The jinni showed me how to pry the gems from their soft, white beds. I smashed most of the juice-filled jewels as I retrieved one.

Fingertips stained red, I placed the seed into my mouth. It burst with sweetness and leaked coolness onto my tongue.

"Do you like it?" He asked me as I chewed.

I crushed the tiny, hard pit between my teeth and hunted for more of the turgid seeds.

"More than I love baths," I groaned.

He let me try them all, taught me their names. I tasted wet orange slices, the soft flesh of apricot, and shining cherries with cores like rock. I stuffed myself with the sweet fruit, gleeful as he described the trees that bore them. It wasn't just pomegranates: all fruit glistened like jewels amongst the velvet green of the leaves.

"Where do they come from?" I asked, my eyes were wide with child-like curiosity.

"Far away from here. Traders cannot make it this far with fruit still whole. It rots too quickly, but, sometimes, it is dried and preserved or turned into spirits. Like wine." He pointed to a cluster of grapes.

I sat back on the sand, leaning against a stone. I ate so much, my belly ached with each breath.

"May I sit beside you?" The jinni asked. He had maintained a careful distance from me.

"You may, but don't forget I'm an ahira, eh? You can't touch me lest you've a plan to woo me." I raised my eyebrows at him, but when I saw the pain flash in his eyes, I stopped and mumbled, "Of course. You don't have to ask."

Seated beside me, he was still careful to keep his distance. Unsure if it was because of what I had said, I felt foolish for trying to joke with him.

Through several breaths of silence, only the rustling of the leaves and songs of lucky birds could be heard.

"I have never done this before. Simply sitting with someone in a quiet place for no reason but to sit. It is," he hesitated, "very nice."

"You and I are the same in that way. It is nice."

"No, I imagine you wouldn't have this luxury. Your father is careful with you and your sisters. But what of your friend?"

"Firoz?"

"Oh, is that his name?" He rubbed the cuffs on his wrists.

"It is different with him."

We sat in unhurried silence for a while more, our eyes staring at the city that lay fixed amongst the dunes.

"You have been very kind. Why?"

"You are one who released me."

I was disappointed by his answer, some small part of me hoping there was something more. Something that made me special.

"But you said I am no longer your master."

"True, but I've promised you wishes."

The sun dipped toward the horizon, the shadows growing long. I felt drunk on the sugary fruit and the afternoon warmth, and my eyelids grew heavy.

"I see that you are tired. Will you stay a little longer?" He said it so gently.

There was a poorly concealed vulnerability that made my chest ache. Just that afternoon, I had felt trapped with my father. The jinni had taken me from that which oppressed me, and now I was sitting in the shade, full of sweet fruit. I wanted to ask him then—can I have my freedom? But I did not want to destroy this peace, the ease of our time together. It was the closest to freedom I'd ever had. I didn't want it to disappear. And, he had been so vulnerable, I did not want to remind him that he was a slave to grant wishes, just as I did not want to be reminded that I was an ahira used to benefit my father.

"Truthfully, I see no reason to ever leave." I smiled at him as I lay down on the sand. I could smell him: jasmine and desert dust laced through with a scent of something unfamiliar. "But why do you want to stay?" I said drowsily.

"When I am with you, I am not with the King. I have never spent time with someone who does not own my actions, who does not only care about my magic. And—" He stopped talking. The word hung between us for some time, before the warm breeze blew it away.

Today would not be the day I wished for my freedom.

I MUST have fallen asleep, because when I stirred and opened my eyes, the sky had begun to purple, the orange of the fading sun was like fire against the few clouds.

"I will take you home now," the jinni said from beside me. He had not moved. He stood fluidly. I followed, slow and dazed from sleep.

"I will return you to precisely where I took you. Move quickly to catch up with your sisters and you will not be missed."

He held his arms open before him, as he had done earlier that day, and I stepped into them.

The jinni wrapped his long arms around me, and pulled me to him. Earlier, the intimate gesture had given me pause. It felt indecent—too close. This time, I understood its purpose. Just as I breathed in, the ground shifted from under me, and I felt the air change, noticed the light brighten. We were back in the stuffy confines of the palace.

I kept my eyes closed, savoring what the jinni had just given me. When I opened my eyes, I would be drawn back to the life that was not my own. A bird shoved back in its cage.

"You should go." He dropped his arms and stepped away from me.

Feeling chilled at his leaving despite the warmth of the midday sun, I looked up at him. I found I already missed him, the freedom and the stories he told. I longed for his attention again and was horrified at the thought of returning to my life, returning to the monotonous days of listening to my sisters, weaving, gossiping, idling.

"When will I see you again?" I hated how desperate I sounded. Perhaps I had made a mistake not to ask for my freedom. Next time. I must ask for my freedom the next time.

"Emel, you must go. Time moves once again." His words were stern.

"Will I see you soon?" I tried again, prolonging the time I could stay in the hallway with him, pushing away my return home. I did not want to go back to my sisters and that life. Not yet.

"I hope." He started down the hall, the opposite direction I needed to go. I watched him and felt despair.

"Wait!"

He turned back to face me, his eyes questioning.

"I wish—" I stumbled, unsure of how to speak what it was I desired—how did I say I didn't want to return to the life I knew waited for me? "I wish to not yet return home."

He looked pained at my words. He whispered, "It will be as you wish."

Then, with a warm wind that came from nowhere, the jinni transformed into golden dust that dissipated into the air. He was gone.

I stared, confused, at the place where he had just been. Nothing had changed. A deep ache pressed against my gut. I had held freedom only briefly, yet the feeling of it had fastened itself to me like a metal cuff around my wrist. Heavy, unforgettable, and drawing me back.

I turned to where my sisters had disappeared days, moments before. I stared at the hallway around me. Why hadn't my wish worked? I began to walk back to the zafif to find my sisters.

An angry voice sounded behind me.

"Stop!"

I turned back, alarmed. It was a voice I knew. It was a voice I did not want to hear in that hallway, alone.

Nassar stood at the entrance, the tent still swaying behind him. He was looking all around me, manic. "Who was here with you?!"

I stammered. "No one."

Still, he looked around, as if someone could be hiding in the folds of fabric. Then his iron gaze settled on me. "You are not to be out by yourself," he hissed. "How dare you defy the King's rule." He turned and shouted through the walls to the soldiers that waited on the other side. "Take this ahira to the King!"

Two guards burst into the hallway behind Nassar and approached me so quickly, I had no time to respond before their hands were clasped to my arms and they were roughly dragging me back toward the Salt King.

11

TADHALAQ
—·—
SACRIFICE

Edala,

In response to your question, remember it is a waste for man to pray to Masira. There cannot be understanding between a worshipper and Masira as there can be with her Sons, who are much closer to us. She listens to none but herself, does only what She desires.

But if you must petition, remember that She will hear sacrifice. Have you heard the salt chasers' idiom, *douse a flame with salt*? Perhaps not—I know your father keeps you sheltered from desert woes—but it means that one must give something he needs before She might listen.

Do not be discouraged. You are learning quickly. Continue to study the Litab, and your ability to reach Masira will grow.

Zahar

—Found parchment detailing discussions of the *Litab Almuq*

8

"SHE WAS OUT BY HERSELF," Nassar said excitedly as the King blundered into his throne, two of his wives trailing like obedient dogs.

"Tramp." The Salt King's voice was honed with fury as he looked at me. "First, you reject Qadir, and now you're caught trying to go off on your own. What would cause you to be so bold?"

The light sparkled cheerily through the tanzanite gems on my father's slippers as I stared at them. At the edge of my vision, heaps of salt sat around us in the room—none still tarnished with blood. Did my father throw out the spoiled salt? Or did he wish the blood away? My thoughts strayed to the jinni. Where had he gone?

"You were distracted with Qadir," he said. "He complained that your mind was elsewhere, that you spurned him, seeking someone else." He stood, nudging one of his wives aside with his foot, and walked toward

me. "And now you're found by yourself. Were you trying to run away? Or perhaps you are trying to find those traitorous men to flee with?"

With a delicate cough, Nassar stepped into my father's line of sight. "We know that the Altamaruq are no longer an issue. Your soldiers took care of all that remained. It would be impossible for Emel to flee to them. More likely, she goes to another man."

The King gave Nassar a sidelong glance before he grabbed my face, crushing my cheeks between his fingers. He jerked my head up so my black eyes met his. An icy terror washed over me, and every breath burned. He was furious.

"Choose your words wisely, Emel, for I will only grant you a few." He released his hold on my face, but continued to stand before me, the jagged stones on my bodice catching on his tunic.

"I was with my sisters. I had fallen behind . . ." I paused, trying to slow my breath, trying to find an explanation. "The vizier found me as I was catching up."

"Lies!" Nassar erupted from beside the King. I cringed. "I heard you with a man! And where was the trailing guard?" He turned to his King, waving his hand at me. "The guard would have been with her unless she hid and evaded him. Or maybe he was the very person she sought?"

The King nodded in agreement. "There is something amiss, Emel. What or who is it you find so distracting? What could you value more than your family?"

"My King, there is no one—"

A swift, unyielding slap wrenched my head to the side. The hands on my arms tightened their grip, preventing me from falling. My eyes watered, and my chest heaved as a sharp pain erupted at my temple.

My mind whirled. The sequence of events was incomprehensible. The happiness I felt in the oasis was like a dream—a blurry memory too good to have been real. Sons, I'd been a fool not to wish for my freedom then. I could be gone from here. Wetness trickled down my cheek. Blood. The skin on my face torn by my father's ring.

Was my father going to kill me? I was not ready to die. I wanted some sort of real life before I was given to Masira. I thought of the jinni again. I dared not look around for him, the echo of my father's accusations ringing in my ears.

"You lying whore," he spat. "There has been talk of an ahira leaving her quarters, of bribery and consorting with commoners. You will be made an example of to your sisters. If there is one among you who has dared to disobey me, it ends now." The King, his chest rising and falling with the effort of his diatribe, turned back toward Nassar. "Fetch the rest of them."

His words were a lash, and each threat left behind shining, crimson terror.

Sycophantic glee smothered Nassar's face.

"My King!" Another guard, followed closely by Sabra, barreled into the throne room. Everything disappeared—the throbbing pain at my temple, the raging king who paced in front of his throne, the wives who watched with secret smiles, Nassar's delight—when I saw Sabra. She had no good reason to be seeking an audience with our father.

"What now?" The King collapsed onto his throne in a mound of flesh.

"The ahira has an urgent message for you," the guard said, his eyes on the ground. Sabra moved to stand in front of the throne at my side. The King's wives, so much younger than my mother, were draped drunkenly at his feet. They made an apparent effort, as evidenced by the creases in their brows, to observe the scene unfurling before them, to remember all so they could tell the other wives, with twisted pleasure, of the foul deeds being done by another's daughters.

Sabra hesitated when she saw me.

"What is the message?" The King barked.

"I . . . forgive me, I can see that it is not a good time. I beg your forgiveness, my King. I will leave. Forgive me." She said her words in a hurry and fell to her knees in a deep bow, continuing to mumble for forgiveness.

"Stop your groveling and spit it out!"

"I came to tell you that Emel was missing." She turned toward me. My mouth dropped open, and I shook my head, imperceptible to all but Sabra. The softness of her face hardened, and she turned back to our father. "I can see that she was here all this time. But you should know this is not the first time she's been gone."

It took all of my strength to keep me on my feet. How could she?

The King was struck silent by the scene before him, bemusement clouding his anger. I could see his struggle. He had wanted to punish me for my possible disobedience for pure fun; however, the revelation that I had actually broken his rules was beyond comprehension. His plodding, alcohol-laden brain could not keep up. His glassy eyes moved from me to Sabra and back again.

I quaked inside.

"I am finished with these squabbling cows." He stood, swaying slightly. "This is a family matter." The King turned to the numerous servants who stood on the perimeter of the tent fanning the room or carrying trays of untouched food and drink. "Leave us."

A disobedient daughter was an embarrassment to the King. Before, I had been only a disappointment. Now, I was shameful, too.

The servants shuffled out of the tent, but surely most stopped and waited, hidden behind tent walls, to listen to the spectacle, ready to spread word about what had happened.

I thought of the jinni again. Was he amongst them? Could he not help me? Or did I have to wish for it first?

We waited in silence while the King sipped his drink, my mind spinning with impossible solutions. Soon, my sisters filed in with Nassar, most wearing their bright fustans and silk slippers, some still wearing bejeweled ahira attire. They had not even donned robes. Nassar must have extracted them from the zafif. I saw their dread as their gazes darted between Sabra and I.

"Nassar," the King said tiredly, "retrieve my whip." The vizier scurried from the tent and was back within moments carrying the iron-handled weapon, a long, leather strap wrapped around it. In his other hand was coiled rope.

I closed my eyes and prayed. *Eiqab, show my father that I see how I've erred.*

"Daughters, I have brought you here to remind you of your role in my palace," he began as he took the whip and rope from Nassar. "In her vanity, Emel has demonstrated blatant disregard for my rule. She has disrespected me, her mother, and all of you. She cares not for my generosity—the bed I provide, the food I give, the shelter I offer. Therefore, for her punishment," he paused and took a drink, "she will be imprisoned for one complete cycle of the moon, and she will receive thirty lashes."

My sisters gasped. My breath caught. For the King to be willing to scar one of his ahiran, to ruin my future with a suitor by marks of disobedience . . . and thirty times. There would be no future with a muhami now. None would choose a marked wife. The sand threatened to swallow me whole as my knees weakened, desperate to collapse.

"Bring her to me," the Salt King commanded the guards holding me. He held out the rope. "Bind her."

Desperate, I shoved my elbow into the chest of one of the guards while my other hand pushed at the face of the second. A heavy blow landed against the side of my head. Black bloomed in my vision, and pain radiated down my neck and spine. I fell onto the ground. I was hoisted upright, my hands and feet bound. The coarse fibers splintered against my skin as the rope was tightened.

Please Eiqab. Please. I begged, closing my eyes. *I will burn in the desert for you. I will never step into the shade again.*

My father stepped slowly behind me, making no sound save the whisper of his sirwal with each step. The afternoon sun burned into the tent. Sweat dripped down my neck and fell into the beaded ivory of my bodice.

Eiqab, guide my father, save me from this. I prayed and prayed, repeating the entreaties over and over.

Until it began.

The first sharp slice of the whip fell onto the skin between my neck and shoulder, tender flesh deeply cut by the leather strap. I cried out at the sharp sting, tears filling my eyes. I wanted to be strong, to be silent. But I fell to my knees, and I cried.

"One," said the King.

I had been abandoned by my god, so I turned back to the jinni. *Please*, I thought, *please come. Help me. Please.* I thought the words so fiercely, I almost spoke them aloud. He had to hear my pleas.

I wish for safety, Saalim. I wish for you to save me. I wish to be away from here. I wish to be in the oasis. I wish to be in my bed. I wish to start today again, to make different decisions. I wished for every possible thing as the whip carved down my back over and over again.

My eyes squeezed shut as I bent forward on my knees, back exposed and stretched. I fell to my side, but the guards pushed me up again. Blood dripped from my back to my neck. My face tight in agony. I focused all of my attention on what I wanted, needed. I hoped it would be enough to call the attention of the jinni.

He did not come.

The King fatigued midway through. The time between the lashes longer, the bites less sharp. He complained of cramping in his shoulder, his aching neck.

My sisters suffered, too, as they watched me crumple. Many cried as they listened to the King's count. Some jumped in surprise with each snap of the lash while others stood silently and trembled. Maybe some thought sadly of the scars that would be left on my beautiful skin, while others thanked Eiqab secretly for my punishment: perhaps now they would have a better chance with the next suitor. I knew they imagined themselves in my place but found relief that it would never be. They were not such fools to break rules as their willful sister did.

I know they felt shame for those private thoughts. They would not soon forget the depraved feeling of being a voyeur to their sister's abuse while they thought idly of the wedding bed and my bad behavior. I knew all of this because I would have thought the same. I bit my lip as I waited for each lash, my teeth cutting into my skin with each crack of the whip.

My thoughts rambled in a thick fog of delirium, and I thought of Aashiq's burial. How the King's guards had dragged the bodies of the dead into the desert and thrown them in two piles. Matin's men, they lit to flame. They burned like the wounds on my back. The smell of scorched flesh had hung thick over the settlement for the rest of the day.

Aashiq's robes were unbelievably bright that day. How could a color be so vivid when there was no life to leaven it? Soon, a vulture had circled overhead. Then another and another. They grew in numbers, just like the lashes. The first vulture dove and landed on Aashiq. The others followed. They devoured him, devoured all of the King's men, piece by piece. Masira's feast. Just as I felt to be a feast for Masira now.

The King's men sang the melancholy song of the committal of the sky when the birds began, one after another, tearing the flesh from the earth and carrying it into the heavens. No one was singing for me now.

That day, I had cried first with relief, and then in sadness, because oh, how I wished to follow him there. But now, I was Aashiq, each lash a bird's beak ripping my flesh.

Then, I was a bird flying low over a village being pelted by sharp rocks.

I was a goat with my limbs tied to a spit, the greedy flames licking my spine.

I was a cloud in the sky, the strike of lightning singeing my fleece.

The King declared the thirtieth lash with enervated triumph. He barked at my sisters about the lesson they had learned that afternoon.

On my side, I shivered with pain. The air was like cold fire on my flayed back. Sabra was still beside my horrified sisters. Her eyes met mine briefly. I saw no remorse, but she had paled.

The King walked near, and I flinched, curling into myself, my lashed skin shrieking in agony at the movement. His tunic was tucked behind the articles at his belt, and that was when I saw it. The glass vessel.

I squeezed my eyes closed and curled my hands into tight fists. I wanted to scream, to beat the floor in my frustration.

Within the vessel, golden smoke swirled in a frenzy. The jinni was locked in his gilded home, blind to the world around him.

"It brings me pain that I must punish your sister so," the King continued his self-indulgent speech of which I heard little. The forged compassion might have repulsed me, but I was so tired. "I trust this has been a lesson to you all. Now," he continued, "your lesson is not through."

My eyes shot open. A gust of horror swept through me like a storm. I choked on it, a wet breath rattling in my chest as I inhaled. My sisters' expressions mirrored mine. What else could the King have for me? Even Sabra looked appalled. I wanted to scramble up to her and claw her face, wanted to scream at her for her betrayal. But the energy was not there, nor the spirit.

"Emel has faced the beginning of her punishment for her disobedience, and it will continue in the prison. But," the King stepped slowly toward the eldest ahira, "Sabra, you have not yet faced yours. Nassar, please." The King held out his bloodied weapon to his vizier, who stepped forward to take the whip. "Sabra, you will receive ten lashes. For being a rat."

9

M Y SEVENTH MORNING AS prisoner was markedly cooler, and the normal yellow light of the morning sun was a soft gray. My blanket, usually twisted and kicked to the other side of the tent, was wrapped tightly around my shoulders.

I awoke later than normal, too. The comfortable, cool darkness of the morning allowing me extra sleep. The metallic lidded pot was already sitting at the entrance of my tent, and I couldn't believe I hadn't woken when it arrived. My day's rations, unfailingly delivered every morning. I sat up slowly, wincing from the slowly healing wounds on my neck and back.

I was glad to have much time left before returning home. Enough to figure out how I would navigate returning to my sisters. I did not know how I would face Sabra again. My fury at her betrayal consumed me until I was exhausted by it. Then I would think of Father, and what he did to me. How scarred would I be? There was no chance for me as an ahira now. Aashiq had been my last.

Men murmured outside. I strained to listen.

"They found two more by the circling of the birds," one said. "Dead for some time."

"Another message?"

"Similar. About the old desert, the trade."

One of the men moaned sadly. "They must want the salt. Explains why they kill those that guard it."

I rubbed my eyes and slowly crawled to the entrance of the tent to hear more. My knee knocked the pot, and the metal lid clanked loudly against its base. The conversation stopped abruptly.

"It is a beautiful morning, Emel," a man said through the tent.

I smiled despite myself. "Lateef, I am happy to hear your voice." My only full brother was guarding my prison tent again. While he did not give me any more allowances than the others, he was at least kind. Peering into the canister of food, I grunted. A large handful of olives, several thick pieces of meat, and many slices of plain flatbread soaked in oil. I chewed the greasy bread and a piece of meat slowly. The rations were similar to those I received at home. I knew how to savor them.

Hunching was almost unbearable, the stretching wounds across my back ripping apart the little threads of skin that had managed to stitch together overnight, so I was eager to stand.

"May I come out?" I said softly, and almost immediately, Lateef pulled open the tent.

"You might want to bring your blanket. It is a cold morning."

Wind rushed into the tent bringing with it the smell of impending rain. Shivering, I inhaled deeply. Wet, metallic earth. Moving carefully, I collected my blanket in one hand, the clay pot in the other, and walked outside.

I stepped out to an infinite horizon—flat like the palm of a hand with only a few dunes breaking up the expanse. The sky was a soft gray muddle of fluffy clouds. At the horizon, dark clouds bore rain.

Rumors of the prison's horridness—the isolation, boredom, starvation—were not what they seemed. When I arrived, in pain and so weak I had to be carried to the tent, I thought I understood. The prison was a cluster of small, ill-maintained tents at the village's edge. Its perimeter was lined with so many scowling guards, there could be no escape. But then, I found the isolation comforting. Hurting and tired, I curled up on my mat. Alone, no one asked me questions I did not want to answer. When I closed my eyes, there was no youthful chatter distracting me from sleep.

I was even more surprised the next morning when food waited for me.

"How long is this to last?" I asked my guard, scared to hear his answer.

"The entire day," he said. "Conserve it."

If I had the energy, I would have laughed aloud. It was not much less than I received at home.

Some food and a quiet place to sleep? This was not so bad.

"You empty your pot yourself," the guard said, more gently, as though he were sorry he told this to the King's daughter. "You tell me when you're ready to come out."

I did and was let outside. Moving slowly, I stepped out of the tent and into the sun, the open air. I marveled at my allowance to go outside, walk freely to the settlement's edge that before I had to sneak to, but I hid my contentment. When I walked back, the guard stopped me. "You will not be let out again until midday, and then once before at night, so plan accordingly." It was unbelievable. Those who whispered to the ahiran the horrors in these isolated tents must not have realized that the King's daughters were just as imprisoned: unable to go outside the palace, equally underfed, and isolated in our own way.

That cloudy day, I walked several paces from the tent, Lateef monitoring from behind. No prisoner was daft enough to flee into the desert unless he sought death—if not from lack of water and food, then surely from the insanity of illusions that rose up from the sand, the whispering hatif, and being unguided amidst shifting dunes.

Dunes that were held away from my village by the jinni's magical hands.

I thought of the jinni often, wondering where he was, if he thought of me, if he knew what happened. I was sure he did. Still, I didn't understand what happened that afternoon. He said he granted my wish, but here I was.

My knees pressed into the ground as I dumped the pot into a hole. A strong gust of wind blew, and I wrapped the blanket more tightly around my shoulders, wincing as it scratched against the wounds on my back.

A loud yelp rose up from behind me. I turned back, alarmed by the fear in the cry. Two guards pulled a man out from his tent and dragged him toward the village. By his dark clothes, I could tell he was one of the soldiers from Matin's army. Nearly every day, he was taken from the tents, and, at dusk, he came back mumbling incoherently. Though sometimes I understood his words—something about a missing king, about Wahir and water, about returning things as they were. Every day he was tortured, the King's men trying to pry his secrets from him like I had pried seeds from the pomegranate. My heart ached for him, especially when he cried for his home and his family, but then I would remember what his people had done to my family, what they'd done to my future.

Finding a small slope of sand, I sat down and stared out at the shadowed desert. Coaxed by the wind, clouds rolled overhead. The graceful silhouettes of twin vultures circled above. The line where the land met the sky seemed impossibly far away. Was there an end to the desert as the legends said? As Rafal claimed? I tried to imagine water that spoke and salt that shimmered on stone, but I could not.

"Come back, Emel," Lateef called. I rose as quickly as I could, the wind whipping my hair above me. We nodded to each other, his head and face uncovered as he, too, enjoyed the weather.

"And Mama?" I asked as I passed him.

"I haven't seen her yet, but I promise I'll give her your message once I do," Lateef murmured as he closed the tent. It was not so easy for sons to see their mothers. They could not walk into the harem as I could.

I lay back, willing myself to think of anything but Sabra. The sun had a long journey before sleep would come again, so I found the loose threads at the base of the tent. I braided them, pulled them loose, then braided them again. I once tried to talk to my neighbor through the fabric walls, but my guard—it was not Lateef—screamed at me, warning me against doing so in the future. I would not make that mistake again.

The *pat pat* of rain tapped the tent above me, so I rolled onto my back to see the wet spots shining brightly. Rain, finally. There was nothing more miraculous in the desert. Had I been home, I would have heard shouts of rapture, squeals of glee, as people abandoned whatever they did to run out and taste the divine gift.

The dull, wet sound slowly increased in frequency until it battered loudly, obscuring all other sound. The smell of dirt and metal rose up at the downpour. I closed my eyes, relishing the scent and sound, the coolness of the air that permeated the tent. The deluge so strong that drops of water leaked through the poorly oiled goat-hair tent and dropped around me.

A warmth crept up my arms, and through the scent of rain, there was something familiar. My eyes shot open expectantly, but it was only my tin of rations and waste pot in the tent with me. My shoulders sagged. I began to pull the blanket over my legs when I felt the warmth again. This time, I saw golden dust coalescing in the air before me.

I gasped. "Oh!"

Soon, the jinni was inside my tent. Even kneeling, his tremendous form made the space feel even smaller. I scrambled to pull the blanket over my bare legs, wincing through the movements.

"What are you doing here?" I asked quietly.

He looked me over intensely: his eyes scanning my face, arms, and shoulders. His expression bordered on despair.

"What's wrong? What's happened?" I rose to my knees, starting to panic.

"Nothing," he said. His shoulders eased and face softened. The rain pounded the tents, hiding our voices from the guard outside. "Nothing has happened. I wanted to see if you were okay. I am sorry I did not come sooner." He leaned forward, reaching his hands out as if to touch me but hesitated and pulled them back to his side. "I could feel your agony that afternoon." He spoke like the words were heavy to lift. "I could feel the strength of your desire. It pulled on me but I could do nothing about it." He clenched his fists tightly. "I am so sorry."

The strength of his remorse and the urgency with which he made his confession surprised me.

"There is nothing to apologize for. Nothing was your fault." He was so defeated, I felt a strong urge to comfort him. "I am fine."

"All of this is my fault." He smiled somberly. "If I had better explained the cunning of Masira . . ."

"What do you mean?"

"I told you your father was a smart man. That the wishes he crafted were specific enough to propel him to power without having to deal with unforeseen consequences. I did not tell you that he learned this for himself."

"Then tell me now," I said, pulling the blanket up to cover my arms, now wet with rainwater.

The jinni crossed his legs beneath him, still appearing too large for the small space.

"When he found me in the oasis, he first wished for a meal. It was simple, it was granted. I think it was a test—just like yours. He ate silently, surely thinking of the possibilities, of my potential. He did not think of Masira's. After some time, he told me his second wish: 'to be the lone desert ruler.' Do you see how this could be interpreted by a guileful god?"

I did not. There were so many desert rulers, it made sense for a power-hungry man to wish to be the only one.

"Masira did not think to make him the only ruler in the desert as your father wanted. When his wish was made, a keening shriek erupted from outside the oasis. Your father jumped to his feet, looking back to the caravan. He ran, urgent with concern. He had recognized that scream. When he arrived, he found the people he traveled with surrounding a woman on the ground. His lover, his wife."

Wife? He was not married when he found the oasis. At least, none of the tales mentioned a bride.

"You must understand, she was his entire life—the reason he sought the edge of the desert, why he wanted to be a powerful ruler. The cause for everything he did. He wanted to be the source of her comfort, her happiness. He wanted to give her everything.

"When he saw her, he panicked. He squeezed her arms, slapped her cheeks. He screamed at her to wake up, to be well again. He yelled at the villagers, begging someone to explain what had happened, looking for someone to blame, someone to help him. But your father arrived too late. She was lifeless in his hands, white foam spilling from her mouth.

"He tried to save her. I felt his desperate desire, strong like a storm of sand. I felt how he loved her. I felt his tearful wishes that she be revived, that she live. I also felt how he wished for his child—still warm in the womb of his dead wife—to be alive, to be born so that he could have at least that part of the one he loved. But it could not be. He was too late. As you know, you cannot wish for the return of life once it has been surrendered to the vulture goddess. Masira guards her souls with wings stretched wide. He lost his wife and his unborn child that day. He lost everything. With a single wish."

I was stunned. The rain poured.

"Masira granted his wish, you see. He was already a ruler, though not a very powerful one. She granted him the isolation he had unintentionally wished for. He became the only ruler in the desert who had no one."

"How have I never heard this tale?"

"When a wish is granted that causes an impossible rift—an unexplainable, subtle, or momentous change in our lives—the memories of all that saw are taken. Those that would have no other explanation than magic won't remember anything. But memories are like a spider's web, and their removal can sometimes leave a sticky trail behind. Only the one who wished and the jinni who granted it will truly remember what was before. It preserves the secret of the magic, you see. It prevents the disturbance that a wish could cause. Your father did not yet understand what had happened, that it was his wish that had caused the deaths. He lashed out, killed two of the nomads in a rage. But no one confessed, and they all grieved genuinely. The villagers loved her almost as much as he did.

"Once his dead wife and child were taken to the sky, people began forgetting they ever existed, treating him as though he had always been alone. Soon, no one remembered the family he lost. He thought he was mad until finally, he asked me. I told him of Masira's volatility, of his intention when he makes a wish. Had he an argument with his wife that day? Was he frustrated with her and had the foolish thought that he'd be better without her? Don't we all indulge in fantasies when we know they would not bring us true joy? I did not ask your father these things—his guilt already burning through him. The consequence of his wish, the reality that he was the cause of his wife's death, was a heavy burden. And he would carry it alone, share his memories with none.

"He was never the same man again. He shed his grief and past like a snake's skin, and in its place, he wore the thickest armor. Having nothing more to lose, he wished and wished again. He became the Salt King.

"Emel," he continued, "do you understand why I tell you this?"

I shook my head.

"When I saw you last, you wished to not yet return home. Do you remember?"

I remembered my wish. I did not remember my thoughts that day, how my words and how I felt led me here, but I understood what the jinni meant. And I understood how a single wish, seemingly so simple, could be so dangerous. "It is as I wished. I have not yet returned home," I whispered.

"I should have better warned you."

"Even if you had, it was a mistake I would have to learn myself." A terrifying mistake. What else could I have asked for that could have led to worse? Where would a wish for freedom lead? Suddenly, Masira's magic seemed too volatile, too risky. Did I want to bargain with a fickle goddess? I shivered.

The rain slowed slightly.

"Are you okay here?" His words were quiet under the battering of rain.

I shrugged. "I am. Truly," I added, seeing his doubtful expression. "Do you know of my mother? Is she okay?"

He rubbed the cuffs on his wrists. "Yes. Your father told her what happened."

My eyes widened as I imagined how that conversation carried through the walls, shrieking how my misdeeds were her fault from all the poison she siphoned into my ear.

"Is she okay?"

"She is. Though she mourns for you. She will be relieved when she sees you again. You have dealt with this much better than I expected, than I am sure any of your family expect. I will give word to your mother and sisters that I have seen you and that you fare well." He saw my confusion. "As a guard, of course."

"And what of Sabra?" I asked, fixating on my fingers.

He sighed. "I can't pretend to know how she feels. But I have spent a long time around people, knowing what they feel and watching what they do. While she carries much pain from her own punishment, I think the weight of her guilt is greater."

"That, I doubt."

"She is in a dark place, but even she would not wish harm upon you. Not really. She does not understand your father like you do. Whether that is willful blindness or self-protection, I don't know."

Hearing him defend Sabra when I was lashed and scarred and imprisoned because of her was too much. I could admit I knew she did not want me to receive my punishment, because I knew no matter how much I loathed her, I wouldn't want her to experience the same. But I could not forgive that she let her fears and jealousy alter my fate—destroy my future. It was unforgivable.

As if sensing my frustration, he said, "Can I see your back? Your face is healing well."

I touched the raised crescent on my temple left by my father's ring.

"Why?" I was sure I wanted no more of his sympathy.

"I can ease the pain."

With my back to him, I pulled my hair over my shoulders. He exhaled at the sight of my crusted, raised flesh that extended up my neck beyond my plain fustan. "I will trace the path of the wounds. Like before." Before, when he had cleaned the blood from my face and hands.

"Okay."

With the slightest touch, he traced over the visible wounds. I winced, waiting for pain, but immediately, an itch spread across the scabbed wounds that soon gave way to intense relief. I reached up to my neck. My skin was smooth, painless.

"Sons," I breathed.

"If you want me to take care of the rest, you will have to let me see them."

I wrapped the blanket around my hips and pulled the dress over my head. When the cold air and raindrops touched my back, I tensed, my arms curling up to cover my chest. The jinni murmured something quietly to himself, then took the tendrils of hair from my back and draped them over my shoulder. He placed his hands and mercifully traced the wounds, erasing the pain. The heat went deeper than the wounds, and soon, my entire body felt warm, as if I were sitting in front of a smoldering fire in wintertime. The rain chilled me no longer. I sighed.

"I must leave behind scars. If I don't, it will look suspicious."

"That's okay," I said but felt a flicker of chagrin. My future would be better served without them. I pulled my dress over my head, the relief from the pain so liberating I laughed.

When I turned to face him, our knees almost touched.

"How are you able to do what you choose with the magic?" My gaze dropped to his hands resting in his lap, and I reached for him, curious.

When we touched, heat rushed through me like water. I met his gaze, his eyes sparking like flames.

"Masira's will and mine are intertwined. Because I am her conduit, I can act on her behalf. I can do what I please, with limitations."

"So, she wanted my wounds healed?"

Deep lines stretched across his palm, and I traced them with my fingers. A drop of rain fell into his open hand, and I placed mine over it.

"No. I wanted that for you." He folded his fingers over mine and held my hand tightly, the drop of water pressed between us. I held my breath. It was so chaste. It was so intimate.

"I will not forget this," I said, nearly inaudible. I hoped he could feel the intensity of my gratitude in my touch, my thoughts.

He lifted my hand to his mouth and lightly kissed my knuckles. A deep, forbidden longing bloomed in my core.

"I am sorry," he said, seeing me still like stone. "I should not have. I will leave."

The edges of him started to blur, fine golden dust swirling off of his shoulders.

"No. Wait!" I cried, too loudly. I slapped my hand over my mouth. The jinni stopped abruptly, appearing whole once again.

"Emel?" Lateef shouted over the rain. "Did you say something?"

"Ah, I . . . was sleeping," I shouted back. "Perhaps a dream."

The jinni and I stared at each other in silence, waiting for Lateef's attention to drift elsewhere. Under his gaze, I was suddenly aware of my unwashed face, unclean hair, and my blood-stained, filthy dress. He studied me carefully, appearing intrigued. I studied him in return, admiring that though he seemed so hard and severe, he had a gentle softness to him. I imagined myself in his arms. He smiled, and I frantically looked away, brushing at invisible sand on my knee.

"How did you get away from my father?" I said, eager to change the direction of my thoughts.

"He is still sleeping in his room, as he is wont to do after a night's heavy drinking. I was guarding his tent. I simply asked another guard to take my place for a bit. I told him my wife was ill and I was to check on her." He looked impish.

"Then you should be leaving soon," I replied.

"Yes, I should."

"Okay."

"Okay."

I began. "Saalim . . ."

His smile widened. "Yes?"

"I'd like it if you came back to see me."

"You would?"

"Yes. If you'd want to, that is."

"Of course. I will return when I can."

I rose onto my knees. This jinni, I liked. I did not understand him nor his motives but I knew I could trust him.

Leaning toward him, I felt the heat radiate off him in waves. I brushed my lips across his bearded cheek, feeling shy and foolish. He lowered his eyes, a small nod of acknowledgement, and perhaps appreciation. Then, as the rain slowed to a sprinkle, the jinni was gone.

10

LEANING AGAINST THE CENTER POST, I stretched out my legs. It was hot again, the cool weather gone with the rain, but I was grateful that summer had passed. Autumn was still warm but at least sweat did not pool at my elbows and knees.

The sloppy remains of sliced fruit was on a platter at my side. My eyes trailed over the wood beams framing my tent—dented with whorls and little bows from bored fingers that left behind desperate drawings—until I looked again at Saalim.

He sat across from me, chin resting on his hands, elbows on his knees. He had visited often since the rainstorm. Each time was rigid, fragile. Like we were both tiptoeing around something unacknowledged. Typically, he came to provide me with food. Mostly exotic fruit and usually in quantities in excess of my appetite. He felt responsible for my imprisonment, so he never wanted to stay long. I think he did not like the reminder of where

I was. He only came to ask after me and ensure I was well. Even though I knew this, I couldn't resist drawing him into conversation, pestering him with question after question or asking him for tales to keep him there longer. I was desperate for company, and he always obliged.

"You are nearly done with your imprisonment. The moon waxes," he said. We no longer had the rain to disguise our conversation, so he used his magic to mute our words to others.

"Only a day or two more now." I pushed my nails into the post, creating a trail of undulations that arced up the wood.

"You don't seem happy."

I shook my head. "I am happy. Of course, I miss my sisters, but I will miss the quiet here and seeing out there without having to sneak or bribe my way out." I hesitated, then gestured between us. "And I will miss this, you know."

"I'll bring you fruit whenever you desire it."

I said, "That is very nice. But it isn't just that."

He waited.

"We won't see each other like we do now, and I won't be able to leave the palace. Not with Sabra around." And really, I just didn't want to see Sabra again. Nor my father.

"You don't know that. Maybe she feels—"

"I won't risk it."

"And when the caravans come?" He smirked. Twice, a caravan had arrived. The first time he told me, I threw a tantrum like a child. I almost asked that he magic me a way out so that I could go, anxious about all the blanks on my map. Though I was more composed the second time, still, he saw me blink away tears.

I groaned. "Not fair."

"What is it you find so interesting about them?"

"Everything," I breathed. My smile was so broad, even Saalim grinned. "They carry so much life on the backs of those camels. I love seeing what they've made, the food they cook, and if I'm lucky, hear stories about what their homes are like."

I told him about Rafal and his tales. "He's traveled all over the desert, like you."

"I've told you about many of the places I've been—"

"No, you haven't. You've told me fairy tales and legends."

"If you say so," he smirked. "But I can tell you about all the other places I've been, if you want."

Empathic, I pressed my hands together. "Tell me everything."

"Right now?"

"Right now. If you have time."

He leaned back onto his hands, saying he did indeed. What did I want to hear of first? The north, I said, telling him what Rafal had said about the desert's edge.

"Is it really like that?"

Saalim grew serious again, and he suddenly felt unreachable. He pursed his lips as if trying to remember. "Yes." I waited for him to tell me more, to elaborate, but he didn't say anything for a long time, so I didn't press.

It was only the space of two hands that separated us, but it felt much farther. The chasm between us grew deeper and more treacherous each day that passed. I did not want to be the first to traverse it, unsure of our intimate exchange the first morning and where that left us now.

Silence settled between us, and I worried he would leave. I did not know when I would see him again.

"I am scared to see my father again."

"I can imagine why."

"Do you think he'll act differently toward me?"

"I don't. Your father lives moment to moment and thinks little of the past. Whether that is by choice or due to drink, I cannot say. I have seen him mete out many punishments, but never have I seen him consider them later. At least, not aloud."

"Does he normally talk to you about things?"

"Absolutely not." His words were heavy, and anger darkened his eyes.

I fumbled with a small piece of fruit stuck to the tray.

After watching me attempt to grab a slippery sliver of honeydew for the third time, he said, "What I mean is that you cannot forget I am a slave to your father. He does not treat me as you do. He does not interact with me beyond what he needs. His relationship with me is different from yours."

I raised my eyes, curious. "And what is our relationship?"

"Perhaps it is you that should answer that question."

"I would call you my friend."

The jinni smiled, but it was a smile that guarded something. He rubbed at the hammered gold that shackled his wrists. While I had grown more comfortable with the strange jinni, he had only just begun to shed his guard with me. I knew very little of his life.

"I would say the same." His fingers trailing along the edges of the metal until they vanished into his hands.

"Can you take those off?" I asked.

"No," he said, his voice strained. "They mark me for what I am. They cannot be removed, see?" He held out his wrists. I tentatively touched the cuff, dragging my finger along the metal until it softened into his skin. I peered at the golden veins. "I can hide those," he said, referring to the paths twisting down to his hands. "When I am disguised as a slave. But I cannot hide the cuffs. Those are always there."

"Are they uncomfortable?"

"They are heavy."

Another story I felt was not my privilege to hear, so I grasped the honeydew I had been fishing for and held it in front of me. "Do you ever eat?" I popped the fruit in my mouth.

Saalim laughed, sounding relieved. He shook his head. "No. I do not need to eat. It holds no interest for me."

"Really? That is too bad. This is delicious," I said as I licked the juice off of my fingertips, smiling. "You are quite good at choosing excellent food, for not knowing anything about it."

"I did not say I knew nothing about it. I have tasted food before. I remember it quite fondly."

I arched an eyebrow. "So you *can* eat then? Why don't you now?"

He lay back onto the sand. "It was another lifetime. Before I was who I am now."

Suddenly, I was again an ahira, tailoring my words for a desired outcome. I drew slow circles in the sand with my finger. "Do you mean, before you were a jinni?"

"Yes. When I was human."

My mouth fell open as dozens of questions flung themselves at me in a frenzied attempt to find their answers. "How?"

"I was changed. I remember some things from when I was human. They are from long ago, but I still remember the pleasures of food."

I wanted to ask him so many things, to press him further. I was so eager to glean some understanding of this jinni—this man?—sitting with me. But I knew he was not ready to share those things, nor was I ready to know them. "Do you miss it?"

The jinni considered the question. "I miss the freedom. But there are times when I am grateful for the powers Masira has given me." He looked at me.

"Mmm, like when?"

"Do you know what happens to water when it gets too cold?"

I shook my head.

"It turns hard as a rock."

"No it doesn't," I laughed.

"It does. One of my masters had an ill child. His body burning with disease. They thought he would die if he did not cool, so I fetched the only thing that would soothe him."

"Which was?"

"There are mountains far from here, tall and made of stone. They reach so far into the sky, they are covered in frozen water."

I stared in disbelief, thinking of dunes that the wind kept clipped.

"Sometimes," he said as he fanned out his hands as though revealing the ending of a marvelous story, "the pieces of the frozen water are so small they are soft like powder. You can crush them in your fingertips and they are a single drop again.

"And there are places where the trees are so dense, you can't see the sky. Animals with branching horns walk through the forest. Their steps are silent, and when they hold still, even if you stare at them, you cannot see them. There, when the nights grow long, the tree leaves are green no longer. They change to yellow and orange and red until the whole forest looks aflame."

"Lies!" I cackled. "What else?" I asked, eager to be back on the path of tales.

He told me of places where women had hair the color of dried grass and draped only their shoulders in silk because the sun was kinder, and where men used swords that were straight as a bone. That there were places where women ruled or men had only one wife. Where different gods were worshipped and cities were made of stone. His tales were endlessly fascinating, though, like most of his stories, I did not know if I could fully trust them, so inconceivable were some.

"If I wished for my freedom, could I live in one of those places?"

He straightened. "Yes, and no. You can wish for your freedom, but know that wishing for something as broad as freedom is volatile. Masira might set you in the middle of your settlement, the wife of a good man and mother of three children, your sisters and mothers in neighboring tents visiting you every night. But She might place you in a village far from this, with no family or spouse but all the jewels in the world."

That did not seem so bad. "But I guess then I'd come back to my sisters, sell my jewels for a camel, and see them whenever I wanted."

"It would depend on the life that Masira grants you. You might be placed in a life where you have no sisters, no attendants, no friends, and you're an orphan child. Freedom from one thing does not guarantee freedom from another. So, if you desire to be free, you must be specific in your words, sure of what you want freedom from. And be prepared to face the risk of having no part of the present in your future."

"Including you," I said, remembering what he told me of Masira separating the jinni from his master.

"If She wills it, then yes. Including me. That does not always happen, but it is a risk you must be prepared for."

Unease gnawed at me. I could not fathom saying goodbye to my sisters or mother, to Firoz. I wanted to be free of my father and his palace, but I did not want to lose the rest of my family. If I lost them and the jinni's magic . . . unable to wish back to the way things were . . .

I arranged wishes in my mind, testing to see all the ways Masira might interpret them. But I would never speak them aloud. It was as Saalim had said of my father, I was indulging in fantasy. Masira was too dangerous, and I did not want my fate determined by her whim.

I was uncomfortable thinking of what could and might be, straining under the weight of the unknown.

"In some ways, it is very tempting, but too, the risk is scary," I said. "But it doesn't matter anyway. How can I leave when I have so many unanswered questions? I want to know more of this powdered water and trees with leaves that fall off, then regrow."

He grinned. "Your interest knows no bounds I am afraid. Eventually, I will be like an emptied goatskin, nothing but echoes inside. I suppose then you'll move on to someone else or wish for your freedom finally." Genuine concern flitted behind his eyes.

"I'll just run off with that other jinni I've been meeting with in the afternoons. Come to me, Aten!" I called out toward the sky. I giggled.

Saalim laughed, too. It was a beautiful sound.

The laughter in his face died, and he grew serious. It was an expression I was familiar with. He felt the stirring of the Salt King, the arousal of his master's fetid consciousness as it pulled itself free from sleep desperate to have the jinni at its side. Soon, the King would call, and he would be forced to answer.

"Emel, I must go."

I dreaded those words every morning he was with me.

"Is he awake?"

"Not yet, but sleep is leaving him."

There was a pause.

"I will likely not see you again for some time."

"I know." An unyielding ache filled in my chest. I did not trust myself to speak again knowing that if I did, my words would betray my melancholy.

The jinni moved into a kneel. He waited. I looked up at him. There must be a farewell more appropriate for this moment than a small smile and swift goodbye.

"Goodbye," Saalim said finally.

"Goodbye then." My words were sticky in my throat.

Outside I heard the piercing cries of an eagle.

"Emel." He spoke my name softly, and there in his words was longing. His eyes held a question. His arms parted ever so slightly, an echo of the gesture he had used not too long ago to take me to the oasis. This time, I knew I was going nowhere except to him.

I threw myself into his arms.

Heat enveloped me, crackling like fire around my scarred back and neck. He pulled me tightly to him, an unguarded desperation in his movements, and I clasped onto him with equal intensity. My chest firmly against his, the warmth of his skin comforting in a way I did not expect.

I wrapped my arms around his neck and pulled his head next to mine, his bearded cheek scratchy against my own. "I'll miss you," I said into his ear.

Saalim shifted and pulled me onto his lap. We held each other in a helix of heat and longing and something like despair. His heart beat wildly against my own.

He pulled his head back to look at me, perhaps to say goodbye one more time. But I did not want to hear it. I did not want him to leave. I did not want the next time I saw him to be unknown. I wanted him to always be near. I wanted his wisdom and kindness and concern and stories and . . . I realized that far more than his magic, I wanted him. It was a heady feeling.

Unthinking, I pressed my mouth to his.

Flames licked up and down my spine. The warmth of his mouth, tasting like dust and flames, stoked an unfamiliar desire in me. I pressed on hurriedly and ferociously with the movements I had learned as an ahira. But Saalim took his fingers and pushed my face from his. Saalim was not a muhami looking to bed a woman. There was yearning in his eyes, but it was tinged with sorrow.

"No, not like this."

Humiliation flooded me and burned through my cheeks.

"Sons, I—I'm sorry." I tried to pull away. "I'm so embarrassed, I shouldn't have . . ."

Saalim held me tightly. "Wait. Stop," he begged.

Locking my stare on the tent behind him, I stopped fighting.

He loosened his hold on me and slowly reached back up to my face, turning me so that I looked at him again.

"Like this," he murmured.

With an aching tenderness, he touched his lips to mine. He pulled away, then kissed me again, though with more insistence. Again and again, he kissed my mouth. He kissed my cheeks, my forehead, my neck. Each kiss radiating heat that settled in a deep, desperate part of me. It was nothing I had experienced with a man, and I melted in his arms at his quiet devotion. A tear fell onto my cheek, and he kissed that, too.

"Emel," he said hoarsely between the pressing of his lips to my skin and mouth. "I am sorry, I now must—"

And as his words fell upon my ears, so did I fall upon the sand.

He was gone, having been called by his master. I sat, unmoving, as I caught my breath, as my stirring body quieted. I was chilled at his sudden departure. My mind swam as it did when I smoked Buraq or drank goblets of wine, except this time, it had only been the jinni's touch, the taste of his mouth on mine, that left me whirling.

Sitting upon the mat's surface, where I had left the near-empty platter of fruit, was a small mound of the finest golden sand I had ever seen. Curious, I rubbed it between my fingers. It was so soft. I carefully scooped the small pile into my palm. Holding it tightly, I lay down on the mat. I painlessly folded my knees into my chest and pressed the dust to my heart, letting it fall through the coarse fabric and onto my skin. A part of him against the part of me that now, I realized with a complicated mix of fear and excitement, longed for him in a way that I hadn't longed for anyone before.

My thoughts drifted to the life that awaited me in the coming days: my sisters, my father, the muhamis. But between it all stood the jinni, like the sun's golden shine through clouds.

"EMEL, COME."

Wavering between excitement at seeing my sisters and mother again and nauseous fear of seeing Sabra and my father, I laughed when I heard Hadiyah call my name. My imprisonment was finally finished, so it was time to face my life again. My heart thudded as I left the tent for the last time.

"My child!" Hadiyah cried, her smile creasing her glistening eyes. She wrapped her arms around me and held me tightly, her hold easing my worries. She swayed back and forth, repeatedly pressing her cheek to mine. Finally, she stepped back. "Look at you. You look . . . well!" She did not conceal her surprise. She raised an eyebrow. "I won't ask. Let's get you home." She clasped my hand and led me away from the tents.

We were alone as we returned to the palace, and it felt wrong. "No guard?"

She peered at me. "Can't imagine why you'd need one. You've learned your lesson, haven't you?" I said nothing, but considered whether that was the whole truth.

Never had I been away from my village for so long. To a foreigner, nothing would seem different. But to me, it was obvious. The rows of homes we passed were all closed. There were no friendly visits between neighbors or children.

"It's so quiet," I said.

Hadiyah tutted, "As it should be. The sun sets. People should be home preparing dinner for their families, not out gossiping with neighbors."

No, that was not it. Something was different. It was far too quiet. I peered inside the only home we passed that had its entrance drawn open and saw a man and woman who looked not much older than me. They sat side by side at a table playing a game with beads on a long wooden board with shallow grooves. They watched us as we passed as though they were assessing us. After a pause, they smiled and went back to their game.

Hadiyah said, "I have a surprise for you."

"What is it?"

"A bath." She covered her mouth with her hand as she laughed. I had never seen her in such good spirits and told her so.

"It is because you are finally free, my pretty child. We'll get you cleaned up before returning to your sisters. Now, don't hate your Hadiyah for saying this, but you smell something foul." She fanned her nose, laughing again.

The attendants cooed and wiped their cheeks when I arrived. They touched my shoulders, face, neck. Their ebullience a welcome homecoming. Though pleased to see them, nothing excited me as much as the sight of the tepid bath that waited in the center of the room—its copper side reflecting specks of light onto the floor. Happily, I stripped the filthy dress from my body.

"You have gotten so soft!" Adilah exclaimed at my nudity.

"Indeed! I thought the same. Breasts larger, bottom fuller. What were they feeding you, a full plate of dates for every meal?" Hadiyah added.

"Something like that." I smirked.

I stepped into the metal basin. The scent of roses and vanilla drifting to my nose as I relaxed into the cool water. When I pulled my hair over my shoulder to submerge it in the water, gasps and groans surrounded me.

"Oh, your poor back."

"What horrible scars!"

Then Hadiyah exclaimed, "That's enough! Silence!"

Her voice was stern, angrier than I'd ever heard it, but the attendants listened. Silently, they scrubbed my hair and body, removing the grime caked onto my skin. Sweat glistened on their brows with the vigorous movements of their arms, their colorful fustans undulating.

They prattled on about my health, on what I had missed while gone. I was grateful for the distraction. It prevented me from thinking of my impending meeting with Sabra and of seeing my father again.

"It has been a good month for the King. Kadri and Yasamin have both been wed," one chirped, and the other women murmured happily. "Yasamin to a local nobleman whose family spans the desert. She's his first wife. If we are lucky, we will get to see her on occasion."

Slowly, I dragged my fingers through the water. I was unable to say goodbye. I would never see either of them again regardless of how close Yasamin was to the palace.

"And what of the Altamaruq?" I said it innocently enough, but I was eager to piece together the fragmented rumors I had heard while imprisoned.

Hadiyah clucked her tongue. "Emel! You know you should not be asking about such things. It is no business of a king's daughter."

"We are safe under the King. There is no threat," another added.

I did not press as I pulled on a clean fustan. Though worn, it was so much thicker and softer than what I had been given to wear in the prison.

Night had fallen, and stars flickered into existence one by one overhead. My hands shook as I neared my home. Sabra waited behind the fabric walls. What would I say to her?

The familiar cadence of ahiran voices drifted out to the path. I listened to them for a few moments more, seeing if I could hear Sabra, before finally stepping inside.

"Emel!"

"Oh my, it's Emel!"

"Sister!"

Their joy collided into me so fully, my concerns for my older sister were briefly forgotten. I was home with sisters that loved me. We clustered around each other, hugging fiercely. Sabra was not amongst them.

"How are you?"

"What was it like?"

"Are you okay?"

"What happened to you there?"

"Find me a man? I'm not picky."

I turned to Pinar and laughed. Only when I had placated them, ensuring them of my health and promising that we could talk about it later, did the chatter die down. I retreated to my bed, removing my coverings.

Without hands to sweep it off every night, my bed was nearly covered completely in sand. As I wiped it clean, I noticed it was unexpectedly flat. Too flat. I hurriedly pulled up my mat—where was my salt? Where was my map?

They were missing.

I looked around at the beds surrounding mine, hoping beyond reason that I had chosen the wrong one. My head swung back and forth across the room, my hands swept furiously across the sand.

"I have it," Tavi said as she kneeled beside me.

"The salt? My map?"

"Yes. I took them after you . . . I didn't want anyone to find them. I worried about Sabra . . ."

I dropped my head into my hands, overwhelmed with relief. "Thank you Tavi." I sat down and searched for my older sister through the tables and wandering sisters in our room. She was lying on her mat, across the room from mine, with a blanket pulled tightly over her shoulders and head. So, she wanted to see me about as much as I wanted to see her.

Tavi said, "Don't thank me. I used half of it seasoning my meals each night."

My eyes flashed to Tavi's, but I saw she was smiling.

"What happened that day? After?"

Tavi scooted close beside me, tucked her knees up to her chest, and laid her cheek against them. "She was in so much pain," she whispered. "She didn't want any of us to help her. She spoke only to me, and even then, it was only a few words at a time."

"Painful, eh?" I said.

"Oh, Emel, I know you fared worse." She placed her warm hand on my back. "It's easy to forget what you went through since we did not see it ourselves. I'm sorry." She didn't say anything for a long time as she turned in the direction of Sabra. "It broke my heart to see her. It still does. I don't think I could have borne it to see you both like that."

"Well, she did it to herself, didn't she?"

"How can you say that? She had no idea what would happen."

"How can you defend her?" I replied, speaking more loudly. A few of my sisters turned toward us. I lowered my voice. "After what she did? It was cruel."

Tavi nodded, but it was insincere, only to appease me. "I'm not defending her. She didn't want that to happen. She has not had it easy, remember that."

"You must be joking," I said leaning away from her, growing angry that I was to be made the enemy from this. That somehow, I was wrong to seethe.

"She didn't have Father's favor, Mama's indulgence—and don't you even start with that. We all know that Mama loves you best. Emel, you're just more resilient."

My mouth hung open, unbelieving that I was hearing those words from Tavi's mouth. "None of that excuses what she did, Tavi." She opened her mouth to respond, but I did not let her speak. "And I won't let you hold me to a higher ideal because you think she's had it harder. It's not fair to me, and it's not fair to her. We all are sitting in this tent together—enduring the same life."

Tavi looked at her feet, chewing her cheek. "I know."

"I can be angry, Tavi. My future has been taken from me. Do you understand I will never be wed now? There are thirty scars on my back."

Tears pooled on her lids, and when she blinked, I saw one fall.

"I'm sorry," she said finally.

"I know."

"I've missed you. And," she cried harder, "when you were gone, I—I was glad you would never be married. I don't want you to leave; don't ever want to say goodbye to you. At least if you're banished, you'll be near. I thought maybe I would do what you did and visit the village to find you. I had it all planned out." She took gasping breaths, crying into her hands. "It's terrible, I know. I'm sorry."

I held her close, laying my head against hers.

"It's okay," I whispered. "I missed you so much."

When Tavi had settled, when our anger had lost its fuel, she asked, "Where were you that day? Why weren't you with the rest of us?"

"Well . . ." Of all of the conversations I had planned to have when I was finally home, I had not once considered what I would tell my sisters of that afternoon.

"Were you with someone?" she gasped.

"Shh!" I hissed. "I don't need those sorts of rumors floating around. Father thinks I was. I wasn't. It was all just being at the wrong place at the wrong time."

She sighed. "I'm so relieved nothing happened to you while you were there." I asked her what she meant, and she looked at me as though I were brainless. "Because of the deaths, of course. Perimeter guards have been killed."

"What?"

"Traders found the first group a few days after you were taken." Her face lit up with the self-importance one gets when sharing particularly good gossip. "Several more have been found since."

I couldn't believe it. My hand covered my mouth, my eyes wide.

"None were our brothers, don't worry. But Father has called on our sisters' husbands in other settlements, asking that they send soldiers. You will start to see more unfamiliar faces around." She said it like a warning.

"Why has no alarm sounded? When the soldiers have been found dead? When the soldiers attack? Why has the city not been warned?"

"They've only discovered them long after they've been killed. And I'm sure Father does not want to alarm people."

Or, he did not want to reveal any weakness, any vulnerability in his invincible facade. Neighboring sisters joined our conversation with their theories. I barely heard their words. My mind was spinning through my own ideas about why the Altamaruq would continue to kill our soldiers.

"I'll get you some dinner," Tavi said. I watched her walk away and scoop the dregs of their meal that night onto a tarnished silver plate.

"Sorry that things didn't work out with Qadir," I said between bites, looking to Raheemah.

"I don't know why he chose me. He spoke of you half the night and how you irritated him. It seemed like he did not understand why he was with me either. Sometimes he would look at me and then seem startled, as though he expected me to be someone else. I would rather marry a man who wanted me."

"I'm sure he wanted you, Emah," I said, not believing the words myself and remembering what Saalim said of magic and the traces it left behind.

Raheemah looked at me crossly, irritated by my coddling. "You know as well as I that we can tell when a man desires us. Qadir did not."

I smiled and pushed my empty plate to the side. I did know what it felt like to be desired by a man. My thoughts drifted to the jinni and the feel of his lips moving carefully on mine. I lay down on the mat, my mind swirling with thoughts, skin tingling with delicious heat.

Extending my toes and reaching my arms overhead, I yawned and closed my eyes. The muggy warmth in the room, scented with sweet oils and sweaty bodies, was familiar and welcoming. I stuffed my blanket behind my head.

Shadows fluttered across my closed eyelids, and conversation rattled in my ears, making sleep difficult for me. I was surprised to discover that I missed the silence and darkness of my small prison tent and already missed the feeling of hope that would greet me every morning as I wondered if that day would be a day Saalim would come to me.

I adjusted my mat so it was next to Raheemah's, and I pulled her to my chest. There was no replacement for her, for Tavi, for all of my sisters whom I loved so dearly. When I had nothing else, I had them.

At some point in the night, the quiet muttering came to an end. The dinner bowls were removed and the torches doused with sand by an attendant. I heard the occasional swishing of limbs across a mat, a gentle cough of my sister or nearby servant, the murmuring of late-night chatter in neighboring palace tents, and the strums of a distant oud sending music into the dark sky. I listened to it all, holding my sleeping half-sister. I took a deep breath and let the noisy comfort of home soothe me.

11

THE HAREM WAS HAZY WITH SMOKE of burning frankincense. I went to my mother's bed, but it was empty, her blanket folded neatly atop her feather pillow, a luxury for the King's wives. "Emel, you're home!" One of the wives approached and embraced me. "Are you looking for Isra?" I nodded, and she pointed behind me. "The kitchens."

Thanking her, I looked back to the empty bed. Before I left, I felt under the mat and pillow, felt through the small basket of things she kept. I found no stories, no letters.

The kitchens were on the other side of the palace, so I followed the long curving path of tents until I saw the plumes of gray smoke and smelled the stewed barley and smoked meat. The kitchens were made up of a large tent that opened on one side to an even larger, uncovered area. I walked through the tent, past shelves stacked with gleaming metal trays and lidded pots

similar to the ones in which I received my rations. There were black kettles, glass decanters, and goblets. Another corner housed enormous copper pots with thin lids, cold in their disuse. At the center of the tent were thick stone slabs, stacked with steaming food. Servants shuffled in and out of the tent, grabbing empty serving ware and kneeling to fill the trays and bowls. Women husked and winnowed millet in the corner while shouting at the men who collected food—demanding this bread be placed that way or this sauce be placed in that bowl. I did not see my mother.

"Move aside!" A man shouted at my back as he turned into the tent with three empty goblets and two trays in his arms.

Startled and eager to be out of his path, I rushed and fell to the side. When he saw my adorned veil and abaya, he understood who I was. He groaned, appearing horrified. While it was tacitly understood that ahiran did not wander through the servants' quarters, it was explicitly understood that servants did not yell at them.

"Ahira! I am so sorry. I beg your forgiveness." He kneeled, setting down his serving-ware.

"There is nothing to forgive," I mumbled. "I am searching for my mother." Shaking the sand from my robe, I stood and went to the outdoor kitchen.

Outside, men and women huddled around flames, hooking the kettles to pull them from the fire or stirring enormous pots. Some dug through sand to pull wrapped meat and bread from hot coals. Goats and chickens were scattered, nosing around for food.

Though she was wrapped in dark, plain clothes, I recognized my mother immediately. She sat with two other women at a fire. They were close together, as if sharing secrets. One was pounding sticky dough on a small stone block. The other eyed angry flames shooting out from beneath a wide metal dome with flatbread sizzling on its surface.

"Mama!"

Nearly all the women turned toward me, but it was my mother who jumped to her feet and ran. "Oh, oh!" We collided. "Sons, Emel! I did not expect to see you so soon." She sniffed and wiped at her eyes, and I was alarmed by her sudden emotional display. She was always so stoic, I did not know how to respond to the sudden deluge.

"I am okay, eh? Everything is fine."

She sputtered a laugh and pulled me to the other women, seating me beside them as she introduced me. They knew who I was, they said, and proceeded to tell me how as a child, I'd stolen bread from their stack frequently. "It was your favorite," one said as she fanned out the cooked bread she'd just pulled from the dome, then tossed it to my lap. I tore a piece and brought it to my mouth.

"This is perfect," I moaned through the buttery bread.

The cooking fires were hot. Even though the air was cooler, how the women could sit beside the fires all day under the sun, I did not know. Shading my eyes, I pulled my scarf down until I could see the small beads swinging in my vision.

"You get used to the heat," my mother said to me. I did not think I ever would.

"What are you doing here?" I asked, watching the woman spoon oil onto the pan before the other threw the flattened dough atop it. It was unusual for a king's wife to be alone in the kitchen, especially mingling with servants.

"Sometimes, I need to be away from the harem. Especially . . . lately. Amira and Yara," she nodded to the two smiling women, and I realized I had forgotten who was who, "are great company. They have worked at the palace since I was wed to . . . the King." Her voice was strained as she spoke. Suddenly, her face pinched, and Amira and Yara began re-stacking the cooked bread with great focus.

"What is it?" I asked as she brought her hand to her eyes.

"I—" she sucked in a breath, "I am so angry with him. How dare he." She took another deep breath. "How dare he do that to our daughters?"

Her fingers trembled, and her shoulders shook.

"It's okay," I said feebly looking from my mother to the women who discreetly paid no attention. I knew it was not okay, and there was nothing I could say to make her hurt less, but it was easier to lie than to see her angry with my father, to see her unhappy.

"It isn't," she whispered. "It isn't. He is a cruel man."

A young boy with a floppy sack around his shoulders glanced at us as he passed by. He tossed the hungry animals some dried grass and seed, and they scurried to his feet.

I balked. Her disparagement of Father in front of the palace servants could end in a punishment much worse than my own. I looked again to Yara and Amira. Their expressions were unfazed, and I wondered if perhaps that was not the first time they had heard those words come from my mother's mouth. I watched the boy—what had he heard?

"Shhh," I said, scooting closer to her. The bread was untouched in my lap now. "You don't mean that."

Mama looked at me. "He is not who he used to be. Every day he is becoming someone else."

I thought of Saalim's story and shook my head. "It is not easy being the King. His burden is heavy with the Altamaruq." The words felt traitorous coming from my lips, and suddenly I understood why Tavi defended Sabra. It felt like it was the only thing I could say to help deflect the hurt, even though I knew it wouldn't help at all.

She winced at the mention of the Altamaruq, then shook her head as if she were shooing an insect. She turned to me, a heavy sadness in her gaze like I had so much to understand.

"Do you know how I was wed to your father?"

I shook my head thinking I really did not want to hear this story.

"I loved him once. Really, I did. When he came to my settlement, he wanted to talk to my father of the salt trade. He wanted my father to cease use of his salt mine, revolutionize the trading. He promised impossible things; that he had enough salt for the whole desert and that he could supply it peacefully if they brought him the goods we had in the west. I now understand those things were not impossible for him.

"He was genuine, enthusiastic. My father hated him, of course, for the threat he posed, but I was fascinated. He walked me under the palms of my father's home and promised me a life that had so much more—a desert that was different. It seemed magical." She scoffed. "How could I say no? He told me of his settlement. That he had three wives at home, and he was looking for someone like me. Someone who knew much about the salt trade—who was brave and strong and independent." She shook her head as she remembered. "I fell easily to his flattery. My father never forgave me. My mother did only what my father did, so, of course, she did not forgive me either. I never saw them again." She spoke with the tight grip of resentment. "That was one of the last times your father went to a settlement to bargain. After that, he just took what he wanted, and now, see what he has done. All dreams of a changed, better desert disappeared with the rise of his empire."

Amira and Yara cooked the bread unhurriedly, their pile growing taller.

Mama spun so that she faced me. "Unlike my mother, I will never follow in my husband's footsteps if it means I must sacrifice what it is I want. And I won't sit here and pretend that I accept what he did to you, has done to others. It is horrific—I will not forgive him. When a muhami comes to court you, you must first watch him closely. See how he treats those who are beneath him." She looked beyond me, at something that wasn't there. "If I had paid attention, if I hadn't ignored that which I saw . . ."

I bristled, hurt in spite of myself. Did she regret the life with my father? Did she regret me, and my sisters? And Lateef?

"Mama . . ."

"I am blathering. Forgive me. It is not fair for me to burden you with this." She grasped my shoulders and looked into my eyes. "You are so much stronger than me. There are so many things happening, and I am so worried. I am so scared . . . I am so hopeful." She clenched both fists. "Just pay attention, Emel. The Sons may bless us yet."

One of the women called to me. "Take to your sisters?" She handed me three large flatbreads.

I took them gratefully. Mama's behavior was strange, unnerving. It scared me. "Mama," I spoke slowly as if to one of the village elders, "I am going to take these home. I need to go." I rolled the flatbreads and tucked them beneath my arm. I nodded to Yara and Amira, thanking them again for their generosity and for their kindness toward me and my mother. But I also watched them closely, wondering if they would report my mother's crazed proclamations to the King.

THE GIRL with the marked face was outside when I walked back to my home. She was sitting on the ground shoving sticks into the sand. When she saw me approach, she smiled shyly and pretended not to see me while watching my every move.

"Hello, little sister," I said, kneeling down. "What are you doing out here?"

"Papa promised that if I let them work for the afternoon, he would play princess with me tonight."

Her parents sewed and mended clothes for the palace. I had seen the inside of their home. Piles of cloth filled the space. With more guards coming from afar, new clothes would need to be made.

"Princess? How do you play that?"

She grinned. "I walk around with pretty clothes and tell lots of good stories. Like you."

I smiled.

"Papa plays the prince and he comes and takes me to his palace and if Mama is done cooking dinner, she'll dress me pretty so I can have a wedding! My brothers never want to play. They say it's a girl game, but I think that's silly because a princess has to have a prince, and in every palace, there are boys and girls."

"I think you're right. Where are your brothers now?" Usually they were running through the lanes and pestering their sister.

Pushing out her lower lip, she said, "They left to go to the market. Traders came yesterday."

"A caravan?" I asked, leaning forward.

She nodded. "Where were you all this time?"

Brushing the hair back from her face, I said quietly, "I have been away, but I am back now."

"But where? I didn't see you forever. Mama thought you had married a prince. I didn't think so, and I will tell her I was right." She poked at the sand with her stick.

"I was visiting a friend," I said, thinking of Saalim. She asked me more. I told her he was a very nice friend who brought me lots of treats and told me wonderful tales. I did not tell her he kissed my lips and had hands so warm, I softened beneath his touch.

She smiled, then eyed the flatbread tucked in my arm.

I took the roll and handed it to her.

"For you and your family." Like me, servants were allowed specific rations and could not visit the kitchens as easily as my mother. Still, they could leave the palace while I could not. Some things they won, some things I lost.

She stuffed the edge of the bread into her mouth, sucking on it until it was soaked and crumbling.

"What stories did your friend tell you?" She asked.

"I'll tell you one, but then I must go." I walked her to a shady area between two neighboring tents and told her of water that when cold enough, turned to stone.

SABRA AND Tavi weren't home when I returned. They went to the rama with some of my other sisters, I was told. Raheemah was there entreating idle sisters to play a card game with her. She looked a little pale and rubbed at her stomach.

"You okay?" I asked.

Her face lit up when she saw me, but it didn't quite hide the pallor. She held the cards out to me. "Me? Yes! Let's play some rounds, eh? You can tell me how your mother is."

"I can't, Emah." I shifted from foot to foot, unsure if I wanted to confess what I was considering, fearing her disapproval.

"Why?" She said flatly, narrowing her gaze.

"A caravan," I whispered. "It's been so long . . ."

She dropped her face into her palm. "Emel! You can't honestly be considering it after what happened."

I shushed her, looking around to make sure our sisters didn't hear.

"If I am quick, can you lie for me? If she asks?" In truth, I did not think Sabra would. In the days that I had been home, I saw that Sabra had changed—like a lamp without oil—she was cold, empty, and dark. Our eyes had met once but no words had been exchanged. Still, I watched her. She was often by herself or Tavi was with her, generous with her love and accepting of Sabra's angry silence.

"Fine. You owe me thirty rounds," Raheemah said brandishing the cards. She smiled, but it vanished quickly.

IT WAS obvious the caravan had arrived—foreign people dressed in beautiful robes and exotic headscarves and turbans occupied many of the bazaar tents. But it was emptier. Villagers did not press through each other bumping shoulders and jostling sacks full of wares as they passed. Still, people were there, and they were exchanging coin.

Cursing, I found Firoz's family shop empty. The sun was already past its peak, so he had likely gone home. Not wanting to waste the opportunity to learn something of the caravan, I strolled through the lanes. There was a small line of people who waited outside one shop. Inside, a man was sitting in a chair while another inspected his teeth. Further, a man sat under dozens of woven baskets displayed on metal hooks. A woman with a basket of iron spearheads caught my eye. She was familiar, as were her wares. I approached with my head tilted up, like coin was my unlimited resource.

"Tell me of these."

"The finest iron mined from the mountains to the north, smelted by my husband's fires, and honed with obsidian from the south. These are sharp enough to piece the toughest flesh and light enough to throw."

"The north?" I repeated. "You've come from the north?"

She nodded and pushed the sharp spearheads toward me. "Twenty dha or a fist of salt."

"The price is too high," I said and rushed off as she called after me, saying she was willing to bargain. She did not know she had already given me what I wanted.

I tore through the lanes, walking as fast as I could without appearing as though I was running off with stolen goods. Finally, I saw the people surrounding Rafal, the man standing on his makeshift stage at the center of them all. The ghutra wound around his head and neck was the color of an amethyst. I could not see his friend through the crowd, but I heard the drum pattering. The mass of people was no smaller than normal, despite the marketplace being quieter. None wanted to miss the fantastical tales Rafal brought to the bazaar.

"They seek to restore the desert," Rafal said. "Change the paths of trade."

"Who?" I whispered to a woman.

"The Altamaruq," she said excitedly.

"You see, there was a time when caravans did not travel to the heart of the desert to acquire salt. They used to travel to the salt mines or to the desert's edge." He waited while people gasped and oohed. Then he continued. "But the desert's edge is impossible, and the salt mines have been lost under sand from disuse. Who could find them now? The maps are faded; so long has it been since we have needed them. The paths here are easy. The oases are known. *Why* change?

"People are angry with the trade. Why should one man control all of the salt? The heart of the desert is punishing, the price of the salt high. But others shake their head saying they're fools. Even if they wanted change, how could they bring it about?

"Do you know what the Altamaruq call themselves?" Rafal asked. The people shook their heads, enraptured by his talk of change, of rebellion. Putting questions in their mind they never knew to ask. "The Dalmur. The believers." He paused, and the drummer pounded his fists.

"They're believers of the legend of the desert's edge. That there is a better desert hidden beneath the one we are now—hidden beneath magic." The drum thudded. "They seek to restore the desert to what it was."

"Even if what you say is real, how could they do it?" a man asked from the front.

"Rumor is that the Salt King found magic in the oasis. It is what the Dalmur seek. Why the King's men keep dying. They try to stop them, but the King's guards are no match for these desperate believers."

I looked around, uneasy. Rafal was speaking too loudly, too freely. If the Salt King knew of his words, he would certainly have Rafal killed.

"They want to know why the oasis is protected, of course. Why are none allowed there except those approved by the King and his vizier? Are secrets kept there?" Rafal continued. I wondered how he could know so much about the motives of the Altamaruq.

A woman scoffed. "But secrets can't alter a desert."

"No," Rafal agreed. "But what else could erase magic? What could prevent dunes from swallowing the Salt King's settlement? What else could create an inexhaustible supply of salt when no salt mines lie beneath the earth?" Rafal asked the sky. His accusations were too much. I feared for him, for all of the villagers around him.

My heart thudded, and suddenly I was very hot. I began pushing out from the crowd, desperate to get away.

Rafal continued. "Except a wish-granting jinni."

The people gasped loudly as the ground slipped from under me. The clouds spun over my head, and I heard people shouting in fury that he would so casually mention something so dangerous.

A few laughed at the silly children's story.

Suddenly, there were hands on my arms, fingers against my brow.

"Is the girl alright?" Rafal called, and I saw his face over the crowd, peering on tip-toes down to me as I lay on the ground.

Pushing the hands away, pulling my veil up my face and tugging down my scarf over my eyes, I stood in a rush. "I am fine, I am fine. Leave me be." I looked at no one, keeping my eyes to the ground, and I rushed home, praying none saw my face nor the bright edges of my fustan beneath my abaya.

The Altamaruq sought a jinni—sought Saalim. How could they know of his existence? My father hadn't told a soul.

Taking deep breaths, I thought of Matin who died trying to kill my father. Did he know that Father possessed the jinni? Or was it a guess? I thought of the guards who died defending the oasis from the invaders. The poor boys who didn't know why their lives were worth the oasis' protection. They didn't understand there was nothing to shield except my father's vanity and mirage of power.

When I got home, I saw that Sabra had not returned. Raheemah smiled at me and waved the cards in my face again. "You're very lucky. She's still out, so I didn't have to lie. Pinar said she and Tavi went to visit your mother after the rama."

I sat down, exhausted and relieved.

Raheemah asked, "What's wrong? You look as if something terrible has happened."

12

THE DAYS STRETCHED ON AFTER RAFAL claimed the
Altamaruq were looking for a jinni. I worried about what the
Altamaruq was doing, where they waited. People said that the King
was keeping us safe, that everything was fine. But I did not believe the men
wouldn't return. What would they do next?

I spent mornings wondering about Saalim—my mind straying to him
when I saw the white-peaked tents from the rama or when my small friend
asked me to tell her more stories. Did he know the Altamaruq sought him?
I longed to talk with him again. Like we did that last day in the prison, easy
and uninhibited. I wanted to hear his voice, and I was surprised that I even
craved his touch. I grew restless and agitated, thinking of all that I wanted
and couldn't have, knowing that if I wished it, it could be. But I was afraid
of Masira and how my words would be twisted, so my lips stayed closed, no
wishes passed through them.

". . . never get married now," Adilah whispered behind me.

Thoughts of the Altamaruq and Saalim dropped away.

Hadiyah arranged my hair so that it fell in thick waves down my back. "We'll cover them. He won't notice." Her voice equally quiet.

It did not matter how they concealed me for the courting, if the muhami chose me, he would see everything tonight. And tomorrow, he would choose another ahira. I thought of Aashiq with little pangs of grief. Every day I missed him less, but each day I yearned more for what he could have given me. It felt like it was so long ago. How different things had been then—fewer secrets, a smaller world.

"Here, this will help, too." Hadiyah wrapped a gossamer scarf around my neck so that it, too, flowed behind me and covered my back.

It did me no good to dwell on what could have been, though. Weakness was not an option. I could not yet give up—not like Sabra. Even if I had no hope that a muhami might find me suitable, I could not stop trying to win his favor. The necessity for marriage to a muhami had been ingrained in me since I was a child. What I wanted and what I knew my family wanted was a convoluted web of emotions that still required detangling. All I knew for certain is that a marriage to a suitor would free me from the palace perhaps more surely than a wish for my freedom. So I could not stop fighting for that. Not yet.

As we walked to the courting, I stared at my sister's back, heart pounding and sweat sliding down my neck. It would be my first time seeing my father since he lashed me.

When we arrived, the King was drinking with the suitor. His glassy eyes swiftly passed over us as he introduced his ahiran by a sloppy wave of his goblet. He did not seem to notice that I was there, and when the afternoon proceeded without a word from him, my unease gave way to immense relief. Saalim had been right.

The King drank, guffawing loudly about this and that, toasted to the suitor, and sat his prized daughters atop his lap. He ignored me as I ignored him. When my father stood to announce the courting had ended, I huffed, looking one last time to all of the servants and guards. I had seen my father's glass vessel. It was empty, yet I had not seen Saalim.

We were walking back to the zafif when Raheemah stopped suddenly. Her hands flew to her stomach, and she lurched forward. Vomit the color of red wine spilled from her mouth.

"Emah!" I turned, placing my hands on her back.

Raheemah righted herself and continued to walk. "I'm fine," she mumbled. "Too much to drink. How embarrassing . . ." She fluttered her hand and attempted a smile. She looked ill—her skin pale, temples damp. Once inside, I sat her down on one of the mattresses while my sisters changed back into their dresses.

"Hadiyah," I said, "Raheemah has had too much to drink. She should go home, lie down." I looked around at my sisters—slowly disrobing, some lying down to rest for a bit away from the sun before walking back to our tent. Hadiyah clucked her tongue and squinted at the ahiran who moved like they waded in honey.

"Yes. Take her home. Be more responsible, child!" Hadiyah admonished my young sister whose head rested on her knees.

She tossed us our coverings and sent us out. We walked as quickly as we could, guard in tow, small flashes of pink and purple peeking out from under the swishing fabric at our shuffling feet.

Arriving home, Raheemah pitched forward again, and more of the afternoon's wine streamed onto the ground. I hurriedly kicked sand over it.

"What's wrong with you? I know you're not drunk, so don't lie to me again."

"I think I'm with child." Raheemah mumbled the words so quietly, I had to ask her to repeat them.

"How is that possible?" It should not have been. We were taught to meticulously monitor our cycle and know when we were susceptible. We knew that during those times, we were supposed to sit out the courtings and remain with the attendants. This was the only allowance the King made for absences when a suitor had arrived. It worked. Most of the time. The first ahira to get pregnant had told her attendant. It had caused a wild frenzy in the palace, and she was sent away as a failed ahira. To be cast out and left with a child? No ahira wanted that fate for herself. So subsequently, ahiran learned to take care of it on their own.

"I don't know," she sighed. "It hasn't been normal, I have been unable to predict accurately."

I paced in circles around the tent, kicking sand up with every step. I was frustrated; I was trapped. Taking care of a pregnancy was not difficult. There was a village healer that my sisters had seen in the past, but I could not take Raheemah there with Sabra's looming threat, and I certainly couldn't ask anyone else to lie for me.

"How long have you known?" I asked finally, stooping down in front of her with a goblet of tepid tea. She leaned against a table leg, face wan.

"I have not bled in almost two moons."

How had she been able to hide this from us, for so long? I pinched the bone of my nose remembering the times she seemed unwell. And we all ignored it.

"How long were you going to keep it secret, Raheemah?" I pleaded. "We can help you, but you must tell us."

"I worried."

In the aftermath of what happened with my punishment, that was no surprise. I rubbed her back. After a while, the rest of our sisters trickled in, tossing their veils and abayas into their baskets. They cast worried looks at Raheemah, asking after her health.

"Too much wine," I said, wishing that there was some way I could get her to the healer before our attendants, her mother, and our father discovered her secret.

THE TWILIGHT horn rang, and we waited. Before long, the tent opened, and an attendant poked her head inside.

"Sabra."

There were audible gasps as we exchanged surprised glances. Sabra herself looked stunned, her eyebrows arcing ever so slightly above her eyes. It had been over a year since she had been requested, and all assumed she would never see a muhami again, the commencement of her twenty-third year less than a moon away. Tavi burst into thrilled tears and ran to Sabra, hugging her happily.

Sabra patiently listened to Tavi's advice, despite Tavi being six years her junior, before she left to be prepared for the suitor.

I grabbed Raheemah's hand in excitement.

"Tonight," I whispered, thanking Eiqab for the fortunate turn of events. We scrambled up. Pulling my servant's coverings from my basket, I readied myself to leave, discreetly tying the salt around my waist. I motioned for Raheemah to do the same, and when she pulled out her ahira coverings—adorned with beads and embroidery—I realized we were trapped.

We had one pair of servants' clothes, passed between the few ahiran who escaped the palace before me. The clothes had been here long before me, so I had no idea where I would find more. I briefly thought of the clothiers, the parents of the neighboring little girl, but I did not want to put them at risk for helping me. Could I go to Raheemah's mother? I did not know her well. What if she told the attendants?

I certainly could not send Raheemah to the healer by herself, yet I had no idea what he needed to do for Raheemah, so I was not sure I could go on her behalf.

"Hold on," I told my sister as she covered herself. "You can't be seen in those." I pressed my hand to my head, now considering if it would be worthwhile to ask my mother. She had friends who were servants—Amira and Yara—maybe they could help me.

"Wait here," I told Raheemah, who sipped tea.

I hurried to the kitchens, praying I'd find one of the women there. There were not many left in the kitchen, my father's dining and entertaining ending with the day, and the fires were unoccupied except for one. I approached the cloaked figure.

"Might you help me?"

The face that turned up to me belonged to a man. "What do you want?" He scooped sand over the hot coals.

"I am looking for Yara or Amira."

He nodded. "Yara lives four homes that way."

I thanked him and scurried off to find her. The home was open to the dusk, and there was very little inside. I saw her and three others sitting at a low table eating and talking quietly.

"Yara?" I asked tentatively.

The woman rose from the ground. "What is it?" She was wary until I told her who I was. "Emel! Come in, share our meal." She took my hand and began to lead me in.

"No, I cannot." I pulled away and explained that I needed an abaya and veil like the ones I was wearing. I did not say why, and she did not ask. She went to a rope strung across the wall and pulled down the only two things hanging from it. "You have another?" I asked as I took the clothes from her. I could smell the cookfires on them.

She shook her head and smiled. "No, but it seems you have greater need."

Imagining her sitting all day in the sun without them, I promised I would return them that night, and I went back to fetch Raheemah.

Disguised as servants, we slipped out of the tent. I turned to one of the guards. He was unfamiliar and very young—perhaps one of those sent from another settlement. I looked to the other and exhaled in relief. The normal nighttime guard.

I rarely had reason to speak to him, but he had returned my leather sack to me many evenings. "My sister is very sick," I whispered to him, thinking of the dwindling time we had as the sun set. "We must seek a healer. I only ask for an escort out of the palace. We can get back in on our own."

He looked at his feet and said, "We have been ordered to keep all children of the King in their home unless we receive word directly from the King himself."

Children. He was not much older than I. "I will pay you well. Two handfuls, since there are two of us. And a little extra when we return to ensure your silence."

He swallowed.

Inwardly, I cringed. I did not want to sacrifice that much salt knowing the healer would require a large sum, but I could not risk him saying no.

There was a long pause. "Okay."

I delivered my payment to his open sack of coins. His eyes greedily watching the salt fall into his possession. Then he escorted us out of the palace.

With Raheemah's hand in mine, I led her down the narrow village aisles, through the twisting lanes. Orange twilight seeped onto everything and made the fires glow warmly despite the cooling night. Raheemah was in awe, her curiosity slowing us down with each turn.

"It is so alive," she breathed. Every turn she stopped to watch what someone was doing, peering into the few homes that were open for the night. She would pause to peer at yoked camels alongside a small tent or a shop that held shelves of glittering vases.

If only she could see it when the people weren't so full of fear, if she could see it when it really was alive. "Don't stop," I said. "We should get to the healer's before dark."

The healer's tent was tall and lopsided. A patchwork of various fabrics sewn together to create a covering long enough to reach the ground. On both sides of the entrance were two wooden stands that each held an untethered bird. We paused when we saw them, admiring their beauty.

The brown griffon on the left was still, her orange eye following us. The other, a sparrow hawk, was unconcerned with our approach, his wings spread wide as he dug his beak through the black and white speckled plumes on his chest.

Strings of beads and bells hung down over the entrance, and a cacophony of pinging glass and metal sounded when we walked through. A large fire sent heavy smoke into the enclosed room. Through the haze, I saw two iron pots filled with boiling liquid strung above the flames. Behind the fire was a large wooden loft, tall enough to walk under, with a flimsy ladder that leaned against it. Beneath were rows and rows of shelves with an uncountable number of baubles and trinkets: metal pots rolled onto their sides, glass receptacles with chips missing from their edges, twisting golden pipes reaching to the sky, vessels of colorful liquid with corks plugged into their necks.

A clatter sounded from the darkness atop the loft, startling us both. An orange glow moved to the loft's edge, and soon I could make out a gnarled man holding a candle in one hand with sheets of parchment in the other. He leaned over the edge. "What do you want?"

"We need your help. My sister, she . . ."

The man set down his papers and descended the ladder, candle in hand, with unexpected dexterity.

"Can you pay?" he asked gruffly when he was on the ground.

"Yes, I have—"

"Come here."

We followed him to a low, silver table atop a woven rug. He set down the candle and, with creaks and groans, slowly folded his body until he was seated on the rug.

He was a small man, not much larger than me. He wore long, white robes that were much too big for him. When we were seated, he tilted his face toward us. His eyes were nearly all white: the brown of his eyes paper-thin and web-like, stretching to the center of his pupils, which were shockingly bright white.

The parts of his face not hidden in his scarf were covered in severe lines and deep folds of thinning, aged skin. No fat to soften his features. There was no beard on his face, unusual for a man. Instead, he had small astral symbols inked across his cheeks and jaw. He sat silently, staring behind us. Was he blind?

"Who are you?" he said roughly.

"My name is Emel. This is my sister, Raheemah."

"King's daughters then?" He guffawed and scratched at his crotch. "How brave you are. Indeed, you must be desperate."

Our names were not secret, but not many villagers knew the names of the King's many children well enough to recognize them at once. "Yes, sir. So you must know your silence is much appreciated—"

"Don't talk to me about keeping secrets, girl. Why are you here?" He snapped.

I cowered and pulled my scarf away from my face. I gestured to my sister. "We think she is with child."

"Lie down."

Raheemah reluctantly lay on the rug, her face turned anxiously toward me. The healer used his hands to feel the way toward her. He bent over her, his large robes billowing out so his bare, boney chest showed beneath. He felt her body methodically as though orienting himself and then fumbled with the ends of Raheemah's abaya without thought to her modesty. He pulled them up carelessly until her midsection was exposed. Her bright pants were brash in the drab room. If anyone were to walk in, her clothes would be immediately recognizable as belonging to a princess. I shifted so I sat between the door and my sister.

Without pause, the healer pressed his boney, claw-like fingers into her skin with firm, repetitive motions until he grunted in understanding, stopped, and nodded. "She could be. It is early. If her womb takes the tonic, she will be briefly ill and the child will be gone. If the womb does not take well to the tonic, then . . . How will you pay?" He sat back slowly.

I exhaled and dropped my shoulders, worrying over the unspoken consequence. Raheemah scrambled up and urgently pulled her robes down to cover herself. She turned to me and said, "There is no choice. I must."

I nodded and said to the healer, "I have salt."

The healer shifted and looked toward me with his colorless eyes. He moved slowly until he sat before me. He brought his fingertips together before him, studying me. As he did, the sleeves of his robes fell down to his elbows, and I was surprised that more black ink coated his arms: the phases of the moons, suns with thick rays, and stems with leaves trailing up his arms until all was lost into the folds of fabric.

"Salt is a dangerous thing to carry, my child. It is the King's currency. Where did you get it, I wonder?"

I stared mutely, unsure if he expected an answer. The implication in his words unnerved me. Was he suggesting I stole it?

The healer's unseeing eyes traveled over my face slowly. Finally, they fell down to my chest. They lingered there for a moment before he stood, groaning as he straightened out. He grabbed his candle and shuffled to the shelves. He felt his way through the trinkets and pulled vessels of liquid off the shelf. He chose vials and carefully poured precise quantities into an empty silver goblet.

Cupping the chalice carefully, he brought it to Raheemah. "Drink. Quickly, now." She silently obeyed, her face distorting at the foul taste.

"You will bleed heavily, and if there is a child, it will leave with the blood," he said.

"What do I pay?" I pulled the sack from my robes and held it before me.

The healer said nothing. He turned back to his shelves and prepared another vial of liquid. He smelled it, grunted his approval, and placed a cork in its thin neck.

He gestured for me to open the sack I held in my palms. He reached his gnarled fingers into the bag and pulled out a pinch of salt. With his shining tongue, he licked the crystalline granules off of his fingers. He closed his eyes, pressed his lips together, and hummed in delight. I glanced at Raheemah who looked as alarmed as I felt. The healer waved the bag away and took a step toward me, closing the gap between us.

"Remove your abaya, girl," he whispered urgently, eagerly. "You carry life in you as well." His warm, sour breath blew against my face.

Raheemah was scandalized, her gaze flicking from me to the healer. Alarm spiked in me. With child? That was impossible. I had no signs, it had been so long since . . . I pulled off my abaya until I stood in the immodest clothes of court.

The healer smiled widely as he stared at my chest, then extended his hand and placed it carefully onto my breastbone.

"You are marked, just as I thought. I could feel it!" he said, giddy fascination thick in his voice. He tapped his hand against my heart and laughed wildly, excitedly. "This love is like a draught of poison, but She has poured it for you alone. It will not be easy to swallow, oh no. But once you've done it—and you will—you will be changed forever." He leaned close to me and whispered, "Do not hesitate to drink." He dropped his hand and then proffered the small vial.

I took it and moved to uncork the vial, about to drink. I did not understand his words, but I knew that I did not want to be with child either.

"No!" He shrieked and his hand flew to the vessel, stopping its journey to my lips. He grew serious. "This is not for you. This is my gift, to thank you for the gift that you will soon give to us." He smiled, almost crazed, before he took the cork from my fingers and re-stopped the vial. "This is for one who stands in your way. May they fear you."

I took it from him carefully, scared of what it contained. "What does it do?"

"Leave," He turned from us and scrambled up the ladder, murmuring excitedly to himself. "I must tell them the news."

13

RAHEEMAH AND I INHALED DEEPLY, relishing the cool evening air outside the healer's tent.

"What was that about?" Raheemah whispered, eyeing the griffon. She still stared at us, except now, she seemed even more curious.

"Eiqab only knows. He is surely mad. But if it works, it was worth it." I crossed the scarf over my face and tucked away the vial. "Are you okay?"

"I feel a little sick, but it helps to be out of that foul smoke." She coughed and looked back to the healer's tent as we walked away. The glowing orange from the fire within shone through the strings of beds that hung at the entrance. The griffon still watched us. "That tonic he gave me was awful."

"I'm sorry." I reached out and gently squeezed her hand.

"Don't apologize. I owe you a great debt."

"So we're even then? No thirty games of cards owed." I smirked, reminding her of the promise to lie for me the afternoon I left to the market.

"Yes, we're even." She paused, then turned to me. "Could I see it?"

"The bazaar?"

"I just thought, well, I have never been, and I might never . . ."

I laughed. "Yes! Let me show you." I explained to her that without the caravan everything would be quieter, and since the Altamaruq had come, things were even more muted. But I promised she would still be amazed. "If it's okay with you, I have a friend I would like to see while we are there. I haven't seen him in some time. It will not take long."

Her eyebrows raised at the mention of a man, but she agreed. We changed direction to head toward the marketplace.

"What do you think the healer gave you?" Raheemah asked.

"Who knows. Meant for an enemy, eh?"

"Perhaps Nassar will be thirsty sometime soon."

"Emah, hush!" Tavi was rubbing off on her.

"'This love is a draught of poison,'" she repeated like a perfect student. "I wonder what it means. Are you in love? I hope not. It sounds bad." She continued to puzzle over his words as we walked, her mood brightening with each step.

Tendrils of light still lingered in the night sky. We had not been gone long. The walk to the healer's took nearly more time than our visit with the healer himself.

The market was ablaze for the evening: shops illuminated by small torches at their entrances, candles scattered throughout the bazaar lanes. We navigated through the quiet walkways, Raheemah exclaiming her wonder at all of the sights with each turn.

"Amazing!" She cried, watching three musicians laugh and sing together, firelight glittering in her eyes.

"Wait here." I left her beside a large spice shop. The outpouring of herbal, floral, and nutty scents reminding me of the palace kitchens. Raheemah walked through the barrels and baskets that were lined in little rows and nodded distractedly.

I crossed the crowded lane and found Firoz sitting beneath his usual tent.

He crushed me to him amongst the crowd of shoppers. It was a hug so different from what I had shared with Saalim. His was the touch of family.

"It is good to see you, too." I pulled away, gazing warmly at my friend.

"Every time something horrible happens, I don't see you. Twice now I've been worried you're dead!"

Indignant, I crossed my arms. "I tried to see you a few days ago, but you weren't here."

"When?" He asked.

I told him, and understanding cleared the confusion on his face.

"Oh, yes."

"Where were you?"

"I sold everything early that day," he said quickly.

It seemed unbelievable given the quietude of the settlement, but I did not contest. I told of Rafal and what he said of the Altamaruq. Firoz started to tell me what he had heard, but I stopped him.

"I cannot stay. My sister waits for me. I just wanted to see you, ensure you are well and let you know that I am the same."

"Your sister is here?! Why haven't you brought her over to meet me?" He stretched out his neck and peered at the people in the lane. "I can add another elusive ahira to my list of acquaintances," he murmured and winked at me.

"Eiqab, help me."

He waved my words away. "Go fetch her."

Soon, we were all sitting together under the tent—Raheemah with a jar of coconut juice nestled between her palms, a comfort for her unsettled stomach.

"I can't believe all that's been happening. First the guards, and now the prison." He motioned to a part of the village behind him. "I heard nothing about illness or death amongst the ahiran, so I didn't know what to think when I hadn't seen you. Where have you been?"

Keeping my eyes on Raheemah, who sat at the front of the shop watching people pass, I told him what happened with Sabra. Of the lashing and the imprisonment. His face fell, and he grabbed my hands, squeezing them tightly.

He said, "You just missed the prison fire."

"What fire?" I asked.

Raheemah turned toward us, her eyes dropping to where our hands were linked. I pulled away. I did not need the rumors going through the sisters that there was indeed a man in my life.

"It was awful. That whole section of the village was worried they'd lose their homes—people tore apart their tents to get away from it."

Fires were rare in the village, but when they did occur, they wiped away entire sections of our settlements, the wood and animal-hair a perfect feast for flames.

He continued, "The flames licked up the walls, getting bigger with each thing they consumed. They destroyed the entire prison. I heard it roaring into the night, saw the soot and smoke over the orange glow."

Apparently, people from all over saw the shine of the fire at the edge of the village. There had been no deaths, but most of the prisoners had fled and were now scattered throughout the settlement in hiding.

"What caused it?" Raheemah asked, now more captivated by Firoz's story than the marketplace.

He shrugged. "A strong wind and a precariously close lamp?"

I thought of the screaming soldier in the prison. Was he in the village now? Mad from torture and seeking revenge? The thought chilled me.

Aware of the passing time, I said goodbye to Firoz, warning him it would be some time before he saw me again. He hugged me gently and bowed respectfully toward Raheemah.

We walked through the market so she could see the shops. She was looking through a table of embellished veils, fingering the shining ornaments, when a middle-aged woman called to us from across the lane.

"Fortunes for a price!"

Interest piqued, Raheemah turned to the exotic woman wrapped in a myriad of colors, thickly beaded necklaces draped on her neck, and shining metal chains on her wrists that jingled together when she moved. Raheemah left the veils behind and traipsed across the lane.

"Please, sister," she begged me, eyes alight with excitement as she listened to the oracle describe fantasies and futures. "I want to know my fate!"

"Absolutely not," I whispered in her ear, careful no one heard our exchange. "We have no coin." We could not be seen trading in salt.

The oracle saw our murmured exchange and Raheemah's subsequent disappointment. "For the young one," she said directly to me, "I will do it for nothing."

It was an offer that could not be refused. Raheemah's face lit up like a lantern as she followed the oracle into the tent.

I was uneasy. People did not do things for free. What would she want in return? I hoped Raheemah had enough wits to keep her mouth closed about who we were. I fidgeted outside before deciding to wander through the nearby shops to pass the time. I would not stray far. Some vendors still had their wares on display despite the late hour. Most had removed their goods, and the empty tents yawned wide, dark like toothless mouths.

I was near one of the darkened tents thinking of the escaped prisoner when my arm was yanked firmly and I was quickly pulled to its back. A scream tore from my chest, but there was no sound. I clutched at my throat. Why couldn't I scream? I turned to my assailant, and in the glow of the market, I saw his face.

"Saalim?" I whispered. Glee immediately replaced the panic. He pulled me through the back corner of the tent where two panels had been loosely tied together.

We stood in the back of the bazaar, smashed between fabric. I clutched my chest as my heart slowed and peered at the rears of tents around us. I could not see any of the marketplace, but I could hear it: clinking trinkets, pinging coin, and humming voices. I smiled, wondrous.

The faint glow from the open shops seeped through the cloth and illuminated the jinni's face a gentle orange. He was dressed in the palace guard uniform, but his scent enveloped me so surely, I could have closed my eyes and known his presence.

We stared at each other. Moths fluttered in my stomach. I wanted to fling myself into his arms, but his reserve held me back. Why did he stare at me like that? At first, he said nothing. Then, with a light, hesitating touch, he reached for the edge of my scarf. I nodded, and he pulled it away from my face.

"Hello," he murmured, his fingers playing through my hair. I pressed my head into his hand. "I've missed you," he said, spreading his fingers across the back of my head and pulling me to him. His other arm wrapped around my shoulders.

"I've missed you," I said into his chest.

"Before you worry," he whispered, looking down at me. "Your sister is fine. It will take quite some time for her fortune to be told."

I leaned back and saw a wicked smile curving his lips. "The oracle? That was your doing?"

"Indeed," he chuckled, then grew serious. "Now, I have something I must finish. We were interrupted last time." He leaned down and pressed his lips to mine. Like a pot shattering on stone, the days of pent up yearning for the jinni exploded from me. I reciprocated his movements with the same desperation, clenching the back of his uniform in my hands. We were tangled together, the urgent tension between us crackling and snapping. The tent walls flapped against us, a pocket of privacy in the beating heart in the village.

I pulled away, breathless, Saalim's face a palm's breadth from my own.

"How did you find me?"

"After so many mornings together, I know you well. Your mind is easy to find." He kissed my forehead. "Did you get away without trouble?"

"We did." I cocked my head, peering at him.

"When I felt you wish for a way to get Raheemah to the healer . . ."

I was perplexed. I had done no such thing. "I did?"

He nodded. "I guided the suitor's choice to Sabra, hoping it would afford you the opportunity to leave. I also hoped I would have the chance to see you while you were out." His lip quirked, a poorly hidden glint of pride in his scheming.

I sighed. "Why don't you have him propose to Sabra while you're at it? Then I can be done with her meddling and free to leave the tent again."

His voice had a hard edge. "I have some conscience. I can't interfere in one's future like that anymore."

"Anymore?"

"I've done it in the past. I regret it."

"I wasn't serious anyway." We both knew it was a lie. Suddenly remembering Rafal's claim, I began fussing with the buttons on his tunic. "Did you know the Altamaruq seek a jinni?"

"I have heard."

"Aren't you worried? They're killing soldiers, they tried to kill my father . . . and now the prison."

Saalim frowned at the mention of the prison.

"What is it?" I asked.

"They attacked the palace again that night. The prison was a distraction, to pull as many of the King's men to stop the fire, to be away from the palace."

I gasped. "What?" I grabbed his shirt in my fists.

"They did not get far."

My voice trembled. "How do they know about you? What would happen if they took you?"

"I do not know what they know or how they know it. You don't need to worry about me, Emel. If there is a threat to the King, it is my duty to remove it as swiftly as possible to save him. And none can get me unless they first get him."

"But you aren't with him now. You weren't there when Matin attacked," I said in a rush, suddenly fearful that something would happen while he was gone. That the vessel would be stolen before Saalim would have time to return and stop it. If he was taken . . .

"No, I was not there when Matin attacked." He looked away. "Your father learned from that mistake. He could have lost his life, he could have lost me." He added softly, "You wouldn't have lost Aashiq."

"It is okay," I said almost believing it. "I am okay."

"Things have changed since Matin. Your father keeps me out of my vessel nearly always—either guarding him or acting as his slave. If something happens to him, if he needs me, I can be there faster than a soldier can move."

"I'm worried."

"I am not." He said it confidently.

"But what can you do for the Altamaruq? How could you restore the desert? How would it be different?"

He grumbled. "Please, I do not want to talk of your father's troubles when I have you in my arms."

He brushed his lips against my cheek, caressing the valley between my neck and shoulders lightly with his thumb.

The mood had changed considerably. I leaned into him again. "I am grateful you allowed me to help Emah. That you came to see me." I felt him relax against me.

"I must confess, it was partly selfish. Seeing you earlier was not enough for me."

"Were you there today?" I was suddenly anxious. I did not want him to see me as an ahira, fluttering my eyes at another man who touched my hips and waist.

"I was. It took all my power to not watch you every moment." He twisted his finger through a long strand of my hair. "This afternoon, I masqueraded as a dutiful slave." His expression was one of mock excitement until he saw my uneasiness. He looked puzzled, then understanding came. "Ah. Emel, I

have known you as an ahira for many years. You don't need to worry. I know
you have a duty to your father."

"It's different now."

"Are you worried about me?" He smiled, pleased.

I shrugged, embarrassed.

"You owe me nothing, except maybe one more thing . . ." He bent down
and kissed me again. His fingers trailed through my hair, down my back and
waist.

We held each other for a few moments more. My head pressed to his
chest, his cheek resting atop my hair. There was farewell in our embrace, not
knowing when we would see each other again.

"You must return to your sister. She is almost done," Saalim said as
he pulled away. He quickly draped the scarf around my head and face. I
adjusted it, righting what his inexperienced hands failed to do.

"I hope I see you again soon."

"I will try to make it so. And if I can't, if it's some time before we see
each other again, know that I am near and that I think only of you."

I rested my hand against his heart. "I think the same."

"I know," he murmured and kissed my lips, sending warmth like hot oil
down my spine.

He pressed me through the parting in the tent so I was back in the deserted
shop looking toward the bazaar thoroughfare. I found my way back to the
oracle's tent and was just settling into the sand when Raheemah emerged.

"Sister!" Raheemah called. I could see from her eyes that there was a
wide smile on her face.

"I will meet someone soon, and we will fall in love!" Raheemah crooned.
"And she wanted me to tell you something, too." She held her finger up and
closed her eyes, as though trying to get it just right. "She said to beware of
the man in gold, for he will steal your heart."

I laughed to myself and wondered just how much the jinni had magicked
the oracle's words. "Oh, did she?"

"Do you think the man in gold is the same man the healer mentioned?" Raheemah asked seriously as we strode away.

I faltered. Was he?

Raheemah prattled on about the specifics of the prophecy as we wound our way back to our home. My sweet half-sister, to whom life had been so cruel—dreams of love and a hopeful future bursting out of her into the night sky. Though it filled me with gladness to be able to give her that gift, there was also a deep ache knowing that tomorrow, she would again be an ahira of the King, a pawn in his insatiable game of power. And so would I.

14

CURLED ON MY MAT, EYES CLOSED, I thought of Saalim—his lips on mine, his beard against my cheek, his fingers on the small of my back.

A bright wash of sunlight flashed onto my face. "A muhami tonight!" the attendant trilled excitedly before disappearing again.

I groaned.

"Practicing for the bed already?" Tavi teased.

I sat up. "Eiqab knows I need no practice."

She fetched our abayas. "What's gotten into you lately?"

Raheemah smirked.

"I don't know what you mean," I said narrowing my eyes at Raheemah. She and I had grown even closer since the healer.

The first day after the tonic, she had been so ill, I had worried that we'd made a mistake. She clutched her stomach while cramps raked her from the

inside. She bled and bled and ate nearly nothing. I almost wished for her recovery, but selfishness kept me silent. I didn't know where a wish would send her.

After two terrifying days, she began to mend. She smiled more, ate more, drank more. And now, she was nearly herself again. Whatever the healer had given her worked like magic.

Tavi began counting my misdeeds off on her fingers. "You barely try with the suitors. You're restless. You smile more."

Raheemah agreed, and I turned to her. "Don't you encourage Tavi's ridiculous presumptions."

Raheemah used every moment we were alone to whisper about the bazaar, the oracle, Firoz. She'd smile so widely, describing the things she'd seen and the people she'd spoken with. She asked me frequently about Firoz. I insisted he was no lover of mine, only a friend.

"Let it be known," Tavi continued, "if something is up and I find out you've kept it secret, I am disowning you as a sister."

I tied my veil. "Well, when I've finished digging my tunnel to the oasis, you're not coming with me." I smoothed down my mat ensuring the bag of salt, my map, and the healer's potion were not visible should anyone come in while we were gone.

Raheemah watched me intently, the desire obvious in her gaze. Like a drop of honey on the tongue, the small taste of freedom was not enough. I knew she wanted to see more of the settlement she'd lived in her entire life without knowing.

But I think she also needed a reminder that the world she had glimpsed was not a dream. I understood. Living a life confined to the palace, it was hard to believe anything else was real.

"When you've finished the tunnel, I'm coming with you whether you like it or not," Tavi said.

"Me, too," Raheemah added.

"Wouldn't have it any other way," I said.

AS WE made our way to our father and suitor, my only consolation for the afternoon was the hope that I might glimpse Saalim.

Despite the winter chill outside, it was warm inside the tent. The suitor was a young nobleman who stood awkwardly beside my father. The man glanced at us as we walked in, smiled uncomfortably, then looked down at the carpets.

I wandered to the margins of the room and sat with another ahira upon a cushion. We babbled about trivial things—tapestries and blankets and the challenges of specific patterns of the rugs—as we waited for the afternoon to end. Raheemah quickly captured the attention of the suitor. He approached her cautiously, another man drawn to virginal youth. Or really, just youth.

Protectiveness distracted me, and I no longer could speak with my sister. She turned to watch, too. The man greeted Raheemah. He seemed scared to touch her, but Raheemah adeptly met his reluctance with warmth. She leaned toward him, smiling widely, though I could see it was forced. Who was this man? How would he treat my young sister? When he took her hand and led her to a place where they could talk privately, I looked away. There was nothing I could do. She was an ahira, this was her fate.

I peered around the room, from guard to guard, slave to slave. No one gave any indication they were who I sought. Disappointed, I abandoned my search and listened instead to the prattle of my sisters around me.

Thirsty, I began to rise in search of tea or wine when a slave appeared at my side.

"Wine for the princess?" he asked quietly, kneeling beside me and holding a silver goblet before him.

My sisters looked up in surprise at the boldness of the slave. Rarely did slaves speak directly to ahiran during a courting, and almost never did they offer us food or drink. It was the behavior of new slaves who did not realize our role in the court was nearly the same as theirs.

Looking down at the slave's proffered glass, I glimpsed a familiar, golden cuff emerging from the end of his white sleeve. Only now, the cuff did not melt into his skin. It ended at this wrist with no twining gold on his skin. His skin was the color of mine, and his face was that of a stranger's. Only the magicked cuffs marked him as the jinni. As Saalim.

Fluttering erupted in my stomach, but I held fast my features to hide my burgeoning smile. I glanced beyond the slave to my father who sat in intense conversation with the suitor. The muhami sat rigidly upon a chaise lounge, Raheemah still at his side. My father did not notice me nor the slave.

"Thank you," I murmured, and when I reached out for the glass, I trailed my fingers quickly up from the smooth metal at his wrist to the back of his hands down his fingers before finally taking the wine from him. He flashed his golden eyes to mine, and his lips curled in a roguish smile, thrilling at the barefaced flirting.

Saalim stood and walked away. As I watched him go, I noticed Nassar. He stood across the room, in a corner, observing the courting as he always did. Except now, he was turned toward me, his glance darting from the slave to me and back again. He had seen everything.

Tensing, I watched him trying to fit the pieces together, fearing the punishment I would face were Nassar to tell my father what he had seen. Oddly, the vizier did not appear angry so much as curious. What was he scheming? What did he plan to tell my father? He looked back to Saalim leaving the tent, then followed him out.

Fighting the urge to get up and run after Saalim to warn him of Nassar, I sat and clenched my fists. I had to remind myself there was no way Nassar, weak and spineless, could harm a conduit of Masira.

The afternoon came to a close when the suitor announced his intention to court Raheemah that evening. She blushed and looked at the ground, but I could see a hesitant smile on her face. Imagining my sister at the mercy of an uncaring man, I wanted to run and yank Raheemah from his side. I wanted to drag her away from the cage of our father's palace.

As we headed home, I trailed Tavi, who spoke excitedly to Raheemah beside her. A guard followed us some ways behind, distracted as he fiddled with his scimitar. It was quiet in the palace, many of the servants home for midday meals.

My mind churned with thoughts of how I could prevent my sister's courtship, thinking of ways I could craft a wish that even Masira could not alter. How could I wish that she marry a kind man instead? One who would let her traipse through village streets and pet neighing horses and taste glistening fruit. Someone who would take her to oracles and let her gaze at herself in bejeweled mirrors at the bazaar.

Staring at the ground, a familiar smell met my nose: jasmine, dust, and . . . I looked up. Everything around me was unmoving. Time had stilled. Grinning, I began to look for Saalim, but it was his words that reached me first.

"He is a good man," he whispered into my ear as he reached his arms around me, pressing his chest to my back. We stood in the middle of the street, frozen sisters in front, an unmoving sun above.

"Do not worry." He kissed my temple. "He will not hurt your sister. Let them be wed. She is unlikely to find someone kinder."

I sifted through my thoughts of the suitor again, allowing myself to see what earlier I had willfully ignored: how he smiled respectfully toward all of us. The way he hesitated around the ahiran, fidgeting with his hands as if unsure where to place them, because he was uncomfortable placing them on us. How he politely asked our names, complimented our hair or scarves or jewels without touching them.

"Did you arrange it?" I said breathing in the scent of him.

"No. He chose Raheemah himself. I was absent for most of the courting, at least until a certain someone longed for a drink." I heard his smile. "I was patrolling the village."

"I looked for you."

"I know, I felt it."

I warmed and leaned into him, thinking of how much I liked this man.

"Nassar," I said, remembering and turning to him. "He followed you out—"

"He followed me, yes. He told me I was not to be speaking to the ahiran."

"Is it safe? That you have done this?" I said, looking at the still village around us. I looked for the trailing guard, but he must not yet have turned the corner.

"If the timing is just right, if no one is looking, I believe I can alter time without consequence." Saalim had stopped the world at the perfect moment. No one would notice the rift he caused. He continued. "I don't want to wait to see you, I don't want to wait for Sabra to look away. I want to see you more. If that means I must steal time from the gods, then I will. If you'll allow it, that is."

My pulse quickened. "It's what I want, too."

Saalim pulled the scarf from my face and kissed my lips. We lingered together, feeling brazen out in the open, whispering into each other's ears, sharing chaste kisses.

"The next time you are alone, the next time no one is watching, think of me. I will come. Please." There was a deep longing in his eyes. He looked so sincere, filled with so much yearning, that I wanted to grab his hand and run off with him at that moment. *Let time stay still forever.* Instead, I took his hand, pressed it between my own, and promised I would.

DESPITE RAHEEMAH'S concern that the nobleman did not want to bed her after spending two nights together, "Talking and . . . and . . . asking me questions!" she lamented after the first night, worried she had done everything all wrong, he asked for the King's permission to wed Raheemah. I cried tears both happy and sad as Raheemah shared the bittersweet news. The sisters laughed joyously and shared advice generously—how to converse with him, how to entertain him, how to laugh and smile and flutter her eyes as wives ought to. Each sounding more authoritative than the next on a subject of which they knew nothing.

I sat back, watching the exchanges affectionately, when one of my sisters walked in. Her face was pale, eyes wet. She clasped at her abaya, her gaze darting around anxiously.

"What happened?" I asked, rising up. Everyone was silent, the sudden tension snapping through the room.

"Six more deaths." Her voice was tight. "Three attendants, three villagers. They were drinking together in a small restaurant last night. Sometime later, they grew sick. They died this morning. Even the healer couldn't save them."

We huddled close as my sister spoke.

"What do they think happened?" One asked.

"Poison. They think it came into the village from the Altamaruq," she spat the words. "My brother said the King ordered that all the wine from traders be dumped."

"Which attendants?" I asked.

My sister hesitated some time, her eyes glistening before she named them all. Each spoken like a devotion. I closed my eyes, hating myself for my joy that Hadiyah and Adilah were not listed among them.

"If they are searching for a jinni," I said, "why would they kill innocent women?"

My sisters spun, and even Sabra, I noticed, looked at me aghast.

"Emel!" Raheemah exclaimed, appalled.

"Eiqab protect us," another murmured.

"They're searching for a jinni?" Pinar said, and the sisters shushed her too.

I resisted the self-reproach that wanted to smash a hand to my face. "That's just what I heard. Of course, I'm sure they don't even exist."

It was too late. The mood in the room changed. Half of my sisters mumbled about needing to pray at the rama, while the others talked louder and more excitedly about the possibility of a jinni. What if it were true? What if one existed?

"Sons, the things I'd wish for . . ." Tavi looked off wistfully.

"The biggest tent in the desert."

"The man with the biggest—"

"Turban," they snickered, careening off into wilder desires.

"What if the wine was meant for the King?" I said, desperate to draw their attention away from the jinni.

"Maybe," Tavi agreed.

How else would they try to get to Saalim? Everything before had felt separate from me, from my family. But the death of villagers, our attendants? It was too close, and I was scared. I hoped it was an accident, that the wine had been intended for my father.

That it was not for the innocent, the Altamaruq hoping if enough of the King's guards and villagers died, he would surrender his jinni to protect them. I prayed to Eiqab that was not their aim, because if it was, they did not know the Salt King.

That night, I sat with Raheemah and in the firelight, unrolled my map.

"Where does he live?" I asked, my throat aching as I fought my sadness.

"He said something about how he came here using the southwest route," she murmured, pointing unsurely at the map. "It is different there, he said. There are more trees and flowers." She smiled. "He said they have mostly settled, because there aren't dunes, and they have a large water source—I think he called it a river?—not far from his home." After using snippets of what she described, I made a guess where on the map she might live.

Dipping my reed into the ink, I drew a tree with small waves beneath it along the southwest trade line.

Then, I handed the reed to my sister.

"What is this for?" she asked, holding the reed awkwardly.

"You must write your name, or, at least, the first letter. So I always know where to find you."

"I can't . . ." Her eyes filled with tears. "I don't know how to write like you do."

"You will be a royal's wife. You must practice."

Raheemah dipped the reed into the ink with an inexperienced hand, the ink dripping from its end. Let some drop off, I told her, so it didn't smudge on the parchment.

She waited, and then with a shaky hand, bent over the map and wrote a large **R** by the tree and waves. The reed was still a little too wet, and the first line puddled.

"Perfect," I said, wiping my cheeks. I took the map and blew on the ink.

"Will you come see me one day?" The words were tight in her throat, tears flowing down her cheeks.

"I will."

Raheemah fell into me and sobbed into my lap. I bent over her as if to protect her from the world, trying, and failing, not to cry.

"I believe you," she said through gasping breaths.

When the fire was doused and the ahiran had fallen asleep, I clutched Raheemah close against my chest. Tomorrow we would say goodbye.

"I have never wanted to stay here as much as I do tonight, I have never wanted the sun to wake late. I don't want to leave," Raheemah whispered.

"Yes, you do. It's hard now, but it will be wonderful tomorrow. The Altamaruq won't hurt us. Don't worry." I tried to believe my words.

"It isn't fair that I'm to be wed before you."

"That isn't true. You deserve every happiness that exists in this world." I combed her hair with my fingers and twisted it into soft plaits. I stroked her back and neck telling her how good she was, how lucky her husband was to have chosen someone so sincere.

When she could not rest, too worried of the future, I told her Saalim's stories. I threaded together his tales of magic and chance and freedom and love while she closed her eyes, finally at ease as she let her mind wander, let herself dream.

When Raheemah's breathing slowed to the familiar rhythm of sleep, I murmured one of my favorite stories of Saalim's—one of a faraway place where there was a golden king with a powerful queen and vast pools of water that lapped against a castle of stone.

TO THE center of the empty rama, I carried the oil-fueled lamp. Its flame was too small to serve as light or heat. It had only one use: sacrifice.

A cold purple washed over the sky as the sun set. I pulled my heavy cloak tightly around my abaya as I set down the flame. I adjusted myself so that my back was to the guards, my cloak fanned so they could not see my hands nor the flame.

Searching between the layers I wore, I found the sack of salt. I grabbed a large pinch between my fingers and closed my eyes.

Masira, I give you my currency for freedom to protect my sisters, my mothers from the Altamaruq. Let them find nothing and move on, move away. Please guide the Altamaruq from here, let them pass us by.

I dropped the salt onto the flame, but it was not enough. I took a fistful and slowly poured it onto the flames until it was doused, hoping the sacrifice was enough to be heard.

Masira protect us.

The salt was stuffed from view, so I grabbed my lamp and rose.

Raheemah had left that morning, and all day I had avoided my home. I did not want to see her empty mat, some day to be replaced by a new, bright-eyed sister. It was the hardest goodbye. She was my half-sister, but she had my full heart. Despite promising I would try, I knew there was little chance I would see her again. So it was a forever farewell, and that was something I could not endure. I thought of what it would be like to say goodbye to Tavi, and I could not bear the thought. I thought of Saalim. No, that was enough thought of goodbyes.

I stopped at the harem in the evening. My mother was sitting with a handful of the King's wives, all surrounding one who cried into her scarf. Raheemah's mother. She had lost her child when Raheemah left with the prince. Of course she was inconsolable. The other wives were quick to remind her of the blessing that having a daughter wed to a nobleman was, that she should be grateful, not sad.

My mother sat with her hands on the woman's knees. "It is okay to weep, to scream. Your only child has been taken from you."

I cringed and walked toward the women. "Mama," I said, tugging on her arm, leading her away from the emotional women. "How are you?"

She looked tired, dark circles under her bloodshot eyes. No makeup was on her face, her hair was unbraided and uncombed. Even her dress was dirty. She brushed aside scattered pieces of parchment covered in her handwriting, and we sat at the edge of her low bed. She stretched out her fingers, then curled them into fists. Again and again.

Wrapping her arm around my waist, she said, "The days are shorter now."

"Yes, winter has come. Even the nights are cold."

"That is not what I mean. The days are going by quickly." She rubbed at her eyes and brushed back her hair, the faint scent of frankincense wafting. Her foot bounced on its toes like she was excited, or nervous, or–

It was Sabra. In ten days, she would be exiled from the palace. I would never see her again, and neither would my mother. I clutched my mother's hand tightly. How could I tell my mother it would be okay that her first-born was soon to be gone from her grasp? I couldn't. Just as none could tell it to Raheemah's mother, not sincerely.

"I feel like there is so much I want to tell you. So much that you need to know. But," she looked up at me, "you keep so many secrets, how will I know what words you need to hear?"

"What are you talking about?"

"Tell me, is there someone that you see? Someone you love?"

I dropped my head into my hands. "No!" My chest and neck grew hot. "I can't believe you would believe Father's lies."

She rubbed her hands on her knees and shook her head, mumbling to herself. "See, we can't know for sure. I don't want to be around all of this death. It is too much. I am scared. I'm—I'm worried. I need to go. Go somewhere and wait."

"What are you talking about? Wait for what?" Who was this woman, and why was she crazed?

She looked at me sympathetically and cupped my cheeks with her palms. Kissing my temple, she said, "It's okay. I'm okay. Go home, brave Emel."

15

SAALIM AND I STOLE BRIEF MOMENTS together when we could find them. Whether his warm hand softly nudged me awake in the unmoving night to ask me if I was okay, if I needed anything, to kiss my lips and touch my neck and hair. Or when I was walking to or from a courting, intentionally lingering behind, and my sisters suddenly froze before me.

Our meetings were always brief, the furtiveness thrilling. Neither of us dared to give in to the temptation to spend longer together, to lay together, so that I could sleep in his arms. Even in a world where Saalim existed, I had a duty as the King's daughter. I was not brave enough to wish my being an ahira away, and I feared things would become complicated if our relationship went farther. So instead, we shared sweet words and passionate kisses before Saalim would disappear, time would press forward once again, and I would return my thoughts to that of a successful courtship with a muhami.

We thought we could endure that way, always ignoring reality, pretending that our relationship was easy, carefree. But we were fools. After all, I was an ahira destined to wed a nobleman. He was a jinni destined to be a forever slave.

And one day, that reality was swept before us like a sand dune. I was requested by a muhami.

The prince was a welcome visitor, the son of a monarch and long-time friend of the King. My father spent two days drinking and sharing stories with the young prince before we were finally called to court. The prince was drawn to me like a moth to flame, and when he chose me, I realized I was going to have to face a suitor for the first time since Aashiq . . . since Saalim. To fight my despair, I reminded myself that this is what I wanted. This was my way out. If I wouldn't risk toying with Masira to gain my freedom, then I would earn it.

Saalim had been locked in his vessel during the courting. He had no ability to stop it even if I had wished for it. I couldn't understand what Father was thinking, keeping him locked away. When I saw the vessel, I wanted to berate him—who would protect us from the Altamaruq should they choose to attack? Who would protect me?

I lay on the thick mattresses as my attendants worked my body with wax and oil. My mind navigated through the deep, dirty waters of infidelity, thinking of Saalim.

I was clothed in carmine, golden whorls spinning throughout the fabric. My hair, pinned off of my face with flaxen barrettes resembling gilded palm fronds, flowed down my back, covering my scars. Braids of golden chains swung down to cover my nose and mouth. That night, I did not feel beautiful. I felt sick. This was the right thing, wasn't it?

After Aashiq, I had turned from drink and Buraq. I had not wanted that false comfort anymore. But that night, I allowed drink to be the crutch against which I leaned. Arak swam through me, and I inhaled the Buraq over and over. I hoped each breath would push Saalim from my mind. When I finally met the King, my eyes were glazed, and my words a sticky mess.

"I am pleased to see that you are not a ruined ahira after all," the King spoke icily as I bowed before him. "Omar is close to our family. You can expect I will hear about how things go tonight." It was the first time he had spoken to me since he carved the marks on my back.

"Your highness." The words dripped from my lips. "I am here to please." We were alone in the throne room except for a single guard and a slave who dutifully waved a wide leaf. My eyes fell to them several times, but they showed no indication of being something they were not. The jinni's vessel was not visible beneath the King's robes. Eiqab, let him stay locked in his prison tonight, let him not see me nor feel my thoughts.

The King stared at me, watching me sway slightly as though the gentle breeze that flowed through the room was a sandstorm's gale.

"Careful, Emel," he said, watching my drunkenness. "You don't want to embarrass yourself with the monarch's son." The King rose, bored with me. Once a flame ablaze with promise of fortunes and high-bred connections, I was now a marked and tattered rug upon which he was forced to stand.

"Isra," he called. My mother came in slowly, clothed in a pale beige dress with a matching veil, strung with red beads. Dark rubies hung heavy down her chest, soldered into a thick gold necklace. It was piled on other beaded necklaces, all bright red like drops of blood in sand.

The King paused in front of his wife and bent his head forward to kiss her brow. I watched, remembering the story Saalim told of a young ruler who once loved a wife. Did he love his current wives as much as he had loved his first?

"Mama," I said hesitantly as the King left with the slave, trying to see through her sparkling facade.

"I have heard . . ." she paused, as though unsure of how to continue. There was a lucid urgency in her tone that snagged my wavering attention. It was so different from the anxious woman I had seen days before. "I need to ask you again. I must know if . . ." she hesitated and then spoke so quietly, I could barely hear her. "Who is the man you see? Do you *know* him?" This time, it was less of a question and more of an accusation.

"What? I see no one. Why do you keep asking me these things?" The lie was easy. I certainly would not confess to seeing a magical jinni that belonged to Father, nor would I confess to leaving the palace and seeing Firoz. Not when the walls of the palace were made of cloth. I swayed from foot to foot. Did she know, or was it the vestiges of the rumor my father had started? Who was telling her, and perhaps more importantly, who was watching?

My mother peered at me as if she were trying to see my thoughts. She reached beneath the layers of necklaces and pulled on a chain until a familiar golden medallion revealed itself from beneath her dress. She pulled the necklace over her head.

"I want you to keep this now." Her hand trembled as she gave it to me.

The metal disc was warm in the palm of my hand. She had worn that necklace since my earliest memory of her.

"Why are you giving this to me?"

"So if Masira needs proof, she will see it. Carry it with you, on your neck, against your chest." She tightly squeezed my hand that held the necklace. "Don't be distracted by untruths. There are no such things. Give your heart to that which is real. Don't think of me, of your sisters. Just go."

Confused by her words and dazed by drink, my feelings were volatile. I choked back a sob.

"What is it?" She asked, her eyes swinging back and forth, trying to understand my upwelling emotion.

I missed my mother. I didn't want this person who kept pushing me away. I wanted to be a child again who fell into her Mama's open arms and soft lap and cried about life: my father's punishment, of Sabra's cruelness, the deaths of the people around us, of Firoz, of Rafal and his map. I wanted to tell her how the pressure for me to be wed was too much and I was breaking under its weight, and how I wanted to be free of my life in the court just as she wanted, just not in her way. Tell her I wanted to see the desert that was hidden beneath our own, and tell her how I did see a jinni and he made me feel cherished. Tell her how I wanted to feel that again and again.

Sobs racked me with each thought.

"Emel, stop!" My mother said sharply. She grabbed my wrists tightly, too tightly.

My tears quelled as her nails dug into my skin. I steadied myself, staring at her wild eyes.

"You are an ahira of the King! You are behaving beneath your position. There are girls out there who do what you do and have nothing over their head, nothing to eat. Keep your head high, Emel. There is none here who will feel sorry for you." She waved her hand around us furiously. "Remember that no matter how trapped you feel, you have control over this." She tapped my chest with her fingers.

As my mother spoke, I saw that beneath her anger, there was fear. She wanted me away. She wanted me safe. She wanted to shake the fantasies, the distractions, from me. Did she know I dreamt of real love in a world unlike my own? She wanted me married to power, to protection, someone she could trust.

She was right. My deluge of emotions trickled away until there was nothing left.

I was an ahira. I had one purpose: bed, wed, and arm my father with a strong, loyal, lifelong ally. It was the only way I could protect my family, even Saalim, from the Altamaruq. I took deep breaths as my mother dabbed my cheeks, scared of the place my mind had been drifting. Those wistful hopes of freedom, of life without constraint—that was not my life, and it never could be.

"I am sorry," I said. My mother kissed my forehead gently then pulled me into a tight embrace. Her familiar smell filled my nose. I thought of my comfort in her arms, and then, unwillingly, thought of Saalim.

"Do what needs to be done and be free," she whispered into my ear. "I love you so, so much. Remember that everything I have done, I have done for you, your sisters and brother."

Finally the guard spoke. "He waits."

We separated, and I followed the guard. But something felt different, strange. I turned back around. My mother still stood there, watching me. Her cheeks were wet. She smiled sadly and raised her hand to me. "Goodbye," she mouthed.

"Come on," the guard said. I waved to my mother, unease mixing with the liquor in my gut, and turned to follow the guard out of the room. I had to make my family proud. That night, I was determined to wed the suitor, so I let go of my desire for a life untethered to my father. Let it disperse like ashes in the wind. Wordlessly, I hung my mother's chain on my neck.

As we moved through a narrow hallway, a heavy hush fell upon me, and the fabric stilled. The air around us was static. If I had not been staring at the guard in front of me, I would have walked straight into his back. He was frozen in place, unmoving as stone.

Sons, not now.

"Sorry I was delayed," Saalim said easily. "It's not too late, though. I can still change his mind."

My gaze lingered on the guard. I didn't want to turn around, to see him. I had a purpose and I had just resolved to fulfill it. I could not let lust and a pipe dream distract me.

A wish for freedom was too complicated, too unknown. So then, what could Saalim do for me? What could come from the endurance of us? Love wasn't enough. Not when it was fettered. I had to choose the simpler decision, the fate that was sure: the back of the guard leading to the suitor in bed.

"Not tonight, Saalim."

He said nothing, and in his silence, I felt his confusion.

I turned slowly, unsteadily. "It is what I must do. I must protect my family." My words were sharp.

"We have talked about this, Emel. That is your father's delusion talking. Your family is protected without you—I protect them. You do not need to do this for them."

"Is it a delusion? What about our relationship? Isn't that too, just a dream? What is the right choice, Saalim?" My words were too sharp, my intoxication sending them spinning like swords.

"A dream? It hasn't been one for me," he said softly, stepping toward me. "The right choice is the one that feels right for you." His words were an echo of my mother's.

I pointed behind me to where the suitor waited. "This is what feels right."

Understanding crashed into him, and the jinni, who had been so confident, so sure around me, seemed to crumble into the broken, wretched slave I had seen the afternoon I released him from his vessel. I, the knife, he, a block of wood.

"Please, not tonight." He pressed his hands together. "I cannot watch you go. Not with him." He groaned. "Don't give him your body. I can give you the next suitor and the one after if that's what you want. Just not this one. Anyone but him."

I didn't listen, wasn't hearing him. The arak sloshed in my ears. Buraq pressed against my chest.

"You said you've watched me these past years. Haven't you seen it? No one chooses me, Saalim. I can't afford to say no to a single suitor."

The gap closed between us, he dropped to his knees, shoulders bent forward, his face twisted with a desperate plea. He clasped my hands, bringing one to his mouth and kissing my palm gently, the coarse hair on his face tickling my skin. He spoke quietly, his eyes staring through me, seeing something I could not see. I could feel the heat of his face, his breath against my palm.

"He is a monster, Emel. His filthy eyes upon you, foul hands on you . . ." He gripped my hands tighter, his words a whisper. "Your fingers against his skin, your lips on his. I cannot bear it. Not for you." His amber eyes simmered, but there was a heavy darkness in them, a familiar darkness. There was guilt.

Not understanding, I pulled my hands away from him. "You can't think of that," I choked. "It will drive you mad! I am an ahira, Saalim. I have a duty."

He looked like I'd slapped him.

I stared, frustrated by how he complicated things, angered at myself that in some ways, I felt more loyalty to him than to my family and had known him for a fraction of the time.

He treated me better than most, yet I could not choose him. I could not live the life I wanted with him. We could never be. My rage bubbled over. My mother was right. Saalim was a fantasy, an untruth. My life as a daughter of the Salt King was real.

"I can't choose you," I said. "Because then I will be back in that reeking tent with my sisters day after day. Will I say no to every muhami until I'm cast out and on the street like Sabra is soon to be? What if you're taken by the Altamaruq, if you are passed on to someone else? Like Aashiq, you will be gone, but I will still be here." I wildly gestured as I spilled the words I did not want to believe onto the ground between us. "You are a jinni. I am an ahira. Our lives are in the hands of my father or whoever our masters will be. There can be nothing between us. There can be no future."

We stared at each other, our chests heaving with hurt and anger and throbbing hearts.

"Go, Saalim," I said flatly, praying that the hurt of my words drowned out the desire I felt for only him. *Sons, let him feel only rejection. It will be better that way.*

He gave me one last, withering glance before his eyes dropped to the ground.

"If it pleases you." Then, he was gone.

Shivering in the suddenly cold hallway, the air moved around me again, and the sound of the palace night converged upon me. Quickly, I turned to the guard, who was pressing forward, unaware of the disturbance. I followed him to my muhami.

"HELLO, EMEL," Omar said silkily.

"My prince." I bowed, shutting my eyes tightly and fighting the swells of sorrow. "How about some wine?" I cooed, pouring us both a glass. I drank mine quickly and began to pour myself a second glass.

"Sit down," Omar said, pushing my hand away from the decanter.

I did.

"Your father tells me that you are the most beautiful daughter but in desperate need of breaking. I thought," he continued, "that this might be fun. Perhaps if we can make some progress tonight, we can try again tomorrow. And if, after the third evening I am satisfied by your obedience, perhaps—" he paused, taking a swig of his wine, "perhaps we can be wed." His freezing words slid down my spine. I fidgeted on the mattress.

"Oh, I hope that I will please you," I purred, understanding what he wanted from me. I leaned back onto my elbows. Omar smirked and walked over to stand between my legs. He leaned over me and roughly pulled the veil from my face.

"Better," he said. "Now, on your knees."

I obeyed. Omar fumbled with his waistline and pushed his pants down to reveal the part of himself that he wanted me to attend to. He thrust his hips forward toward my face.

I thanked Eiqab I was numb from the liquor, from the Buraq, and I took him between my lips.

I closed my eyes and imagined a vast empty sky that I floated through. A gentle sky where I felt nothing. I imagined this, and nothing else.

"Yes," he hissed, his voice thick with lust as he clasped my arms, tugging me to stand. His eyes were glazed and sweat glistened on his brow. I stared at his chest covered in a white tunic and thought of fluffy clouds. He grabbed my face and pulled my gaze up to his. Our eyes met, and I saw lust so much different from Saalim's.

I shook my head imperceptibly, ridding myself of thoughts of the jinni. "Take off your clothes," he commanded.

I did as he asked. He surveyed my nudity, his eyes lingering on my chest, my legs. He followed and came to me, pushing his body onto mine. "This is nice, isn't it?"

I hummed in agreement. I closed my eyes and again, thought of the sky. Were I a bird, I would soar so high, none would catch me.

He clutched the back of my head, moving me like a doll, and his mouth fell on mine. I felt nothing as I climbed through the sky.

He reached between my thighs.

I thought again of Saalim. Did he know Omar's intentions? Is that why he begged me not to come tonight?

I was a means to an end for Omar. An outlet for greedy ardor. He cared not for me, only the space between my legs.

He turned me so I faced away from him and pushed me onto the bed. My hair fell over my shoulders. The scars on my back shone like signal fires at night.

Snarling, he rolled me onto my back again. "I don't want to see that." He mounted me. Through my hazy vision, I could see his expression was crazed. As he forced himself hard between my thighs, I closed my eyes, moaning as I was trained. He squeezed my body until I bruised and shoved into me over and over and over.

I tried again to think of the sky, to think of the uncaged bird I wanted to be. But I could think of nothing but Saalim as tears fell down my cheeks.

THE TWILIGHT horn rang through the village. Minutes later, an attendant arrived.

"Emel."

Omar had requested me again.

"Good girl," my father hummed as he fondled his glass vessel, empty of tarnished gold smoke. He sat on his throne, the jinni's salt surrounding us like an audience. Two days' worth of sand was in the top of the hourglass beside him, its gentle stream filling the bottom far too slowly. He sipped his cloudy arak and sent me out the door to my suitor.

Emboldened by the bruises he had left the night before, Omar was rougher, meaner. I lay back, letting my mind travel to the worlds I had heard the jinni speak of. Places where homes were built of stone and flowers bloomed like weeds.

That night I did not think of Saalim. No, I would not violate my memories of his safe hands while tumbling with that monster in his muddy pond.

Sticky and sore, lying next to the sleeping pig, I resolved that I would not let a third night happen.

Not like that.

No.

I would have my say.

"A THIRD night, Emel? My, do you please him so!" My father's voice boomed with pleasure. He clapped his hands. I was bruised and weary and aching, but there was no liquor or smoke in my blood to dull my pain.

Only one day of sand remained at the top of the hourglass. Omar had the journey of the moon and sun left to decide if he would choose me as his bride.

My father dismissed me, and I was sent off to bed the savage. And finally, I was not helpless.

Tucked carefully away was the small vial I received from the healer. Omar sat against a pile of cushions when I entered the tent. The air was hazy from Buraq smoke as it had been the nights prior, and he was already deep in his drink. I greeted him coolly, and he laughed.

"How are you feeling, my dove?" I could hear the amusement in his voice as he called me the same name often used by my father.

I did not answer. I went to pour him another drink as I had done the nights prior.

I arced my body so that the scarf draped over my shoulder and down my back concealed my movements from him. I uncorked the vial and tentatively smelled it, scared to get it too close to my face, but it smelled of nothing.

Nervously, I tipped its entire contents into his goblet of wine. Nothing happened. I exhaled, relieved, then began to worry what the healer had given me. Had it been nothing more than water?

I turned back to Omar and smiled lazily at him as I handed him his sullied wine. I watched him fearfully as he drank, waiting for him to pause, to notice, and fly into a rage.

But he did nothing. He drank it in one swallow.

"Sit with me," he ordered and grabbed my hand, pulling me down toward him. My full goblet of wine spilled over the sides onto his pants. He huffed angrily but said nothing as I sat beside him.

He began to talk of our future, speculating that perhaps I was not the best choice for him, casually insulting me and the scars he found so unsightly. Sitting rigidly, I was unable to listen. All I could do was wait.

Not much time passed before his words began to slur. I grew tense hearing the change in his voice. I watched him closely. His eyelids grew heavy, and he began to blink more and more, slower and slower. The space between his words lengthened.

Though dazed, understanding furrowed his brow. He looked bewildered, then peered at me, wary and suspicious. He tipped his head back, eyes closed, and fell deeply asleep.

I waited through the night, silent as a scorpion, but he did not stir. At dawn, I gently pushed at his shoulder, seeing if he would rouse. He did not. When the light through the tent changed, when the sun was beginning to rise, I returned home.

Though I was exhausted and sore, depleted and hollowed, there was a lightness to my steps. In the only way I could, I had said no to a suitor, and I had won.

I had won myself a small reprieve. My duty to Omar was finished.

And of my duty to the Salt King? I realized I owed him nothing.

THE FOURTH night came. The base of the hourglass was full. Omar's time was up.

At the blaring of the twilight horn, I steadied my breathing, staring at the sand on the ground between my feet. Tavi sat beside me, holding my hand tightly. She saw my bruises, she saw my face. She knew the cost if he wanted me.

The attendant came. "No summons from the King tonight. I am sorry, Emel." She sounded so sincere.

My heart beat wildly against my ribs, exaltation pumping through me. He did not want me. There would be no wedding. Omar would not return to court for another year. He could not hurt me, or my sisters, until then. There was a flicker of fear. Though he had no proof, would he tell my father what had happened?

My sisters clucked sympathetically, thinking they understood how I felt. They only saw that I had been close to a proposal. They did not see that my soul hurt more than my body. They could not see the relief that emerged like a shadow with the sun.

I did not understand the full weight of the burden that had been sitting upon my shoulders until it had been lifted by the attendant's words.

When I was not called to the King and the looming promise of proposal was pulled away like a scab, I cried. My sisters thought it sadness. I said nothing to dissuade them. They did not need to know that it was joy, it was restoration.

True, in some ways I was sad. I was sad for the girl that I had been just two nights prior. So weak, so helpless, so confused. Because of my father and the thorny court he created. Because of men like Omar. I cried when the attendant left, because I felt grief for that girl, for me.

But I cried, too, because I was changed. Through Firoz, through Aashiq, through Saalim, I had glimpsed a part of me that I had never seen, did not know I possessed. Though I could not control all, I could and *would* control some things. I did not have to be a willing participant in my father's court.

Sorry, Mama. I do not care what you envision for my future. I don't want it.

Sorry, Father. Your thoughts of my worth don't align with mine, and I will have the final say.

Sorry, sisters. You may find the easier path the one that has the fewest turns, but that is not the path I will choose. I can't sacrifice myself for you or for anyone.

I looked at Tavi, whose soft eyes glistened in response to my tears. She gave me the smallest smile and winked at me. I knew she understood. She and I were cut from the same cloth, and she dreamed my same dreams. We clutched each other.

"I can't endure this anymore," I whispered to her.

She nodded, knowing.

And with that realization was strength. Finally, I glimpsed my own power. Now, I needed to learn how to wield it.

III

QAWI

POWER

Wahir crafted beasts of the ground and watched them pace. He crafted beasts of the sky and watched them flap their wings.

Eiqab laughed and struck the animals into the dust.

He said, Brother, you think you are powerful because you can create life, but remember, I am stronger, I can destroy it.

Wahir did not stop. He continued to make life, even when Eiqab took it.

Masira watched her sons closely, but she did not interfere, for it was a discussion to be kept between brothers.

Wahir pointed to his beasts. He said, But look at the camel that stores my water for the length of the moon, see the vulture that feeds himself on the death you cause, watch the fox that finds its meals beneath my pale light. Life is wise.

Your life may be wise, but still, it is weak, Eiqab said, sending more beasts crashing to the ground.

The beasts grew in numbers, and soon Eiqab could not kill them all. Brother, Wahir said, you are mistaken. Life is not weak, it is infinite, and when faced with trouble, life endures.

—Excerpt from the *Litab Almuq*

16

I KNEW THE HEART OF WINTER had arrived when the fires were kept burning through the night. With the season of long nights came the anticipated winter festival, the Haf Shata: a seven-day revelry surrounding the massive desert-wide market that culminated with a private party at the King's palace. The poor and the wealthy alike traveled from across the desert with their own goals in mind—whether it be to line their pockets with dha and fid, cart away rare gems and salted meat, or to see the King's famed wives and ahiran.

The village was abuzz with excitement in preparing for the festival. Shop owners bulked up their supply, cleaning their tents and shelves. Guards combed the village ensuring livestock was tethered, clothes were pulled from drying lines, and homes and shops were rendered immaculate. They ineffectively removed the beggars from the streets, as most retreated at the sight of them, only to return moments after they had passed. When the

guards weren't busy pulling the scrupulous mirage over the settlement, they were planning the ways to best protect their king. The threat of the Altamaruq lurked, and we all worried an influx of people traveling into the village would better hide the lurking rebels, would better conceal another attack.

But the threat was not enough for the Salt King to call off the Haf Shata. The festival must take place.

The palace swarmed with servants who meticulously arranged decorations, planning elaborate fare and drink, preparing every under-utilized tent for guests or to house and train new slaves recently bought from southern traders. The last time I walked by the kitchens, there were so many people shrieking at each other, I thought it to be a brawl—but no, only discussing who would use which cook fire. The clanging of the hammer at the metal-forgers went nearly through the night. The click-clicking of needles and the whoosh of fabric had been incessant from our neighbors' home as they prepared costumes. More and more pots were lined outside the potter's as he waited for the sun to dry them before he shoved them in his kiln. Looms rolled carpets out of tents like tongues as more and more were woven for the palace floors.

It could have been a heady chaos, but this year amongst the ahiran, the Haf Shata was of little concern. Instead, we focused on the twenty-third anniversary of Sabra's birth. In the days leading up to it, we tiptoed around her, fearful of stoking the anger that threatened to boil over. She had grown taciturn and hermetic, unwilling to speak to the family that would soon be forced to abandon her. It had been nearly three moons since I had spoken with her. Since we stood before my father and she threw the fledgling to the foxes. The enmity was heavy, and each day we shared in our home together was harder than the previous.

Tavi was relentless, begging each of us in turn to move beyond our bitterness. "You don't have to hate each other. You both are being absurd," she would say. I would shake my head and say, "Sabra first." I am sure my older sister did the same. I knew in a couple of years, I would suffer the same fate.

But watching Sabra sulk around the tent, I allowed myself the indulgence of feeling pleasure that my sister would suffer after being so vile. Even if that feeling left trails of guilt.

When Sabra's final morning arrived, the disquiet in our home was a knife's edge. I couldn't stand it, so I lay on my mat staring at the fading marks that still lingered on my arms and the map held open between them. It had been ten days since Omar. My bruises were sinking into my skin, now only a soft green.

I refused to think of Saalim, flinging myself toward any other thought when he crept his way into my mind. We had not spoken since that night, and I was not sure we would ever speak again. Would he come if I called? I feared he wouldn't, and I would never be able to tell him that I was wrong. He had been right all this time. I owed my father nothing if it was at the expense of myself.

Three scimitar-clad guards walked through my stirring thoughts and into the ahira tent. I sat up, the map rolling itself up with a snap. My sisters gasped at their boldness, pulling down their dresses and yanking blankets over their bare legs. Men did not enter our tent.

Unless they had orders from the King.

"We are here for Sabra," one said. Their faces were uncovered, so we all could see they were our brothers. The King had sent his family to banish his family.

It began: the muted whimpering that escalated into deep sobs as my sisters cried for their eldest. Sabra's face crumpled. She closed her eyes, chest heaving, then slowly rose. Sabra would not fight her fate; she was too proud. By the time she was standing, the hurt was buried.

I watched her closely, trying to know what was beneath her expressionless gaze. She moved slowly, first kneeling to roll her mat. Tavi rushed beside her to help. I saw our young sister's shoulders shaking from across the room.

"Leave it," the same brother said. "You will take nothing with you to the settlement center."

Tavi turned with a scowl. Sabra did not rise from her kneel. She paused, carefully controlling her words. "Not to Father or my mother?"

"No."

One of the guards handed her a thick camel-fur cloak that was not dissimilar to what they were bundled in. It was newer and thicker than the second-hand ones we possessed. It would keep her warm in the winter days, but she would still have to find fire in the night. Tavi rushed to fetch her abaya and veil. Everyone would know she was a castoff ahira.

Sabra stoically dressed, finally throwing the cloak around her shoulders. They would take her to the bazaar where she would be released from their guard. She was to have no contact with her sisters and was prohibited from returning to the palace. If she was caught in the area, she could be sent away with traders to distant villages, or, sentenced to death. It was our father's decision and depended heavily on his mood. She was no longer a part of the family and should act as such.

Sabra had never been into the village, and I thought of Raheemah walking through with me—how she clung to my arm, frightened of being separated. How despite all of her wonder, she was terrified of its enormity. My chest tightened as I wondered how scared Sabra felt facing a world of which she knew nothing. I regretted my smugness, my secret thoughts that in many ways made me no better than Sabra. I was not a fledgling. I was a bird with strong wings, and I could endure. It was Sabra who could not.

"Am I to have nothing? No money then?" Sabra spoke softly, but we could all hear the ground-splitting crack that broke through her voice. Tears welled in her eyes, but she stood tall.

"Don't worry," Tavi said, fussing with Sabra's cloak. "We will get you everything you need. We'll figure it out. Won't we?" Tavi looked at all of us. No one said anything.

"You are to have nothing, and since ahiran are forbidden from leaving the palace and consorting with commoners at the risk of their own exile—" the guard stared pointedly at Tavi, "—I would not expect to receive anything from anyone." Though his words were harsh, there was a softness underlying them. He did not want to be telling these things to his half-sister. I could see sympathy smudging away his stern guise.

There was a long pause. Sabra stared at the ground. Tavi kept fussing and fussing. Looking around for food, for a sack, for anything to give Sabra even though she knew the guards would say no.

And I don't know if it was Sabra's strained forbearance or Tavi's frantic helplessness, but I could not stay silent any longer. "Don't be cruel. You can let her take the mat, at least."

"You are out of line," the other guard snapped.

"It won't keep her alive," I said sharply. "She will still suffer, don't worry. But you won't have to live with such a leaden heart." None of the sisters, including Sabra, looked at me, embarrassed by my blunt tongue.

"You will take nothing. We will give you a few moments to say farewell." The guards left to wait for her outside.

One by one, the room fell apart anew. My sisters went to Sabra, hugging her and filling her with ridiculous promises of finding her on the streets, of sharing their food, of having their prince take her into their home, perhaps as a maid or cook, of talking to the guards to see what favors they could extract. The promises all empty like shop tents at high moon.

Tavi would not leave her side, racked with sobs as she clung to Sabra's arm.

Sabra stood still while our sisters flocked to her, touching her like worshippers of an idol. Sabra's eyes stayed trained above the tent's exit, keeping her head unmoving so that no tears fell despite their pooling on her lower lids. My sisters sobbed and clutched Sabra's robes, keening as though she were dead already, not understanding that the worst part was not her leaving but not knowing what would happen to her once she was gone.

Most had not been present when our older sister had been cast out six years ago. They had yet to know the grief, the heartache that trailed in its wake. I remembered that day well, but I had forgotten that it would hurt as much as it did watching Sabra face her ultimate fear. Her ultimate failure. Last time, it took two years to learn of the fate of my banished half-sister. She had struggled to craft together a semblance of a life, impossible without a consistent source of money. Begging had not proved profitable that fateful day. Hungry, she attempted to walk off with a loaf of bread. She was caught, and the shopkeeper beat her violently in the middle of the market. The spectators and shop owners shouted in approval. Teaching the vagrant daughter of the king to mind her manners was a lesson that all in the village wanted to witness. A King's daughter was lazy, she was entitled. They would show her as much compassion as the King showed them.

How little the villagers understood.

My half-sister did not die from that beating, no. That would have been too merciful. She found shelter in an abandoned tent at the far end of the village; how she had managed to crawl there, so broken was her body, I do not know. She lay sick for days. The filth that seeped into her open wounds found an agreeable home, and before long, she became a vomiting, febrile creature with no awareness of the life that passed around her. It was some time before her heart, weary from suffering, stopped.

Two years it took for this story to reach my ears. Two years for the family of the dead to learn of her passing. Once out of the palace tents, she'd had no one. She had been forgotten. How could any sister survive? To have had so many in such a small world and suddenly to have no one in a big place? It was the fate that terrified me, and it was the future I knew Sabra was thinking of as she stood listening to her weeping sisters' desolate words.

Had our mother come and seen her these past few days? I had not seen it. I am sure Sabra did not go to her, she was as stubborn as me. What was it like to leave home without a goodbye from your mother and father? The indignation I felt toward my father, the resolution that I owed him nothing, suddenly rekindled. Just because my father declared it did not mean we had to let Sabra go quietly.

Tavi's face was wet, and she gasped like the air would soothe her. Watching Tavi's misery was almost worse than seeing Sabra go.

I was not close with Sabra, but she was my sister, and I could not watch her face this fate, not if there was something I could do to prevent it. I could not shrink back from my father anymore. He was not my master.

I moved from my mat and pulled the sack from beneath it. I looked at it longingly, already mourning the loss of small freedoms that would come with giving it away. I would never possess this much salt again—how many more muhami would request an older ahira? I did not know if I would see Saalim again. There would be no more magical salt and certainly no more stolen salt.

Standing, I called to my sister. "Sabra," I repeated more loudly when she did not turn. I was next to her now. She pressed the sleeves of her cloak to her cheeks then looked at me with blood-shot eyes.

"This will serve you better than it does me," I said cautiously, quietly, aware of the guards that stood outside, though they chatted loudly amongst each other. I described how the salt was used and the careful way she should trade with it, my voice growing stronger with each explanation. "Villagers will take advantage of your ignorance. A pinch is all you should need for food, drink. A place to stay may cost you two or three. Don't let them ask for more." The words tumbled out of my mouth as she watched silently. "Go to my friend, Firoz. You'll find him every day in the market. He sells coconut juice, is not much older than Lateef. He is kind and will help you learn the village, where to sleep, and where it is safe." I rambled on, trying to cram as much useful knowledge about the village as I could in those few moments.

It was almost thrilling, teaching her everything my father didn't want us to know. I hoped my sisters listened. I wanted them to learn, too.

Sabra took the bag into her hands, opened it, and peered curiously inside. Her shoulders dropped and brow smoothed as she understood that such an immense quantity of salt would be invaluable to her. With it she could survive.

Suddenly, the reasons we had fallen apart were forgotten. I wanted to mend everything in that moment, to make up for lost time. If I could give her the gift of salt, I could, too, give her forgiveness.

"Sabra, I am sorry for what happened between us. I—"

"I don't want it."

"What?" I fiddled with my fustan as I looked from the salt to my sister.

"Do you think you can just give me this," she raised the bag into the air, "and everything will be okay? That I'll forgive you for everything you've done?"

I recoiled. Forgive me?

"Because I won't. You are a foolish dreamer, and you put everything you want before everyone else in your life. You're selfish, and you give me this to make yourself feel better. So, know this, Emel. I don't want your charity, and I don't need it." Sabra turned her palm over so that the sack fell to the ground, half of the white granules spilling out onto the sand.

Furious disbelief choked me, and I stepped forward, about to shout about what she was losing, what exactly she was turning away. But I caught myself. She would not hear it even if the words were screamed into her ear.

I had done what I could. I would not beg. She needed the last say because that was all she could take. So, if that made her feel better, if rejecting my gift eased her even a little, then I would let her have it. She could have that with my pity, because she was making a terrible mistake.

Sabra turned away from me, our sisters, and walked out of the tent. She said goodbye to none.

Most were silent, in disbelief that she could say no, that she had turned down that which would have changed her life, maybe even saved it. But some murmurings about my selfishness echoed through the tent. I did not look and see who sided with Sabra. I was sure I already knew those sisters, and I would not expend more of me worrying about them.

Only residual sniffling and questioning whimpers were left in Sabra's trail. My cheeks were hot, and my hands shook as I scooped the salt back into the sack and returned to my mat.

Tavi followed, pressing against me as she cried and cried. I tried to console her, to soften to her agony, comfort her like a mother would, like I knew she needed. But I was cooled iron, hard and unyielding. I was angry at my father, frustrated by Sabra.

I stared at the salt beside me, wondering what I'd do in Sabra's place. At least I would finally be done guessing, I'd know what my future held, and I'd know what I had to do to survive. And I could survive—I'm sure I could, because I knew how to wield my selfishness. That which Sabra, my sisters, claimed was my problem.

I laughed to myself, and Tavi looked up at me, bewildered. Poor Sabra forgot that pride, not selfishness, is the most dangerous thing for an ahira. Her pride would be the death of her. Of that, I was certain.

17

VISITORS CAME IN DROVES for the Haf Shata. The wealthy and well-known sent flattering letters to the Salt King when they arrived, hoping for an invitation to the culminating event of the festival: the infamous, erotic party with fountains of arak and clouds of Buraq. For those who were not invited, the revels of a festival in the prosperous settlement of the Salt King were justification enough for the trip through the desert. Firoz said the baytahira was busiest during the King's final party, so apparently no one went unattended.

The village was teeming with people out to buy wares to take home, people in search of healers, people gambling in game houses and drinking in the bazaar. An exorbitant amount of coin was exchanged.

Until the King's private party at the end, the ahiran were absent for all of the Haf Shata: we missed entirely the celebrations hosted by the wealthy when darkness fell, the swirling dances that rippled alongside the market in

the afternoon, the long hours of drink and games played by friends until sun rose the next morning. We remained in the palace and only heard of the festivities from the servants, who happily detailed their evenings to one another as they passed us by.

The Haf Shata was more exciting even than the arrival of a caravan, and with Sabra no longer present to fault me for my small escapes, I refused to miss it. No court was held during the festival, so I had no reason to linger in the palace until the midday horn. Jael and Alim still guarded my tent at sunrise, so every morning of the Haf Shata, Jael escorted me out of the palace so that I could visit Firoz.

That afternoon, Firoz and I tried to find Rafal. "He has to be here! Everyone else in the desert is," I said eagerly, pulling him through the bazaar. Most people we asked looked at us as though we were speaking another language, which I suppose was entirely possible, and shook their heads. Finally, we found a local who knew Rafal.

"You didn't hear?" the man asked gravely. "Killed."

My breath caught. "Impossible. Why would the Altamaruq kill him?"

The man looked perplexed, then laughed. "No girl, not by them." We waited. "By the Salt King."

Firoz said, "But why?"

The stranger lowered his head, his turban nearly touching Firoz's.

"For spreading lies and degrading the King. He was a fool—spoke too loudly and too confidently in the middle of the bazaar. He was bound to be caught eventually." The man crossed his arms and leaned away, smug with gossip.

"No . . ." I stepped away from them both, bile rising in my throat. My map, the whole desert. Gone.

Firoz thanked the man and dragged me away. "Emel, stop." He put his hands on my heaving shoulders when we found a quieter spot off the path. "It's okay."

"My own father . . ."

"Your father is fierce and cruel—those scars on your back are testament to that. Rafal was not stupid. He knew what he did was risky. But to him, it was worth it. He accomplished his aim."

"What do you mean?"

"Because more people know about the Dalmur now."

"The who?"

He pressed his fingers to his brow. "The Altamaruq. More people are asking questions. Perhaps we don't have to live like this—don't have to stay under the Salt King's thumb simply because he's the most powerful man in the desert. We don't have to live this life under his reign. Why can't we see the oasis? Because he says so. Why can't we build sturdy homes? Because he says so. Why can't we leave the settlement, and why is it so expensive to go with the caravans? Because he says so. Why can't we visit the palace, why can't you leave, why are you forced to defile yourself night after night? Because he says so." He spat the words.

His anger distracted me from Rafal. "Quiet." I didn't want to lose him, too.

"No. I won't be quiet about this. What Rafal said was true. I have to believe it. I've been talking to other people who are a part of the Dalmur, other believers. There is a better desert, a kinder place. We just have to find it. And if we want to find it, we have to find a jinni."

I swallowed. "What do you know about this 'better desert'? It's all make-believe, like jinn and winged-steeds and Si'la. You're throwing your hopes into a fire. I don't want to talk about this for another moment longer. Either you're coming with me to see the shops, or I'm going by myself." I stormed off, slamming my feet in the sand. Firoz followed.

Later that day, he took me to the baytahira.

"Why are we here?" I groaned, stuffed with sweets. He led me past the few men and women who called to us. I noticed Firoz had been right about it being a busy time. There were few people still inviting visitors—most of the tents were occupied.

"I want you to meet some people," Firoz said, too innocently.

We walked through the ribald quarter, further than I'd been before, until we were again amongst homes. Firoz turned into the space between two tents that opened unexpectedly—a secluded square where I could still hear the music from the baytahira. A large blanket skewered on poles protected the rowdy group sitting around a table at its center.

"Firoz! About time," one shouted. The people called to him, then turned their cheery faces to me in question.

He greeted them and held his hand out to me. "This is . . ." he hesitated.

"Isra," I said uncertainly. Firoz did not normally introduce me to other people.

They welcomed me like an old friend and scooted their dusty cushions until there was a space between them. Next to Firoz was a handsome man who grabbed two cushions for us and introduced himself as Rashid. He and Firoz seemed very close, mumbling to each other about things I could not hear. There was a handful of others whose names I forgot as quickly as they said them. They all talked more loudly than the next in an effort to be heard, slamming their cups on the table when making particularly important points. I did not understand half of what they spoke of, but all the same, I was filled with warmth at being included amongst them.

Across from me was a quiet couple. The woman leaned lazily into the man whose arm was around her shoulder. They did not say much but laughed at the others or nodded at opinions. The woman's eyes were a striking green, bright against her skin. Her eyes met mine, and I flushed. But she smiled, and it was sincere.

I did not want to stare, but I could not tear my gaze from the couple. The man dotingly pressed his lips to her veiled hair every few moments. I watched his fingers clutch her shoulder with intention, how he seemed to orient around her and she him. It was beautiful, and I ached with envy.

I imagined leaning against Saalim, yearning for that easiness, that closeness. How freeing it must be to walk hand in hand together in a village that swarmed with activity, pulling each other to and from the shops. Perhaps they even shared a home together. When I considered this, the ache grew. It would never be with Saalim and me, not in a world where he was a jinni and I an ahira. Perhaps if his magic could change the desert, his magic could change us. I had thought so much about my freedom, but what about his? The thought chilled me when I thought of how Masira might interpret freeing a jinni.

There was so much causing me to turn away from Saalim—that our relationship could not be what I dreamed, that I owed allegiance first to my father and family. But Saalim had been right, and I owed my father nothing. Just because things with Saalim were not like love stories shared around fires, it did not mean I had to turn from him. Even if it was just a moment, if we could make each other happy, wasn't it worth it?

I stared at the wooden table, splintered and bowing from age, and thought of him—of how much I wanted him beside me that moment. I regretted everything I said the night I saw Omar.

I want you back, Saalim.

". . . executed. King's orders," Firoz said. My attention was pulled back to the group.

"He knew it would happen," the man named Rashid said, and the others nodded sadly.

"This has to end," the green-eyed woman added, grasping her lover's hand. "The violence is disgusting, and the King won't stop until he is the last one standing. We know that."

A man spoke. "There are rumors there may be one who will do it."

"Do what?" I interjected, both desperate to know and terrified to hear. They all turned to me, then looked to Firoz, alarmed.

"It's fine," he said, and looked sharply at me. "You can trust her."

The man explained. "Steal back the jinni, so that we can change the desert."

We can change it? I bristled. "You think the jinni is real then?" I asked, my hands shaking.

They laughed, and my neck warmed. "Oh yes," the lover said, unwrapping his arm from the woman and leaning forward. "That, we know for sure. The King has too many impossible things, and there are a few who believe they've seen the jinni with their own eyes."

Him? My whole body quaked.

"What is this better desert like?" I asked. The people again looked at Firoz like I was daft. Like he was daft for bringing me there.

Rashid sighed. "Salt can be traded all over the desert, like it was long ago. Wealth is earned from hard work, not from magic. Rulers are benevolent, they listen to their people." He placed his hand on his chest and clutched something beneath his robes. "We're getting close, I know it. We'll get what we want soon. There are too many of us here, too many signs. We already outnumber the guards. The King can't keep the jinni from us forever." He put his elbows on his knees and rested his chin on his hands. "I can't wait to get out of here." He nudged Firoz, grinning. "North, yeah?"

Firoz beamed back and nodded. "It will be a spectacular journey. We'll leave, and we won't look back."

I leaned away, feeling more and more apart from these people, from my best friend. Won't look back? Firoz, what about me? With stunning clarity, I realized that Firoz had a larger life than the one I saw. He loomed so large in mine, I had not realized I was just a very small part of his, perhaps the least important part of it. The betrayal I felt was stoked by the embarrassment that as much as Firoz meant to me, I was not his equivalent. But beyond that, how could Firoz align himself with these rebels, these people who killed for greed and myth? After they killed Aashiq?

It felt dangerous sitting amongst them. I glanced to the tents around us and wondered who lived there, and who shouldn't be listening to these words.

"I don't understand why people think a jinni is the answer," I said, irritated by their gullibility—surely I would have been more skeptical before I met Saalim—but more so because, understanding Saalim's magic, I could not deny they were right. If anyone could change the desert, he could.

Rashid's face softened. "We know this because of the legend, of course."

My frustration dissipated. I remembered Rafal mentioning something about a legend.

"What does it say?"

Behind me a man shouted, "What are you doing back here?" I jolted, and the people at the table stiffened.

A guard I recognized strode into the clearing. I had seen him on a few occasions talking with Kadri—he was one of her brothers. Rarely around the ahiran, he would not recognize me.

"Sympathizers?" He said, narrowing his eyes at us. I looked again to the surrounding tents. Who had told the guard? Fear shook me, and I thought of what my father would do to me if I were caught amongst them. And then I thought of Firoz, and his friends—surely, they would be killed. I could not allow that.

"I'm so glad you've come!" I squeaked, getting up from the cushion. "Yes, there are sympathizers!" Firoz's friends grumbled behind me as I ran to the soldier. "I spoke with a guard about it. Bahir, I think his name was?" I thought of my half-brother whose gloat was too big for his ghutra. "He must have got the message wrong."

The guard looked perplexed. "That is not what—"

"Yes, I'm sure he did." I pointed in the direction of the baytahira, explaining I had heard rebel talk that way. "I told him if he needed to find me, I'd be here. Surely that's why you've been led here. Like I said, he got the message wrong."

"It was not Bahir who spoke to me."

"Probably sent the message through others. He seemed uninterested in what I told him. But I'm so grateful that you have taken it seriously." I bowed. "Thank you for everything you do to protect us. It is your bravery and selflessness that brings me peace." I let my voice crack the last words, feigning tears. I straightened up, dabbing under my eyes. "Shall I take you to where I heard those vile people?"

The guard leaned back, fearful of the tears. Stepping away, he shook his head and said, "I know where to go." He turned and left the clearing as quickly as he'd come.

My heart raced, and I swayed, dizzy with my defiance.

I'd stood up to a guard. I'd lied to a guard.

When I turned around, Firoz was behind me, beaming from ear to ear. "I think your acting might be better than mine." He pulled me into an enormous hug, and even though I was angry at him, I could not help it, I laughed and listened to his friends cheer for Isra.

I said, "I need to go." It was too dangerous to be seen with his friends.

"Promise you'll come find me again tomorrow."

He looked so hopeful, so pleased with me, that I could not resist. I nodded. "Of course, we still have much to see."

"DANCE WITH me!" Firoz yelled over the music a few days later, pulling me into the crowd of people, light on their feet.

The sun was high. Each morning, Firoz sold his coconut juice so quickly that I did not have to wait for him long. We were always celebrating by the midday horn.

"I don't—know this—dance," I panted as I bounced on my toes, watching the feet around me and trying to mirror their movements.

Firoz locked his arm in mine and spun me in the direction opposite the other pairs. Laughing, we made ourselves fools.

We skipped away to other parts of the bazaar, and I'd search carefully down each lane. I carried with me a small bag of salt, just in case I saw Sabra, just in case she changed her mind. But I never had the chance to ask. I never saw her in the market.

Our fortunes were read by oracles, and though none mentioned lovers of gold, I kept hoping they would.

A man changed a woman into a grasshopper with the clap of his hands. I shrieked, and Firoz nearly collapsed onto the sand cackling.

We saw a monster in a cage with no eyes to see and no tongue to speak.

"It looks like a child," I said quietly of the pale creature the handler fastidiously kept in shade.

Firoz peered at it closely, his nose scrunched. The monster hit the metal box it clutched against the cage bars, a loud clang ringing in our ears. The black-robed handler turned to us and screamed that we get away from it. We scurried from them, biting our tongues until we were out of reach, then laughed until we cried.

A man played a pipe, and a snake rose at its song.

"Unbelievable!" I exclaimed.

"It's magic," Firoz said.

I thought of Saalim as I watched the pipe player. Was he amongst us, or was he at my father's side? I felt a pang of guilt that I was having so much fun when Saalim was stuffed in the palace, shackled to his King. It wasn't fair. What if it were him I walked beside or danced with? I looked at Firoz and imagined Saalim as a man instead of a jinni, laughing and dancing and doing whatever he pleased because he was simply a human enjoying human things. If I ever saw him again, I resolved that I would ask if he could be freed. Was it possible, or was his future an eternity of servitude? Perhaps it would be my gift to him after all that he had given me.

"We're so alive, Emel," Firoz said through a wild grin.

"You're drunk." I shook my head, smiling.

"You're different." His face was close to mine as he stepped in front of me. I could smell the liquor on him.

Walking around him, I continued our stroll. "So are you. I'm sure the wine has something to do with it." We stopped and looked at jewelry from the South. Bracelets made with the same glass beads and cowries I gambled with, thick beaded necklaces the same color green as the girl's eyes. "How are your friends?"

He looked at me, confused. "Can't say. I haven't seen them since we were there together. Why?"

I stared at the sand as we walked from the shop. "You seem like you are all close."

"We're friends, but not that close. Not like I am with you." He pushed his shoulder against me.

My belly tingled with happiness. "Really?"

He laughed and again, looked baffled. "Yes really. Why?"

"I don't know," I said, still staring at the ground. "You and Rashid talked of leaving . . ."

"Emel," he stopped and held me in front of him. "If I ever leave and you haven't already gone from here on your own, I'm strapping you to my back and taking you with me. You're my best friend, and I'm not going anywhere without you."

Even if the words were just air that blew away as soon as they were spoken, they held me up like a home's wooden posts. Someone, finally, I could lean against, assured that I was not alone in this desert. Firoz, I could rely on. I wrapped my arm around his waist and walked with him. I could not speak for a while, worried that my voice would betray my overflowing emotions. "Well, we at least agree on that."

We stopped at another shop where villagers crowded. A foreign man was selling small tastes of pomegranate wine. I convinced Firoz that we must try it, and he agreed when I dumped the scoop of salt into his palm.

He drank the wine in one gulp and looked at me excitedly, "Emel, I'm in love."

"It is delicious," I said, sipping mine.

"No, Emel. I mean with someone. I am in love!" he said smiling widely.

My heart pounded. "Oh . . . you are?" I asked shakily, leaning away from him. This was not a conversation I wanted to have.

He spread his arms wide. "I am!" he yelled, then spun in a circle. When he saw my face, he laughed. "Not with you, you fool!"

And then I laughed, too. Relieved.

"But you, Emel. What has changed?"

My cheeks were sore from beaming as I thought of what was different. From the outside, everything was the same, life exactly as it was. Yet on the inside, everything was new. I was in control. "This is what feels right." Then I thought of Saalim. *Almost* right.

FINALLY, THE festival was at its close. It was the night of the King's private party and, though I was sad to see the end to the village merrymaking that had offered some relief from the worries of the Altamaruq, I hoped that finally, I might see Saalim. The ahiran walked in a crowded line through the narrow halls smelling like sugared flowers.

The party commenced when the sun began its fall from the sky. I could hear the rhythmic music bleeding through the walls as we were led through the palace. Our clothes hissed and chinked as we walked—the sounds becoming more muffled with each step we took toward the vast entertaining tents.

Though the ahiran went to every one of my father's private parties that ended the winter and summer festivals, the decadence always astonished us. We strode into the behemoth of a white tent and slowed our steps as we gazed at the room, completely transformed from when my father addressed his people those many moons ago. Deep cobalt swaths of fabric twisted above my head, reminiscent of a cold wind. Thick, newly woven rugs of similar blue hues were piled on the ground. Between the chilly twilight and the blue surrounding me, I felt I had waded into the cool, sapphire pool of the oasis.

The tent's sides were strung open to the unblemished desert, letting in the wintry wind to cool the revelers. The sky was a deep orange as sunset began, the ground set aflame from the light. Though I saw none, I knew guards were stationed outside.

The loud music from the musicians scattered throughout the room drowned out the nervous patter of my heart, and I gazed at the partygoers around me. I hoped would find a way to blend in with them that night, that I would find Saalim. Sons, were there a lot of people. Hundreds gathered in the two tents that stood side by side. Robes of vermillion, jade, cerulean, ivory, and rose blurred across my vision as the men and woman circulated through.

More slaves than I had ever seen roamed the halls holding goblets and decanters of wine, arak, and other spirits. I stepped to the center of the room toward a large banquet piled with food. My eyes roamed over the offerings: small dumplings wrapped in leaves, flaky pastries dusted with sugar and nuts, steaming piles of roasted meat, stacks of fresh flat bread.

"If you lose me tonight, you'll know where I'll be," Tavi mumbled beside me, staring at the tiered trays.

"I'll be right alongside you," I said.

"It counts if I kiss my dinner, right? I promise I'll use my tongue."

Guests murmured as we spread ourselves through the room. Soon, the rowdy crowd was hollering in delight, some already flinging coins at their favorite ahira. The Salt King, sitting atop a silver chair on a small stage, called for the attention of the crowd. Silence poured over us, and all merry faces turned toward him.

He stood slowly, leaning against his wives for support. He wore silver and navy colored robes that matched the great tent. His blue turban, studded almost entirely with diamonds, resembled a heavily starred night sky.

"My friends," he said. "Thank you for coming to my winter celebration!" The people yipped and hooted in delight. "My beautiful daughters have arrived." He gestured to us, brightly colored and scantily clad. "Now the party can begin. Praise Eiqab for his mercy this winter, and play nice with my girls!" He laughed loudly to himself and downed his drink. Guests holding goblets followed suit.

We were released into the party to mingle, flirt, and tease. It was our role that night: partygoers could caress and kiss as they desired so long as they could pay. After shoveling two pastries into my mouth, I sauntered slowly through the crowd, matching the beat of the music. Compliments were purred for my breasts, my hips, my eyes, my hair, but I barely acknowledged them. My father's game was not one I wanted to play anymore.

Before long, a middle-aged man approached. "A dha for the first kiss, my dear?" I could not refuse outright, the man might complain to a guard or Nassar. But I could resist, just a little.

"One dha only?" I raised an eyebrow. "I am worth far more."

He reached into his purse and pulled out three.

I dropped my chin, and the man handed me three golden coins. I slipped them behind the fabric covering my breasts. He grabbed my neck and pressed his mouth against mine quickly, a chaste kiss. I tasted the arak on his lips. The surrounding crowd clapped and laughed in approval, and before long, a line of people waited for their turn.

"That man looks like he may offer me more, I choose him," I'd say to a handful of people, turning from them toward a man who looked kinder.

"I like the look of that woman's purse," I'd say, nodding toward a woman who walked away from me.

When I was alone with a guest, it was harder to say no, but when a crowd wanted attention, it was easy to deflect. The more coy I played, the easier it became to say no. I tingled with pleasure at each refusal, each assertion of my choice. In previous years, I offered guests whatever they wanted so long as they paid something. It was what was expected of us. For the first time, I dictated how the night went: how much they paid, how they touched me, whether or not they were allowed to kiss me. They happily listened, because, I realized, they relished the chase. And I thrilled at being in control.

Large bowls sat upon the small stage by my father's chair, empty as he mingled with his guests. The guards allowed me to approach the stage and dump my coins. They clinked against the metal as they fell to the bottom of the bowl. Other sisters did the same. Throughout the night, the basins filled.

I turned toward the crowd, surveying the room from the stage. The sun, now sinking into the horizon, shined its dazzling light into the open tent. Everywhere its glow did not touch appeared black.

A face in my periphery caught my attention. I turned to meet the gaze. A slave holding goblets of drink stared back. We stared at each other for several moments before the slave turned away, continuing his task. His eyes did not glow, and I saw nothing to mark him as the jinni, but nonetheless, I hoped. My heart quickened as I descended the stage and followed the slave, ignoring my duties to the guests, desperate not to lose sight of him as I weaved through the dancing, laughing, groping, and drinking bodies. Where was he? I stopped in the midst of the crowd, head whipping back and forth as I stood on my toes.

"A drink for the princess?" The words, almost identical . . .

Wild-eyed, I whirled around to face the man.

"I beg your forgiveness. I did not mean to startle," he mumbled. His eyes stared down toward the clinking chains circling my waist. I took the goblet of wine and examined him quickly, tilting my head from side to side. There was nothing familiar about him. No heat, no smell, no golden cuffs around his wrists.

I sighed. What was I doing, and what could I even say to Saalim surrounded by all these people?

The crowd spun around me, the music loud in my ears, drums vibrating through my chest. I brought the wine to my lips, and I swallowed it in one drink.

"Slow down, Emel," a familiar voice said.

Cold fear crept up my spine. I turned, and there was Omar. I silently cursed having forgotten that while he was not allowed to court for a year, he was welcome at the summer and winter festivals. I had not seen him since our last night together. Had he known that anything had happened? I peered at him nervously, but all I saw was an intoxicated man.

"Prince," I nodded. "It is a pleasure to see you."

"Quite the fun we're having tonight!" His words were slurred, and relief washed through me. If he knew something was amiss, he did not let on.

He leaned toward me. "Though I do think that my time spent with you was better. This is all so . . . chaste. Don't you think?" He smirked and edged closer.

The tent suddenly felt like a net. I leaned away, trying to step back.

"Ah, Emel. You wound me," he said with mock pain. He frowned. "I know you must be broken-hearted I did not take you as a bride, but you see, I could never have taken someone like you as a wife. As a plaything perhaps . . . I cannot deny you were fun. Maybe when the private tents open later, I'll look for you. Until then," he pulled out two large golden coins, "a kiss will do."

"Actually, I was going to tend to another. You've interrupted me," I said, attempting to slip past him.

He raised a hand to me as if to strike me, but instead, grabbed my arm and pulled me to him. I squirmed under his hold as he squinted at me, as if trying to figure me out. He pressed his lips roughly against my own, then placed his mouth on my neck, his teeth pressing into my skin.

Finally, his hold loosened. I spun away, and without looking back, disappeared into the crowd.

"Just as delicious as I remember," he laughed behind me.

Night had fallen, and the King again called for attention. The volume of the party dimmed alongside the music until there was only the hissing sounds of rustling robes and hushed whispers of guests.

As though he forgot that he had just called to his guests, my father hollered at a servant.

"Come! Tonight is a night for fun to be had by all. Including you!" The King pointed at the servant then clapped his hands. A smattering of chuckles rumbled through the people.

The servant shuffled toward the King, head bowed low.

The King took two glasses of wine from the tray and offered one to the servant.

"Drink with me!"

At first, the man refused, shaking his downturned head.

"Ah, I'm wounded." He turned toward his guests. "Who would refuse a drink with the King?"

The servant reluctantly took the glass.

"There you go! Now . . ." The King clinked his to the servant's, laughing horribly, then downed his drink.

The servant hesitated, then moved to do the same. Offense shifted the King's features, and he grabbed the goblet from the servant's hand and splashed the red liquid onto the poor man's face, spilling drops of wine onto the tray and staining his white tunic. I warned myself not to look too closely. It made no difference whether I knew him or not. But as I told myself no, my eyes wandered to his wrists.

"No king drinks with a slave," the King hissed.

A glint of gold peaked out from his sleeves. Saalim. My chest tightened as the crowd laughed at the man's humiliation. I clenched my jaw, furious.

The King continued loudly. "We do not mix with the low. Eiqab has blessed us with fortune, and we will not waste it." The people yelped their approval.

Pushing the servant away from the stage with his foot, the King turned back to his guests with his arms spread wide. The man stumbled and fell to his knees, his tray and empty goblets spilling across the rugs. The guests laughed harder, clapping in wild delight at the spectacle. I turned away, seething—unable to see anything but my blinding fury. I tightly folded my arms across my chest to prevent myself from doing anything else. I wanted to go to Saalim and reveal to the crowd how weak my father was who relied on magic for power. I wanted to run to Saalim and hold him, shelter him from the fools who did not know his worth.

My father did know Saalim's worth, though, I realized. He knew exactly what he was doing and to whom. Of course he would lord his power over the only thing that was more powerful than he. The one thing that could not fight back. My nails dug into my skin.

Once the laughter died down, the King announced to his visitors that he and his harem would be spending the rest of the evening in the neighboring tent. All were welcome. The panels of fabric that had been open connecting to the two tents were promptly closed for the privacy of those who would watch the King's lechery or participate in their own. Guards quickly followed their king and his harem into the space. I did not watch them go. I had not seen my mother all night, and I did not want to see her amongst the wives soon to bed the King in some atrocious display of power. It was the only time I was grateful to be his daughter and not his son. We did not have to watch him befoul our mothers as the guards who protected them did.

Less than a quarter of the crowd followed the King. Perverse curiosity, engorged and shameless from liquor, leading them to the enclosed tent. When the panels opened as they passed through, I could already glimpse thick Buraq-rose clouds sitting heavy on the shoulders of the visitors inside. Mercifully, I saw nothing else.

For the rest of the guests, the music returned and strummed along. Drinks circulated, food was consumed, dancing began again. For those that desired, the private tents were now opened, allowing guests short, intimate encounters with the ahiran if their pockets were deep enough.

I lingered by the open wall of the tent, peering out at the night. My thoughts fixated on my father's cruel treatment of the jinni.

As the night pushed on, the crowd in the main tent thinned, some finding ahiran to join them in the private tents, others reclining on the large cushions and benches scattered about the room. I watched my sisters flirt and touch coaxingly, some sitting on the laps of men, others locked in heady embraces, coins sparkling at their breasts and hips. My eyes scanned the slaves and guards, but I did not see the one for whom I searched.

About to turn back toward the desert, wanting to glimpse the white-freckled sky once more, I saw Omar approach from amongst the crowd. I turned my back hoping he wouldn't see me.

"I thought it was you," he said, suddenly next to me.

I let out a breath and stepped away from him. "Mmm," I hummed. A guard stood just outside the tent. I had to be careful now. If the guard saw my refusal, I felt certain my father would hear of it.

Omar carefully stroked my arm, his fingers tangling in the gauzy fabric of the scarf on my shoulder. "Your father is enjoying his wives tonight," he said, staring out into the night. "You should visit, observe," he whispered. "I desire you, Emel." He moved so that he was behind me, both of our faces turned to the onyx desert. His body concealed mine completely from the company inside. His stomach against my back, his robes brushing against the soft fabric around my legs. His rapid breaths blew against my hair.

"Perhaps you could learn some things from your mothers."

I feigned a laugh. "Me? I think perhaps it is you who could learn something. Like how to please a woman since your manhood couldn't manage it on its own."

He wrapped his arm around my waist and yanked me toward him. I could feel the hardness of him pushing against me. He roughly stuffed his hand beneath the fabric covering my breast. "You whore. How dare—"

"Prince Omar," I said loudly so that the guard standing near would hear. I shoved away from him, relieved he made his reckless move. "The King's rule does not allow this behavior without first your payment for a private tent. I am not your ahira tonight."

The nearby guard heard me and shouted at Omar. "This is no courting. They are not free!"

Omar pushed away from me, mumbling to the guard about misunderstanding and dramatics and of course he was going to pay. He strode back into the party. I stepped out across the threshold and into the desert, enchanted by the darkness around me. I let myself linger in the night until I was sure Omar had lengthened the distance between us. I closed my eyes entertaining thoughts of running into the inky night, disappearing forever. But no, not yet. There were still things I had to do, frayed edges that needed mending. I had to find Saalim. Back inside, I saw Omar had not gotten far. His back was turned to me as he watched the lazy partiers. Smugly, I saw that his shoulders rose and fell with heavy breaths, surely enraged by his humiliation.

Smiling to myself, I sauntered by. "You may think you hold the winning hand, my prince," I hissed, "but the cards I have, I play well. Better luck next time." I winked, and walked away.

18

OMAR FOLLOWED ME. I hadn't considered that he would, and had the words not felt so good, I might have regretted them. I quickened my steps, but he kept my pace. Neither of us ran, not wanting to attract undue attention. Searching the guests for those that seemed unoccupied, those that might find my company desirable, I heard Omar call behind me.

"Emel," he said loudly, "you cannot say no to my coin."

So he was playing this game, too.

I pretended I did not hear, acted as though I was not running from a guest but rather searching for someone. If a guard heard Omar, they did not act on his words.

Glancing to my side, I saw that Omar was right behind me. He reached out his hand, fingers spread, and firmly grabbed my arm. Sons, now I was in trouble.

"Ahira," a man called as Omar pulled me to him. Eagerly, I turned in the direction of the voice. A handsome, young nobleman came toward us, robes of white and gold undulating around him.

"There you are!" I said brightly, tearing my arm from Omar's grasp. The nobleman faltered at my unexpected response.

"Actually," Omar said, "we were just heading to a private tent."

The man's eyes darted between Omar's hand on my arm and our faces. "That is impossible. The ahira promised me an evening in a private room. I have just spoken with Nassar. It is already arranged." The man stepped close to Omar, nearly a hand taller than him.

Omar sneered at him. "Do you know to whom you speak, salt chaser?"

The nobleman's face hardened to flint. He stared at Omar as an eagle would a rodent and squared his broad shoulders such that Omar appeared a child beside him. Though the nobleman said nothing, Omar seemed to be struck dumb.

He looked away and said, "She bores me anyway." Huffing he retreated to the party.

I dipped my head to the nobleman and offered him a tired smile. "Thank you."

"You do not have to thank me. I have come with coin."

Between Omar and the other guests I'd tended to that night, I was tired of the act. But how could I say no when I could feel Omar's eyes on my back, certainly watching to see if what the man said was true.

The man led me away from the center of the room. He held three dha out to me. "Will this do for a kiss?" He was close to me now, speaking in my ear so I could hear him over the musicians playing nearby.

"The night is not young, sir. A kiss on the lips will take quite a bit more."

"Well, perhaps just a touch then," he said and pressed the coins to my palm.

I closed my fingers around them. The nobleman reached toward the chains encircling my waist and touched them lightly, letting them drop one by one back to my navel. He touched the top of my brassiere, tracing his fingers along the whorls of the design. He paused, hesitating just for a moment, then collected himself and said, "The gold is lovely on you."

"Thank you." I closed my eyes, exhausted, but not daring to turn this man away.

While he reached into the purse at his hips, I scanned the room. Omar stood at the room's periphery, staring at us. The nobleman pulled out five dha. "Enough for a kiss?"

"That will do," I said smiling, taking the gold coins. I arched my neck, a show for Omar, and waited.

The man leaned forward and, with unexpected gentleness, brought his lips to mine. I felt his lips part just slightly, but there was no urgency, no hunger to his movements. Nothing like the other guests that evening. It was pleasantly familiar, reminding me of the morning in my prison cell those many moons ago . . .

My breath caught, a deep chasm wrenched open, chest tight from the pressure. My eager ahira facade crumbled. The man trailed his lips across my cheek to my jawline to the place just under my ear, his touch feather-light. He let his mouth linger above the bruised area on my neck left by Omar earlier in the evening. His warm breath and beard tickled my skin before he kissed me there softly, just once. He kissed me everywhere I had been kissed that night, gently, slowly. As if he had seen it all and was there to erase it, replacing it with something soft and kind—or claim it as his own. His hands held my head and shoulder attentively.

Feeling myself soften at his touch, I stepped back. "Saalim—?" I whispered, hopeful. Though my chest burned with longing, we had too much to discuss. I needed to apologize, to explain. And it couldn't be here, out in the middle of the party.

"Ah, my time is up, is it? Very well, I can pay more." Scorn fell from his lips, and I recoiled from it. I didn't understand where his contempt was coming from—was it my behavior tonight? What had I done to upset him? Then I remembered the last time we spoke. He had not forgiven me.

He held his empty hand in front of me, and, at the slightest movement of his fingers, another golden coin appeared. He deftly tucked it behind the cloth on my breast, letting his fingers linger on the skin of my chest.

Heat flooded through me, but it could not battle the cold iron that held fast the memory of our last time together. The poison I spat at him. He kissed my mouth again, carefully and tenderly, holding my head in his hands.

He presented more coins. He was intent, almost frenzied, tucking the gleaming coins wherever they fit. His fingers caressed my skin each time, heat radiating out from each touch. He bent to kiss me again.

"No," I whispered into his lips. Each moment a stinging reminder of what I was. "Please."

He spoke with his brow pressed against mine. "Why not, princess? I can pay. You cannot refuse me." Suddenly, he was angry.

"I can't . . . I want to talk to you."

Through gritted teeth, he said, "After I have had to watch every monster at this insufferable party place his paws on you, I think you can stand a bit more."

He kissed me again, but now he was fiercer in his movements. He held my face firmly between his fingers and pulled my hips roughly to his.

"In fact," he said, "how about we collect our little privacy, like we promised your dear Omar?" He grabbed my hand and pulled me to the guards who stood alongside Nassar and the basin of glinting coins.

"A private tent, please," he said to the vizier.

Nassar squinted as he looked at Saalim, his lips pursed as if about to ask a question before satisfaction eased his features. "Oh yes, Emel is quite experienced. Enjoy!" Nassar did not care that he did not know who this man was. He had money, and that is what mattered.

Saalim held his hand over the bowl and coins spilled from his palm. Once his price was paid, he turned and strode toward the private tents, taking me with him.

We stepped into a room that was not dissimilar to the tents that I often shared with muhamis: gauzy fabric hung from the ceiling above a large mattress piled with colorful pillows and thin blankets.

Once inside, he turned toward me. He had shed his disguise. His skin dark gold beneath the nobleman's robes, his face held the familiar planes, and his eyes, though shadowed by anger, flashed bright yellow, like lightning splitting the sky.

"Saalim, wait." I begged. I held my hands before me and backed away. "I need to talk to you."

"Talk about what, exactly? You said it yourself. You are an ahira, I am a jinni. We cannot be together. But you forgot one thing. I am magic." A large leather sack appeared in his hands, and he dropped it onto the bed. Coins clinked together loudly. "And I can pay for my whore."

I flinched. Hearing Saalim call me the same thing as Omar was worse than his anger, and tears filled my eyes. "This isn't you." My words came out in a gasp. "I can't watch you pay for me like they do. You're better than that." I flapped my hand toward the tent we had just left. My throat was tight, aching like a fist clenched it. "You said you wouldn't be jealous."

"Jealousy. Is that what this is?" His ferocity cleaved my sadness. "So they can grab you and touch you as their coin will allow, but I cannot do the same?" He laughed. "What was it you told me? Your duty lies with the King. Here I am, allowing you to fulfill that duty. Give yourself away for the King, Emel. Isn't that what you want? So long as he benefits?"

I watched rage distort the kind, gentle, thoughtful jinni I had known. Was he jealous? Or was he giving me exactly what he said he was, exactly what I had claimed I wanted?

"You could at least act as well around me as you do around those savages." His chest heaved with exertion, fury.

Tears rolled down my cheeks, and I shook my head over and over again. Every word he spoke was a knife sliding deep between my ribs, but I realized it was a different sort of pain. Not the pain caused by violation like Omar's, by the tedious stripping away of pride, but rather by heart break, the visceral pain that gnaws and chews until there is nothing but pulp left inside.

"Saalim, I am sorry for what I said. I am sorry for what I did. You were right about him, about everything. I was wrong." I wiped at my cheeks. "My father deserves nothing from me."

He hesitated, and it fueled my resolve.

"It doesn't have to be like this. You are not them. You are better. I know this . . ." I hesitated, looking around and trying to find the words. "I was a fool—thought I could be done with you, could move beyond what we had. But Saalim, you mean too much to me. I was wrong." Not ever in a world in which I knew he existed, where he was trapped by magic and an uncaring god, held in chains by my father, could I be done with him.

I remembered what my mother told me: *Don't be distracted by untruths. There are no such things. Give your heart to that which is real. Don't think of me, of your sisters.* Saalim was what was real, and whatever the cost to me, to my family, he was who I chose, even if it was only for now.

"You do not need to pay for me, do you understand?" I moved toward him, pleading. "Because Saalim, you already have me."

The truth of the words hit me as hard as it hit him. Did I love him? I did not know. But I knew I wanted him in a way that I had never wanted another. Not for lust, but for companionship. For an honest intimacy that I had never known before the stolen moments we had together, talking of every thought that came to my mind or embracing each other feverishly. I wanted him because with him, I smiled freely and often. His touch one that inflamed as much as it comforted.

The sharp anger of his face softened.

"You see?" I repeated gently, like I was soothing a scared animal. "You have me. I am here." I am here. I am here. I repeated the words over and over, terrified and relieved by their truth. I sat back onto the ground, mind wracked with shame, with confusion, with fear of what I was, and what I wanted. Of how I felt when men touched me.

Of how differently I felt when Saalim touched me.

Of course he was angry with me—I had rejected him and chosen my father, chosen the man who kept him enslaved. Of course he was furious. He was scared, he was helpless, and he had made a fatal error as a slave—wanting something. We both had.

He wanted someone I was not, probably someone I never could be, and he wanted a life we could not have. Hadn't I wanted the same? What would be the cost for me to be what he desired or for him to be what I desired? How could I wish away my being an ahira without saying goodbye to everything I knew, without saying goodbye to Firoz, to Saalim? Could I wish away Saalim's chains without losing him? I was ensnared in the sticky web of my father's court, and the harder I fought to free myself, the more entangled I became.

Saalim looked down at me, silent. His anger had dissipated, and in its place, I saw shame. He took several paces back from me, his features re-arranged into that of the slave. All details precisely as they were, down to the irregular blotches of red stains spreading from his shoulders to his chest.

"Stay here tonight," he said, his voice unfamiliar again. "I will keep you safe from the others."

He did not touch me again, did not tell me how he felt. He left, and I cried.

I AWOKE to silence, cocooned in unbelievable softness. What was so soft? Where was I?

As I sat up, the night returned to me in a rush. Ah, yes. The King's concluding party of the Haf Shata. Where were my sisters? Had they already returned home?

Back in the main tent, a number of people lingered, withdrawn and exhausted. Outside, the desert was still black with night, or was it morning? I had no idea how long until sunrise. I shivered in the cold room and looked around for my sisters. The musicians had their instruments tucked under their arms and were receiving payment from Nassar, who sat groggily in the King's chair. The metal basin that sat beside him had glinting coin piled high within. Servants scurried between tents, picking up goblets, bringing guests sage tea or wine, and serving trays of flatbread and pastries to those who needed it.

Men and women were draped across each other on benches and on the ground. Dried vomit stuck to the chin and chest of one, another slept beside the pile he left on the midnight carpet. So many sleeping soundly. In the other tent, where the panels were again strung open, I saw half-naked bodies huddled closely, most unmoving in sleep.

Head aching and stomach churning, I turned away.

Tavi was standing alongside the table where the food had been diminished to shallow, collapsed piles.

"How was the night?" I asked, grabbing a date pastry.

"I promise I wasn't actually here for the entire thing," she said through a mouth full of food. "Though the evening may have been more enjoyable if I had."

"Yours, too, eh?"

"At least it's over. We all need sleep." She nodded to a bench where a few younger sisters huddled together, eyes closed. Other ahiran slept alongside men and women passed out from drink.

"Any sign Father plans on leaving soon?" I asked. "Where is he, anyway?"

"With some of his wives in there. Drinking, of course." She raised her eyebrows and plunged a piece of meat into a thick yogurt sauce.

My father's belly jutted out amongst the bodies like a dune of sand. He had a goblet in one hand, the jinni's empty vessel in the other. "We'll be here a while then." I sat down on a bench and leaned my head against a wooden post, my eyelids growing heavy.

"Did you see Mama tonight?" Tavi asked as she sat beside me.

I shook my head.

"Me neither."

"That's good. Maybe she stayed home."

As we spoke, I watched the slave that hurried from task to task with wine-stained shoulders. He did not look at me.

Tavi followed my gaze. "That was cruel."

"Hmm?"

"What Father did. To that slave."

"It was." I took a deep breath. I almost told Tavi everything in that moment. I wanted her to know that though Father did not care for him, I did. That the slave was not alone, no matter how alone he felt.

But I said nothing more. I hung my head forward and closed my eyes.

I do not know how much time had passed when Tavi spoke again. "They're certainly well-rested."

My eyes shot open. I had fallen asleep. When the haze cleared from my vision, I saw that Tavi referred to two men walking swiftly through the large room.

They were foreign which was not unexpected for the party, but there was something else unusual about them. Both wore traveling robes and headscarves of muted brown and black rather than the bright formal robes and elegant turbans most men wore that night. Shining metal bounced on their chests. Large golden pendants, I realized, hung from long chains. I squinted to better make out the details as they crossed the room. It was not until they were nearly in front of me, passing swiftly, that I saw the design etched deeply into the metal—a large sun enveloped by a crescent moon.

The medallion reminded me of my mother's that lay hidden beside the bag of salt beneath my mat. After that night with Omar, I never wore it like she asked. It reminded me too much of her volatility and defiance.

"What?" I breathed, staring at the men's backs, trying to piece it together.

"What is it?" Tavi turned to me.

Like they passed some unseeing threshold, the men sprinted forward suddenly, straight for Father. They unsheathed long, gently curving swords from their belts.

"Sons," I said as I jumped to my feet. No one moved, everyone seemed as if in the clouds. "No!" I shrieked.

People heard my cry and looked in my direction, cloudy and confused, before realizing what I shouted about.

"Stop them!" Nassar said, not loudly nor quickly enough in his exhausted daze.

The King's soldiers, eyes half-closed, leaning their aching backs against tent posts, slowly lifted their heads. As though wading through quicksand, they started toward the men from the various corners of the room. But it was too late, the predators had already reached their prey.

My father, bleary-eyed and dampened from his indulgences, watched the men run toward him for a few moments too long. He attempted to stand, but his girth and the softness of the cushion made rising difficult.

I watched in horror. One of the men pulled his sword behind his head and, in a large sweeping arc, brought it down at a sharp angle toward the King's neck, poised to slice through the tunnels of life-giving blood and air.

Screams pierced through the room—one of them was mine. I squeezed closed my eyes and then slowly opened them, peering through nearly closed lids, to see the aftermath of the strike.

My mouth fell open. The blade had not touched the King's neck at all. Had my eyes not been closed, I might have seen what happened. Did my father move in the last moment? Did another guard parry the blow? Or had the blade hit an invisible, magical shield, a finger's width from his soft flesh? A guard was beside the King now, clashing his sword against one of the foreigner's.

Guests were shrieking and fleeing the room. Those who had not witnessed the attack certainly heard the panic and roused themselves from their stupor. Tavi was hysterical.

She yanked my hand. "Let's go! Come on!"

"Here," I said, pulling her along as we scurried behind the table of food where I could still watch everything. My mind was spinning as the foreign man who was not fighting the guard screamed at the other in a thick accent, his words impossible to understand. His eyes were wide with excited triumph, a look that did not match their failed attempt at murdering the King.

I was sure these men did not want my father. They wanted Saalim. They were the Altamaruq.

The man's gaze traveled around the Salt King as the King held his hands before his face like a coward. The man saw the empty glass vessel cupped in his palm and easily pried it from my father's grasp. The other still swung his sword in broad strokes, warding off the enervated soldiers that clustered around them.

When their vile fingers clutched Saalim's vessel, I could not stay hidden. I jumped from under the table. "No! Stop them!" I screamed, panic flooding me. Tavi shouted at me to stay quiet, but I did not listen. *No, no, no, I could not lose Saalim.* I began to run after them but stopped myself. What could I do?

The man with the vessel shouted to his comrade, laughing maniacally as he wrapped his hand around the lid. He just had to open it, return Saalim, then release the jinni once, and Saalim would have a new master. Saalim would be gone from me forever. The attacking man evaded the soldiers and joined his partner as they sprinted, golden sparkling on their heaving chests, toward the black desert.

Frantic, I searched for the wine-stained slave. I had to see him one last time.

"I wish for them to be stopped!" The King boomed, his voice desperate and crazed. He rose from his chair with a strength and urgency I never before saw him possess.

The slave was there, standing beside the stage, passively watching the fleeing soldiers. The fool Nassar sat upright and helpless in the silver throne behind him, fervently scanning the tent, panic-stricken.

And then the man holding the vessel began to cough. It started small, but then it escalated into desperate, gasping chokes. The man ceased his running, clutched his chest, and fell to the ground. The guards descended. In one final, desperate effort, the man flung the vessel to his companion. Then, he was pierced by the guards' scimitars.

In the midst of the chaos, the jinni stood calm and poised.

The foreigner's partner ran back toward the empty gold and glass jar that spun away on the rugs. He bent to retrieve it, but the delay was too great. The guards reached him too.

With a surge of nausea, I listened to the blades penetrating flesh over and over and over again. When the guards were satisfied, they walked away with vigor, energized by the conflict.

I looked back to Saalim. He stared, emotionless, toward the bodies, his arms straight at his sides. None would know that he was the cause of the cough, that magic had killed the men. I began to move toward him, to collect the vessel, but Saalim looked at me for the first time since we had spoken in the private tent and shook his head.

He was right, what was I thinking?

Saalim went to the still-warm heaps of men, and carefully stepping over them, bent to pick up his home.

Never before had I been so relieved for the death of a man. Not even Matin's.

Saalim bent over and saw the pendant, pausing just a moment before he stood again, vessel in hand. He looked at his glass home, and I wished I knew what he thought while holding his prison in his hands. Hating myself for how glad I was that he was still there, still my father's, I sat down and leaned against the table's leg. I slowed my breathing, letting my heart calm. Tavi cried into her knees, her whole body shaking.

With his shirt, Saalim wiped the vessel's surface. The blood stained the fabric more darkly than the wine. The King went to the jinni. They met not far from me. My hands were clenched together, fingers bloodless. Saalim fell onto one knee and bowed his head. He reached his arms forward, sleeves falling back to reveal the golden petals encircling his wrists, and handed my father his vessel. The King grabbed the jar roughly and spat at the jinni's feet.

"Too close," the King snarled. "That cannot happen again."

The King turned away from the kneeling slave and faced what few guests remained. He rearranged his features and was suddenly smiling, arms open. He laughed, an edge of hysteria in the sound.

"Men and women! Get up from your hiding places. There is no harm. This was purely a game! Simple fun—our concluding entertainment!" He clapped his hands wildly. The guests peered around, confused. Their gazes darting to the mutilated corpses on the ground. They would not understand why the men wanted the vessel, would only think it a valuable piece of treasure some beggars wanted to sell for coin. If they had seen that the blade had been prevented from slicing my father's neck by magic, they would not remember that now. Masira would be sure of it.

"The party is finished!" The King said. "Now, return to your beds and sleep the rest of the day away." He reached up and wiped his brow, and I saw that his hand shook.

The guests adopted my father's joy. They began clapping with enthusiasm, mirroring the King. Soon, everyone was laughing, back-slapping, and retelling what they just witnessed with wild pleasure, hands grotesquely shooting in the air around them in echoes of the violence.

Saalim returned to fetching empty trays and goblets. I did not see his face, but I saw the deaths, his imprisonment, weighed on him as he walked.

The remaining guests began to file out, leaning on each other while laughing and crying and smacking their lips in drunken nausea. The ahiran clustered together, waiting for our father to send us home.

A guard ran in, sweat dripping from his brow.

"My King!" he shouted as he ran past us. People paused their egress to watch.

"What is it now?" The King whined.

My eyes fell to the floor as I strained to listen.

The guard was at the stage where my father stood by Nassar. "Your Majesty." He took deep breaths, hands on his knees. "Some of your wives," he paused for breath again, "they are missing."

Missing? I reached for Tavi, who linked her arm in mine. We hadn't seen our mother that night. Though there was no reason to think it, my mind wandered to the Altamaruq. I prayed they had nothing to do with it.

But a sharp, nagging fear told me they did.

Was a magical jinni—the promise of a better desert—really worth all this? Pressing my eyes with my fingers, I nearly screamed. To cause so much hurt—so much chaos—for some silly legend.

Was I surrounded by fools? I thought of Firoz and his friends, Rafal, the burning prison, the slain guards and attendants, Matin. I remembered the shining, cold scimitar piercing Matin's heart, the muddled blue of his robes, the golden sun and crescent moon on his collar, stained with red.

Suddenly, I realized why the men's medallions were so familiar. Horror, thick and suffocating, rose in my throat.

The two images embroidered on Matin's robes were the same as those etched on the medallions belonging to the men. The engraving identical to the medallion belonging to my mother.

19

LATEEF'S CRIES WOKE US AT SUNRISE. "Emel! Tavi!" Tired from the party, I roused slowly. "Emel! Wake up! Tavi!"

The urgency in his voice peeled away the fatigue. I sat up, most of the ahiran mirroring my confused concern. Pulling my cloak over my fustan, I slipped out of our tent with Tavi at my heels. It was cold outside, and I could see my breath. I almost spoke, almost scolded him for shrieking and waking the entire section of the palace. But then I saw his face.

"No," I said, shaking my head and backing away.

Quietly he said, "We should speak in there." We looked to Alim and Jael, who shrugged.

He came into our home, expression strained. His gaze trailed along the girls scattered around the floor in the dark tent, blankets pulled over them. The filtered morning cast dark shadows under their eyes and onto the hollows of their cheeks.

"Mama?" I asked, my voice thick.

Lateef's face fell. He nodded. It was a small nod, barely any movement at all, but it cut like a sword. His eyes were wet, but he was composed. A cry tore from my chest, and I fell to the ground, Tavi clutching my shoulders. We sobbed into our hands, barely hearing Lateef's stumbling explanation to the sisters who asked.

During the party, four wives had fled. They escaped with the help of kitchen servants, easily missed in servant's robes. The women went to the village edge to meet a caravan that would be leaving with the Altamaruq, so sure that this final attempt at the Salt King's life would be successful, so sure they would finally get that which they desired.

Lateef did not speak of the jinni, perhaps he did not believe in his existence. But I knew it was what they wanted even more than they wanted my father dead.

But the men who tried to steal Saalim had failed and were killed. They would not know that the King was a step ahead of them. The jinni could never be taken while Saalim was out of his vessel. The King's wish that Saalim protect him would always prevent his death, and if they tried to take the vessel as they had, the King could easily wish for their demise. Just as he had. Matin was their one chance, but Aashiq had stopped him. The King would never let his guard down again.

I slammed my fists into the sand thinking of Aashiq. Sons, if he hadn't intervened, if he'd let Matin win, I'd be with him now, never having met Saalim. The Altamaruq would have won. Mama would still be here. All would be fine.

But there was no relief to be found with that conclusion. Fine was not good enough.

After the two men were killed, the King's guard had left the party to find if others of the Altamaruq were close by, waiting to do that which the first men had been unable to do.

None should have been assembled at the camels that time of night.

So when the guards saw people huddled around their caravans, throwing their packs onto the camel's backs, they knew something was amiss. The wives saw their approach and in their foolish panic, fled into the desert.

"Nothing signals guilt like fleeing," Lateef said, his voice trembling. "They were killed. The guards didn't know they'd slain the King's wives."

I could not concentrate on his words. The breath was pulled from my chest, and I struggled to keep it, wheezing and choking and crying and spitting.

She planned this. She had known she would leave. It must have been why she gave me the mutinous necklace. Suddenly, I was furious. I stood oblivious to Tavi still leaning on me. Had sanity fled with the summer? How could my own mother leave her children, leave her husband, her security for a wild dream? Briefly, I thought of how unhappy I would have to be to leave my family, my home. It was an unwelcome thought that smothered my fury. I wanted—needed—to be angry.

Of course, I had thought to do the same—wish for freedom. But I had chosen to stay, because I could not leave them behind. I was not so selfish. Pacing through the room, I rubbed at my cheeks, angry at my mother for what she had done. Angrier at myself that I had not been brave enough to do it myself.

"The King wants them burned."

I spun to Lateef, aghast. "His own wives?" To burn them instead of giving a sky burial was the greatest show of disrespect.

Solemn, he clasped his hands and looked at his feet. "But I will not let our mother burn, Emel. That's why I came. Today we send her to the sky at the sun's peak. South of the village."

IF THE guests of the Haf Shata party believed the King's lies about the men's deaths being an act, they beheld the truth when they learned of his missing wives. When they saw his mask fall. Word spread through the village, and panic ensued. Guests promptly packed their things and were gone by midday. The Altamaruq were wild, ruthless. None wanted to be caught in their fray.

Being out of the palace that day was like moving through a terrible dream. It was so unlike what it had been the days before and even worse than what it had been in the autumn. Shops and homes closed and people quiet behind their walls. No one walked the lanes, no children sped between homes. It was the largest threat to the king yet, so they would hide away until the rift was gone and wait for the traitorous hope—yes, surely this was the last time—to settle in.

At the southern face of the village, there were four bodies wrapped in pale cloth placed next to each other. It was a great risk performing a sky burial for the King's wives when he demanded otherwise. But Lateef was brave, just like his mother. Just like I was learning to be.

Eight guards, surely sons, clustered around the dead, unwrapping them carefully. The vultures were already circling, knowing a feast when they saw one. Deep and slow, the men—the boys—sang their plea for Masira, beseeching that She take their mothers to Her sky, take them into Her arms.

Tears were a resource I no longer possessed. Exhausted, I slid to the ground. Tavi did not want to be there, she said. Never having seen a burial before, she did not understand what I knew. That it was beautiful and elegant. That each time the vulture landed, it felt like Masira herself was there, collecting the soul for safe-keeping. The ache would dull, the sadness would be stripped away like the vultures' meat. In its place, relief and peace would come. I waited for the vultures to land. Waited, and waited. Come, birds, give us a rest from this grief.

I wished Saalim was there to sit beside me so that I could rest against him. So that I could say, let us forget. Let us forgive.

A golden eagle cried above me, joining the vultures. It circled with them, once, twice, three times. Then, as if it had spoken, it flew away, and the circling vultures fell into a glide, fluttering feathers and outstretched wings, onto the dead. Piece by piece, the brave, foolish women were carried to the mother of gods.

DAYS PASSED, and there was no word from the King. If not for Lateef, we still would not know of the passing of our mothers. My grief at my mother's loss was surpassed by my anger. We should have been told by the King himself. By our father. I felt as though my days were fueled by my fury. I seethed at his neglect, at everything.

The ahiran wallowed in their sorrow, in their fear. Those who had not lost their mothers were careful and quiet around those of us who had, and our home became a strained and volatile place. If one tear fell, it brought on a deluge of others. They expressed their pity for what we'd lost, then babbled about being next. Surely, the ahiran would be targeted by the Altamaruq. They implored we all stay within the walls of our home, but others had shaken their heads. Our father did not care enough about us for our deaths to be worthwhile to those soldiers.

Listening to their ceaseless fears was insufferable. I knew their ignorance about what the Altamaruq were really after was our father's fault, but still, I paced through the palace as much as I could, praying at the rama, watching men spin pots on the heavy stone wheel, or listening to the clanging of metal as swords were forged. But there was only so much I could take.

Saalim had not come to me, and I had not called to him no matter how much I wanted to. Where did we stand now? Did he know of my mother's rebellion, of her death? I grew anxious again thinking of my mother, of Saalim. I managed to lose so many things in such a short amount of time. Now there was only Tavi, only Firoz. I pushed the palm of my hand into my brow, closing my eyes and rocking on my hips as I sat on my mat.

I was suffocating. It was too much. I needed to leave the palace.

Tavi said nothing as I rose.

The others watched me silently, surely thinking me idiotic or cold-hearted or selfish or any number of things I did not care about. I had not seen Firoz in days, and I missed him.

It was nearly sunset, so I was not surprised when I found Firoz's shop empty, but I was disappointed. Undeterred, I went to his home. The intrusion would be highly improper, but I was desperate. I wanted to see him smile, wanted to hear someone talk about anything else. I didn't want to think about Mama. I was tired of the Altamaruq and its disruption of our lives. I was exhausted by the panic—however appropriate it might be.

His mother was outside tending a pot that sat above the fire in front. Her soft, worn face glowed in the orange light.

"Excuse me," I said, carefully lifting my voice so it sounded sweet and harmless. "I am looking for Firoz."

"Firoz, eh?" she said as she surveyed me. Little faces poked from the tent when they heard their mother speaking. "Who are you?"

"My name is Isra."

"He hasn't mentioned you," the woman said, not unfriendly, "but he tells me that if anyone were to call when he's not in, he'll be in 'his talking place.' He said his friends know where that is." She raised her eyebrows at me, as though trying to discern if I was a real friend and knew this place. Luckily, I did.

"Thank you, I will search for him there." I nodded gratefully and turned away. The children screamed goodbyes at my retreating back while Firoz's mother aggressively shushed them and told them to get back inside.

Even the baytahira seemed subdued. Though the music still floated into the sky, it was quieter, and I could not hear it until I was nearly within the quarter. I always visited this place with Firoz, and being here by myself was unsettling. It was unusual for a woman to be by herself here for any reason other than the obvious. I could not be caught.

Uneasily, I walked down the passageway, carefully scanning the people I passed in hopes of finding Firoz. Men and women called to me, desperate for coin. The shouts were sickening as I was reminded of the King's party and everything that happened in its aftermath. I passed quickly, heading toward the tents for hire. Firoz and I had used those to talk many times. Was he with a friend there? I scanned the handful that were closed.

No, this was absurd. If he was with a friend in one of the tents, I could not go and interrupt. What if he was with the woman he loved? I had never asked him about her, unsure that I wanted to know who I shared Firoz with.

I squeezed my temples with my fingers, feeling incredibly foolish. I needed to return home, but I decided to check the last place I could think of. I walked through the rest of the baytahira and turned between the familiar two tents until I was at the square with the table at its center.

A pair of men locked in a fervent kiss clutched each other on the ground, leaning against the table.

Their flagrant disregard for propriety and their enthusiastic passion was so intimate, I felt as an intruder. Yet I could not turn away. In our settlement, it was frowned upon for people to display their love so openly—though, of course, this part of the village was itself discreet. These men's maverick behavior was dangerously thrilling, and I smiled beneath my scarf.

They were lovers, I could tell, and I yearned for the same. Could Saalim feel my thoughts reaching out to him, the small flickers of my heart before I stamped them out?

The men unabashedly ground their hips against each other, their hands clasped furiously at each other's backs and thighs. Finally, they parted for breath, and one of the men looked right at me.

"Oh!" I gasped and turned, about to scurry out. But then I realized that I recognized his face. "Firo?!"

The men separated rapidly, and Firoz, hair messily trussed by his lover's hands, turned toward me, fear etched into his face.

"It's okay. Just me." I raised my hand and lowered it back down.

"Emel?" he mouthed silently, tactful for once.

I nodded, and he laughed with relief. "What are you doing here?" He turned toward the man. "Rashid, come with!"

"Rashid?" I choked, looking beyond him at the man I now recognized. "I didn't realize . . . I didn't know . . ."

"Nice to see you." Rashid nodded, brushing back his hair and readjusting his tunic.

Firoz chuckled at my bewilderment. "Rashid is the one I was telling you about . . ." *The one he's in love with,* I realized. Firoz wrapped his arm around Rashid's waist as Rashid brought his arm around Firoz's shoulder. "I met him a while ago, in the market. Rashid introduced me to the others. He's one of the Dalmur. He keeps us informed of what they're doing, what they plan, so we can be prepared."

I groaned and looked at the tents around me. Firoz spoke too loudly.

"I don't want to hear about that," I said.

"Don't worry, it's safe here," Rashid said. His voice was deep and strong. I could see how Firoz would be comforted by it, how he could listen to his words and believe each one.

"So, what's going on? Why're you here?" Firoz asked.

"I was looking for you," I said quickly, feeling foolish as I explained my convoluted and desperate path to him.

Firoz saw my face, certainly heard the ache in my voice. "What's happened? Are you okay?"

I wanted to tell him then that Rashid's people attacked my father, were the cause of my mother's death. But I bit my tongue. I watched the pair, teeth gleaming in radiant smiles, and realized how selfish it was of me to come see him, wanting to offload my pain. It was not Rashid nor Firoz's fault that my mother was dead. That the village was locking themselves away. That everyone was scared. It was not their fault that I was an ahira. I could not blame them.

Sighing, I shook my head. Firoz was ebullient with Rashid. I would not be the one to tarnish his happiness with the strain of my troubles. "Nothing, Firoz. Just wanted to say hello, tell you about the party. We will see each other sometime soon." I leaned forward to hug him goodbye, and as we embraced, I could smell the other man's spicy scent on him.

"Be careful, Firoz," I whispered in his ear. "People listen."

"I'm always careful. Come find me again soon. You know I want to hear all about it." He planted a wet kiss on my cheek before sending me off.

So Rashid was the man who held Firoz's heart. Though it was unfair of me, I could not help feeling territorial, like Firoz could belong to none else. I looked at the man again, trying to fit my new understanding of Rashid into the place of the man I thought I'd known. Rashid stood confidently, his arms crossed as he watched me and Firoz. His lips were curved in a soft smile that widened as Firoz approached him again. I hoped Rashid was kind, but more importantly, I hoped he was right about their safety.

Walking back through the baytahira, I had a vague sense of unease. That someone watched me.

I looked around, but Firoz and Rashid were back in the private square. Continuing my search, my gaze fell upon a woman sitting quietly amongst a group of moving and jeering people. This woman did not holler, did not cry out, did not stir as I met her stare. She simply sat still, looking at me. Despite the cold, her body was draped immodestly in the thin clothing of her profession, alerting the pleasure-seekers to what she did, of what she could be paid to do.

I was pinned by her stare and felt as though quicksand pulled my feet into the ground. With all of my effort, I tore my eyes from hers. Movement returned to me, and I walked away as fast as I could. I prayed she did not recognize me. Prayed she had not seen from where I'd come.

Because even in the dim light, I could see that it was Sabra.

20

S TORMING THROUGH THE SETTLEMENT, I could only think of Sabra. My own sister in the baytahira doing exactly what she had wanted to escape from. Vexation spilled from me, oozing out of my fingers and my toes, seeping into the sand and pulling me down. I walked on, my heart beating thunderously. A baby cried in a nearby home, and a tired mother cried in echo. Sons, why was there so much sadness everywhere?

What a fool I had been to want a few moments away from the palace. Away from thoughts of my father, my mother, my life as an ahira. Even when I fled the palace to be away from it all, I had walked right back into it. My father's influence was everywhere—in Sabra sitting destitute as a giver of pleasure, in Firoz having to love Rashid in secret while wishing for a better life, in families that tucked away because they didn't feel safe. He was the fabric of our settlement, and no matter how much I wanted to shred it into pieces, I was powerless to do so.

Sure, I could say no to the suitors, reject my father's rules. But to what end? I had a thin line to toe—he could not catch wind of my rebellion or I'd be finished. No matter the choices I made, even if I owned them fully, I was still bound by silk chains. Running away was no option either. Even my mother died trying. A muhami choosing a scarred ahira was impossible. So what was left for me to find my freedom? Magic?

I needed something, anything, to distract me from my life and the brutish father that controlled it. Something to shake from me the images of my mother, bloodless in the sand; the feeling of unwelcome lips and hands on my face and body; the gloom on my sister's faces when they returned from their suitors or when they learned of the death of their brother, their attendant, their mother. We were supposed to be happy, appreciative. To relish the life of an ahira. But there was no amount of untruths we could tell ourselves to feel happiness at the prospect of being pawned off like precious stones.

I wanted something that I truly loved. A life that was my own, something where I was in control. Life as my father's ahira was not endurable. My mother was gone, Raheemah wed. I had Tavi, yes, and my other sisters, of course. I loved them, but did I stay for them? Or do I do as my mother did? As my mother said—don't think of anyone but myself. Could I wish everything away? I was beginning to think I should.

And even if I was brave enough to throw my future in the unknown and ask Masira for my freedom, where was Saalim now? Would he honor my wish if I asked him to be free? I could use him, as my father did, for his magic. I could let him grant my wish only to return to his glass home, to stay for the rest of days.

My thoughts swirled in a tempest. I cried out as I grabbed fistfuls of my robes. I took steadying breaths, trying to prevent the panic from pouring out of my eyes and mouth. Time and space is what I needed. I wanted to be somewhere far from this infernal village even if just for a moment.

Stopping in an empty lane, I closed my eyes and leaned against a sturdy post. I thought of how I felt when I stood in the oasis or on those occasions when I had gazed at the horizon or when I watched a bird soar across the sky. What would happen if I walked out into the desert tonight with nothing but the moon and stars as my companions? What if I went to the perimeter of the village and just ran? I would run until I found the desert's edge. And then, I'd jump into Rafal's angry water and let it swallow me whole. If it even existed.

Sons, I wished I could just see the desert's edge for myself.

My breath slowed as my heart calmed. Keeping my eyes closed tight, I didn't want to see anything but the desert's edge, anything but freedom.

At once, everything was quiet, as if a thick scarf covered my ears. I opened my eyes.

A preternatural stillness had pulled its cloak over the village. The air was quiet, no breeze blowing through the thick fabrics hanging from wooden frames, no hum of quiet voices trying to keep their secrets. I spun around, looking for the source of the unmoving world.

Saalim leaned against a post across the lane, arms folded across his chest. He was entirely a jinni in that moment: skin iridescent under the moonlight, bare chest rising and falling with each breath, cerulean sash wrapped snugly around his hips. He was like an elegant statue, but it was his face that drew my attention. His golden eyes held the same darkness I had seen the night of the party, but now the shadows that rested beneath his brow were darker, his gaze sullen.

"You have wished, and I am here to obey," he said from across the lane, answering my unspoken question.

"Wished? For what?"

"To see the edge of the desert."

I had?

I had.

"You can take me there?" I was breathless, eyes wide. I never thought it possible.

"Of course," he nodded, "if you'd like me to, that is."

"Yes," I said, without a second thought. "Take me."

His face rose slowly, his gaze full of questioning surprise. I unwound my scarf from my face, letting it drape over my shoulders and walked to the jinni until I stood before him. Tentatively, he held his arms open. Worried that if I hesitated for even a moment, he would change his mind, I stepped into the jinni and wrapped my arms around his waist.

I felt so whole in his arms, so normal, so comfortable, that I pulled him more tightly to me. I pressed my cheek to his chest, inhaling the warm, dusty, jasmine scent of him. Not wanting to forget the feeling, the smell.

Tentatively, Saalim wrapped his arms around my shoulders. It was not intimate, it was functional, and the rejection stung. Waiting for the ground to shift beneath us, I closed my eyes. But there was no change in the air. Nothing happened. I loosened my arms. So, he had decided against it after all. Why had he come? Just to give me hope and see it taken? Embarrassed and angry, I unlatched my hands.

He took a deep breath. "I am sorry, Emel," he whispered. I heard the pain in his voice. "For everything." His arms finally tightened around me.

The torrent of emotions whirling inside me came to an abrupt stop, and as if it were the wind that had been holding me up, at its cessation, I crumpled. Tears spilled from my eyes as I cried into his chest. Tears of yearning, sadness, and relief rolled down my face, spilling onto Saalim.

He held me as though he was responsible for keeping me whole. And I wondered if, perhaps, he was.

"Oh, Saalim," I said through my tears, "so am I."

We stood for a long time, clutched to each other.

It wasn't until I quieted that I felt the world shift.

THE GROUND beneath my feet was more solid than that of sand or wood or carpets. The air was thick and almost wet, like a recent rain passed through. An unfamiliar, undulating, crashing sound echoed around me, and a heavy, cool wind whipped up and encircled me carrying a scent that I recognized immediately. One that had been so unfamiliar before.

My sandals clapped loudly on the hard ground as I stepped away from Saalim's embrace. Unsure, my arm stayed around Saalim's waist as I peered around.

There was nothing. We were in the mouth of the black sky surrounded by emptiness. Just two people in an endless night.

My eyes soon adjusted to the pale silver glow cast by the crescent moon. There was something . . . A large, stone structure, its edges a chalky white in the moonlight, materialized to my right. As I examined it, I saw it was damaged. Almost like pieces of a puzzle, segments of it lay in clumps surrounding its large, square base. Circular domes sat upon tall towers, the asymmetry suggesting that some were missing. Pairs of slender columns stretched up to jagged, broken walls and supported crumbling vaults of stone. Away from the large, broken structure, solitary columns and arches stood alongside shattered walls and cracked roofs.

I was amongst ruins. A grave of a city, just like Rafal had said.

"What . . . Where?" The words floated quietly from my lips and disappeared into the crashing sound.

"I have brought you to the edge of the desert," said Saalim. He gazed wistfully around us, his arm tight around my shoulder.

"It smells like you."

He did not seem surprised. "This was my home. Madinat Almulihi." He looked at the crumbling stone. "It is only ruins now."

I spun to Saalim, looking at him questioningly. "What happened to it?"

"An arrogant prince destroyed it." He took a breath, then continued. "When I was human, I lived amongst these streets. Can I show you?" There was a sadness to his words, but there was something else, too. He reached up and scratched his cheek, his gaze flitting down to me as he spoke, his fingers clenching on themselves. Was he nervous?

I nodded. Holding my hand tightly, he led me through the ruined streets. He described buildings with wide windows and open doors that allowed the breeze to waft through. He spoke of stone streets and sorrel horses that pulled rolling wagons over them. He talked of spongy, green velvet that spilled from the crevices between bricks and coated giant columns, of twisting vines that broke through the cracks in the ground and crawled up the walls of homes. Of ivory flowers that grew like weeds in fragrant clusters and spread their petals for the moon. We wound our way through the remains of Madinat Almulihi, and with his words, Saalim gave life to the perished city.

"If you lived here, and now it is like this . . ." I paused as I thought. "How long have you been a jinni?"

"I have lost count."

Sorrow pulled at my chest. Confined to a glass cage for so long.

He pulled me toward the large, fractured structure in front of us. The palace, he called it. Even derelict, it was more magnificent than my father's. He told me of the colors splashed through the interior, tiles against the light gray bricks, and of the water that trickled in its fountains and collected in tiled pools. He described powerful yet benevolent rulers that once lived behind its walls, and the children they had who were wild and spoiled and imperious.

We came to the end of the stone road that ran alongside the dilapidated palace. I looked up at the massive wall with small keyhole-shaped windows letting the moonlight shine through. Turning away from the palace, I looked to where Saalim had been leading me. My mouth dropped open, and I stopped in my tracks as I faced the source of the ceaseless roaring.

Saalim looked at me with a cautious, boy-like smile, feeling my insecurity through my tight hold on his hand.

"This is the sea," he said finally.

I gaped in terror at its immensity, in curiosity at its wetness. "This is the angry water?"

Sons, Rafal had been right. There really was water at the desert's edge. No myth of the desert's edge spoke of water that roiled with life and had a voice which cried out into the night. None except Rafal's tale.

Saalim laughed. "Angry? It is not angry, Emel. It is beautiful."

Watery blackness met the star-filled night and stretched before us. It surged rhythmically, its rise and fall revealed by the pale light in the sky whose reflection left a trail of silvery droplets on its surface. The waves crashed and rolled onto themselves to create a white, frothy disarray illuminated by the moon. Saalim was right. It was not raging.

It beckoned.

Saalim stepped down off of the road toward the sea, gently pulling me with him. Cautiously, excitedly, I followed. We walked down battered stone steps that led to the shore. The sand would completely cover them, were it not for the ocean wind that ripped through the steep slopes. I pulled my scarf and cloak tight around me as I moved slowly down the stairs, watching my feet carefully. Between the stone steps were small flowers that grew in clusters. They quivered in the wind.

I bent to examine them. They had thick, long petals that surrounded a large, circular center. Their stems sprouted from the sand, and thin leaves reached up as though to buttress the white bloom.

"Pretty," I said.

Saalim knelt next to me and gently tapped the petals.

"The moon-jasmine," he said. "They open only at night." He pinched the base of the stem and plucked it from the sand. He brushed the hair away from my face and tucked the flower behind my ear. As it passed my nose, I caught its scent—jasmine. My smile was a reflection of Saalim's.

Once upon the shore, Saalim gestured to more pieces of the fractured castle that had fallen from the cliff and were half-buried in the beach. Nearest was a large, onion-shaped dome nestled in the oceanside, the waves splashing against its tiled surface.

"I thought we could rest there," he said.

I was puzzled by his familiarity with the ruins. "Do you come here often?"

"I used to."

"Not anymore?"

"Not anymore. I don't need to be here like I once did. I don't miss it in the same way."

We walked along the sand, and I looked nervously between the waves that crept too close and the looming structure we moved toward. We walked to its base, and the cavernous maw opened before us. The curved walls that barricaded the wind allowed sand to pile high within. We stepped inside.

The sound of the ocean was amplified in the dome, and when we spoke, our voices echoed around us.

"What is this?" I asked.

"It's fallen from the palace—a dome from one of the towers."

He kneeled and pushed sand around to create a shallow groove. He did not look at me as he did it. He was nervous. I watched him as he worked, puzzled.

Within seconds, a large, magical fire filled the groove. Chilled by the wet, ocean air, I moved gratefully toward it. The orange glow of the flames illuminated the interior of the dome. Along the surface of the sand were black and white shells and trails of vines washed in by the sea. I stared at the fire tossing its sparks, mesmerized by the warm light. The jinni sat beside me, his warmth a further comfort. He handed me a thick, blue blanket that materialized in his hands. I wrapped it around my shoulders, continuing to stare at the fire before me, unsure of what to say.

"Emel," the jinni said after a long silence. "Your mother . . . I am sorry."

Staring at my fingers, I said, "I don't know what to think. I waver between fury, sadness, and jealousy."

"Jealousy?"

"That she could be so brave as to leave everything behind. I could never."

"I disagree. I think you are very brave."

I smiled.

"Why are you angry with her?"

"For the same reason I envy her. She left her children behind to follow in the footsteps of the Altamaruq."

"Ah, to find the hidden desert."

I turned to him. "They're so desperate to find you, Saalim. To use you to get to it."

"I've already told you they won't get me."

I thought of my father. "He uses you like you're nothing." My gut tightened, and I clenched my hands. "Does he always treat you that way?" I asked, thinking of the wine-stained tunic.

He looked down to the cuffs around his wrist, the golden veins on his hands, glinting golden in the firelight. "Rarely, but if there are guests to witness it . . ."

"He is a monster."

Saalim looked at me earnestly and scooted closer. "Emel, I am the monster. My behavior toward you that night . . ." His voice was heavy with self-reproach, and he winced, pained by the memory. "I will never forgive myself for how I've treated you."

"Stop. We both made mistakes. I treated you horribly the night I went to Omar. I said terrible things. You were angry." I took his hand. "I've forgiven you, so please, forgive yourself." Tracing the edges of the golden cuffs with my fingertips, I brought his hand to my cheek. "I know it's hard to do," I whispered, inhaling deeply the dusty jasmine and what I now could identify as the ocean scent he gave off. He smelled of Madinat Almulihi. Of his home.

Letting go of his hand, I reached tentatively for his face and trailed my fingers down his temple, his cheek, his bearded jaw. In answer, he took my hand from his face and kissed my palm. We stared at each other in the orange glow.

"There is something I need to tell you." His voice trembled.

I sat upright. "What is it?" I could not take another surprise.

"You once asked me why I stay with the King, your father. Why I don't still time and live elsewhere?"

My hands held Saalim's, waiting for him to continue.

"I gave you a reason, but it was a lie. I have so much to explain." He took a deep breath and looked to the flickering flames.

"Okay." I let go of him and clutched my hands together, thinking of what he might tell me. "Wait, Saalim."

He looked at me uneasily.

"Whatever you are going to say . . ." I squeezed my fingers together. "If it is more bad news . . . I don't think I can bear it." I bit my lip.

He nodded slowly. "I hope you can bear this." He continued. "When you were born, there was great joy in your father's court. He loved Isra more than any of his wives. I think she reminded him of his first, the wife he lost, because she was willful. Much like you.

"Isra providing him with a beautiful daughter was the greatest gift she could give him. Sabra was a quiet child, and she was not drawn to him like his other daughters, and though it is hard to believe, the King loves his daughters. When you were born, I think he placed all of his aspirations on you. I was there when he named you. Emel . . . it means ambition in the old language. It was the name he was going to give the unborn child that died with its mother, had she been a girl. You were special to him. I think you still are, which is why you anger him so. He knew you would be his most beautiful daughter, so black were your eyes, your hair, so lovely and fierce was your mother. You would be powerful." He looked at me cautiously.

A pang squeezed my throat at the mention of my mother, of Sabra.

"I watched as you grew. A headstrong child." The corners of his lips turned up as he remembered. "You flitted from room to room, running about your father's court without a care. He gave you allowances sanctioned for none other of his children. And as you grew into a woman, Emel, and began your ahira training, your beauty was unparalleled. So was your stubbornness." He smirked.

"If anyone cared to look, they could see that being an ahira dismayed you, but still, you acted tremendously." He reached for my face and touched my cheek sadly. "You flourished as his ahira, but," he pressed his hand to my chest, "it was not you. Like this flower," he moved his fingers to the flower behind my ear, "you bloomed at night. Every time you were called to court, you were like a queen, beautiful and elegant. But you were also fragile. Each day, you closed up, protecting yourself fiercely. You hoped for something more."

I was stunned that he had known me so well without knowing me at all.

"The suitors were drawn to you, like waves to the shore. You stirred in them something that they had never felt, and they were pulled toward you. Again and again."

His voice hardened. "I could feel their desire, and though I hated watching them with you, I found I could not look away. I, too, was entranced, fascinated by that which you protected so intensely. I dreaded when your father returned me to my vessel. I agonized over what I would miss. Would you be there when I came back to your world?

"I became greedy when I was around you. Every time I felt a suitor desire you as a wife, I redirected his thoughts. To your other sisters, to his home. Anywhere else." He confessed this quietly, ashamed. "Emel, you could have been wed over three dozen times by now. Men would have dug through dunes with nothing but their hands to have you."

I looked up at him, mouth agape. All of my failures because of him. I bristled at the confession, thinking of what I endured as a failed ahira. Saalim nodded, as though feeling my ire. He looked so sad, so regretful as he stared at the fire. "I am so sorry," he said.

And I felt his apology deep within me. It softened my anger, my hurt. I was at the desert's edge seeing something I thought was only legend. Was I angry? Yes. But would I have changed my past knowing this was my present? No.

"Aashiq?" I asked.

"I stopped," he said and looked up from his cuffs to me. "First, with Aashiq. He was a good man, sincere and full of love. I thought he was perhaps the only one who I would allow to take you from me. And he chose you. As you already know, I was not there the day he was to receive you, but I wonder if I could have stood and watched it. I like to think I could—that I'd be selfless enough to let you go—but I wonder if I would have diverted him in that final moment." He shook his head and looked back at his hands. "But after that, once I truly knew you, I could not meddle in your life anymore. Once I understood how you felt about the world. Once I glimpsed your ferocious independence myself."

"Omar . . ."

"Yes. No matter how much I wanted to, I would not change his mind. It had to be your choice. It was not my choice to make. I had already gone too far."

My face filled with heated shame as I thought of my obstinacy that night. What a fool I had been.

"Emel, you asked why I don't leave your father. It is not your father I cannot leave. It is you." He shifted himself so that his knees touched mine, and our eyes met. His golden irises were molten, gleaming yellow in the fire. He tentatively reached for my hands. I did not pull away. "Why still time and live a different life, if it means I must leave you behind? A frozen ahira in a court of pleasure. It is cruel, and I cannot, will not, abandon you unless you ask it of me.

"After Matin's attack, when you released me from my vessel, I knew something had changed. When I entered your world, it felt different. Whomever had released me was not your father.

"When I saw that it was you, it felt as though Masira herself had wound the threads of fate in my favor. I had been fascinated by you for years, and then you were standing before me with blood on your face and hands. I wanted to hold you then and there, make sure you were okay. I wanted to confess to you everything, to kiss your hands, your face—erase the blood, the hurt. To touch you, to embrace you. I wanted to do what I had seen the suitors do. But you were so scared, so unsure. A dove apart from its sky. I worried I would scare you away. So I did what I could to ease your fear and impress you. I wanted you to see how I could help you, for you to keep me near." He squeezed my hands in his when he said this as if he was still scared I would run.

"And when you asked me to bring Aashiq back . . . Your first wish and I couldn't fulfill it." He dragged his hand through his hair. "I hated that I was powerless to help you, but even more, I hated myself that I didn't want to bring him back. I didn't want you to love anyone else." He stopped and looked at the fire.

"It's okay," I said shakily. "Go on."

"Once you released me, I had this connection to you. Suddenly, there was something between us, and I relished it. I felt your love for your sisters, your mother, your brothers, for Firoz. Even Aashiq. You had so much to give in a world that preyed upon you insatiably. I envied all that received your attention.

"And then the afternoon of the courting with Qadir, I felt you desiring my presence. I went wild with anticipation. I wanted to give you whatever it was you needed and more. When you wished for me to prove my intentions— not for freedom, for wealth, for power—I was even more captivated. You reminded me so much of your father, only your heart was so good.

"Prove my intentions? How could you not see I was desperate to give you everything? I was so eager to help you, to be someone to make you happy. I told you that you could wish for whatever it was you wanted, and then you wished again . . . to not return home. I was ashamed. In my eagerness, I had not explained well. I had failed you, and you were manipulated by Masira." He raised his hands to his face, anguished by the memory. "You were so forgiving when I saw you in the prison. It was then, Emel, that I realized why I had been mesmerized by you for so long."

I stared at him, entranced by his tale, my anger long replaced by the careful warmth of his words.

"Emel, it was because I loved you." He paused, then said it again as though he still couldn't believe it. "I loved you. And I still do. Every day I love you more. Not as a desert ruler loves his wife. Not as a greedy man loves his sparkling diamond. I love you as a musician loves his hands, as a nomad loves his feet. I cannot describe how it is that I love you, but I can say that I would be lost without you."

Heat spread from my chest to my toes as I watched him in the firelight.

"I love you like I have loved nothing before. It is like nothing I felt as a human, like nothing I have ever felt in my lifetime as a jinni. When I realized it so many moons ago, it drove me mad. To fall in love with a woman who pleases other men, who must make them believe she loves them. It was the choice of a fool, but I did not care. At least I would be a happy fool. I did not know then how you felt about me, did not care. Did not even begin to hope that . . ." He paused before continuing.

"Every so often, I felt your mind reaching for me, small tugs throughout the day, and it gave me hope. And then, when you kissed me that morning, I was tormented with longing. I could not bear to watch the suitors touch you, to look at you. I wanted you for myself, wanted to protect you from everything, to kill them all. I wanted to crush your father with only my hands." He exhaled, frustrated. "But I am limited in my power, and in my discontent, I became a monster. Someone that I never wished for you to see.

"So, I will apologize once more and beg for your forgiveness again. I have interfered in your life in ways you have not asked. I wish I could say that I regret my actions, but it would be a lie, because I am here with you now. I only regret that I treated you abhorrently." Saalim lowered his gaze to my hands.

There was a long pause while I considered my words. My eyes wet and brimming.

But before I could speak, his voice, hoarse and deep, rumbled around me. "Though I am a jinni who fulfills desires, I am first a man. Like all, I am selfish, and I have shamelessly allowed myself to fulfill my own wish. Being with you is my greatest want. I ache with hunger, Emel. I yearn for you."

A tear slid down my cheek.

21

THE WORDS LEFT SAALIM'S LIPS and drifted into the night, mingling with the crashing of the ocean, the roaring of the fire, the pounding of my heart against my chest, the rush of blood in my ears.

Saalim had shown his hand—he was as exposed and vulnerable as I had ever seen him. I knew if I wanted to leave in that moment, he would take me home. If I never wanted to see him again, he would honor it. He was at my mercy—not because he was a jinni and I the woman who released him from his vessel but because he was a man in love and I the recipient of his devotion.

But I would not run, because at his confession, a liquid heat pooled deep in my gut, warm and smooth. It was addicting, and I wanted more.

Pulling together all of my memories, I tried to make sense of everything. I could see it now, how he behaved around me—tentatively, trying so hard

not to scare me away. I thought of how I mirrored his hesitance, thinking I would do the same. How I thought of him and longed for him—wanting him near not because of the comforts he shared but because I wanted him. When I saw him in the prison and he told me of Masira's caprice—when a wish for freedom became something that scared me more than it enchanted me—I still wanted him. Not for his magic, because I was not my father.

Though it shamed me to admit, if I were to never see him again, I would feel an aching hollowness perhaps even deeper than the loss of my mother. It would be unlike anything I had felt before. Sitting with him, I was safe and I was sure. I trusted him like I trusted none else. Even more than I trusted Firoz. He was my equal, my perfect half. I was not alone when I was with him. My dreams of seeing the desert were heightened, were made better. Because now, I wanted to see it all with him.

I wanted this life more because of Saalim. The desert was an amazing thing, but it was nothing compared to the people that were in it. Nothing, compared to Saalim. So if for now we could only be slaves, we were at least in love. It was an acceptance both terrifying and exciting, and I craved it.

Without a word, I rose to my knees. I dropped the blanket from my shoulders and let my scarf and cloak fall to the ground. I pressed my hands to his face and neck, tracing my thumbs over his jaw, fingers tangling in his hair. I brought my lips to his and kissed him softly. His hands found my waist, and the warmth of his touch made me shiver. Our mouths parted. He tasted of the desert, of the sea.

I moved to his lap, wrapping my legs around his waist. He stilled—the new intimacy giving him pause—but I did not stop. I circled my arms around his neck as he pulled me closer, and we continued to press our mouths to each other, desperate to convey the feelings that words inadequately expressed.

Saalim removed the flower from my hair, setting it atop the twisted fabric on the sand. His hands slid up my thighs slowly, questioningly. I pulled back from him and reached for the hem of my abaya. Together we removed it so I was only in my dress.

Holding me to him, Saalim reached for the blanket. With easy movements, he flung it open so it laid flat on the ground. He lay me gently atop the soft sea of sapphire, his eyes sweeping over me slowly, examining the fustan bunched up at my thighs, watching my chest heave.

"I like blue on you," he murmured as he crawled over me, placing his hands beside my head. "But perhaps not as much as I like gold." He smirked and I reached up and pulled him to me, our mouths meeting urgently.

He groaned, lying atop me. The heat of him enveloped me such that the cool ocean air became a welcome respite.

"Emel," he whispered my name between frenzied kisses. My heart fluttered every time. As he melted into me, I felt his longing, hot and unyielding and true.

Never had I felt more desired as I did in that moment. The object of someone's lust, not because I was a means to an end but because I was a half to make another whole. I trembled under the heat of his passion, of the immensity of his love, and I pushed my hips into his, desiring, for the first time in my life, to fit to another in the way only lovers could.

Saalim pulled away from me at the movement, his eyes glazed with need. He stared at me, savoring me.

I sat up, pushing him away slowly. Kneeling, I pulled the dress over my head. I had never been nude in front of a man whose opinion I cared for, and that vulnerability carried an emotion I had never felt: uncertainty. Was I enough? Would he like what he saw? I thought of the scars across my back, shame stoking the insecurity.

Saalim's breath caught as his eyes took in every peak and valley of my body, everything he had never seen but had for so long wanted to glimpse, to touch.

"Sons," he whispered before he pushed me back down onto the blanket and explored my body with his mouth. His hands following, fingers trailing down my chest, along my breasts, my waist, and down to my thighs. His fingers circled and touched and teased, exploring my body until finally, they dipped between my legs and found that there, too, they were welcome.

He touched me reverentially. An unfamiliar, pleasurable ache blossomed in the deepest part of me at his movement, his gentleness, the devotion he conveyed in his every touch. An unfeigned moan left my lips as his mouth and fingers moved over me. He drew himself above me and kissed my lips. I raised my head to meet his, reaching my arms to his neck, but he pulled his mouth away. He pressed his lips to the corner of my mouth, my cheek, my jaw, my neck.

It was like the final night of the Haf Shata, where his every kiss erased what another had done: every stroke, caress, and pass of his lips seemed to erase the cloudy, degrading memories of the nights I spent with other men. Each careful veneration by Saalim revealed to me what it was to be respected, desired, loved. The heat of the fire from Saalim's touch brought me to a precipice to which I had never journeyed. I stood upon it, overwhelmed by an exhilarating fear as I was filled with desire to fling myself off.

I writhed beneath him. His movements echoed my urgency, and at his quickened, roughened touch, I felt inundated with a freedom that provided all the push I needed. Hurling myself from the cliff face, I cried out in agonized pleasure. My body quivered, and I pulled Saalim to me with a fervor I did not understand, shuddering against him as though he was the only solid thing in my liquid surroundings.

"Saalim," I breathed and pressed my mouth to his hot neck, breathing all of him in, all that surrounded us. He held me firmly until my quivering ceased.

When I had stilled, he pulled back to look at me. I smiled at him, my chest rising and falling with rapid breaths, and reached down to his waistband. "Let's make this fair," I said and carefully began untying the blue from his hips.

He leaned onto his heels, effortlessly unwrapped the sash, and stepped out of his pants. My gaze wandered over him as he stood above me, his skin luminous over his carved body, the sharp angles of his face. He was entirely naked, the golden cuffs at his wrists the only thing embellishing him. He appeared unlike any man I had ever seen, nearly glowing in the firelight. His eyes, full of lust and affection, held mine as they devoured me.

I crawled to where he stood and pressed my hands to his thighs, feeling the muscles tense beneath my palms. He closed his eyes at my touch, and I explored him with my mouth and my fingers as he had done to me. When my fingers trailed away, teasing, he opened his eyes and looked down at me.

"Please," he exhaled.

I pulled at the backs of his knees until he kneeled before me. I reached up and pressed my mouth to his, the new intimacy of our naked bodies pressed against each other creating the delicious tension in my body again.

We fell upon the blanket, legs and arms entwined, mouths locked, hearts pounding frantically against each other's chests, and finally, when our desire to be close had crested, Saalim seated himself into me, filling an emptiness I had not realized was there. We moved together in a perfect rhythm, as though the motions we had practiced in our previous lives, in other beds, had been in preparation for each other.

I found myself at the summit again, only this time, Saalim stood beside me. We thrusted and pulled and kissed and moaned and breathed into each other intimately as only those who have caressed and explored and exalted each other will. We stood atop the peak, the ocean wind swirling wildly around us, and together, we jumped into the abyss, clinging to each other as we shuddered with fear, with ecstasy, with love.

A GENTLE light pressed itself against my eyes closed tight in sleep. It pressed and pressed until finally, I stirred. For the briefest of moments I felt nauseated, thinking myself waking in the bed of a suitor. Feeling the heat of the muhami at my back.

But then, the memories of the night rushed back, and I smiled with relief and pressed my back lovingly into the man who cradled me.

We were sleeping upon the blanket, and another that Saalim must have created in the night rested atop us. Our clothes still sat in twisted piles on the sand. The ivory flower that was laid atop my robes appeared as alive as it had the night before, though now tightly closed. Saalim felt me wake and pulled me to him; his arm wrapped around my waist, his metal cuff warm against my skin. He leaned up onto his elbow and gently kissed the hollow between my neck and shoulder across which a purple scar stretched.

"Good morning, Emel," he said, his beard tickled my ear.

"Hmm . . ." I sighed happily. "Good morning. Did you sleep?"

"No, I do not sleep," he said contentedly. "I was blissfully aware of every moment that I held you."

I smiled and turned to him, burying my face in his neck. I felt the day brightening, the gray light trickling in and illuminating the red sand. The waves still broke upon the shore over and over again.

"Is time frozen still?"

"Mmhmm." His chest rumbled against mine.

"The sea . . ."

"It speaks because I like its voice. I could never stand being where there is water without waves."

"Like the oasis and the wind through the trees," I said. "Can we just stay here forever?"

"Yes, forever." He kissed my neck and back.

I shut my eyes tightly, thinking how much I wanted it to be so, how happy I could be.

"Let's go outside," Saalim said after a while. "You have to see the ocean in the morning."

Slowly, I sat up and looked out from the dome, seeing only the steep, sandy slope we had walked down the evening before. Saalim stood, and offered his hand to me to do the same. He led me outside, and the wind blasted us both. I curled my arms into my chest, teeth chattering. "It's so cold."

He laughed, unbothered by the chill despite his nudity, and hurried back into the dome to fetch me the blanket. Wrapping it around my shoulders, we stepped around our shelter. I saw the true immensity of the ocean for the first time. The sky was a graying purple as the sun washed away the night. Birds the color of the moon and wings the color of ink soared above us, cawing out into the early morning. Beneath the lavender sky, the ocean churned a deep slate, reaching for the red, sandy shore. The waves rose and fell and crashed onto themselves, into each other. Soft green and white foam floated away from the wreckage.

I stared across the sweeping ends of the ocean where it met the sky, unbelieving that it was as large as Rafal had claimed. I watched the waves, enthralled by their rise and fall. The night prior, the ocean's voice scared me. That morning, I appreciated its song.

"Does it ever stop?" I pointed to the heaving sea.

Saalim smiled. "The waves? No. They are the heartbeat of the ocean. They are what give it life."

"Can I touch it?"

"Of course." He nodded, but quickly added, his face growing serious, "Be careful. They are powerful and can pull you in."

I walked away from him, taking small, cautious steps toward the water lapping at the sand. Pulling the blanket more tightly around me, I walked from him. Turning back to him, I saw he stood a man anew as he watched me. His shoulders were relaxed, his chest pressed forward. I wondered if he felt as I did—satisfied with his life, proud of his love, grateful for his fortune. A smile stretched wide across his face, and I replied with the same.

I turned back toward the sea, letting my toes sink into the cold, wet sand. I waited for a remnant of a wave to reach me. When the smallest trickle of ocean water pushed at my toes, I squealed. "It's cold!"

I ran excitedly back to Saalim, then repeated this several more times, getting so bold as to let the water splash up my leg and wet the blanket. I reveled in the freedom, the whimsy, and the privacy of that sacred place.

The ruined city hovered above us on the sandy hill. Its gray stone was bright in the soft light. On the crumbling columns and arches, green smudges emerged from their cracks and surfaces. Moss, Saalim had called it. The dome we slept in the night before was coated in a slimy, umber film where the water crashed against it. Black shells stuck tightly to its wet surface.

We dressed and traveled back up the battered steps to the stone street we walked the night before. Brightly colored tiles were in small piles along the ground next to castle walls. A few were still in their original place neatly around windows, arches, and doors. Small squares of oranges, yellows, blues, and greens glinted brilliantly as we passed. Green stems pushed through the gaps in the street, white petals at their ends pressed together to conceal their heart from the day.

In the light, it was apparent that Madinat Almulihi was enormous. Broken buildings led far out into the rocky desert, stone streets half-buried in the sand stretched out toward the tall cliffs opposite that of the sea.

"What happened to it, really? What did the prince do?"

Saalim sighed. "It is a sad story that perhaps one day I'll tell you in its entirety. But for now, know their rulers were lost. The city fell because of their son. A strong army came to attack it, desperate to absorb its power. Most of the people of Madinat Almulihi fled, turning back to their ancestors' nomadic way of life."

We sat at the base of a column, Saalim providing me with a feast of my favorites. I leaned against him, his arm curled around my shoulders, and picked at the pastry in my hands.

"It would be nice to live here."

"Would you really like it?" His eyes were wide, a tenor of worry in his voice.

"Yes, I would be very happy." A gust of cool wind blew, and I closed my eyes. I leaned against the column, the sun warming my skin.

He placed a kiss on my brown. "You would have loved it when it was whole." He clenched my shoulder with his hand. Contented by the ease of us, I couldn't stop smiling. As I finished my meal, he described what we would see on the street had the Madinat Almulihi been alive. He talked about the sounds, the smells, the life of the city.

He loved his home, and my chest clenched with grief for him that it was lost, that it was never to return again.

"Do you think it could be true that there is another desert, a better desert? Because maybe then we could restore your home, too." Suddenly the rebels did not seem so imprudent, not if it brought back this beautiful place.

"What would it be worth if there was? If it could?"

"If we could live here together, it would be worth everything."

"The loss of your family? Of Firoz? Of me?" Saalim smiled sadly. "If only we could tell Masira to give us exactly what we wanted. You'd have to give it much thought before you wished it. Remember we could be thrown across the desert from each other, you know, if the desert was upended."

I curled my arms around my knees and leaned further into Saalim. I said quietly, "I don't like thinking about that." Anyway, the Altamaruq were fools, and I couldn't believe I was indulging in their fantasy.

Staring at my feet, I saw that white, glistening dust was stuck to my toes.

"This doesn't look like sand," I said as I drew my finger across the tiny white crystals. I held my finger in front of my eyes, examining them closely. "It looks like—"

The jinni pulled my hand to his mouth and briefly closed his lips around my finger, sending tendrils of heat down to my elbow. I felt his tongue push against the pad of my finger before he released it from his mouth.

"It's salt," he declared, smirking and smacking his lips.

I gasped and reached down to find more of the fine powder. I tasted it, too.

"Salt?" I exclaimed in disbelief. "Like what my father has?"

"The same."

"It's just like Rafal said!"

Saalim groaned. "If I hear you mention that man's name again, I'm leaving you here by yourself."

"You wouldn't dare." I glared at him. "Rafal, Rafal, Rafal."

He stood up and stormed off, then turned back and ran to me, tackling me to the ground in the gentlest way, attacking my neck and chest with his mouth.

"Wait!" I said, sitting atop him as he lay on the stone. "Salt comes from the sand?" I narrowed my eyes.

Saalim roared with laughter, pulling me close. "No, not from the sand. From the sea. The water is so salty, you can't drink it. When it dries, it leaves a residue of salt. Besides mines, the sea is the only place it can be found. That is why it is so rare and part of the reason why Madinat Almulihi was such a wealthy city, as your favorite story teller said."

I ignored the jibe. "The tale of my father . . ."

"What?" He sat up, bemused.

"'The man who from the sand of the desert, found the salt of tears.' It's the ending of his story, but it has always seemed . . . wrong. Now I understand why. 'The man who from the sand of the desert, found the salt of the sea.'"

I stared at the sky, thinking of the tale, of the role the jinni played.

"The horrid man who from the sand of the desert found an amazing and handsome and quite perfect magical jinni who gave him the salt," said Saalim. "That sounds the best, don't you think?"

I shoved my elbow into his ribs. "And here I was being serious."

"You're too serious."

I gasped. "No, you're too serious!"

"If I am too serious, I will not tell you of Almulihi's salt trade."

Urgently rescinding my declaration, I begged him to tell me. Saalim explained the city's trade—how it was before my father's settlement was at the heart of it. That people came from all over to collect salt from the inexhaustible supply at the city's shores. He said there were salt mines, too, owned by smaller settlements not far from here where people could acquire salt. It was a kinder trek for many, the coastal climate easier on the people and the camels. When he made mention of floating ships that carried in stone and other rare goods, I was nearly vibrating with fascination. The questions tumbled out of me. Ships? Travel by water? There was no water on my map. How much was missing? After answering quite possibly one hundred questions, he closed his hand around my lips, silencing me.

"You ask so much. When can I kiss you if all we do is talk?" He declared with a wide smile before he removed his hand so that his lips could take its place.

"You are so happy today," I remarked, looking up at the joy creasing his temples and mouth.

"I am very happy. I am home with a woman I love very much." He looked down at me, his golden eyes bright.

I smiled, but it disappeared quickly as a sorrow settled upon me. Our evening, that morning, it was all so temporary, fleeting. Soon we would return to my settlement. To the unknown. To my father. We can't stay forever, Saalim had reminded me. We had to go back to real life eventually. The longer we stayed away, the harder it would be to return.

"Stop," Saalim said. "That life is there whether you think of it or not, so don't think of it. Let us enjoy this moment together. Without anything else in the way. We can always come back."

"Do we have to leave?"

"Say we stop time. What happens when you grow old, Emel? And you take your last breath? You would close your eyes only to wake up back in your settlement. For life to start all over. Only then, you'll carry with you the happiness and freedom of dozens of years back into that fettered life. It would be cruel, and no matter how selfish I want to be, no matter how much I want to give you what you want right now. I can't do that to you."

So we sat and watched the sun pull itself high into the sky, feeling the air warm around us. We watched birds settle atop the towering walls, dive into the surging sea. Saalim told me more stories he remembered from life in Madinat Almulihi. Nothing that revealed who he was within its walls or what his life was like. Always stories of other people, of someone else's home. But I was satisfied by what he told me, captivated as I was by the unbelievable world he described.

We shared tales and food and fondness as a couple: a golden jinni bound by magic, a dark-eyed ahira shackled by a king. Dreams of joy despite our impossible love.

22

THE SUN DROPPED BACK INTO the horizon, the ocean air dried, the wind ceased its motion, and the ground softened to sand once again. The night returned and tents were back in their place lining the quiet lane. I clung to Saalim, holding my eyes closed, already desperate to return to the desert's edge, to anywhere that was not where we now stood.

My stomach churned with anxiety. I did not want to return to home, to the court, to another man's bed. Every toxic thought rushed back to me as if trying to smother my happiness.

"I don't want to leave you," I whispered into his chest, tears slipping out from my closed eyes.

"I know." His voice was strained. He held me as tightly as I held him, his laughter gone with the waves.

"I want to go back. Stay there. I don't care about the consequences."

It was childish and pathetic in its desperation, but as real life trampled on my joy, I clung to the sweet memories as strongly as I could.

He frowned. "I want the same. I want to give that to you."

"Then do it."

"You know why I won't."

"If I wish it?"

"Please don't," he said, defeated.

I took a deep breath. "How will we do this?"

"I don't know," he said after a pause. "But I will find a way to see you as often as I can. I promise it." He clutched me more tightly, murmuring in my ear. "Are you ready, my love?"

I shook my head, but I reached up and kissed his mouth one final time. Then, time moved again.

Swiftly, I returned home, fighting my tears as I wound through the lanes. I mourned the loss of what had been and what I returned to, disbelieving that I had seen the desert's edge known in the village only as legend. It was as real as the jinn.

IN MY hands, I held the frame of a tapestry depicting the dunes against a backdrop of dusk as my sisters guided loose threads through its taut bands. A commotion of men's voices penetrated our tent.

"Emel!" A man cried through the din outside.

My head shot up. Oh, no. The last time a man had shouted my name outside the tent, I learned my mother had died. What would it be now?

I searched for Tavi, but she was still there, sitting at my side. At least she was safe. I would not lose another sister.

I waited.

"Emel!" he cried again. The voice was familiar. It sounded like Jael. I strained to understand the words being said but so many men were speaking at once. I shoved the frame off of my lap and went to the entrance. A handful of guards were huddled together, loudly talking over each other.

Behind them, the little girl watched with wide eyes. She saw me and waved excitedly. I gave her a small smile then turned to the men.

"What is it?" I yelled over them.

"Emel—thank Eiqab!" he cried. It was Jael.

Another guard whipped his head around and shouted, "Get back inside! You are forbidden from leaving!" I did not recognize him. With the unusual cadence of his voice, I knew he must be a soldier from a distant settlement.

I scoffed and tilted up my chin. "You overstep. I am a king's daughter and can go where I please in the palace." My air of superiority diminishing his own, I approached Jael, his expression alarmed.

"What is it?" I asked.

"They've just come from the village to tell me," he panted nodding to the two young guards who stood still shouting with the foreign soldier. "It's Firoz. He's in trouble."

I did not wait to hear more. I rushed inside and rapidly dressed. Flying back outside, I shoved my entire bag of salt into the angry soldier's chest, a currency I now knew was as abundant as the sea. "To thank you for your silence," I said pointedly to the power-hungry man. "Split it amongst yourselves." I turned to the young guards. "Thank you for coming to tell Jael."

Running down the lane, I was stopped by a horribly familiar face. Nassar. He stood to the side of the passage with another man who looked toward me with white eyes and a tattooed face. The healer? From Nassar's baffled expression, it was clear he saw what I had just given the guards. Both men looked at me intensely—did the healer see? Could he see? Nassar's gaze shifted back to where the guards were still hollering at each other, now excitedly, as they ran their fingers through the salt. I held my breath, waiting for the vizier to shriek at me, to grab me and take me straight to my father.

Nassar's expression changed from confusion to anger to understanding and back again. He stepped toward me. "Where are you going?" His voice was hard, but it was not threatening. Almost like he was trying to distract me. Like I had caught him doing something he shouldn't, just as he had with me.

The healer murmured into his ear. Nassar turned to the healer, looked at me one more time, then backed away and disappeared into a billowing tent. The healer regarded me with his unseeing eyes before turning and following Nassar.

My heart pounded in my chest. I couldn't understand what the two were doing together or why Nassar hadn't taken me straight to my father. What had the healer just told the vizier? Was my father sick, or Nassar? Would he tell him of Raheemah's secret? Of mine?

I shook my head. Too much time had been lost already, I could not spare another moment worrying about my father or his vizier. If it was the last thing I did, I would find Firoz. I would not lose anyone else. I sprinted through the palace lanes.

"Wait!" Jael shouted at me from behind. "Emel, hold on!"

I stopped abruptly and turned to wait. He caught up quickly, sweat dripping down his chest, ghutra askew. "You can't just run out of the palace! You don't even know where to go!" Struggling to catch his breath, he managed an explanation at last. "He has been sentenced."

"Sentenced! For what? Where is he?"

"For being a part of the uprising, for colluding with the Altamaruq," he said, then leaned in and placed a hand on my shoulder. "Soon he'll be at the grounds."

My hands flew to my mouth as his words settled over me: the execution grounds. He had behaved so recklessly—they all had. I warned him, and he hadn't listened. I wanted to scream.

Jael seized my wrist, and we hurried to the servant's passage. He barked at the other guards stationed at the palace entrance—we were on an important errand for the King. Finally, he let me go. "What will you do?"

"I'm going to find him, Jael. I have to see him . . . have to do something."

"See him if you must, it's why I came. But what do you think you're going to do?" he cried. "There is nothing that can be done. The vizier has given his verdict. It is an unpardonable crime."

"I can't let him hang, I just can't." *Not after everything that has happened. I can't lose him, too.*

He looked uncertain. "Go then. But please, be safe."

I turned from Jael, not knowing what it was I would do.

"Emel." Something in Jael's voice startled me, and I looked back. "I don't know what you can do or how," he said, "but if there is any hope, it lies with you. You're the bravest and—" he chuckled mirthlessly—"luckiest person I know."

I clasped his forearm and squeezed it lightly. "Thank you, brother." Then I ran, uncaring that my bright fustan flickered beneath my abaya, uncaring of anything except Firoz.

Coughing from exertion, sweat spilling down my brow, I found myself at the arena. I had been there once before, but I had been a child, when the wives had more allowances. It was so much smaller than I remembered. There was an oval patch of sand with a ramshackle wooden fence lining its perimeter. A smattering of people had gathered around its edges. I did not remember much from the execution I had seen, but I remembered the electric energy, the loud, crazed voices, the jeering and booing and hissing. The people that afternoon chatted too calmly, too idly for any execution to be occurring soon. The arena was empty other than a single structure—a wooden platform that stood a hand's height above the ground. From its surface rose the gallows, a lone rope hung from the crosspiece.

Maybe the guards had been mistaken?

I dashed back toward the village center, hoping for a mistake. I wove through the villagers and tent-lined streets, through the quiet marketplace, anxious at the sight of Firoz's shop standing empty despite the early hour. I went to his home, but it was closed. Fearing to disturb his family, if Jael had been correct, I continued on to the baytahira in hopes of finding him there. If not Firoz, someone who knew of his whereabouts, or his sentence.

In the confined byway of the baytahira tents, I looked from face to face, desperate to see one I knew. They had few visitors this early in the day, so they all called to me. They were not the people I wanted.

I spun around seeing no one I recognized. I spun and spun and spun, looking for anyone to help. Sons, where was he?

"Girl, there are plenty of dance partners here. You just have to pay," a voice slurred. The cluster of men and women seated along the fringe of the byway tittered.

I knew that voice.

"Sabra?" I turned slowly toward the approaching figure. In not even the full cycle of the moon, the woman who was once my sister had been transformed into a sickly creature. She had always been thin, but now she was even thinner. Her hair was filthy and clumped, her eyes were bloodshot, arms bruised, and her clothes—not the clothes she had left with—were torn and soiled.

"Emel?" she sang loudly, artificial sweetness coating my name. "Sister?" Sabra shouted it, drawing the attention of those who had not already turned in our direction.

Ignoring her jeers, I ran up to her. "Have you seen Firoz?" I began rattling off a description of him—the color and length of his hair, the way he wore his trousers, how he tied his turban. I babbled on until I realized that Sabra was laughing.

"Have you seen him?" I nearly screamed it.

"That boy who desires other boys? Who sells drink in the market like a child? Who talks to all who will listen of a better life if only we'd get the jinni from the King?" she pressed a finger to her chin as though lost in thought. "Oh, yes. I have seen him. Many times. I even once saw him with you." She said the words sloppily, leaning in toward me as she spoke them, pushing her finger into my chest. Even through my scarf I could tell her breath was sour, body unwashed. "Though you paid me no attention that day. Did you even see me?" She asked to the sky, eyes searching the clouds maniacally.

"I thought," she continued, her words garbled with drug or drink, "I should tell my beloved sister more about this boy. She seemed so surprised when she saw him with another man talking as one of the rebels who tried to kill Father."

My breath caught. Had she been in one of those tents when Rashid and Firoz talked to me of the Altamaruq? Had she followed me?

Yet Sabra made no mention of these things. "Maybe she did not know him as well as she thought. She thought him to be such a good friend—or was he a lover? Was he the reason she was always leaving us? To get her fix from a village boy? I thought she must want to know more. But," she pouted, "I couldn't find you, so I went to the palace and told a guard who promised he would tell the vizier. That way, he could share it with you." Sabra batted her eyes innocently.

I looked her up and down, horrified. "You risked your life going to the palace, just to punish me?"

"Punish you? Emel, no! I wanted to help you know more about your friend, eh?" She waved her hand. "I never thought it would have resulted in all of this!" Pretending astonishment, she flung her hands wildly in the air. "Now, poor Firo is in trouble."

"Don't you dare call him that," I spat, stepping toward my sister, malice rolling off of me in waves.

Sabra laughed again. "What would you rather me call him? An abomination? A cow? A rebel? Oh, or a *believer*? Well, don't worry." She stepped back, beginning to walk away from me. "Soon he'll be trussed up like the animal he is. Feet hung over head, throat sliced from end to end."

A foreign rage poured itself through me, blurring my vision. In that moment, I was nothing but a channel for wrath. All I saw, all I could think of, was every foul thing my sister had done. Every wrong to me or my sisters, every vile word, every odious look.

"Is your hatred of me worth this, Sabra? Worth the scars on your back? Worth risking your life to hew down my friend? Firoz is a good person, kind and generous." My father's court had transformed Sabra into a monster, but the blame did not lie solely there. Sabra had made her choices as all of the ahiran did. I did not care if her face was less pretty, her hips narrower, her legs thin. Mama would have welcomed more of her companionship and conversation, if she had been willing to give it. I would have welcomed that over her jealousy and hurtful barbs. Even the suitors who came to us, for all that we teased one another about their lust, did not always leave with the prettiest girl, or the girl who was most pleasing in bed. Sabra might have won freedom, even love and respect, if she were not always so fixated on what she did not have. There was no excuse, no justification for her wickedness. She had made the decision to be cruel, and I would never forgive Sabra for it. I shoved my sister hard, and she fell gracelessly to the sand.

She was powerless. Frail body and broken soul sitting in sharp angles upon the ground.

"You think my life is worth living?" she screamed, eyes dark with fury and shame. "Do you think I am happy? Have I ever been happy? What do I care if I die? I hope I do!"

Voice shaking, I said, "I hope Masira grants that for you. You deserve everything you have."

THE FEW people I passed on the way back to the arena appeared undisturbed, unaware that anything significant was happening. I wanted to latch onto that as proof that there was no execution at all. But reality tugged. Only the most depraved found joy in viewing the death of another.

Turning another corner, I faced the grounds once again. Dread, heavy and coarse, swept over me when I saw more people had arrived. Voices loud and dissonant rang through the clearing. Covered faces were turned toward each other, wide sleeves swaying with the vigor of the spectators' gestures. I had not seen so many people together since the Haf Shata party, another's tragedy luring people from their terror with promise that the source of their fear would be killed.

As I looked toward the center of the arena, sharp, bitter tears stung my eyes. *No, no, no.*

Firoz stood with several guards. The guards' faces were covered, but Firoz's was left for all to see, an exhibit for the spectators who waited impatiently for the main event.

He stood with his hands secured by rope before him, feet bound as mine had been when I was lashed. He looked as Sabra had—his clothes were worn and filthy, sweat staining the chest and underarms of his brown shirt, hair tangled with grease and grime. His face, crumpled and broken, was bent toward the sand like a wilted flower. I could see the streaks of dirt traced onto his cheeks where his tears had dried.

I ran to the fence and leaned forward, desperate for Firoz's attention. I wanted him to see me, to know that I had not abandoned him.

My tears spilled onto my cheeks. He did not look up at me.

"Firo," I whispered his name, needing to say it aloud, but knowing that none could hear. If I was seen as a sympathizer, I might also be seized and sentenced to death. His family was nowhere to be seen, likely venting their grief in the safety of their home, clinging to each other in sorrow. I peered around for Rashid, the man I had seen with Firoz, sure he had come. There were several companionless people scattered around the edge, faces covered with thick scarves. I did not know Rashid's eyes well enough to recognize him.

But I saw one I did recognize—a small woman with green eyes. She stood alone, her hand clutching something under her robes, something that sat against her heart. I noticed another man, not far away, doing the same thing. And then I realized that there were at least a dozen of them. Standing quietly, some faces wet, others expressionless, all clutching whatever was at their hearts.

The Altamaruq, the Dalmur. There for their friend. They had not left him alone. I hoped Firoz knew they were there.

There was no warning. No hollered announcement, no bell chiming, no solemn cry. There was no procession for Firoz's execution. In the eyes of the monster King, he was an animal and would be treated as such. The guards suddenly pushed him onto the stage. Had I not been staring fixedly at my best friend, I would have missed its beginning. Soon, the crowd caught on, and they screamed taunts at the man who was to die.

Their voices roared in my ears, masking the whimpers that passed my lips. Firoz stepped onto the wooden platform and seated himself before the rope.

I silently urged him to fight them, not to let them win. But he did not. He did not struggle, did not resist the hands in service of the King as they held his bound feet and tied them securely to the swinging rope. As the guards tugged and pulled and looped the coarse material, Firoz took one, slow look over his shoulder. I followed his gaze to a man clad in black; crimson covering his face like a vulture. His eyes were rimmed red, cheeks wet as they disappeared behind the scarf. He tapped his heart once and nodded to Firoz. His shoulders shook as he cried.

The men stared at each other as if their fragile, beating hearts were carefully cupped in the palms of their hands. Here it is, it belongs to you. As if the ground was still so they could stand on its sand together. A pair in the desiccated desert, awash with love.

Firoz pulled his hands to his chest and tapped it once, then he broke Rashid's stare and turned back to the ropes twisted at his feet, shattering their last moment and everything that had been between them. He was a man drowned in his grief, his heart drifting away behind him.

I sobbed. No! It could not end like this. Sabra could not do this to them, to me. She could not win.

I wish, I wish, I wish . . . I screamed the words in my mind, praying not to my gods, but to Saalim.

The guards pulled the rope slowly, Firoz's feet lifting off the wooden stage.

Saalim, please. I wish, I wish, I wish . . .

Firoz leaned back, eyes toward the wide, blue sky. White clouds glided by lazily.

Save him, Saalim. I wish for you to save him. Please.

I closed my eyes, concentrating hard, before opening them again and seeing Firoz's hips rise from the ground. I choked on my sobs.

Save him, save him. Please, save him. I did not think of my words, I only thought of how I could not lose Firoz—full of hope and so deserving of a better life, and of how Sabra could not have the final say when she was so angry and undesiring of this life. I thought of me and that I could not lose my best friend, too.

I wish for Firoz to be saved.

"I am here."

I exhaled, almost weak with relief. No, it was stronger than relief. The feeling one has when awoken from a nightmare that felt so real, so tormenting, that only death would have served as resolution. At Saalim's quiet words, whatever it was, I felt it. The jinni was beside me, his arm brushing against my shoulder, appearing as any other spectator would, but I knew it was him. It was his voice, his warmth, his scent, his comfort.

Firoz's torso lifted from the platform now, his face turning purple. The guard, standing alongside the man who slowly heaved the rope, carefully pulled a knife from his belt. He twisted it before him, the rusted silver glinting in the sun, reflecting the bright, hot light onto the spectators as it twirled.

Suddenly, a golden medallion slipped out from beneath Firoz's tunic. It swung beneath his head like a pendulum. I knew what it was. I had its twin buried beneath my mat. I looked at the Dalmur that watched their friend. Is that what they all clutched? They held their faith so close to their heart.

I could not be angry at them. Not anymore. At least in their urgent need, they loved one another. They loved their friend as much as I loved him. The Dalmur fought and killed and died for their people, their friends. Would I take the risks they took for my family? I knew my father and the people with whom he had surrounded us—the people who assented to my depraved life, who encouraged it regardless of how it made me feel—would not do the same for me.

"Saalim, I wish for Firoz to be saved," I whispered, despairing, not taking my eyes from my best friend, from the gold that caught the reflection of the sun. "Please."

"Masira will give you what you wish."

I blinked, and when I opened my eyes, a woman was in Firoz's place.

Her body rose above the stage.

Then, I realized who it was.

Sabra. I turned to Saalim, who appeared as horrified as I. Looking for the Dalmur, I saw there were none where they had stood only moments before.

My sister rose until she was suspended entirely from the crosspiece. Swaying slightly in the wind, the knife-wielding guard rested a hand against her hip, stilling her, before he bent his knees. He clasped his hand to Sabra's opposite shoulder, bracing himself, and he reached the knife across her neck, readying for the final act.

"No." It was all I could say, and I repeated it over and over. Why was she being killed? What had I done?

"Let's leave," Saalim said, pulling my arm.

"No!" I said, loosening myself from him, staring at my sister, at the glinting silver knife. My body shook, tears spilling from my eyes anew. "No, no, no."

"You don't need to see this." His voice was firm, rough, and he stood in front of me just as the guard pressed the blade to her neck. He turned me around. I could not fight him. I would not have seen even if I wanted to. My vision was blurred with bewildered sorrow.

As Saalim guided me from the arena, I heard one woman say to her companion, "It's what the whore deserves for going back to the palace. A begging tramp, worthless to the King."

I paid no heed to where Saalim took me, but we were soon in an empty tent, everything quiet around us.

"What did I do?" I cried, falling to the ground and pulling my knees to my chest. "I've killed my sister. I've killed my sister." I rocked back and forth, choking on guilt.

Saalim kneeled in front of me, pushing the scarf from my head and face. "You've done no such thing."

"I thought about Sabra. I was thinking about her when I wished for Firoz. I was so angry at her. But . . ." I sucked in a breath, "I didn't want her to die. I didn't want to kill her."

Saalim was quiet. Did he know it was my fault? "Masira does what she will. You can't control it, and you can't blame yourself for it."

I thought of my last sight of Sabra, hoisted into the sky, imagining if it were my own life being taken. I had thought a wish would be my way out of the palace, but if this was Masira's answer, how could I ever risk it? How desperate would I have to be to make a wish that might result in my own death? "I don't want this life," I cried. "I don't want any of this." I looked at Saalim whose eyes glistened. "I killed my sister. I killed her." I cried into my knee, clutching the sand in my fists.

Saalim wrapped his fingers around my wrists.

"Shhh," he said, so gently it sounded like the fall of ocean waves. He pulled me to him, tucking me against his chest. "Shh," he said again and again. I listened to his whisper, I listened to his heart.

I shook, my teeth chattering, and Saalim held me closer. "I want you to know something."

I said nothing.

"Are you listening to me?"

"Yes."

"Sabra has gotten what she wanted. Do you see that?"

Pulling my face away from his chest, I stared at him like he was as crazed as the healer.

"When all she had to face was suffering, death was her escape."

"She didn't want to die." But I knew he was right.

I felt the lie on my tongue.

"Even I could feel her desire."

I thought of what she had said to me when I saw her last. *Do you think I am happy? Have I ever been happy? What do I care if I die? I hope I do!*

"Masira showed her mercy. She was not left to perish on the streets as the other cast-out ahiran. She hurts no longer."

"Strung up like an animal?" I whimpered. "That is suffering. Before all these people who hated her, said cruel things—"

"She was not conscious on the gallows. She felt nothing, Emel. It was like she was asleep and then, without feeling a thing, she was gone." Saalim pulled me tightly to him. "Masira will take her. I will make sure of that, if it means I become a vulture myself and fly her to the goddess."

He was so earnest, so weighed down with grief of his own, that I believed him. Through my slowing tears, I said, "I am no better than my father. I am a monster." And that thought scared me the most. Half of me was my father, and I could never rid myself of that truth.

He kissed my hair and held me, for days, moons, years. Then finally, he said, "It is because you cry that I know you are not."

IV

TADUHAN

—•—

SACRIFICED

Zahar,

I know it has been some time since I last wrote, and for that I am sorry. The desert has taught me much, and I don't plan to return home soon. If ever.

Finally, I have come to understand what you mean of sacrifice. Only, I realize it is much more than giving something you need. You must be willing to risk all that you have for Masira to hear.

Masira heard me, Zahar, and though I did not understand it at first, I understand now. Because I have given everything, she has given me the same.

Edala

—Found parchment detailing discussions of the *Litab Almuq*

23

EATH AND SECRECY AND LIES lurked behind every corner poisoning everyone I loved. I was submerged in the misery it left behind. My mother, my brothers, now my sister. I mourned them all, and I grieved for myself; the life that I was trapped within, that I wanted to be desperately free of.

If it weren't for Saalim.

And it was only Saalim who could quell my grief, help me to forget the life that plagued me.

Tavi was inconsolable at the death of Sabra. At first, I held back from telling her, unlikely as it was that she would learn of Sabra's death otherwise. She might never have had to hear the appalling news that her sister was slain because she had returned to the palace. I hoped not to burden her with that knowledge, that she might live more peacefully than I. But if word got back to us that she was dead, I knew she'd never forgive me for keeping it from her.

"Dead?" She cried. I could see it in her eyes. She felt the same as I—that this was too much, she could not bear another moment. "How? Why?"

I told her what I knew, feeling dishonest and dirty as I left out my role.

"And you hated her!" Tavi said, suddenly angry. "You hated her, and she died with that hatred."

My mouth opened and closed again, surprise leaving me speechless. She was right that there were times I let the bitterness fester between us, and I wondered if perhaps I might do better to temper that malice in the future. But now was not the time to discuss this with Tavi. She needed to be angry at someone since she couldn't be angry at the one person whose fault this was. After all, we were supposed to be grateful for the Salt King.

"Do you at least feel some guilt? Our sister is dead when we haven't even finished mourning Mama yet you still go out prancing around the village like nothing is wrong."

Those were Sabra's words coming through Tavi's lips, and though it stung to hear them, I knew she did not believe what she said. Reminding myself she was grieving—she was angry at this life, at her gods—I did not respond. She could fling her nasty comments. They could not make me feel any worse than I already felt.

"I'm sad, too," I whispered. She did not look at me.

After I had returned home from the execution, I'd discovered a new sack containing as much salt as I had given away earlier that day. My mind went to Nassar and what he might do now that he had seen me with an enormous quantity of salt. I worried about his plan and his motivation for delaying my punishment.

Days passed and no word came from the vizier. Tavi rarely spoke to me, no matter how hard I tried. I refused to give up on her, to let her wrath turn me away as I had let Sabra's. Tavi was the one sister I had left, and I could not abandon her. Like Sabra said, she needed me.

But neither could I sit in our home, letting myself grow miserable at the confinement, for Tavi's sake. So when no suitors requested court, I left. My salt was never depleted; the jinni saw to that. The guards never asked the source of my income, none wanting the payments to cease. They relied on my bribes.

On the rare occasions when the King demanded the ahiran be accounted for, the guards whose pockets I lined were usually the first to volunteer. My number was included, even if I was roaming the streets of the village.

FIROZ WAS in his shop. I had not seen him since he dangled by his feet from the gallows, and it took all of my strength not to hold him as if he was someone I'd lost and then found again.

He was sitting upright, his eyes darting around the lane at everyone that passed. He had tied his ghutra so that his face was covered. When I approached, he barely eased. Nodding to me, he shifted so that I could sit beside him. In silence, we watched the people pass. There were so few, and they all appeared as anxious.

"What's going on?" I asked, after he had said nothing.

He tugged on his sleeves, pulling them down over his wrists.

"Things aren't right around here. I keep getting the sense that I'm being watched or someone is coming for me."

I shivered. "Why?" He couldn't possibly know what had happened.

"I don't know. It started a few days ago. I was with Rashid, and I was overwhelmed with this feeling that things weren't right. Guards came, and they stared at me for the longest time. I got the feeling they knew me, but then they took some woman instead. Rashid feels the same—a sense of unease, of grief—and he doesn't understand why. Started at the same time. Whatever this is, it feels bigger than the Dalmur."

As Saalim had said, Masira was not perfect with her magic. Firoz remembered, Rashid remembered. Well, perhaps *remember* is the wrong word. They sensed what had happened. The magic left its muddy trail through their minds.

"That woman was my sister," I said.

Firoz turned to me, my confession shaking away some of his uncertainty. I told him what happened, leaving out his part of the tale.

"Emel, I'm sorry." He slammed his fist into the ground. "Sons, I wish I'd left on a caravan when I had the chance. You know I almost asked you for salt? I was this close." He held up his fingers. "But I didn't want you to think I was using you. I could have left here. I wouldn't be around any of this. But now they're not even letting caravans in."

"What do you mean?"

"Nassar is still meeting the runners at the oasis, but on the King's order, he is sending them away with only enough water to take the caravan to the next oasis. There is no trading."

"Because of the Altamaruq?"

Firoz glared at me.

"The Dalmur," I corrected. I didn't want to fight with him, too.

"Yes. It's ridiculous. They're already here. *We're* already here, and we're not stopping. What is the King's plan? People will die without salt. The entire desert depends on what he has. We've nothing to lose now, if they won't let caravans in. We have to find that jinni." He turned to me then. "Have you seen anything unusual in the palace? Something that could suggest where the King keeps a jinni hidden? Anything could help us, Emel."

I turned from him, conflicting thoughts rattling through my mind. Who was I helping by sheltering Saalim? "No, of course not."

He was as trapped as I was, as Saalim was, forbidden to navigate life as he wanted, neither to speak nor to love as he pleased.

Could I wish for my freedom, regardless of the consequences to the rest of the desert? What about Saalim? If wishing for my freedom separated us, I could never wish for his. But would I sacrifice myself and the desert for his freedom? Those choices, that reality, I was not yet ready to face. But the necessity gnawed at my heels.

"There's a rumor a palace woman may help us."

He looked at me thoughtfully.

I laughed, a little too loudly, a little too maniacally. "Well, it isn't me. Maybe one of his wives since they're much closer to the King . . ."

A woman and her small son approached Firoz to purchase a drink in exchange for a few nab, a low price but it was all people were offering.

"What am I going to do with Tavi?" I asked Firoz after they left. He stared at the copper coins in his hand as I told him of her grief and rejection of me since Sabra's death, how furious she was with me.

"What do you need when you're angry or frustrated or feeling trapped?"

"To escape."

"Then do that for her."

IT TOOK much coaxing but Tavi came. The promise of a distraction, relief from palace life, was too alluring to forego.

"It will be safe," I said to her. "I promise you nothing will happen to us." When Saalim had given me an extra servant's abaya and veil, he'd sworn he would make sure of it.

Her soul was tired. I saw it in her eyes when I asked if she wanted to come with me to see the village, to see the desert. It was the bravery of our mother, of Lateef, of even Sabra, that finally brought her to agree.

We walked through the village, and I showed her the places I frequented with Firoz, confessed to her why I left the palace. I needed to see that life had joy and that people were strong, capable of enduring their troubles. Being in the village gave me hope.

I told her things I'd told none of my sisters—that I hated being an ahira, and that it was okay to hate it. It was okay to detest our father. I told her how I dreamed to leave our village one day. Of how our mother had told me it's what she wanted for us most. Tavi did not speak much, but I know she listened.

Finally, we went to the village's edge. Tavi peered across the sand for a long time before she stepped out, fearlessly taking one step, then two, then three away from the settlement. "Not too far," I called, warning her of the guards that would be wary of a villager who strayed out on their own. Soon, she was out so far, I was sure she could not see the tents behind her. The draw of freedom perhaps grabbed hold of her too. The meeting of sky and sand looked to be a mouth about to devour her whole, and I wanted to run out and snatch her from it. But she needed this. I'd let her have her peace.

"She is someone else in her grief, a husk of who she was," I whispered to Saalim, guilt clawing my insides. I had called to him as my sister and I walked, sensing I needed his help. So when Tavi walked out into the desert, he was there beside me.

"She yearns for a life different from the one she has," Saalim said, his fingers gently resting on my neck.

I nodded, leaning into him. "I told her of my own dreams." We were silent for some time. Then, "I've a wish."

He looked down at me, surprised. "You said you would not wish again."

"If I've the power to do something to make things better for Tavi, I have to try." I stood on my toes and whispered it into his ear.

He smiled and brought his hand to my face, his thumb caressing my cheek. "Your finest wish yet."

Dark clouds emerged from the horizon's throat, slow at first, then picking up speed. They spilled across the sky, low and thick and black as night, until they swallowed the sun.

Cold wind whipped my robes. A white flash of light cracked through the clouds. The sound of the splitting sky shook the earth.

Then, Masira tipped her goblet, and the rain fell.

The drops were generous, and they came fast. I heard the whoops and hollers of villagers behind me as they ran from their seclusion with vessels to collect the rain, children who shrieked rapturously as they were soaked to their bones.

Tavi gazed upward and stretched her arms out beside her, palms up as if to collect the drops. Her shoulders shook, with joy, with sorrow. I did not know.

There is life ahead, Tavi. Here is life for you now. Cling to that hope, my sister. Don't let go.

The desert received its nourishment, and so did Tavi.

NEARLY A moon's cycle passed, and there was nothing from the Dalmur. Nothing from Nassar. What were they all waiting for? I could not pretend to know, but I waited with them, straddling the wall of incision as the days slid by.

The twenty-second anniversary of my birth came and went. Saalim surprised me with a small square tile, the swirling blue hues of which matched perfectly the ocean that crashed against the desert's edge. It was from the palace in Madinat Almulihi he said. I kept it buried under my bed, wrapped within a small piece of cloth with the moon-jasmine that remained impossibly alive. It was alongside my mother's dangerous necklace, Rafal's map, and my bag of salt.

Some days, after I snuck into the village to see Firoz, I would seek out Saalim too. I called to him silently, beseeching him to wash away my grief. Every moment with him was a beautiful reminder of why I stayed in that savage world, why I was scared to leave.

"Mmmm, Emel," Saalim cooed into my ear one evening as the sun dipped below the sand.

"Saalim," I whispered back, kissing him earnestly. I could hear the sounds of the marketplace, the lively voices of shop goers who had abandoned their fears with the silence of the Dalmur. When there was no rush, when we could afford it, Saalim let time press forward. "So you do not have to relive these moments without me in them," he had said.

The tent we were within was one that Saalim often created—food piled in one corner beside a decanter of sweet, sage tea, lush cushions and blankets upon a soft, low bed, and gentle firelight twinkling through a golden lantern. Our voices were silenced to the outside. To any who walked by, it appeared an unoccupied shop tent. We would undress each other hurriedly, longing to touch and feel and explore each other again. Our bodies would crash together in explosive passion, our cries ringing out into the emerging night, heard by none. Then, we would lie beside one another in the glow of the fire, fingers trailing lazily, talking of anything and everything. When talk of the village grew tiresome, Saalim would tell me stories. Describing things that I could scarce imagine. When there was need to return home, Saalim would still time so we could linger just a little longer.

Saalim was on his back, head resting upon an emerald cushion. I was curled at his side, my black hair twisting amongst his auburn. My arm draped over his chest, tracing his ribs with my fingertips.

"Have you heard anything from Nassar?" I said. "He could have me killed if he wanted to. Why would he delay?"

"Perhaps he does not have the energy to care with all the other, more pressing things there are to worry about. Anyway, I imagine he doesn't want to bring more upsetting news to your father." He pulled me tightly to him.

"Bad news? Nothing has happened, has it?" I sat up, leaning against his chest.

"No, no. Lack of news improves your father's disposition. I'm sure Nassar does not want to be the one to change that."

I was perplexed. The quietude was unnerving. They did not yet have their jinni, and if Firoz's desperation was any indication, they were not satisfied with dreaming. They wanted him. I pressed my cheek more tightly to Saalim's chest. "Do you think they plan something?"

"I wouldn't know," he said. There was an odd hesitation in his voice, his brow creased. "I've only heard whisperings. I do not know what they think nor what they plan."

"Firoz said people will die if Father doesn't allow the caravans to come and trade for salt. Is that true?"

Saalim nodded. "It is a long way off, but yes, people will eventually need salt desperately. They cannot live without it. It's a part of your blood. And they can only get it here."

"It's what Rafal said. People want the routes to change—to find other sources of salt. If we bring Madinat Almulihi back . . . then maybe? Perhaps if I wished for—"

He pressed his lips to my forehead. "Love, would you stop thinking of all these other things and simply worry about yourself? If you won't do it for yourself, do it for me. I am beginning to think I am the only one who worries about you, and it's hard to care for someone more than she cares for herself." He smirked.

Raising my eyebrows, I said, "Find yourself a new someone then."

"A new woman? But I like how you taste best." Suddenly his teeth were on my shoulder, and he had pinned me to the bed. I yelped as he wrestled me with his mouth, and I tried to do the same, drooling on him and biting my tongue in the process. He laughed at me until he was wiping tears from his face.

And then we lay quiet together again, listening to the sitar twangs and tabla drum beats chase each other through the tent. Loud voices and clanging of coins resonated around us. I closed my eyes, lulled to sleep by the sounds, the rhythm of Saalim's rising and falling chest.

"A suitor will arrive tomorrow," he said when I was almost asleep.

I opened my eyes, disappointed by the news of a visitor. Suitors meant spending an afternoon with a man other than Saalim. It meant smiling and flirting with someone I cared nothing for.

"And if he wants you, shall I redirect his attention?" He asked as he always did now.

Staring at the fluttering tent wall, I said, "Only if he bites harder than you. Otherwise, I'll gladly run off with him." Then I raised myself onto my elbow. "Really, how can you continue to ask me? Of course. The idea of spending a night with another . . ." It was so abhorrent, it made me nauseous. "Always, until my twenty-third year when . . ."

He looked at me, eyebrows raised in a way that was familiar to me. "Go on."

"Don't start," I begged.

"And then what, Emel? We cannot ignore the future forever. It comes whether you choose to face it or not."

"When my father casts me out, we will be together. I will live somewhere nice, and you will live with me as often as you can."

"And would you be happy? Living a life alone, waiting for me to come? With only brief moments with me?"

I was annoyed. Why had he ruined our evening with this conversation? It never ended neatly. Always a scramble of frustration and sorrow.

Clenching my fist, I sat up. "Yes, because I would have to be," I said, worrying my lip between my teeth. "I would rather it be brief moments with you for the rest of my life than none at all."

He looked at me sadly as he pulled me back down to him. He rubbed my back and arms with his hands.

"And when your father dies, what happens to me? What if your father hides my vessel with me in it? Or gives it to a favorite son who chooses to move away? What then?" He returned the same argument I had spat at him so long ago.

"I don't want to talk about this!" I shouted. Sitting up and scooting away from him.

"You must!" His voice was loud and harsh. He sat up and glared at me. "You cannot run from this, Emel! You must decide what it is you want so that you can be gone from this place."

"And leave you? Leave us?" Tears pricked my eyes. I buried my hands in my hair as my mind churned with ideas, groping for anything that could serve as a solution to our complicated puzzle. He came over and pulled me to him again.

"Not all masters lose their jinni with a wish. We don't know that you would leave me," he murmured.

I pressed on his chest so that he lay back down.

"We don't know that I won't." I climbed atop him, laying my cheek against his chest, listening to the whoosh of his breaths, the beating of his heart. "Anyway, I am not yet convinced it is my freedom that I want the most."

"What do you mean?"

"What about yours?"

His body hardened under mine. It was no longer welcoming, soft. He rolled me off of him, grunting in disapproval of the conversation.

"No." His words were stern, serious.

"Can I even ask for it? Can I free you from your prison? What would happen?"

"Yes, it can be done, though none but my master can free me."

I slumped forward.

"And once freed, I would certainly be gone from here." He pointed to the village around us. "I would be someone else entirely. I'd remember very little. Like my ability to know the tenor of another's wants, I would just know the sense of my past, none of the details. Even if I was within an arm's reach of you, I wouldn't know you. But you would remember me and . . ." His words trailed off.

"But you would remain a little bit you?"

His expression was agonized at my words, the lines of his face hardened. He hated the path our conversation had taken.

"I will be what I was before and only have the memories that Masira grants me." Like Firoz and Rashid and their hazy feeling of being in trouble.

He took a long breath, his eyes suddenly sad. "And Emel, I am sure they would not be of you. And even if they were, how would our paths ever cross? You'd still be an ahira with the same fate—locked in the palace until a suitor snatches you up, which would happen quickly, I'm sure. So even if I wanted to come find you, you'd be gone by the time I arrived. So please, love, do not think of my freedom." He looked over to me with eyes pleading. "It would be torture to leave you like this."

"You want me to ask for my freedom but I don't know how. I am scared that I will be taken from here, far away from you. Or that when I ask for my freedom, I'll be strung by my heels just as Firoz . . . as Sabra."

Saalim looked pained at the thought. "But remember the intention of what you want. When you wish for something, you are speaking from here." He brushed his fingers against my brow. "But what you feel here is just as important." He laid his hand against my chest. "Had you not just fought with Sabra, had the words of her saying she hoped she'd die not rang loudly in your mind, I do not think she would be gone. Would you have been imprisoned when you asked to not yet return home, if you hadn't been thinking of how much you didn't want to return to your normal life? The result of the wish would have been different."

What he told me was not new. We had discussed this. But still, I cowered at the thought of making the wish.

"So you have to be clear in what you want. You have to feel it here." His words were hard and unyielding, but his lips against my chest were soft. "To give you your freedom, to say goodbye to you, will be the hardest thing I do." He murmured the words against me. "But I will do it, Emel. I will help rid you of your father so that you can take back your life."

"Can't you . . ." I hesitated, "just kill him?" It would be such an easy solution. I felt vile for finally voicing that desire aloud, for talking of my father's murder so casually. I turned away from him, embarrassed.

He was unabashed by the question. "I would have done it already if I could. Remember, I cannot kill my master. I cannot change his fate in any way without his choosing it. I do nothing for him that he does not ask me to."

"But then how can you do all that you do for me without my asking?"

"So long as it does not affect my master, I can use my magic however I please. And it pleases me to please you." He leaned forward and kissed my temple, his hand running down my arm.

My head ached, trying to process the nuances of jinn magic. "So then if I were to ask for my freedom, would I not need to be your master? Wouldn't my freedom change the fate of my father?"

He considered my question, then nodded. "Clever."

I sighed. "I hate this."

"You must become my master."

"That means I would need the vessel." I exhaled and pulled my knees to my chest. All this planning made things too real. I wasn't ready. Not yet.

As though he sensed my disquiet, he said, "Even if Masira separates us . . . if you leave me for a better life and I can see you no longer, I will still have my memories of us and the knowledge that you are hopefully somewhere safer, happier. Somewhere you can be whole.

"Though no amount of time with you will be sufficient, what I have had, even if just a flicker in my long life, in which I was finally able to love you, to hold you and have you . . . that will have to be enough. The thought of forgetting you, having none of our memories together . . ." he stopped, and sucked in a long breath.

"But what about me and what I feel?"

He said nothing and took my hand tightly in his.

THAT NIGHT, Tavi and I sat at the center of the rama, both clutching our small sacrificial flames. She pressed her fingers to the brass that held the oil, closing her eyes, her lips moving to silent words. Our relationship was mending. As her grief abated, it left room for understanding and forgiveness, and in their trail, I found that we were closer than before.

She collected the jar of water she'd brought with her and pulled the stopper from its top.

"Tavi," I said, then reached into my sack of salt. "If you want Masira to hear, then take this." I poured a palm of salt into her hand. "She will listen."

Tavi had never been in possession of so much, and she did not know that my source was unlimited. She had a choice then: keep and spend it—it would get her many things if she braved the settlement again—or sacrifice it.

She did not hesitate. Turning the salt onto the flames, she said her silent plea again. When the fire was doused, her shoulders dropped, and she pulled the doused vessel to her chest.

I repeated her movements and poured the salt onto the flame.

After a moment, I asked, "What did you say to Her?"

She sighed. "I told Her I wanted us to leave here, together." She rested her hand on my knee, and I covered it with my own. "And you?"

I said, "The same."

DAWN WAS brightening the ahira tent. My sisters slept soundly. Gentle, slow sighs around me. My eyes were open wide as I stared at the canopy, at the tiny holes in the fabric that allowed light to seep through.

I did not sleep well that night, tossing and turning with thoughts of Saalim and our conversation. My mind waged war over my two desires: freedom or Saalim.

Why couldn't I have both?

I turned and dug through the soft sand near my mat until I felt fabric. I pulled out the package and shook off the sand. Rolling onto my stomach, I carefully unwrapped the contents.

The long necklace and small tile fell onto my bed alongside the moon-jasmine whose petals were still stretched open in the dark tent despite the emerging dawn. I brought the flower to my nose, closing my eyes and smelling traces of Saalim in its perfume. I set it down and fingered the tile delicately, wondering where it once rested in the ancient castle.

I thought back to the desert's edge and the bustling city Saalim had painted with his words. I replayed my fantasies of a life Saalim and I could share in a city like that, walking hand in hand along a road of horses and busy people, sharing sugar-dusted dates. I replaced him with a nameless, faceless man, seeing if I could find happiness with that stranger. I couldn't. My mind returned to Saalim.

As I gazed at the white flower and the blue tile, I realized that without Saalim I would not have my gleeful dreams, my pools of hope. If I did not have him, I would have neither of the precious things cradled in my hands. I would possess no more knowledge of my world than what I was able to glean from tight-lipped suitors and stories from a trader. I would not have the memories of the sea or the birds that cawed above it. I would not know that ships were things that sailed on waves and that fish were animals that swam beneath them. I would not understand that stone was something to stack and craft homes, not just a weight for parchment. That wives were not something to be counted as objects but something to be revered and held. And I would never have learned that the warmth of being loved was amplified by the terrifying fire of loving one in return.

I spun the moon-jasmine between my fingers, its blurring petals resembling the glow of the sun. I thought of the night I received that flower. The night I spent with Saalim in the fallen dome. Of how he helped me down the stone steps eroded by salty spray and ocean winds. I remembered how he knelt down and plucked the white flower from the sand, handing me a piece of his home. I recalled the moon that night, its pale glow as it curved in the star-speckled sky. How later he gave me the small tile, imperfect along its hand-cut edges, and told me that with it, I could always remember the sea.

My mind wandered and wandered, climbing through memories of Saalim glowing gold, treading around my mother with blood-red stones strung from her neck, stepping over dead soldiers beside a glistening throne. It moved rapidly in the lethargic hours of the morning until it stumbled upon something . . . something that snagged. My mind groped through the haze, finding the edges of a thought, a memory.

The fog cleared as I remembered a golden sun and crescent moon emblazoned on the collar of navy robes. Navy, or indigo, or . . . the color of the tile that rested in my hand. The color of the sea. A golden sun with thick rays was unusual but its portrayal clear when next to its equal, the moon. But there was something about the jasmine in my fingers whose thick petals surrounded a perfectly round center. The flower that, when open, looked unmistakably like the image of the sun that had been threaded onto the blue fabric.

I grabbed the medallion strung to the golden chain and examined the crescent moon and sun etched onto its surface. How pretty I'd thought it was when I finally looked at it so closely for the first time, before I connected it to Matin, to the foreign soldiers. To the Dalmur.

I held the moon-jasmine up to the medallion and peered at the two beside each other.

I sat up, stunned.

It was not a sun that was stitched onto the robes of my father's enemies. It was the flower that grew wildly at the desert's edge. It was an image of the white bloom that I held, magically alive, in the palm of my hand. And alongside it was a crescent moon for whom its ivory petals would spread.

Like shuffling cards, everywhere I had seen those images flashed through my mind—carved into the pendants that swung from the assassins' necks and had rested against my mother's chest, stitched onto Matin's robes, tattooed on the arms of the healer, etched onto the golden bands that wrapped Saalim's vessel . . .

I dropped the objects in my hands. There was more to the Dalmur than wanting the jinni for the wish. They were related to Madinat Almulihi, and if their hopes carried traces of the same sea that surged through Saalim, there was something I was missing.

There was something Saalim was not telling me.

24

S AALIM WAS CORRECT about the suitor, and that afternoon we
gathered in our finery to meet the muhami Ibrahim. I bided my
time, waiting for the perfect moment when I could find Saalim and
demand he tell me everything he knew about the Dalmur.

Ibrahim was older with a long white beard that draped against his chest.
Though he might have been the oldest muhami to court us, I could see he
was a strong man and a formidable ruler. He was vaguely familiar, but I could
not place why. We were told he came from a large city far across the desert.

I could hardly concentrate during the courting, thinking over and over
of the Dalmur and the possibility that they had a deeper connection to
Saalim than I understood. What did it mean that they carried symbols of
Saalim's home? The jinni was disguised as a soldier and kept a close guard
on my father during the courting. I tried to catch his gaze, wanting him to
feel how desperately I needed to talk to him, but he did not look at me once.

It was some relief that Ibrahim behaved so differently than the other suitors or my distraction might have been obvious. He did not get up to speak to us, did not call us to come to him. Occasionally, the King would gesture to an ahira, drawing on the advantages of one girl or the next, as if suddenly remembering the reason the man was sitting in the tent with his daughters. Ibrahim would observe politely, his white beard swaying as his head bobbed.

But I could see that the Salt King was not investing in a political alliance with this man. My father was agitated and distracted, and I wondered if Ibrahim was even interested in taking home a bride, so little did he interact with any of us.

Since Mama's death, I had noticed a marked change in my father. He had grown pale, irritable, and taciturn, his clothing disarranged. The frequency with which he snapped at his daughters, barked at Nassar, or cuffed his slaves had increased, and his volatility erupted from long stretches of apathy. Sometimes, I thought I saw sadness lurking behind his indifference but rage and impassivity were the perfect camouflage for vulnerability.

The muhami asked my father of the people that threatened our village—he had heard the rumors, what happened at the King's Haf Shata party. My father's eyes darkened, but he waved Ibrahim's words aside, shrugging his shoulders, claiming it all had passed. Ibrahim pressed him for details, and surprisingly, my father elaborated on what had happened. He warned Ibrahim to be careful, describing in detail what the savages—he spat the word—had done to the settlement. "Spreading lies to my people, seeding distrust," he said, leaning back into his chair as though tired of speaking.

It was strange but empowering to be in the position of greater knowledge. My father seemed small and weak, understanding so little. Ibrahim seemed genuinely concerned as the King described the details. Ibrahim clucked sympathetically. A similar rebellion was occurring in his home, he said. Strange people who terrorized his streets, leaving behind black marks of their hands as if a threat.

"The Altamaruq think I've a jinni," the King said flatly. A few of my sisters barely concealed their winces at the word. I watched Saalim to see how he reacted, but he was untroubled. Did not even blink.

"Bah!" Ibrahim pounded his fist into his palm. "Mine search for the same. Absurd radicals!" The King nodded distractedly.

The vizier stood by watching my father and the foreign ruler, watching me and the rest of the ahiran. His gaze was impassive. His eyes had met mine once earlier in the afternoon. He had stared, but when my eyes found his, he shifted his focus and continued his perusal of the room.

My father's dispassion, Ibrahim's nonchalance, Nassar's curiosity, the Dalmur and Madinat Almulihi. I was uneasy about it all.

When the ahiran had given up on the muhami and were sitting on cushions talking amongst ourselves, my father addressed us. "Daughters, it is time to return to your home."

Confused, we stood and assembled, ready to follow the guard that would lead us to the zafif to change.

"Emel, you stay."

I stopped, disbelieving that Ibrahim could possibly want to court me— Saalim would not have allowed it—my heart slammed against my ribs. Tavi looked at me questioningly as she followed my sisters out. Soon, I was alone with the King, Ibrahim, Nassar, and a few of his slaves and one of his guards. Saalim. Finally, our eyes met. He was rigid, as unprepared as I for what the King planned.

"You've given up, Emel," the King began when my sisters were gone.

"Forgive me, your highness," I stammered as I fell to my knees to bow before him.

"I don't want you to speak. Just stand and look at me." His quiet terrified me more than if he had shouted. I rose, and my eyes met his.

"I have watched you through two seasons of laziness. You have not tried with the suitors. You continue to fail despite my best efforts.

"Beyond your failure, you oppose me and my law. First, you're out by yourself in the palace. I know that was not the first time. I thought your punishment would remind you of your duty to be obedient, remind you that I am the King. I thought it might correct your behavior.

"But it didn't. And now you flirt with slaves, ignore suitors, and refuse guests at my festival." His voice did not rise. It was level. He was weary. "Yes, Emel," the King continued. "I have eyes everywhere. How long did you think your behavior would escape my notice?"

I looked at Nassar, but he watched the Salt King, and his face gave nothing away. So he had not remained silent after all. He had spoken with his King, and now here we were with this foreign man. I wondered what role he was to play. Ibrahim sat back and watched me, unaffected by my father's charges.

I glanced to Saalim, his eyes were dark as he listened.

"And if that was not enough . . ." The King rose from his chair and walked toward me. I saw Saalim start forward as if to protect me, but he stopped himself, remembering his place. He was bound, helpless to do anything. "You bribe guards with salt you stole from me to go into my village." Still, he spoke softly. Like a hissing snake.

My eyes flashed to Nassar, but his scowl was not one of resentment. He looked surprised, almost fearful, at the King's words. Momentarily, it shook me from my rising alarm.

"For what purpose do you serve me, Emel?"

My attention snapped back to Father.

"You are my ahira, and instead you eat my food, sleep in shelter I provide, wear my jewels, and do everything but the one thing I ask of you."

I leaned back as he approached, anticipating what was to come. I stared at the buttons against his shirt, watching them peek out from behind his beard tentatively as though they, too, did not want to miss the spectacle.

He said, "Look at me, you coward."

Unable to bear it any longer, tears filled my eyes. Not tears of sadness, but tears of rage. Sons, I was no coward. I did not hide behind another's strength because I was too powerless to face things on my own. I shook with fury, and silent, hot tears coursed down my cheeks.

I stared at my father, blurry through my tears. I did not look to Ibrahim, to Nassar, to Saalim. I could not stand to see their faces. I held my head high, my mouth set in a hard line. I stared at him until he looked away.

"You are of no use to me now," he said as he paced in front of me. "I sent word to Ibrahim after I learned of your refusals at the Haf Shata party. We are fortunate for the timing. Ibrahim needs a gift for his son as a congratulations for his first marriage. You will not be that wife, Emel, as you are no longer worthy of that title. Your marks bear truth to that. You will be his son's concubine. You will travel with Ibrahim to his home, live in the palace with the other whores, and when his son needs to be attended to, you will pleasure him as you have been trained.

"Ibrahim knows the details of your deception, Emel. He will see an end to it. He can't have a wayward mistress for his son. Oh," the King paused, suddenly remembering, "I do believe you and his son have met. His name is Omar."

I set my jaw, clenching my teeth as I listened to his words. There would be no reality in which I would leave my village to live the rest of my life as Omar's whore.

Death would serve me better.

"My King," Nassar cleared his throat. "Emel is very beautiful, very skilled. Is sending her away the best decision?" He sounded scared, and the fear in his voice, his boldness at speaking up, again distracted me from my father's sentence. I looked to the small man whose hand was held out before him, questioning, tentative.

"That you think you can continue speak against my decisions shows I may have misjudged you as my vizier," the Salt King said.

"Throw him to the foxes," Ibrahim said, waving his hand. He still had not moved from his chair.

The King looked at Nassar. "We will speak after I am done."

Nassar looked apologetic. "Forgive me, your majesty—"

"Leave here," he said.

Nassar left slowly, looking from the King to me and back again, his brow furrowed, his hands fussing with the air as if trying to do something, anything, to change what was happening. I did not understand his reason for speaking out, but I was grateful for it.

The King turned to me and said nothing, so I filled the silence.

"I am not afraid of you," I whispered through clenched teeth. "You won't win." My voice so quiet that none could hear it but my father.

The King did not flinch at my words. He took my face in his hands. I refused to wince, to cower, though I was sure he would kill me bare-handed in that moment.

"I wanted you to have everything," he whispered just as quietly, and I was stunned to see that his eyes were wet, almost tearful. "You were supposed to be one of the best." His voice cracked. His fingers were soft on my cheeks, nails just barely pressing my skin. "I was a fool for thinking you could be like her . . . was it Isra who poisoned you? Turned you against me?" Again, his voice caught, and he dropped his hands. I heard the ache in his words, and had I not been so angry, I might have felt sympathy. But that pool of water had long dried.

"You think cruelty makes you strong," I hissed, and he glared at me. "But what strength do you have without those of us to whom you are so cruel?"

"Be gone from me," he said. He moved swiftly to the tent's exit before he stopped, back turned to us all.

"Take her to her sisters," he said to the only guard left in the room, to Saalim. "Then I want you back to my sleeping quarters. Ibrahim, the servants will escort you to your room. Emel will be ready for you to depart at dusk."

My feet were heavy as stone, so I stood in the room, unmoving, for what seemed an eternity. Everyone had left, except me, Saalim, and the servants who watched me warily.

"Move," the guard, the jinni, said finally. He nudged me coldly, maintaining his act before the servants. My feet moved me out of the room, but

I don't remember how. My body quavered, my heart thundered, my legs were weak with tremors. As soon I stepped into an empty hallway with the guard at my back, the world froze. I could barely register the change in the air before Saalim pulled me to him and the ground slipped from under me.

And when I felt that we stood in the shade of the trees in the oasis, I cried.

"You are worthy of being someone's wife. You are worthy of love. I love you," he told me over and over.

He held me as I wept into my hands.

"I can't go, Saalim," I said through shuddered breaths. "I can't. I would rather have no life than one as Omar's whore," I said. "I have to make a decision. It can't wait."

"I know."

By the small pool, I paced back and forth, rage and sadness and fear propelling my steps. Ideas streamed out of me, ways to get around the King sending me away. I did not want to make my choice. Not yet. Not ever. But I knew my time was up, the base of the hourglass full. I could wait no longer.

I asked the jinni to change Ibrahim's mind, but he could not. It was not Ibrahim's idea but my father's. Saalim was incapable of changing his master's plan. Could he kill Ibrahim? Could he cause another attack by the Dalmur? Couldn't he do anything? No, there was nothing. This was the King's plan, and Saalim could not interfere with it.

There was no way out. If I did not make my move, the King would make his. He would win. So I would not let him.

Saalim knelt before me, taking my hands in his, and watched me with heedful patience.

I recoiled, seeing that he waited for my choice.

"Do you know what you want?"

"Yes. No." I looked at Saalim, at every angle of his face, the way his lips moved when he spoke, the way his shoulders rose as he breathed. "I am not ready to say goodbye." And I had to prepare for the fact that it very well would be goodbye. If I freed the jinni, if I freed myself.

"There is no rush," he whispered, and I heard the pain I felt in his voice, too. "We will stay here for as long as you need."

We stood in silence for a long time. After a while, the leaves rustled, and the water danced with small ripples. I looked at him, worried that he had done something foolish and allowed time to move forward again, but he had only magicked the wind and the sun as he always did.

He said, sheepishly, "You know I must hear the words of the wind through the trees and see the sun fall into the earth."

We lay down together in the cool sand, and I curled into him, marveling at his ability to be so enamored with the world despite its darkness.

"Saalim," I said after a long silence, my head on the bend of his arm. My mind had been a torrent of thoughts and wild plans when I remembered that morning. It had seemed so long ago when I held the tile and moon-jasmine and golden necklace. A whole lifetime.

"Hmm?"

"The Altamaruq, the Dalmur, whatever they are, they know about Madinat Almulihi. The symbols they carry—it's a moon-jasmine, not the sun. Why are the same images carved into your vessel? What aren't you telling me?"

Saalim studied the cluster of trees above him. He inhaled deeply, revealing nothing on his stone face. His silence made me uneasy. I watched him, waiting for him to say something, anything. When he didn't respond, I stiffened.

"How long have you known?"

"Since your father's party."

I thought back to that dark morning when the men tried to steal his vessel. I recalled the choking gasp and the man's fall, the slice of blades as they were pressed into soft bodies. The jinni's face as he bent over one of them, retrieving his vessel, pausing when he saw their golden pendant carved with the symbols of his home. I remembered the ache in his eyes, the curve of his shoulders as they fell forward.

"When you saw what they wore around their necks."

He nodded. "I have killed so many for your father. It is my purpose as his jinni. But their deaths, I will always carry with me."

"You did not kill them. The guards did."

He laughed flatly. "I might as well have. The man fell to his knees because of me. Everything that came after was because of me."

I wrapped my fingers around his arm that crossed my chest. "He wished for it. You can't feel guilt because you do what your master commands."

"Does that work for you?" He asked.

I thought of the nights I spent with muhamis, forced by my father. I shook my head.

I said, "You still have not answered my question."

He exhaled.

"Why do these people who bear the symbol of Madinat Almulihi search for a jinni who happens to be from the same place? Why have you kept this from me?"

He sat up. "It was not something I wanted to burden you with."

Of course. How could he tell me that the people I once hated most were from the city which I loved? From his home? Maybe he feared I would think he was like them.

"I don't hate them, Saalim. I think, finally, I understand them."

They were as desperate as I, doing whatever they could to find a life they could embrace. Is that not what I did every time I left the palace, risking the safety of my sisters and my brothers, every time I drew another place on my map, and every time I closed my eyes to plan a wish that even Masira could not twist?

"Aren't we all salt chasers seeking freedom, some semblance of control?" I asked.

If I did not look out for myself, who else would? I had only me. And I had to endure. Weren't we all the same?

Saalim shook his head. "That is not it."

I closed my mouth. I waited.

"They carry the symbols of my home because of the legend that has been passed from mouth to mouth for as long as I've been a jinni."

The legend. The one all the Dalmur have mentioned, the one that has them convinced that they will find their redemption.

"What is it?"

"You already may know." He took my hands. "Do you know the legend of the lost prince?"

I thought for a moment before I nodded, slowly. "Of course. My mother told it to me often. The one of the prince who was locked away and the family who perished." I frowned. "I don't understand how—"

"Let me explain." He stood and helped me to do the same. "I think the story is best told from where it took place. If you will allow me to take you there?"

I nodded and stepped into him, closing my eyes, feeling his heart beating against my cheek. When I opened my eyes again, we stood amongst the crumbling ruins of Madinat Almulihi.

25

Saalim

T HE GUILT I CARRY from the fall of Madinat Almulihi is like a scar—it will be with me forever. I still smell the blood that pooled in the streets; still hear the sounds of blades and the screams of neighbors; still see my mother, cold like the dagger she used to kill my father, telling me to run; still bear the shame that I did not stay to protect her.

Madinat Almulihi was my only home, and like all children who grow in one place, I never appreciated the fortune of my life. It was the most prosperous city in the desert, ruled by my mother and father with unyielding justness. I could not appreciate that then. I do now, but it is much too late.

It was no wonder people from all over the desert flocked to see our streets. They had heard the rumors of ocean wind, green that crawled across walls, and flowers that sprouted between bricks. When they came, they were amazed to find more wonders than what the whispers told: massive stone palaces, domed temples for worship, homes with strong foundations and

sturdy walls. They saw the joy of the neighbors who shared food and drink, the people that loved openly, the freedom with which people were allowed to live. It gave them escape from what was, at that time, a lawless era in the desert when it could only be ruled with violence.

But the visitors saw only what they wanted—that there was no violence, there were trees that gave shade, water whose body was larger than the desert's. They did not see, did not want to see, that no matter where one lived, unhappiness lurked like a shadow.

Some of these visitors returned to their settlements and tribes telling tales of this extraordinary place, spreading curiosity and jealousy. But many stayed, and as the village grew, the desert calmed. By the time I was born into the palace, Almulihi was a bustling city, a massive center for trade and travel. The desert was ordered, and men used words instead of scimitars. Because our land thrived, it was only a matter of time before someone tore its roots from the ground.

My father was generous with me as his firstborn. Perhaps it was to make up for his own failures as a husband and king, but he doted on me and groomed me to be his heir. For years, I was a little kingling and paraded through the palace like I wore the crown already. If you had asked me then, I would tell you I did.

I could not be the only heir, though. Two daughters were born, and then finally, one more son. We were celebrated and adored by the citizens as if we were their own. We roamed the streets of the city with guards on our tails. My sisters twirled in bright dresses, vine crowns woven in their hair. My brother and I clanged our dulled swords on the palace steps as we fought heroically in imaginary battles. We grew into young adults who were too distracted to learn our roles as city rulers, to learn to lead as our parents did.

We were naive. We were not prepared for what came.

"Where is your brother?" My mother asked me the morning Almulihi fell. To a servant who headed into the kitchens, she called, "The king needs his tea."

Kassim was only my brother when she was displeased with him. "I am not his keeper," I said.

She looked at me with great shadows beneath her eyes. "Find out where he has gone. Your father wishes to see him. He is having a bad morning." She turned her gaze to the windows, the bright blue sky cut into four arching squares.

The servant bustled out of the kitchen carrying a tray with a bronze kettle and ceramic cup. The queen followed her up the stairs.

I stormed through the palace, my hard-soled shoes clicking loudly against the smooth tiles. I was no servant to fetch my wayward brother at my mother's order. Nadia was in the gardens clipping roses. She looked up at my approaching steps.

"Finished at the docks already?"

Shrugging, I stepped down onto the rose beds, careful my boots did not soil with mud. "I don't see why Father has me performing a hired-man's job. I won't waste my time in dockyards when I'm king, so I don't see why I should do it now."

She raised a knowing eyebrow and turned back to the roses. "Go tell that to Father."

I said, "Have you seen Kassim?"

"He has not yet returned."

"Returned from where?"

She studied the roses, searching for what I did not know. They all looked the same. "To visit some settlement. He left last night, said you already knew."

He'd told me nothing, but this was not surprising. Kassim and I rarely spoke except to mollify our mother at mealtime. He was flippant and inattentive, and I could rely on him for nothing.

"When does he get back?"

"Late tonight or tomorrow I think." She clipped three more roses until she had a full bouquet. Then, she held them out to me, smiling. "Should I take them to Father?"

I turned from her. "I'm sure he'll love to see that his heir has spent her entire morning trimming blooms from their stems."

Passing through the atrium, I flung aside the vines that were left to grow so long they tumbled onto the floor and strode around the fountain whose incessant trickling water drove me to insanity. I climbed the curving stairs and made my way to my father's chamber.

The king was in bed, a frail and sad version of who he used to be. Each breath rattled, his arms held no meat, his eyes were sunken, and cheeks hollowed.

"Father," I said when I entered. My mother was at his side, holding the cup of steaming tea, readying to bring it to his lips. She did not look at me when I entered.

"Son." He began to rise, but my mother pressed her hand against his chest and shook her head. My father listened. "How were the ships? Did Ekram explain the inventory? He was supposed to take you to the storerooms, too." He looked at me hopefully, and I felt a stirring of guilt that I had told Ekram to handle it on his own. I did not need to learn the minutia of ship trade. My father trusted him, so would I.

But I nodded. "It's done." I fished my purse from my hip and pulled from it a small package. Once unwrapped, I showed my father the contents. "Dried meat from the western sea called ham. The captain sends his wishes for your health. Said his mother made him eat this every day he was ill. Cured him of every ailment."

"Good boy," my father said, but he did not ask for the meat, and I, feeling foolish, wrapped and stuffed it away. My father patted the bed beside him. "Come closer."

I did, though I hated every moment of it. Hated seeing my father as a frail man. It did not fit with the man I knew, the man I idolized and loved. My father, the king, was not weak. He was not unsure. He did not rely on others to accomplish his simple tasks; did not rely on my mother to bring drink to his lips.

My mother spoke. "Saalim, we've things to discuss today. Citizen disputes I would like you to assist in resolving. Petitions from merchants and farmers who arrived this morning. Tomorrow, we will meet the keeper of the southeast mine. They're having trouble, though, I'm not yet sure with what. I have not finished the letter. Thought you might help with that, too. We will look through it together." The tasks poured from her mouth like the fountains in our home. The burden of the city fell on her shoulders with my father's illness, and she used the opportunity to supply my siblings and I with the education we had not yet received—a gift none of us particularly welcomed. We did not understand that we had to learn how to be rulers. We thought it came from blood alone. My mother was tireless in her effort to care for our father, for our people. When I collapsed into bed at night while she was still tending to my father or managing the servants, I wished I possessed some of her strength for my own.

"Tell me what needs to be done. I can do it," I said lifting my chin. And I could. I did not know why she thought to assist me still. My father had been sick for nearly four moons. I had taken it all on without issue. Some things, my father and mother held onto too tightly. I did not need to see Ekram when he could manage the shipyard on his own. I did not have to speak with Azim nearly every day to check on his management of the soldiers. No fool would take Madinat Almulihi to war. It was wasted time, so I did not do it.

I did things differently, but I was not wrong.

"Where is Kassim?" my father asked. "I must speak to him."

"Nadia said Kassim is visiting a settlement. He won't be back until late tonight or tomorrow. When I see him, I will tell him you have asked for him," I said watching my mother, waiting to see her approval that I had done what she asked. "If it has to do with palace work, Father, just tell me. I can handle it."

"I know you can, son." His voice was fractured and hoarse. "Maybe he visits Edala. Will bring her home to me. It has been so long."

My mother pursed her lips then turned back to my father. "Take another drink, love." My mother curled protectively over him, her hand behind his head like she forgave him of everything. My father looked so relieved as he sipped the tea like a child, watching her misty eyes. He seemed so grateful for her mercy.

From high above, the horns' blare echoed.

The war horns.

My mother's eyes met mine.

I stood up and briskly left the room. I had only heard the horns' cry once before, and it was when my father had the players blow their curving instruments in the atrium. My siblings and I needed to learn its sound, needed to know to fear it.

I found the narrow, spiraling staircase of the tower. I leapt up the steps, staring at the white-washed walls, glimpsing through the keyhole openings the midday sky outside. Finally, I reached the doorway that led to the platform where three men stood, blaring their horns in succession so that there was no break in the sound. From the top of the palace, I could see other men and women with war horns standing atop their homes, carrying the sound out to the extremities of the city. People emerged onto the streets to see the cause for alarm. None brought their weapons.

"What comes?" I shouted.

One pointed out to the dunes on the horizon. I saw them then—the rapidly approaching army, an uncountable mass of soldiers. The largest I had ever seen, and they were not flying our banners, not fighting for our king.

So swift were they that they had already spilled into our city by the time I returned to my father and mother.

"An approaching army," I panted, the door to the chamber slamming the wall behind me as I burst through it. And as I said it, I heard the cries outside. The cries of war, and the cries of terror.

My mother did not wait, she dropped to her knees and reached under the raised bed. The ring of metal against stone sounded in the room, and when she stood, she held a long straight sword, and a small, jewel-encrusted dagger.

"Find Azim. Assemble the soldiers!"

I ran, searching for Nadia on the way out to warn her to hide, to find somewhere safe. I did not see her. It was not until much later that I learned she was killed in her room defending herself with a sword she could wield only poorly.

Azim was gone from his quarters, and when I saw soldiers of Almulihi out in the streets already defending the palace from the invaders, I understood that he had already done what was needed of him. He had been more prepared than I.

Like a child, I watched them from the balcony, seeing how my play battles with Kassim paled in comparison to the real thing. Real violence was not something I had seen. We had learned to wield swords and how to defend the softest parts of our bodies from the sharpest edges, but we had not seen blood, had not seen death. When I saw it then, I was unable to move to meet the enemy. I was terrified to join my father's soldiers, fearing that in moments, I, too, would be lying lifeless on the steps.

Our men were not ready. They were not strong enough. The people of Almulihi had grown complacent, and we were nothing compared to the prepared army that tore through our streets. Villagers fell easily to blades. Soldiers were taken by one stab of the sword. It seemed like years, like no time at all, before the invading men broke through the palace walls.

"They've entered the palace!" I yelled to my mother and father, bursting again through the door. I do not know why I ran to them, but it was all I could think to do. I was a child, scared and in need of someone to direct me.

Nothing could prepare me for what I saw.

My father lay dead, the hilt of the jewel-encrusted dagger emerging from his chest. Blood was all over my mother's hands, tears fell from her eyes.

"What have you done?" I screamed, dropping to my knees and clasping my father's hands.

"Spared him the dishonor of dying by the enemy's hand." She said it strongly, like a queen. "We will fall, Saalim." She picked up the long blade and moved to the bed to stand in front of the dead king, her gone husband. "Combat will not save us."

"So that is it? Are we to surrender?" I could hear the men's shouts through the palace. They were combing the rooms. They were searching for us.

She shook her head. "I will die defending Almulihi. You cannot. You must try and save her. Run from here. Find Zahar."

"The healer?" I asked, bewildered.

"Go!" she screamed, pointing a shaking finger at the door. She clasped the hilt of her sword.

I did not look back. I hated that I fled so easily, without remorse or guilt. That I could so easily turn from my home in desperation when my mother could kill her husband and stand and wait for her own death without flinching.

That remorse, I carry now.

Soldiers' footsteps clattered behind me as I fled into the hall. I heard my mother call to them. I did not turn. Using the servants' passages of the palace, much as I had when I was a child, I reached the healer's home, tucked into the far reaches of the palace grounds.

Zahar sat at the table of her kitchen as though she were waiting for me. I knew little of her other than the few times I was taken to her as a child with a scraped knee or fevered chill. Before she left, Edala had told me that she was magic and could wield Masira's power. Perhaps my mother had listened to her daughter when she spoke of these things. I never believed a word.

"Please," I said, falling to my knee at her feet. "Almulihi falls. If there is anything you can do to save it, to save us, I beg you." Shameful tears filled my eyes at how desperate and pathetic I must look, when I realized how much had already been lost. Everything my parents had created could not be taken by these people, not if I could stop it.

Zahar peered at me for a long time.

"Please," I said, hearing more screams from the palace.

"I can save Almulihi," she said. "But it will cost you."

I nodded. Anything. "What must I give? I will give it."

"Everything you have."

Everything? I thought she meant the blankets on my bed, my books, my swords and tunics, my boots, my father's gold and salt—mine now, I realized. It was a large price, but it was worth it if it would save my home. "You can have it all."

Zahar cackled and shook her head. "No, boy. I don't want your things. I mean *everything* you have." She pointed at me, at the home around us. "If you want me to save your home, first I will take you from your home, then take your home from you. I will take your family, your friends, your neighbors. You will watch them perish. And you will remember them all. I will take from you your pride and honor. You will be a slave and learn the power in benevolence and grace."

Balking, I stood up. "But how will that save my home?"

"You will get it back. One day." She leaned back in her chair.

I grimaced and began to retreat, deciding that this did not seem worthwhile.

She slammed her hand onto a table. "Boy, this world has been handed to you on a salt brick. It is time you learn to appreciate what you have and earn what you desire so greatly."

Appalled, I asked, "Why make me a slave to save my home?"

"Because those are my conditions. And I will do so with gladness. When you are released from your enslavement, you will be returned to your home, to everything made by your mother and father—" She spat on the ground after she said father, like it was bitter on her tongue, "—and then, you will be fit to rule."

"When will I be freed?"

"When you desire it least. Watch for the one who carries your mark."

I did not understand how she could promise such things, how she had the power to make them so, but I agreed. I would have given anything in that moment. Slowly and with creaking bones, she stood from the table. She seemed older, weaker than I remembered. She brought me a stoppered glass vessel.

It was wrapped in golden bands etched with the symbols of my home. Inside, golden liquid sloshed violently against its unyielding walls. It was like she had known I was coming. She was already prepared.

"Drink it all." She handed me the vessel.

Opening the petaled lid, I smelled inside—ocean and dust and moon-jasmine. It did not smell bad. Jubilant cries of men penetrated the gardens, and I heard the hollering and laughing as they sliced at the rose bushes Nadia had so carefully clipped earlier. If they were finished in the palace, my mother, I was sure, was dead. I had nothing left to lose.

Zahar looked beyond me, fear shaking away the apathy as she shrieked. "Drink it now!"

The men came closer. Blades trailed on stone, nearing the enchantress' home.

I drank. Never before had I tasted something so wonderful yet so repulsive. I craved swallowing it as much as I desired to spit it onto the ground. After the first few gulps, I felt it—tendrils of liquid that felt alive and greedy. Like a hungry fire, they reached all the way to my feet, to my hands. They grabbed hold of me until I was powerless against them. They held the drink to my lips. I could not stop, though now I desperately wanted to as the flames swallowed me. But I was no longer in control.

Zahar watched me with wild eyes. Like a madwoman, she laughed. "Foolish boy!"

The door to her home exploded open and men poured in. But she was already gone.

The fire built and built, and I burned from the inside, until finally, I was weightless, like smoke, like a hot wind that blew across the sand. Then I was moving, moving, moving so swiftly that everything was a blur. Until finally, I saw nothing.

But I could feel everything. I felt sickening glee and triumphant power. I felt agonized horror and the depths of grief. The pain of the city that crumbled around me and the joy of the invaders that ruined it.

Suddenly, there was a pull stronger than I'd ever felt, and I was swept from my weightless blindness. I grew heavier and heavier until I could feel the ground, and I could see the world. It felt different, though, as if I had been bound by the heaviest chains. With great effort, I broke from my kneeling posture and stood. And then, like a claw digging its nails into my skull, horrid and fouled thoughts pressed themselves to my mind. I could not make sense of them—why I felt them, why I didn't feel them, why I understood them.

The fiery hands that controlled me earlier turned up my face until I saw a man. Then, the hands moved my mouth and tongue so that I spoke the words: "Yes, Master?" I stared at a man I did not know. He was sitting on my father's throne spinning my mother's jewel-encrusted dagger into the wooden arm. We were in my home.

But it was not my home anymore. It was a crumbled, hollowed shell of what used to be. There was no roof where once it had been. It was only dusk that covered us like a canopy.

I wanted to fall into the ground, sick with what I had done, with what had been lost. I could feel it around me, Madinat Almulihi was perished, my family with them.

I did not know what had become of my sister Edala, of my brother Kassim, but as I prayed they were spared, I was sure they were not. Had unseeing chains not lifted me upright, not held my face in stoicism, not fixed my attention onto the man, I would have run from there and cried.

Instead, I stood and waited to serve, because the hands taught me that was my fate.

And then it hit me, powerful and unyielding: the man's searing desire for more death, for more victory.

So, I gave him what he wished, and the desert fell, too.

26

SHATTERED TILES LITTERED the ground in what used to be a room for thrones, a room to see the citizens of Madinat Almulihi and deliver edicts and orders. Now, it was a carcass of that place, and there were no citizens to seek its guidance. The jinni's remorse stirred the air around us, crashing into invisible walls and sinking to the earth. Like the mixture he was forced to drink, I wanted to turn away from his tale but found myself transfixed, filled with all the sickening details children never heard.

His story revealed what I had not understood before. It seemed, almost, to explain everything. The Dalmur did not search for a jinni simply to make a single wish, to uncover a better desert they hoped was there. They searched for the jinni to free him because they *knew* that with his freedom, life would begin anew.

They were not rebels. They were believers.

"You forgot one part," I whispered, finally.

He broke his gaze from his fallen home and turned to me. "Did I?"

"The end." The part that my mother had told to me over and over again as a child. She had been a believer all this time, and she had wanted me to be the same. I reached up to Saalim's face and gently touched his cheek. "To be kind to the enslaved man, for one day he may be a king."

He looked at his feet, and I saw that I was losing him in his grief and in his fear.

The city was so different now that I knew Saalim's history with it, not through the pretty tales he told me before. Now that I understood he had been more than a man who lived amongst its streets. I saw it with new eyes. "Tell me more about what the palace was like before," I said, hoping to distract him from his role in it all. Crunching carefully through the ceramic shards, I walked toward a battered wall.

He took me through what would have been the back of the palace. Without the tedious care to preserve the impossible garden at the desert's edge, what would have been the beautiful flowering bushes were now just sand and small-leaved plants.

White birds cried above us as they swooped down to the crashing sea. Seagulls, he had called them the last time we were here.

"I wish I could have seen it when it stood," I said.

"I do, too." He walked away from me beyond the gardens.

"Saalim." I held out my hand to stop him, to beg him to look at me. I wanted to tell him that he need not carry so much guilt, so much regret. But when I saw the fallen city, I saw it was unfair of me to expect him to be unfeeling in the aftermath of his loss.

He turned and told me we stood in the healer's home, where he had been changed into who is he now.

How different this Saalim seemed from the man he described before. I knelt down and pushed through the rocks, imagining that I was touching the same thing that a human Saalim once touched.

I love all of you, regardless of your past.

I pressed my fingers into the ground, hoping that Saalim from the lifetime before could feel it. "What do you think happened to her?"

"Zahar?" He looked out at the horizon, walled by rocky cliffs. "She fled just before the invaders arrived in her home. She was old and tired. She did not get far."

There were some remnants of metal and glass scattered along the ground, and I pushed the rocks aside to peer at them. Beneath were pieces of parchment, unbelievably whole. Their words were mostly smudged and faded from the wet air, but I could see they were old correspondences. Now was not the time to sit and sift through them, though I wished I could. Anything to glimpse the life that Saalim lived, to understand the city that needed to be reborn. "Where were your quarters?"

He led me there, his bare feet stepping easily through the sharpness. He pointed above our heads, saying it would have been there. But now, he gestured to the ground, then stiffened. He knelt down to pick up a small, wooden figure.

"What is it?" I asked.

"A toy . . ." he stared at it for a long time, and I heard wonder in his words. "From when I was a child." He held it out to me. A meticulously carved, wooden soldier holding a long, straight sword at his side. Saalim gripped it tightly. "I can't believe it's here, that I have never found it before. I kept it for so long. When I was a child, I'd pretend to be brave like him. I would stand just the same with my dulled sword at my side." He threw it to the ground, and it broke in half.

He moved on to the edge of the palace where the dunes overlooked the sea. I quickly picked up the now-legless soldier, tucked it beneath the band at my hips, and went to stand beside him.

Wrapping my arm around his waist, I leaned into him.

"You are not the same man you used to be. You are no coward."

"How can I be anything but? I am bound to obey. Bravery is not a choice I have."

"That isn't true." I stood in front of him, between Saalim and the sea, forcing him to look at me. "Bravery doesn't have to be what we hear in the stories, Saalim. Big and heroic. Perhaps that soldier," I pointed back to where he'd thrown the toy on the ground, "was very scared. And taking that sword in his hand was the bravest thing he'd done in his life. Maybe he never went to battle.

"Bravery can be small—like when you came to me that rainy morning in the prison tents because you needed to apologize, to confess. Or when I asked you to let us stay forever here and you told me no. Or letting Aashiq have me, because you knew he was good."

Saalim grimaced at the memories.

"Doing something despite what it costs you. Doing something hard when you could choose something easy. That is brave." *Telling me this tale and showing me, finally, all of you. That is brave.*

He pressed his mouth to my brow but said nothing. His heart pounded against my ear. My heart thudded its reply. They banged on their cage walls, calling to each other. But neither Saalim nor I acknowledged their cries.

Saalim was trapped in the darkness of his home, lost in the dust he'd kicked up from his tale. It was not the beautiful city we had been to before. It was the ruins of a family, of a life, of dreams and a future. Saalim had given everything to save what mattered to him most.

Could I do the same?

Though I did not want to face my choice, we could not stay here. I did not want Saalim to linger in the aching remains of his home any longer.

"Can you take me back to the oasis?"

"Of course." He tightened his arms around me, and we were returned.

I felt like I had been pulled from one world and had been plunged into the next. The images of a roiling sea, a fallen family, and a crumbled home were taken and rapidly replaced with the memories of what happened with my father, with Omar and Ibrahim. They came barreling at me as the fear of my future pummeled my gut.

Saalim spoke. "I am sorry you have to do this."

"What do you mean?" The toy soldier's sharp edges poked into my skin, and I carefully removed it, tucking it beside a rock when Saalim looked away.

"That you have to make this decision. That you have been given no better alternative. I know that you have hoped for something else, a different answer to this problem. And now you are left with no time for that to come. It is not fair—none of your life has been, Emel. I am sorry for that burden."

"Thank you," I said, my voice strained.

Burden. That was the second time he had mentioned my burden that day.

Kneeling by the pool, I dipped my fingers into the water. The sun was low in the sky and shining its light through the trunks of the trees onto my face. My reflection peered up at me from the sapphire pool. My eyes reminded me so much of my father's, I had to look away. Fear gnawed at my insides. The water was cool, and I wanted to submerge myself in it, hoping it would dull the throbbing ache.

"Let's get in," Saalim said suddenly.

"What?"

"I feel how much you desire it." He smirked, his anguish leaving him the longer we stood in the oasis. "I remember the day I brought you here, you wanted to jump right in. Imagine how hard a time I had then, trying not to imagine you without clothes in the water."

"You're trying to distract me," I said, turning to him.

"Is it working?"

I smiled, and his grew wider. "Yes. I've always wondered what it is like. But if I get in," I slipped off my shoes, "promise me you will answer one more question."

"The last one ever?" He said, and as soon as the words left his mouth, he looked to regret them, realizing that it very well might be.

I dipped my toes into the water. I rapidly pulled them out as I shivered. "It's as cold as the sea." I placed a foot in again, stepping further into the pool, and hesitated when the water came to my calves, soaking the hem of my pants. My teeth chattered.

He moved beside me and swiftly unwrapped the sash from his waist and let his pants fall from his hips. The light of the setting sun hit him square in the chest, casting his long shadow onto the rocks, between the trees, and out onto the desert behind him.

I marveled at him in the light. I noted every detail, the rise and fall of his chest as he breathed, the veins on his hands, the length of his fingers. They were not mine to see forever, so I would remember them now.

He stepped past me and into the water without flinching. He sat down, the water coming up to his chest, bright against his skin. So opaque was the azurite water, I could not see his long body beneath its surface.

"Come in," he said to me, his eyes flashing to mine. "It'll get warmer." He raised his hand to me, the water dripping from his fingers.

I laced my fingers in his and stepped into the water, its coldness causing me to tremble. My bottoms were soaked up to my hips. As I stepped nearer to Saalim, I felt the water warm.

"How?" I asked, edging closer.

"Magic." The corners of his mouth turned up with amusement.

Bending my knees, I was submerged in the shallow pool. The water was pleasant surrounding him, and I wondered how much of the warmth was magic and how much was from the heat that seeped from his body. When I was within reach, he unfastened my top and peeled my bottoms from my legs. He took the soaked garments and tossed them behind him. The fabric dried in midair and fell into a quiet heap atop the sand.

The water rose to my chest. My long hair stuck to my skin and coalesced into inky, wet tendrils within the blue pool. The sun's light hit me fully now, and Saalim gazed at me slowly. I wondered if he was noting every detail as I had done to him. His eyes wandered over my hair, my face, my neck, and shoulders. His gaze fell down to my breastbone and he seemed to stare just a little too long, his eyebrows gathering, his lips pursed.

"What is it?"

He shook his head and pulled me to him. "It's nothing."

That was a lie. "There is still something I do not understand," I said. "You told me that you had not wanted me to know the tale of Madinat Almulihi, because you did not want to burden me with it. What did you mean? I want you to be free regardless of whether or not your freedom returns Madinat Almulihi. It changed nothing for me, only allowed me to understand better who you are."

"I thought it obvious," he said, looking puzzled. "The mark, of course."

"My scars?" I tilted my head and reached my fingers back to touch the raised skin.

"No, not your scars. Your mark." He stared at me, and when he saw that I did not understand, he asked, "You don't know?"

"Know what?" I grew anxious. "What are you talking about?"

He reached his fingers toward my chest, pushing my hair away and gently touching the place above my heart.

"Right here," he said slowly, his voice a mixture of curiosity and concern. "You almost glow. I thought you knew—that the healer told you?"

"What?" I looked down.

I could see now, in the direct light of the sun, that there was a radiance to my skin, resembling Saalim's skin in that area alone. A golden sheen invisible out of the sun's direct light. I brought my hand up and rubbed at it, noting the subtle increase in the temperature of my skin. I checked my fingers to see if it came off. There was nothing on my fingertips.

The healer? He had told me nothing.

But then I thought back to that evening, and I realized he had told me. He had pointed to my chest and said I was marked. Then, *this love is like a draught of poison . . . Do not hesitate to drink.*

The pieces were all there, but I could not place them. Could not yet understand.

"What is it?" I asked.

"You are marked by the magic of jinn. By my magic. I first noticed it at the Haf Shata party, but I did not realize what it was then. How it is here, on you, I will never understand. I didn't do that. I would never . . . It is like a part of me was pressed here." He was perplexed as he stared, tracing the area with his fingers over and over. It was like he, too, was trying to remove it.

I remembered the morning in the prison when I clutched the small pile of golden dust that had been left behind on my mat. How I pressed it to my chest in desperate longing for his return. Embarrassment flooded me at the memory. Saalim saw the change in my face and reached his hand to my chin, pulling it up so I looked at him.

"When?" he asked.

I explained. I told him how I had felt so confused yet excited by him. How never, before that morning, had I felt fluttering moths in my stomach that the stories describe of women falling in love. Even Aashiq, though I had indulged in dreams of a future shared with him, did not cause a stirring in me like Saalim.

He listened, taking my hands into his as he did, then his face crumpled, and he pulled me to him and wrapped his arms around me. He clung to me tightly, desperately, like he was scared I was going to fly away.

He said, "Not long ago, I began hearing rumors from the mouths of cavalier guards and servants. Those that serve your father but consider themselves part of the Dalmur. I heard them say that the healer had found the marked one. A woman of the palace would be the one who would right the desert. The healer had told the woman, they said, so she knew. So they had to sit back and wait."

"But that was so long ago. Why did they attack at the Haf Shata party?"

"After the men were killed, I presume the healer told all of the Dalmur about you. They did not want more senseless deaths."

"And now, they wait for me because," I waded through a haze of disbelief and uncertainty, "I . . . I carry your mark."

"Do you see why I am upset? Do you see why I did not want you to know my part of the story?"

I shook my head, pulling away from him.

"All of my life, I have wanted freedom from Masira, from my blind cage. But then I found you, and for once, Emel, I have not thought of it. I have thought of nothing but you. I want nothing more than to be around you, with you. I want nothing less than I want to be free right now.

"I did not understand it before, but when I realized what this was . . . I understood it all, though I wished so desperately for another explanation." He touched my chest. "Your father says you are marked and that is why you do not belong amongst the ahiran. He does not recognize how right he is. Yes, you are scarred." His fingers trailed along the ridges on my back. "But that does not matter. You are marked by the jinn." His fingers pressed mine against my chest. "That can only be sanctioned by Masira. You do not belong amongst the ahiran, Emel, because you belong to something higher. When you chose me, Masira chose you." His eyes were lit with fear, and he looked down to the surface of the water. "And I hate it, because she has taken your decision from you."

When you desire it least. Watch for the one who carries your mark.

All of the pieces slammed into me, together at last.

So I had to free him.

Was I the only one who could? Or was it that there would never be a time again when everything came together as the enchantress described? Perhaps anyone could free him, but only I could resurrect a city, uncover a gentler desert.

How had everything converged at once? Was it that Masira arranged it all? Or was it coincidence and all of these things could have happened at any time? Matin and his soldiers had known my father had Saalim. After so many years in the Salt King's possession, the jinni was no longer a secret. I wondered how they finally learned. What drove them to come? When had my mother learned about Saalim's existence? I remembered the occasions where she asked me if I was in love, if I was seeing someone. Did she suspect that I was seeing Saalim? She must have. She gave me her necklace with the mark of Saalim's home, what all of the Dalmur had, surely hoping that if they carried the mark and found the jinni, they could bring about the change. She must have hoped I would piece it all together. She thought if I held the mark, I could free the jinni to bring about the resurrection of Madinat Almulihi. Maybe she even dreamed I would live there one day.

Mama, if only you knew.

I touched my fingers to my chest where a golden warmth was imprinted on my skin. I was suddenly scared as I understood what I must do.

Saalim interrupted my thoughts. "Emel, I love you. And not because you are marked. I would carve that magic from your chest myself if it meant I could have you forever. I don't care about that. I don't care what Zahar said.

"You are the wind through the leaves, the feathers of an eagle's wings, the current of the ocean, the smell of the desert during rain. You give me life, Emel, so how could I live without you? Please, don't think of my freedom. It is not what I want." In his pleading, I could see that he was desperate, he was terrified.

I said, "You ask too much. To not think of you, to not think of the people who weep with hope that something will change, to ignore the people who will die when my father fails to open the salt trade again. How can I ignore that? How can I choose—"

"Please," he said earnestly as he kissed my face and neck and fingers and hands. His mouth, his touch conveying what he did not say aloud. "You can't stay in this life, Emel. You can't go with Ibrahim."

"I have an impossible choice," I said. "It is so easy for you to ask me to spare myself, damn the desert to Eiqab's sun, leave you imprisoned for eternity. But Saalim, the weight of that decision will be on my shoulders for the rest of my life."

Quietly, he said, "I made the choice for my people and home, Emel, and the heaviness of that decision stays with me. I don't want you to make the same mistake. Don't leave yourself behind for the sake of everyone else. No, you will not carry the same guilt, but you will be miserable in different ways. Choosing yourself can feel wrong. But often, it is the most important thing you can do."

Did Saalim wish he had fought the soldiers? Chosen to face his death in futile defense of his home?

I saw as his eyes met mine how much he meant what he said, heard the pain in his voice. With Saalim, I was loved, I was safe. I thought of what and who I was before him—a small, sad woman. I had not known how much fuller life could be when shared with someone who loved me and whom I loved back. How could I wish for my freedom? How could I wish for his? How would I choose?

Considering how I might craft my wish, the structure of my words and the intention of my heart, I thought of what I could say and feel that would bring about what I wanted. Freedom for us both. I had to believe that we could have a life together, an unbound future. I had to believe like the Dalmur believed. My breath caught in my throat.

He said a future together was impossible, but I did not have to allow that to be true. Why couldn't I fight like the Dalmur? Why couldn't I fight with them?

"Saalim," I said, breathless. "I love you."

I placed my hand on his cheek softly. Though I am sure he had felt it in my longing for him, I wanted him to hear it from my lips. Before I made my decision. As the sunlight reflecting from the water touched his face, I saw that in his smile, there was sadness. The unforgettable impossibility of our love always circling like a vulture.

"You can love a jinni, a man owned by another?"

"I can love you. Even if Masira has given us only this moment, I love you for it all."

And I will find you, Saalim. I will find you no matter what happens to us. I will fight for us, come what may.

He reached his hands around my neck and pulled me to him, pressing his mouth roughly against mine. Unrestrained need broke from him as he held me firmly against his chest. I crawled atop his lap as he leaned back against the sandy bank of the pool. His eager fingers travelled over my shoulders and arms then moved down over my body into the depths of the water. My hands followed in kind, tracing greedily over his jaw, neck, and chest. Feeling him, cherishing him. Echoing his hands beneath the surface of the pool.

My hands found him waiting for me, so I rose to meet him, my chest briefly rising above the water. His gaze traveled across my skin, the golden flare above my heart. He cried out into the sky—a sound of agony and ecstasy and despair. Had the world been awake, had it not been stilled for us alone, all would have heard his call.

I felt the desperation in how Saalim held me, moved against me, kissed me, breathed into me, pressing his cheek to my chest as I moved atop him. I felt the fear in him. A fear that mirrored mine. The fear of goodbye. As if he knew he was seeing me, touching me, and loving me for the last time. I cradled his head and neck in my hands, trailed my kisses across his lips and face.

I love you for now, I love you forever.

Our limbs tangled together as we loved in the small pool, our worship turning a quiet pond into a crashing ocean.

27

W E ROSE FROM THE POOL. The softest cotton appeared in his hands, and he gently pressed it against my wet skin, kissing the dryness it left behind. We dressed together, as partners do. I let him hold me in his warm arms, inhaling the scent of Madinat Almulihi that rolled off of him. When he kissed me, I relished the taste of him, the feel of his lips on mine. I closed my eyes, committing everything to memory.

Then, I asked him to take me home.

THE SUN returned to the top of the sky. I was back to the moment when Saalim had taken me from the palace. Back to when my father had declared I was to spend the rest of my life as Omar's toy.

We were in front of my home. The guards who stood beside the tent entrance were unmoving, unseeing, unhearing, unaware of the world around them.

"Saalim," I said, voice tight with resolve, "keep time still. I have something I must do."

"What do you plan?" He grew more concerned with each request and my sudden change in mood. I did not explain. Even though Saalim was only bound to protect his master from harm, I could not risk that Masira would sense my intention to interfere with the King and disrupt the magic.

"Just give me time," I said, my tone sharper than I had intended.

"Of course," he replied, bowing his head slightly, looking askance at me.

I walked down lanes and through the rings of tents full of stilled people. I walked slowly, but purposefully, each step requiring an enormous effort, each breath requiring control. If I lost focus, if I lost my restraint, I knew I would turn back. The fear of my choice would consume me.

He asked me to tell him where I was going, what I was doing.

I did not, could not, respond.

When I arrived at the first towering, ivory tent, I stepped past the frozen guards into a long room that was clearly used as my father's keep. There were unmoving slaves hovering over gleaming scimitars, polishing thick daggers, sharpening blades. I had never been in this part of the palace before, but my determination prevented me from lingering, from inspecting the unfamiliar surroundings.

Saalim trailed me as I navigated through the palace until I found myself in the throne room. How different—how small and flimsy—it was from the room Saalim described in the palace of Almulihi. A guard sat upon the ground, his head hanging low, chin resting on his chest, deep in sleep. Piles of loose salt and stacks of salt bricks were scattered around the room. So much salt, all in my father's uncaring hands. It added to my resolve. I would fix this.

I glanced at Saalim, remembering when I had first released him from his vessel. How scared I was then, how different I was now. How little I had understood, how little I had to hope for.

"What is it?" he asked.

"Do you remember when I released you?" I spoke quietly, foolishly not wanting to disturb the statuesque sleeper at the edge of the room.

"Yes," he replied, stepping toward me and taking my hand in his. "I could not believe my fortune."

I looked into his eyes. Concern darkened his gaze. He smiled softly, a coaxing gesture and silent request. It was so vulnerable. A deep ache bloomed in my chest when I looked at him, the pain nearly swallowing me whole. I broke my gaze as a sobbing gasp escaped my throat. I turned from him and walked through to the next room.

"Emel!" Saalim cried, hearing me weep.

It is what must be done. It is what I must do.

I shook my head. Tears spilled down my face. My throat ached with the effort of curbing my cries.

I moved forward. If I hesitated for one moment, I would turn back and beg him to take me back to the blue pool so we could string a hammock and dance under the shadows of leaves until the day I died.

Finally, I found my father's sleeping quarters. Steadying myself, I focused on my intention as though Masira was listening. *I pose no threat to my father, I have no need to harm him.* I repeated it over and over to myself, feeling it in my bones.

Nervously, I peered in. If I overstepped, if I crossed the boundary that Saalim must maintain, the magic would be disrupted. The world would move forward once again, and my father would find me in his room.

The stench in the room was thick—the sour, foul smell of unclean bodies, liquor, and smoke. Though little time had passed, the Salt King was already sprawled on a large mat at the room's center, two wives curled beside him. All appeared as corpses in the preternatural stillness.

I surveyed the room curiously, noting the things that my father treasured. Trunks of salt pressed to the edges of the room, more than I realized he possessed. Baskets of glittering jewels and sparkling dha and fid. Another table strewn with arcing swords and delicate knives, some gleaming, others tarnished. Large, ornate tapestries depicting lovers hung from the cross-beams of the tent, lining the walls with vivid colors that glowed orange from the torch fire. A large armoire against another wall, door hanging open with robes spilling out of its cavernous mouth. Books stacked haphazardly throughout the room.

I thought of what I wanted and needed and how it wouldn't affect my father, wouldn't impair him. My heart beat loudly as I waited for the fire to suddenly flicker, for chests to rise. Quickly, I searched through the scattered things beside my father's bed, through the soft piles of robes near the armoire, through the objects on the tables. After failing to find what I sought amongst the trinkets and robes that were strewn about the room, I looked back to my father.

Saalim watched me, fists clenched. I did not know if he was already fighting to keep the world still or if he worried he would be overpowered by Masira as I did.

I crawled onto the mat, exceedingly careful not to touch the bodies that lay there. I pressed my knee in a soft part of the bed, and one of his wives rolled toward me, her eerily warm skin touching my calf. I nearly yelped but remained focused as I knelt beside my father, heart beating thunderously against my chest.

There was a hiss of breath, and I did yelp before slamming my hand to my mouth and frantically inspected the room for signs of life. But everything was frozen still. It must have just been Saalim.

"What happened?" Saalim said, approaching me.

Pushing my hand to my brow, I said, "It was nothing."

Like a trespasser, I felt around my father's hips and waist. His skin felt like mine, his flesh soft and weak as anybody's. He was not invincible. His face was pinched, as though pained. It was strange, touching him and realizing that he, too, was human. He seemed so small. I continued feeling around, reaching into his pockets, until finally, I heard the telltale clink of metal against glass.

I lifted the robe from his protruding belly and found Saalim's prison. It was empty, fastened to the King's waist by a braided leather belt.

I am no threat to the Salt King, I mean him no harm.

I unbound the vessel and took it into my hands. The clink of the metal chain hitting the glass wall was the only sound in the room to accompany my ragged, uneven breaths as I stepped off of the mat.

We waited, and still the world was unchanged. I relaxed. Now, it was time to act.

"Emel," Saalim said cautiously.

I closed my eyes, steeling myself. Though time did not move, it moved too fast. My time with Saalim disappearing like sand through an hourglass. The agony chased me, desperate to sink its claws in my back.

I inhaled . . . exhaled . . . opened my eyes.

"Before you do anything, tell me what is it you are planning to do." He stepped toward me, pleading.

"I will tell you everything. But first, take me back to the oasis. It is not safe here."

His hands quivered like leaves in the wind as he pulled me into his chest.

WE WERE back where we had been moments before. The world was still, as though everything that was happening would never exist at all. The trees above us were immobile, the water at the heart of the oasis like glass. Everything stood at a standstill while I, at the mercy of Masira, decided my fate.

"Saalim," I whispered, mostly to myself. Silent tears rolled down my face at his name, at what was to come.

He eyed the vessel in my hand, wary.

"Saalim," I said again, louder this time. "I won't let this be your life. You cannot continue to be a slave to every man who finds you. I love you too much."

"Emel, stop this." He grasped my shoulders tightly, fear etched onto his face. "I have told you this. I don't want my freedom. I don't want it." He spun away and walked out into the desert.

"Wait!" I called after him, my tears slowing as my resolve hardened to iron. "Listen to me. We must restore your home. You must return to Madinat Almulihi as its leader because I love the people in this desert."

He turned around, returning to me with a shaking head. "No. I do not want it. I do not want anything without you in it." His hands reached up to my face, his thumbs tracing over my drying tears. I stared at his chest, not daring to look in his eyes to see the pain I heard and could feel.

"No, Emel," he whispered. "I do not want my life back if it means that I am to forget you. I can't leave you here in the village at the mercy of your father. I can't let you do that."

"You misunderstand me."

He paused. I looked up to him to see hope breaking through the fear on his face like a sun through clouds. "You mean, you will ask for your freedom?" He sounded so relieved.

I began to pace back and forth in front of him, clutching his vessel tightly in my hand. I fought to string words together to explain. "You made a bargain, and it will be fulfilled."

"I don't understand." His hope was gone. "What are you saying?"

"I have agonized over what I would do about us, thinking it to be an impossible choice. How do I choose between the freedom of a man I love—a man who will become a king and return the desert to what it deserves—and the freedom of myself, an unknown future promised by Masira? How can I choose, knowing that we could lose *us* in the process? I misunderstood the entire time, Saalim. Perhaps just like you.

"It does not have to be one or the other. We do not have to be lost. We can both be free, together." And I felt it then, I believed it with every thread of who I was.

In his eyes, I saw that he felt the same thing I did—the promise of possibility.

I stopped pacing and stood before him.

"Because I am marked, Saalim, everything changes. I will choose us, Saalim." I took a deep breath. "But first, I must choose myself." I continued. "You speak of bravery when one faces an enemy head-on, knowing they are doomed to fail. I do not think it brave. Had you run out onto those steps and fought those soldiers only to die, it would have been a foolish sacrifice. You gave the enchantress everything to save your home. Running from battle to seek her help did not make you a coward. You were smart.

"The tales we tell in my village would paint me to be selfish for my choice. For first choosing myself over a great civilization and King. Or they would say I was a coward for wishing for my freedom rather than earning it with cunning or sword. But I am no fool. To choose to fight my father? I would die. And that is a fate I am not ready for.

"So if I have only the choice to run or fall, I must choose to run. So I will run from here, Saalim." I grasped his hands in mine. "If Masira is generous and allows you to go with me, then I will free you, too. But if we are separated . . . if we are a world away from each other—"

Saalim opened his mouth as if to object.

I did not let him speak. "We have to prepare for that possibility." I gripped his hands more tightly. "If you aren't with me, I will come back, because I will join the Dalmur. I will fight for you. Forever. Because I am making my choice for you, for me, and for us.

"All of the people who carry your mark are waiting, Saalim. They are looking for their king. And when I am free, I will join their hunt, because I understand now that I am the only one who can succeed.

"Because I will be the one who wishes, and you are the one who grants it, we will still have our memories of each other. It will be just like you said. And so no matter what happens, we will always be linked. And you will feel me when I call to you. You can find me, so you will help me, right? We will circle each other like vultures in the sky."

He nodded, smiling with understanding.

"I will do everything I can." Hope was there again, bright and shining.

"I promise you I will set you and this desert free." The more I spoke, the stronger I felt.

Saalim pulled me to him and clasped me as tight as he could, breathing me in.

"You are as fierce as a hawk," he murmured into my ear. "So go and be free of your cage." He brushed his fingers against the fabric covering my chest. "Everywhere you are, I am. I trust you, my love, and I will wait for you always."

And so this was it. Tears fell from my face anew as we held each other for the last time. Then I stepped back and opened his vessel.

"Saalim, I wish for you to return to your vessel." If I was going to wish for my freedom, I was going to be the master of Masira's magic, not just a recipient of the goddess' fickle generosity.

The jinni looked up at me, eyes full of sad hope, as he disappeared into a cloud of dust that slowly fell into the sand.

The wind blew, the leaves rustled. At the return of the jinni into his prison, time could no longer be held at bay.

I clutched the vessel, now closed and filled with swirling golden smoke, and pressed my mouth to it. "I love you," I whispered, hoping he felt my devotion.

Then, I opened the jinni's prison.

I did not know that it would be for the last time.

I did not know that nothing would go as planned, that Masira could be so devious.

28

THE GOLDEN SMOKE BLOOMED out into the oasis until it slowly coalesced down into the shape of the jinni. Seeing him like that, with his head bowed and shoulders curved forward, I wavered. Would it be better to free him? Could I live another day knowing he was still a slave to Masira, to his master, trapped in his prison?

"Emel," he said quietly, breaking through my doubt, "have you a wish?"

I sucked in a shaking breath. I hoped that I was not wrong, misled. I hoped I would still have him with me when freed, but if not, I hoped I would find him.

Only the one who wished will remember what was before. The one who wished and the jinni who granted it. Saalim had told me so long ago. I was relying on that truth.

"Emel?" Saalim asked, sensing my reluctance. He looked up. "You must do it. You must be free."

I looked into his eyes and saw his heartbreak, his hope, his fear. I ran to him, tossing his vessel into the sand beside us, and fell into his arms.

"I hope—" I began.

"It will work," he assured me.

"If we are apart, I will miss you. However long it takes for me to find you, I will miss you every moment." My tears came again. "I hope I find you," I whispered, and I felt Saalim pull me even closer to him.

I was sure I would be sent far from my home—how else would I reach my freedom? I did not dare to hope that I would be freed and still within reach of the vessel. That would be much too simple, and Masira was not so generous. Would Saalim and his prison be left in the oasis? Surely he would be found by someone else. Would it be the Salt King again, Nassar, or someone else entirely? I only hoped it was someone kinder than the King, so that while I joined the Dalmur's hunt, he did not suffer.

"I love you," he said to me. I heard the aching sadness in his voice.

Finally, I pulled my head back and looked into Saalim's agonized face, his glistening golden eyes. I held his face in my hands and mouthed, *I love you.* I kissed him, just once, on his cheek.

Masira did not care about small sacrifices of water and salt. She heard real sacrifice. So I would sacrifice everything I had, just like Saalim had once done—my family, my home, my love. *Take it all from me, Masira, if it means you will listen.* I hoped She heard. I hoped She would deliver. I soaked in everything I wanted to come from this wish, let it saturate me—my hopes for Saalim, for myself, for my home and sisters. And I couldn't resist, I thought of my father. That one day, Masira would give him everything he had given us.

With indisputable resolve, I leaned to Saalim's ear. "Saalim, I wish for freedom from the Salt King." My words were simple but my heart said so much more.

Had his mouth not been near my ear, I would have missed his words. "Master, I obey."

Still holding the jinni, I waited to feel something—a tingling in my chest or my toes or my fingers. But I felt nothing.

Suddenly, Saalim's back arched. A gut-wrenching scream ripped from him, and he clung to me as though I were an anchor to a world that he was being washed from. He roared a single broken *no*.

"Saalim?!" I shrieked, pushing away from him.

"Emel!" He cried, staring at his hands.

It was the last word he would speak to me, and it echoed into the desert for only a moment before it was snuffed out like a flame.

The jinni held his arms before him, looking with terror at the changes in his body. The gold of his skin was leeched from his body into the golden, petaled manacles. And when they had swallowed all, they fell from his wrists and dropped dully onto the ground.

"No, no, no!" I yelled. "What is happening?! I didn't wish for this! This isn't what I wanted!"

Saalim could not respond. His hands, then arms, feet, then legs, began to swirl violently with a hot wind that seemed to tear him apart, removing him one grain at a time. His extremities disintegrated into dust, swirling wildly around him. Saalim spared his limbs only a moment's glance before he looked back to me, a tortured expression on his face.

I tried to grab him, prevent the magic from taking him away. But when he was only dust and wind, there was nothing I could take hold of. I screamed, tormented as I watched Saalim being pulled apart, as I watched him splinter into dust.

I couldn't make sense of it. I had not yet wished for his freedom. It couldn't happen yet. How would we find each other?

"Saalim!" I cried again and again until there was nothing left of him. The golden ash fell without a sound, leaving not a single trace.

Had I misspoken? Had I said *your* freedom?

As I gazed at the empty place where Saalim used to be, I began to understand implication of what I had done. I felt like a fool. I had been so confident, so sure that I was doing the right thing. That my fate was in my hands when I held Saalim's vessel.

I was so wrong. My fate was in the hands of Masira, and She was a fickle goddess. She might listen, She might hear, but She would do as She pleased. Like the card games with my sisters, unless I held the strongest card, I could never be sure to win. Masira would always have that card. Why did I let myself forget it?

Enormous regret crushed me, and I collapsed onto the ground where Saalim had fallen, clawing at the earth to find some part of him that proved to me that he was not gone. I found his vessel, and when I saw that it was empty, I sobbed.

I looked down at my clothes, the same clothes I had worn when I saw Ibrahim. They were unchanged. My fingernails were the same, my black hair still long. I looked up to my village, also unchanged. Still a massive huddle of tents with a white palace at its center.

Saalim was gone, and I was still an ahira. I would never be able to find him. I would never see him again. And I would be sent to Omar to live the rest of my life as his whore. I scooped the sand where he had fallen into his empty vessel, apologizing to him through my cries for my foolishness, that I had done wrong, that I had misjudged everything. I clung to the golden manacles that lay unmoving on the ground, still hot from his skin. I pulled it all into my chest as I curled into myself.

When I had no tears left, when I was filled only with dry, aching grief, I rose from the ground, covered in sand. I winced in pain. How long had I lain on the desert floor? My muscles were cramped, my shoulders tired, my skin rubbed raw from the sand.

But that was nothing compared to the agony in my chest.

With a small glimmer of hope, it occurred to me that if Saalim was no longer a jinni, perhaps he had returned to his home. Did Madinat Almulihi stand once again? But I could not get there. I would not be able to find him. I had no camel, no direction-telling bawsal, no caravan to take me.

The desert had not changed. There was no new sand beneath my feet, no great rumble that brought forth a kinder desert from beneath the one I knew. Saalim was gone.

Fear began to rise. If time was moving forward, if I was still an ahira, I would soon be missed. I considered the amount of time that had passed. The sun dropped from the high point in the sky. Dusk would arrive soon, and I would be delivered to Ibrahim.

I found the broken soldier toy stowed beside the rock. Staring at the small carvings a knife long ago had made, I touched the planes of his face, the hilt of his sword, holding it like it was the most delicate thing in the world. It was. The hammered gold that had encircled Saalim's wrists was now cold, and again, I felt the visceral ache of grief. The pain all lovers dread—the mourning pang of a forever goodbye.

If Masira would not allow it, then I would find my freedom another way. I would not return home. I would not return to my father. I would either find somewhere to live uncaged or let Eiqab turn me to dust.

Holding everything that remained of Saalim to my chest, I took several measured steps toward the emptiness that waited on the other side of the trees. I could run. I could be free.

Then, I saw smoke from the depths of the desert. It startled me back to reality, and I stared at it. A narrow, billowing cloud rose up from beside a dune. Then, a blur of black emerged, the dust it kicked up rising like a specter.

Someone on horseback, I realized. Probably a runner, as they were the few who used horses. My heart raced as my gaze flashed from the approaching runner back to my village. Runners always approached the oasis, and Nassar always came out to meet them. I could not linger. I had to move. I glanced once more at the empty horizon behind me—did I walk into its yawning jaws? Let it take me forever?

No. This life deserved one more try. I would not leave it yet. I would hide in the village. Firoz would help. If another caravan approached, I would escape with them. I didn't care what the cost was, I would find a way to pay it, and I would take Firoz with me. Tavi, if she'd come.

I sprinted back to my home. The gold manacles, toy soldier, and sand-filled vessel were pressed securely against my chest as I sprinted back to the tents. They chimed together in a percussion that matched my footsteps and quick breaths.

When I came upon the edge of tents, several guards ran out to me, shouting. "What are you doing? How did you get out here?" One barked, baffled by my bright ahira clothes and lack of coverings.

"A runner comes!" I yelled, pointing to the horizon. I ran between the guards. They made little attempt to stop me, the approaching runner of far greater interest.

I tore through the village. The few people outside stared at me with mouths agape.

Firoz was not in his shop tent, so I ran to his home. I did not care about propriety anymore.

"Firoz!" I called outside his home. "Firoz!"

His mother hustled out, flustered and obviously annoyed. Her eyes widened when she saw me. An ahira with tear-stained cheeks, clutching treasure and screaming for her son was not a sight she expected.

Firoz fell out of the home behind her. "Emel!?" He cried, equally surprised by my state. "What's wrong?"

I broke down again. "I had the jinni, Firoz. I had him! And I could have freed him but I chose to free myself instead, and it didn't work." I sobbed, proffering the jinni's things as if it explained everything. "And I'm going to be sent away. A runner is coming—another caravan is near. Nassar won't let them in, so we will need to go out to meet them. Ready yourself! We will run away together."

His mother's face whipped between her son and I, alarm keeping her silent.

Firoz placed his hands on my shoulders. "Slow down, Emel. Explain it all again."

"I did everything wrong." I again showed him what was in my hands. "And I lost him."

Turning back to his mother, as he felt my shivering, he said, "Mama, can you get her something to cover herself?" She obeyed wordlessly and returned with a worn abaya before she retreated back into her home. Firoz took my things from me so I could dress.

"Be careful!" I said as he cradled them. I didn't care that I sounded crazier than Rafal.

Firoz was mesmerized by the vessel—the flowers and moons that were carved into its metal bands. "There was a jinni?" He asked. "He was in here? You knew him?" His eyes grew wide with disbelief.

As I pulled the abaya over my shoulders, I began to explain. But I was interrupted by the clamor of tolling bells.

The warning bells.

Firoz and I looked at each other, and I took Saalim's things from him again.

"Not a caravan then," Firoz whispered.

"The Dalmur?" I asked, daring to hope. Maybe they'd rallied after all, decided not to wait on the girl from the palace, and come to find the jinni. I could make myself known to them, tell them I'd already freed him! They could take me with them back to Madinat Almulihi.

Firoz's brow creased in concern. "I haven't heard of any such plans."

"I have to get home," I said. "I have to find Tavi."

"Emel!" Firoz called at my back as I fled the tent.

I stopped and looked back to him, chest heaving.

"If you've a chance to leave," he said as he ran to me. "Come find me. Take Rashid and me with you."

"I won't leave you," I promised.

Tearing through the village, I wove between the people who had stepped out of their homes to locate the source of the alarm. My frantic sprint through the lanes only heightened their panic. Some rushed into their homes, desperately closing the fabric of their tent in a hopeless attempt to protect themselves from whatever was coming. I remembered Saalim's story of the day Almulihi fell to attackers, of a people whose king had not adequately readied them to defend themselves.

The king died, and the city was destroyed.

I ran faster.

ENTERING THE palace was too easy, under the circumstances. I tugged up my abaya so they saw my ahira clothes and told them I'd no time to answer questions. The guards were far too concerned at the prospect of war to care about a king's disobedient daughter. When I arrived at the tent I shared with my sisters, there were no guards out front. I slowed my steps. My thoughts raced through the wording of my wish again. Had Masira taken my sisters from me when I wished for freedom from the Salt King? Or did not even the King's daughters matter when there was a threat? Wary, I peeled the fabric apart and stepped into the room.

It was empty, but my sisters' mats were strewn about in a familiar way. I exhaled. They still existed, they just weren't here. I ran to my mat, lifting it from the ground. I found the tile, necklace, and flower folded inside the cloth beside the rolled map. But where was the salt? I frantically searched for the sack the jinni had given me. I tore into the ground as the salt suddenly became pivotal to my believing the jinni had ever existed. I flung sand behind me. *No, no, no. I could not lose him again.*

Finally, my fingers snagged on camel's wool.

With quivering hands, I pulled the sack from the sand. Salt was still piled within. I turned it over, dumping most of the salt into the sand— useless to me if there was no caravan to pay for my escape. I kept a little, just in case. I stuffed my tokens of Saalim inside, then slung it over my shoulders with a leather cord.

"Job well done," an age-hardened voice spoke into the tent. The bells clanged loudly around us.

I gasped and turned, wiping my hands on my clothes. The healer stood just inside the tent, white robes bright in the crimson room.

"What are you doing here?" I asked, backing away.

"I've been waiting for you. I sensed what you did. Felt it right here." He hit his chest with his palm.

I turned my hands up and out beside me. "I didn't do anything. Nothing turned out right."

"It took you a while, yes. It is why they felt they needed to intervene, although they failed as I warned they would. Far more deaths than I wanted. So many innocents lost." He took mincing steps toward me. "Child, if only you knew how many letters we've written about you and the jinni! How long we've hoped for you to understand. We wondered if we should show you the path, tell you what you needed to know. But Isra said you were too stubborn, that you must learn it on your own."

Isra? My mother? She knew this entire time?

He continued, "If we told you how to act, she said you'd do otherwise. Isra is a smart woman, Masira carry her soul."

I staggered back.

He nodded, a toothless grin spreading on his face, his eyes trained on my chest. On my mark. "Child, you were splendid!" He beamed. "You freed him!"

"But I didn't wish for his freedom. I failed." A cry ripped through me. "And now he's gone."

"Masira sees intentions. She saw yours, smart girl. She will deliver us back into the hands of Wahir, Eiqab be damned!" The healer chuckled to himself. His milky eyes danced. He clapped his hands together and laughed louder. "Good girl! Good girl!" he bellowed into the tent, his inked face and arms causing him to appear as a shadow in the white robes that swung around him.

"I don't understand," I said through clenched teeth.

The healer's laughter stopped, and his face softened as if he finally comprehended my bewilderment. He came closer, and leaned toward me. "Perhaps, if you look at your map, it will all make sense." He began to walk away, then stopped. "And once you do, I suggest you find the King. *Your* king," he said, laughing again as he left my tent, leaving me alone.

Kneeling onto the ground, I carefully pulled out my map and unrolled it. I gasped.

It was a still a map of the salt trade, still a map of the desert with all of the settlements I knew. It still had my hand, the ink I'd placed.

But the lines were different, the routes were changed.

Because now, they did not lead to my settlement. They were different, as if turned by invisible hands. They all arced north, to a place that had no cliffs barring its entrance.

They led to a glistening city that sat at the edge of the sea, the words Madinat Almulihi written beside it.

He was home. Now, finally, I laughed, too, rolling my map and stuffing it away. "He's home." I said aloud, and left the tent.

The healer still stood in the lane, his unseeing eyes turned toward the sky, his arms held up in joy. I ran past him, shouting about Saalim's return home. Through the din of the bells, I could hear him behind me.

"You did it!" He cried. "Now we are free!"

As I rushed toward the heart of the palace, the servants' shouts broke through my glee. "A challenger to the throne! The King has been challenged!"

I ran like I raced the wind.

29

"THE KING HAS BEEN CHALLENGED!"

"The Salt King will defend his throne!"

"Did you hear? There is a challenger to the throne!"

As the bells clanged loudly around me, I sped through the palace, tearing through the crowds of servants who cried the news to each other, to their families. Some were concerned, others excited by the impending spectacle.

A small girl stood at the edge of the lane. She watched the panicked people with liquid eyes, her hand in her trembling mouth. She stretched her neck in all directions, and I realized she was lost. When she turned toward me, I saw the red that curved around her face. My neighbor. I didn't want to stop, but I could not leave her behind.

"Little sister," I said, kneeling down to her. "Are you looking for your family?"

She nodded, edging close to me. She leaned against my knee. I pressed my hand to her waist, and she clutched my abaya with her small fingers.

"Your family will find you at home. Know your way back?" I asked hopefully, so she could hurry home and I could hurry to my own family.

"Yes," she said, but she looked in terror at the masses of servants moving toward the heart of the palace to watch the King.

I sighed. "I'll go with you," I said. "Quickly now." I took her hand and began to lead her home, but she took slow, scared steps, so I lifted her onto my hip and carried her.

When we stepped inside her home, her fear transformed into enthusiasm. "Do you want to see my things?"

I was breathless and fatigued from carrying her at such a swift pace. "I can't," I began, but she was already digging through a basket and pulling out a piece of thin parchment and small metal toys.

The bells still clanged, and I bounced on my toes, needing to hurry. I worried about who was coming. What would they do when they got here? Would they tear through the village, through the palace? If it was truly a challenger to the throne, it should not be an attack on the village. Tradition dictated that they would arrive, challenge, and leave if they failed. That was desert rule.

But if they won, what happened afterward was the choice of the new ruler. I did not want to be caught in that fray. I wanted to be there to see the challenger for myself.

The little girl shoved a poorly drawn map in front of me, distracting me from my thoughts. "Like yours," she said proudly.

With awe, I saw that she remembered every detail I had told her of our desert. In her young, inexperienced hand, she had drawn it faithfully.

"This is amazing," I told her, and she beamed. "But there is one more thing you need to add."

I told her of the city that sat by the sea, her child's mind easily forgetting the distress outside to think only of the whimsical city. Despite the urgency of the voices that ran past the tent, despite my desperate need to join them, I pulled out my map to show her what I meant. She took it in her hands, her eyes roaming over it greedily. Pointing to the north, I showed her what she was missing on her own. She nodded, absorbing everything I said.

"Maybe one day you'll see Madinat Almulihi."

She nodded. "When I am big, I am going to have a camel and go all over the desert. I'll find more places and put them on my map. When I come home, I'll show you, so you can fix yours."

I smiled. "That sounds nice. Now, I want you to add the city to your map with as much detail as you can. Work on it until your family gets home, eh? It's important that you stay here."

She agreed.

"If it quiets down out there, you can do one more thing. But *only* if it gets quiet."

She stared at me, listening to my every word with whole attention.

"If you go to my home, you will find a pile of salt in the sand. Collect it in a bag if you have one, or a piece of cloth. I know you have those." I smiled and brushed the piles of clothes around us. "Then, take it back here. Hide it until your parents and brothers come home, and then you can tell them it was a gift." The salt would serve them well, perhaps even buy them a way out of the palace servitude, maybe even a camel to travel with. The girl bobbed her head importantly, taking her two tasks very seriously. I pressed my hands to her cheeks. Then I ran from her tent. I realized I might never see her again, and I did not even know her name. I prayed that she would be safe, that she would not be scared.

In the zafif, I found a single attendant, hustling as she collected various items, locking them away in a chest. She turned toward me when I entered.

"Emel?" Hadiyah relaxed when she realized it was me.

"Hadiyah! Thank Eiqab! Where are my sisters?"

"They are with their mothers, of course. Why aren't you with them? Haven't you heard? There is a challenger to the throne."

"Yes, I've heard! Where are their mothers, then? Where is everyone going?"

"To see the challenge. In the great tent. More men are following the messengers, I believe the challenger is among them. Find your sisters. Find them quickly. Whatever happens . . . you will want to be with them, I think."

My spinning thoughts caught on to Hadiyah's tone, her frantic behavior. "You think the King will die today."

She looked up at me with scared, sad eyes. "Your father is old, and he's sick with grief and gluttony. I don't know what will happen."

I looked to my attendant one last time. I hesitated, unsure if I should say goodbye. I had been so preoccupied with thoughts of Saalim, of myself, that I had not once stopped to consider what it would mean if we had a new king. What would happen to my attendants, my mothers, my sisters. He could be as vile as my father. Or worse.

Running to Hadiyah, I pressed a gentle kiss to her cheek.

"Be safe," I whispered. I found a black scarf and rapidly tied it around my face and hair before heading to the palace tents.

I found my sisters, their mothers with their young children—future ahiran and soldiers—gathered in the tent with my father and his guard, the very tent where the Haf Shata had taken place. A large number of villagers had also joined my family there.

All awaited the arrival of the challenger. The room was bare, no blue carpets piled on the sandy floor, no sapphire fabrics strung on its towering beams.

People streamed into the tent, awaiting the event with nervous excitement. I remembered the challenger of ten years ago—the man plunging to the ground in a graceless death as cries of fierce joy were raised for my father. Would this challenger meet the same fate?

Finally, the bells' toll diminished until none sounded. An eerie silence fell upon the tent, the entire village. I slid beside my silent sisters, my hands pressing to the sack of metal and glass at my waist, preventing them from clanking loudly amongst the murmuring voices.

"Thank Eiqab," Tavi said when I appeared next to her.

Her eyes were red from tears, and she threw her arms around me. "I didn't know where you were. I was so worried."

"I'm here now."

"What's wrong?" She pulled away, looking at my face. "Are you okay? What happened with Father?" Her eyes were round with alarm.

With Father, Ibrahim, and the courting. Sons, that felt like so long ago. I shook my head. "I'll explain later."

Tavi's arm brushed against the sack that I had slung across my shoulders. The metal clanked quietly together. She could feel the jagged edges.

"What do you have?" she whispered, but sensing my reluctance, she bent to my ear. "I love you. Like the desert loves her sun."

I found her hand and squeezed it. "Like the fox loves his moon." It was what our mother had told us when we were children.

We turned to face our father, our hands clasped tightly.

The Salt King paced back and forth. He had hurriedly dressed. Had he still been lying with his wives when the messenger arrived? He wore white robes embroidered with gold that marked him for what he was: the leader of his army, the Salt King. Atop his head was a small golden turban, tied sloppily in his rush. His scimitar swung from his waist as he paced. His guards lingered near him, all clad in white.

There was a loud commotion from outside the tent. The guards were shouting, and unknown men yelled back. The deep sounds of horses chuffing echoed the barking commands of the foreigners. Within moments, the fabric was strung open. Sunlight spilled into the tent along with the dark shadows of men.

In the very place where, months before, I had stood to look out into the desert night, I now saw horses carrying unfamiliar soldiers in tunics of dark gray, black, deep blue, and red. These were the colors of well-traveled men to whom uniforms were unimportant. Flashes of silver shone from their belts and across their chests. Their faces were covered with dark scarves. Their ebony horses, covered in ornate gold and silver tack, danced restlessly

A. S. Thornton

over the sand. Horse travel was not easy in the desert with so few places to graze and drink. These men had planned their journey well, and I wondered where their camel caravans waited for them. The King's guard stood warily beside the intruders, bright in their uniforms of white.

Where had these men come from? If these strangers were to challenge my father and win, we would have a new leader, a new king. I was uneasy, and so, too was my family and the villagers surrounding us. I could feel it in the silence that pervaded the tent, the uneasiness of the people who stood watching, shifting from foot to foot.

The foreign men dismounted from their horses. They took their time settling and tying up their steeds. A few of their men began to remove the tack. So, they planned on a long stay. Wearing the same tunics and headscarves, none stood out as their champion. I felt foolish as we stood and watched the men unhurriedly go about their chores.

When the men had all assembled before the entrance of the tent, a man walked up from the rear of the group. Grasped firmly in his hand was a long wooden pole with a bright blue flag attached to its end, flapping toward the ground. I stilled when I saw the golden details—a flower opened for its crescent moon. My hand flew to my mouth.

So the Dalmur had come again, after all. They had decided to challenge my father officially, surely to win his jinni. Sons, why now? Masira had been flawed in her plan—failing to tell these traveling men that their king was already returned.

I brought my hand up to my forehead. Had I caused this?

If the challenger won, giving me freedom from the Salt King as I wished, what would they do when they did not find the jinni here? I edged away from Tavi and tunneled through the people until I stood at the edge of the ring we had made around my father and his challengers. I could run out, explain that they would not find what they were looking for, that he was gone. Tell them to return home because Saalim was there waiting for them, that their palace and homes would be waiting for them, too.

I tightly closed my eyes, pressing my fingers to my temple. What was I thinking? They would never believe me—I was no one. They wouldn't believe any of us. If they learned there was no jinni to be found, these foreign men might kill us all unless the Dalmur hidden amongst us could convince them otherwise.

"Which of you comes to challenge me?" the King bellowed. "I will not be kept waiting as you delay, fussing with your pets. You are lucky my men have not slain you on the spot for the atrocities your people have committed against mine—a respect not given to my people. It is honor that keeps me standing before you now. Something you know little of." He strode up to the men, babbling about integrity and bravery, his guards flanking him heavily. The King readied his scimitar, holding it low at his hip.

One of the men approached my father alone. He wore dark blue and black, and carried a long straight sword at his side. The King's guards stood erect as the foreigner stepped toward them, their own scimitars ready in their palms. I could not make out the words, only the rumble of men's voices.

I was so focused on the intruders, I had not realized how many more villagers had arrived at the tent, their whispers an incessant hiss behind me. The warmth in the tent climbed as the bodies crammed in. Beaded sweat fell down to my neck, my legs, my arms.

Finally, the King stepped away from the man, his guards at his heels.

"Clear more space!" the guards bellowed at us, and quickly we stepped away, creating a large oval where none but the King, his soldiers, and the foreign men stood. The villagers were packed together now, and I felt people pressed against my back at all sides.

As the white-clad soldiers separated from those in black, my father laughed as though great fun were to be had.

Small children clinging to their mothers looked up in confusion, wondering why they heard laughter when there was so much fear.

The King turned to his audience. I fell back with the crowd, hoping he would not see me. "My people! Thank you for your unwavering support, your loyalty. It has been years since anyone has threatened our village, challenged my throne. Few have been so foolish! But not these people." He cackled at the men clustered together watching his speech without any indication that they were affected by his words.

"Finally, they challenge us like honor demands. No more of their futile, subversive attempts at my life. Today we *will* be victorious." He said calmly to his audience, a wicked smile stretching across his greasy, jaundiced face.

The villagers shrieked their approval, startling me as I watched with breath held.

How could he stand so confidently without the jinni at his side? He did not really think he could out fight the challenger? I shifted my gaze from my gloating father to the eerily calm men who watched him.

"From the barren desert, I have created a kingdom that rivals those of legend! I have spread my seed across the desert, and my power has grown. And you, my beloved people, have stayed by my side, trusting in my strength. Believing in the safety I have provided, in the strength of my army. *Your* army." His arms were stretched wide as he made drunken circles through the sand. "Born from the sands of the desert, I am the strongest king who has ever lived. In the light of Eiqab's sun, I will never fail you."

The people roared their approval. On my toes, I turned to peer behind me. Dozens more villagers had arrived. I was shocked that so many could fit within the tent. The bodies were crushed together, and I clasped my bag tightly as the people pushed closer to their king, pushed at my back, shouting his name in exultation.

"Salt King! Salt King! Salt King!" Their heaving chests pressed against me, their voices loud in my ear.

I held my bag at my chest, clutching Saalim's things tightly. I glanced at my sisters and my father's wives not far behind me. Did they feel the same fear? Most stood wordlessly, dread in their eyes. Only a few had joined in the frenzied chanting of the villagers.

The King gestured for silence.

"Let's end this dallying and get on with it." My father spoke to the crowd, bowing his head subtly, the people hushing their voices one by one to hear his words. Somewhere, a baby cried. The Salt King asked the challenger, "What say you to my people?"

This was the opportunity for the challenger to convince the people that he would be a worthy ruler should my father fall. After his speech, my father and his opponent would release their birds to Masira. Their final sacrifice before battle.

The man spoke to the King, and his words were sharp, vicious. "I am not here to convince your people of anything. I don't care to own this settlement, your people. You have stolen from me, and I am here to take back what is mine."

Gasps emerged from the crowd. The King laughed to himself, waving a hand at the challenger. "On to the birds then. I wish for a rapid victory against this man!" The Salt King said these words carefully, turning toward his adversary. These words were something different, something that his audience did not understand. To them, it was a simple hope. But not to me. I heard it for what it was. It was a desire. A wish.

My mouth fell open.

He does not know. How can he not realize he doesn't have the vessel?

He indeed must have been lying with his wives when he learned of the challenger. He dressed in a rush, assuming the jinni's vessel was still attached to his hip, the jinni still waiting outside his sleeping quarters.

But it wasn't, and the jinni was gone forever. But how did the King even remember the jinni? Shouldn't Masira have erased Saalim from his memories? Maybe Saalim wasn't gone after all. Hope took flight like a broken-winged bird. The cold cuffs and empty vessel dug their hardness into my skin, and I knew I was being ridiculous.

My father stood, chin jutted forward with the ignorant confidence of a child. He had cast his wish, like always. He did not have to wonder if it would be fulfilled. It always was. His jinni was always there.

Of course he wished for his victory. He was an ill, weak man who could never defend the throne on his own. Without Saalim, he was nothing.

I bit my lip to keep from laughing aloud, humor emerging from the sea of hysteria. *Eiqab help us all for what we are about to witness.*

I looked behind me, seeking an exit. Could I still escape? I could run from the tent and hide before my village fell to these wild men who furiously destroyed everything in their hunt for the jinni they would not find on the Salt King. People were crushed together, hopelessly close from where I stood at the edge of the oval all the way to the tent's exit. I could see people had even gathered outside. There would be no fleeing.

The Salt King stepped toward his challenger, the faceless, nameless man. He explained the ceremony of the birds, spitting the words at the challenger while we all leaned in, desperate to hear this meeting of light and dark. It struck me then—surely, I was watching my father's last moments.

I hated the King and the court he created. I hated everything he believed in and fought for. But he was my father. I remembered what Saalim told me of his beginning, that he was not always an evil man. He stood before the challenger so confidently, so foolishly. Tears filled my eyes as I understood that I would lose him that day. I would be someone's child no longer. And it was something I had done to myself. If I hadn't made the wish . . . if Saalim hadn't been freed . . .

But then I thought of my mother, of my sisters, of my villagers, of the desert, of the Dalmur. All harmed—or killed—because of my father's greediness, his need to put his possession of the jinni over everything else. We had all been dealt hands by Masira at birth. Some may have had it worse than others, having to do more to get less. But one could not judge a person by the hand they were dealt, only by how they played it.

My father had become a monster from the choices he made. He was a cruel man who had doled out his savagery willingly. He warranted no sympathy of mine.

He deserved the fate Masira devised for him.

30

T HE KING SPAT ON THE GROUND at the challenger's feet and turned away. "Nassar! Bring the bird!" The King commanded. His gold-topped head swiveled back and forth, searching for his vizier. "Nassar!" he tried again.

The challenger's men stirred, many eyeing one man among their ranks curiously before looking to the King again.

The King waited then stormed to his guards.

"Your highness," a man stepped forward clutching a small wooden cage, ignoring the King's blunder. "I am here, I have it." The man held the cage forward, revealing the agitated quail inside its walls.

"Who are you?" The King spat. "Where is Nassar?"

The man was taller than my father, but he looked very small as he bowed his head forward.

"I am your vizier? Ah—Ahmed?" He said sounding as confused as my father.

"Nassar, do you know this man?" The challenger said to one of his men. There was a mockery in his tone, a simmering violence behind each of his words. I was chilled despite the suffocating heat.

A small man stepped forward and went to the challenger. When he turned in my direction, I gasped aloud.

But I was the only one.

"No, sir, I do not." It was Nassar, the King's vizier, wearing the enemy's clothes, covered in dust like all the rest as if he, too, had ridden into the village on an enemy horse, his loyalty pledged to another. Aside from my own confusion there was no reason to believe it a charade.

The King saw it, too. "Nassar?" he boomed, furious. "Eiqab's fury! What pathetic act is this? You will be sent to death for this treason!" The King backed several steps away from the challenger, from his vizier, outraged. None of the King's guard went to him, none offered their support.

None but Ahmed, who seemed desperate to rein in his King's madness. "Shall you release the bird now?"

The spectators murmured to each other, confused by the turn of events. The people looked at their king, looked to the man named Nassar as if they'd never seen him in all their lives. The guards dithered beside my father, unsure of what to do. Villagers and guards alike all nodded their heads at Ahmed's suggestion, eyes wide. *Sons, let us move this shameful spectacle along.*

My hand shook as I pressed it to my chest, disbelieving what I saw. None knew who Nassar was. It was like he had never existed.

They were not confused by the blatant rebellion of Nassar as I was, because they did not know him. In this new reality, in this world where Saalim did not exist as a jinni, Nassar was not a part of the King's most trusted men.

My mind spun. What was Nassar doing with them? Why, in this changed world, would he be loyal to them? I ran through my memories of him. How he came to the village, how quickly he ascended to the role of vizier. His sycophantic behavior as the King's second in those early days, compared with how he had acted in the recent past, so incongruous with the malevolence I had come to expect from him.

Was Nassar the missing piece? Was he the reason the Dalmur knew of the jinni? It had to be. It had to have been him all along. My fingers clasped the metal through my bag as I realized Nassar was never loyal to the Salt King. He was always loyal to the people of Madinat Almulihi, to the Dalmur.

Nassar, like the others, was searching for his lost king, his better desert.

The attacks, the poisoning, the undermining of the Salt King's sense of security . . . it all began with Nassar.

Rumors of the King's impossible wealth and sudden termination of his nomadic ways surely had drawn the attention of those legend-seeking people. Nassar's unknown history, his arrival on camelback *alone* all those years ago. My mind whirled. He must have been a spy for the Dalmur to learn if the King had called on magic to obtain his power. Had they spies in settlements all over the desert?

Once he became the King's vizier, surely he had seen the immense piles of salt, the King's impossible, unflagging strength, heard tales of his improbable feats. Did he glimpse the jinni? Or did he just see the same golden cuffs on different slaves and soldiers? Either way, Nassar—at least the Nassar I had known—must have come to find the jinni, and he found him. And once he was sure, he had summoned an army of navy and gold to come fetch their prize.

After all, was it not Nassar who was responsible for meeting the runners and messengers, approving or denying their entrance to our home? Matin had been only the beginning. I remembered how Nassar had led the man into the throne room. How he had seemed so oblivious to Matin's agitation. Of course, it was all an act. He was leading the predator right to its prey.

Then why hadn't Nassar simply stolen the jinni when he learned of Saalim so long ago? I considered my father and his obsession with the vessel. That it was always to be found in the palm of his hand or fastened to his waist. It was a mere accident that he had left it behind when Matin attacked, the suddenness of it all causing him to forget himself. His beloved vessel, lost amongst the fray. There had been no attack since the last challenger to the throne ten years prior. Of course the King was caught unaware, careless. Otherwise, he was never without it. There was no way Nassar could have stolen it short of stealing it off the King's own body, which he never could have done with sentries standing guard around him. He could not have killed the King, either. Not with the jinni who was commanded by a wish always to protect his master from death.

Nassar could not have taken the jinni by himself. He needed the help of others. Matin, the Dalmur. But really, he needed Saalim.

Only I could do it, because I had jinni's magic at my fingertips.

My mind raced through the last few moons, when Nassar's harshness toward me whittled away to something akin to benign neglect.

What changed? I tore away at my web of memories, trying to understand. I bit my lip, eyes shut tight, rubbing my forehead, tearing, tearing, tearing . . . My hand dropped to my side. I looked up.

He had known this whole time.

Nassar knew I was meeting with Saalim. He must have suspected it after I had arrived back in the palace from the oasis, when he heard me speaking with a man but found me impossibly alone. But, of course, he was not yet convinced. No.

Not until he saw me speak with the slave who wore Saalim's golden manacles at the courting or until he saw me fling an unfeasible amount of salt into the chest of the guard as I fled my home in search of Firoz. The day he had been standing with the healer.

Surely, too, the healer had told Nassar a king's daughter was the woman they sought—the woman bearing the jinni's mark. So then, they just needed to wait. They placed their hope in me, trusting I could do it.

And I did.

But, what about *this* Nassar? Why was he here now, with these men? Why didn't they know?

"Bring me Anisa," the challenger called. A man from outside walked in with an enormous golden eagle on his forearm. Whispers traveled through the crowd. Eagles were not easily manned. And to have traveled such a distance showed a well-trained bird and an expert falconer.

The challenger took the eagle's jesses from the man and coaxed her over until she stood on his arm. He slowly removed her hood, speaking softly to her.

Ahmed handed my father the caged quail. "Whenever you are ready to release, your highness."

My father's face was pinched, lips pursed as he looked from the golden eagle to his quail. He opened the cage and shoved his hand in, grasping the frightened bird. He held the weightless creature to his mouth and closed his eyes, murmuring his words for Masira.

The challenger continued to whisper to Anisa as he carefully untied her jesses.

"Go to the goddess," my father called, throwing the quail above him. It fluttered its wings, panicking at the enclosed space, flying in jerks and spasms above the crowd, who yelped when the bird came too close. We waited for the quail to find its way out and carry the King's message to the sky. But it was frightened by the people and the confinement. So instead, it made tight, panicked circles above the King.

"Go to the goddess," the challenger said, and the eagle stretched her wings, and flapped them once, twice, then rose from the man's arm. She was not alarmed by the enclosed space, at the spectators who screamed and ducked when she neared them. She knew her exit. Hovering above the crowd, she glided to the opposite side of the tent, gaining speed, then circled around. We all watched the predator with wonder, and I held my breath as I watched to see her fly out into the day, into the sky.

Her wings beat slowly, but her flight was swift. She headed to the opening, and I waited to see her disappear. But then she rose up and snatched the quail from its panicked flight with her great claws. She drifted out of the tent, her easy prey held tightly by her sharp talons, and vanished into the day.

The crowd was silent. Never before had the King been unable to give word to Masira. It was an ominous sign.

"I won't continue like this," the King barked, glaring at Nassar, at Ahmed. He stepped from the challenger and unsheathed his scimitar. "I wish for this to end," he cried into the air.

There it was again: a wish. The Salt King touched his belt, looking for the jinni's prison I had stolen from him. I reached into my sack and cupped it in my palm, watching the filtered sunlight glint off the etched flowers and moon. My father would never have shown his face in battle if he knew his jinni was gone.

What an elaborate deception this was. My father was a doll on strings in Masira's wicked hands. What a fool he had been to hold on to the jinni for so long. Masira had been patient, calculating. Like a scorpion waiting in the sand to seize Her prey.

The King spun when nothing happened, stumbling slightly in the uneven sand. He peered around the room. "I wish for this to end!" He screamed. Spit flew from his lips, his cheeks purpled as he grew enraged.

The challenger pulled his sword from his waist and held it ready.

"Where is he?" the King shouted, backing away from the long blade. "Where is he?" He turned around, looking from face to face. The rage that had consumed him was like fire without oil, and it dwindled quickly, fear taking its place. His eyes narrowed as he examined his own people suspiciously, rolling his shoulders forward in a protective posture as he realized just how vulnerable he was.

"He is mad," one villager said loudly to another.

"What has gotten into him?"

"Too much wine!"

The villagers mumbled to each other in their confusion. This was not the behavior of the King they knew.

Despite every aching pang of grief that had racked me that morning, I smiled.

Ah, Masira. What a cunning goddess She was when crafting destiny. To take and take and take, but then to leave just a little, just enough. How wickedly cruel it was to take from my father his only confidant, to erase Nassar's existence in the eyes of the King's people, and to leave those memories intact for my father alone. To take from him the foundation of his strength, the fountain of his power, his jinni, and to leave him with only the memories. So that he, too, could feel what it was to be laid bare. To feel the terror of vulnerability and the degradation of being power-less to another.

"Let us end this," the challenger announced, and he stepped toward the King.

The man moved like a shadow across the room. Years of training had taught him how to swing the sword, and a lifetime of living in the desert had taught him how to navigate the sand. He moved effortlessly.

"No! Stop this!" The King backed away from his pursuer. "I wish for this to be stopped at once!"

The spectators lining the ring opposite me stepped away from the King as he neared them, but the crowd was dense. They could not retreat further. The King got closer and closer, until finally, one man pushed the King's back so he tripped forward into the arena.

"Fight, you coward," a villager cried.

And just like that, the loyalty to their king was lost. Life in the desert is not one that makes allowances for valueless allegiances. Desert rulers played a game of strength, and the people followed its victors. If they did not, they, too, might die. When their ruler was a ruthless tyrant, the choice was even easier. When they saw their king's weakness, they were quick to abandon him. Surely, some even took joy in it.

"Fleeing like a mouse!"

"Eiqab will guide us to the true champion!"

"A fool!"

"Kill him!"

The hunter approached his prey, swinging his sword elegantly through the air. This match was too easy for him; he would play with his food. Swiftly, he wielded the sword around him. Its fine point sliced across the top of the King's golden turban, knocking it to the ground in an unraveled pile.

The King brandished his scimitar, wagging it back and forth before the challenger as he spat powerless words at him. The man swung his sword overhead and heaved it down onto the King, who defended the blow. The clash of metal rang out into the tent, silencing the whispers and shouts of the fickle villagers.

The people watched as the men swung their blades, the King's training as a youth returning to him as he parried several more of the man's swings.

But there was only so much that a sick, drunk, and weakened King could do to evade the blade of a young, well-trained attacker. Soon, a slash of silver sliced down into the soft spot between the King's neck and shoulder.

An agonized scream tore from the Salt King. He dropped his sword and fell to his knees. Wordless, he reached up to his wound as the blood spilled into his ivory robes. The challenger's back was to me, so I could not see his face, but I could see my father's. He looked at his bloodied hand, horrified, before he looked to the man standing before him.

The blade of his sword left a trail through the sand as he approached the King. With his other hand, he reached up and unwrapped his ghutra from his head and neck.

"I want you to see the man who has brought you to your knees," he hissed. Had the tent not been so quiet, I would not have heard the hushed words. A desert wind blowing over the sands.

Terror, deep and far-reaching as the ocean, transformed my father's face when he saw his challenger. And it stayed there as he made the last choice he would ever be allowed—he begged. He dropped his gaze to the ground and placed his palm into the sand while his other arm curled into his chest.

"Please," the King mewled into the sand. "Be merciful. Spare me!" The King babbled his pleas, his eyes searching those of us who stood at the circle's perimeter.

As his gaze neared me, I stepped forward, slowly pulling my own scarf from my face. It was a small step, a tiny movement, unnoticeable to others who stared at their king, but it was enough to draw my father's attention. With a wry smile, I pulled my hand from my sack and turned my hand over so that my father could see the item I cupped in my palm.

So that he could see that I had the jinni's prison.

That I had won.

His face paled when he saw what I held, when he recognized who I was. When he realized everything he had lost.

The challenger said, "Anisa did not let your bird carry your message to the goddess, so I will let you tell Her yourself. Masira sees not the moving; She devours only the souls of the stilled. I will hurry so that you can take your journey to her sky, if She will even receive you."

The King still stared at me, his mouth agape. Did he hear the challenger's words? Did he know what came? The man raised his sword over his head and plunged it through the King's back, pinning him to the sand.

The villagers stared in stunned silence as their king ended his thirty years of reign by vomiting blood into the sand that had birthed him. The strongest King of the desert. The King who would never fall.

They were shocked, but they were not stupid. The silence gave way to cheers for their new king. Many were quick to leave the great tent and palace, wanting to be the first to share the news. Their excitement spilled out into the village. The men who guarded the Salt King's throne room, his keep, and his quarters, along with all the villagers who remained in their homes, swiftly heard the cries of the finished battle.

"A new king!" the people shouted through the streets.

Some of the old king's wives and children cried, others simply stared, dumbfounded at their slain husband, their murdered ruler.

I felt nothing.

"Bow before your king!" Nassar thundered into the tent as he held the flag of his people aloft.

One by one, the villagers and ivory-clad guards kneeled as though pressed down by the gods' hands. I followed, the people nearly on top of each other as we found the space. I stared at the ground, my mind reeling at the motive of this new ruler. The Dalmur thought they accomplished their aim. Yes, Father was dead, but that which they sought was gone. Why had the threads of fate failed to guide these men back home? Back to where I hoped Saalim sat upon a carved throne in a stone palace beside the sea.

"My people." Our new king's voice rang out like thunder. The venomous malice had left his words, and in its gentleness, there was a familiarity that snagged my attention. "You may rise."

Slowly, we did. I desperately tried to see our new ruler, but still, I could only see his back. His brown hair was shorn at his shoulders, and it fell down in sweaty strands by his neck.

Several of his guards approached him carrying large trunks. The people parted for them swiftly. The men set the trunks at their ruler's feet, and our new king dropped to his knees and opened them. They were filled with salt.

His shoulders tightened as his fingers trailed through the white crystals.

"This has been stolen from me, and now the price has been paid. You may return to your families, but carry with you tales of his treachery and what happens to those who take what they do not earn." He spoke sharply to the spectators who remained, staring angrily at the salt in the trunks.

People filed out of the tent, sifting through the palace, their voices growing quieter and quieter, until they had returned to their homes. With some of my father's guards and the foreign men, our new king left.

The rest of my father's guard, my sisters and I, our mothers and their young children stayed behind. Tavi found me.

"What do we do now?" she asked, "Where will we go?"

The voices of my family grew louder as they all began asking each other the same. No one knew what came next.

"If no one comes, we return home," I said. "Then, we wait until we hear word from the king."

"I can't believe Father is gone."

We looked at the ground where our father was slain. Now, there was only red-stained sand, and a path leading from the puddle to the outside. The new king's men had dragged his corpse out into the desert. They, at least, had given him the gift of a sky burial. It was not something Father would have gone out of his way to do for them.

Tavi said, "Emel, would you think me a monster if I told you I don't feel sad?"

"Only if you promise you won't think the same of me," I said.

"What will happen to us?"

"I don't know, but we will withstand it."

We joined our sisters, watched their fear multiply as they shared their worries with each other. My sisters did not know how to be anything but ahiran. What if we were asked to do something else? We grew restless, considered returning to our homes, when finally, the king and white-clad guards entered the tent again.

"These were his wives and children, his daughters—the ahiran," the guard said. "They belong to you now. What will you have us do with them?"

As the king approached us, I could see him wholly. Despite the dust of the desert and wear of the sun, I could tell he was young. The sharp angles of his tanned face, his long, straight nose, and roughly bearded jaw was unmistakably familiar. Even his hair, now that I saw him straight on . . .

Impossible.

The king scanned our faces, his eyes briefly passing over us, unseeing.

"Send them home. I don't keep women from conquests," he spat. A roguish smile emerged on his lips. "Though if some are willing . . ."

His men laughed, and the king's eyes flicked around the women and landed on me.

Ice drove straight through my spine when our eyes met because, even from where I stood, I could not mistake his eyes were the color of liquid gold. The same eyes that my father looked into before he died.

Surely, he had recognized them too.

A rush of hope rose in me. My hands shook, my heart thundered against the roar of blood in my ears. *It can't be.*

But then he turned from me and continued to appraise the women before him, like I was just another ahira, indistinct and unmemorable. My hope plummeted, the pain of my loss, my heartbreak aching anew. He did not recognize me at all. *Even if I was within an arm's reach of you, I wouldn't know you.*

"I will soon return to my home in the north." His tone had changed. He sounded almost kind. No, not kind. Obliging. He was fulfilling his role as our new king. "I have enough camels and stores to take you to my home if you desire it. It is a large city, called Madinat Almulihi. There is enough work and lodging for everyone."

He continued. "Though you are not my daughters nor wives, I have taken from you your father and husband, and I recognize my duty to provide you shelter and a life of at least nominal comforts. Should you choose to make the passage with me and my men, I warn you it is not an easy journey— forty days on foot with dangers beyond the harshness of the desert.

"If you choose to stay, I will leave you with a small sum of coin so that you may attempt to forge a life for yourself, as you will be asked to leave the palace."

Tavi gripped my arm tightly and leaned into my ear. "Do we dare? Have we found a way out?" I looked at her, confused by her meaning. Out of the palace? Her eyes were so bright, so full of optimism, they softened my ache. Tavi, brave as our mother, quicker to see it than me. She was right, this was our chance to leave the settlement.

The goddess had not ignored me after all. She heard me, and She listened. I had wished for freedom from the Salt King, and I was given just that. My father was gone, the monster put to death at last.

"You would leave here?" I asked, disbelieving that this was my same sister who had chastised me for wishing for the same.

"If you are with me, yes." Her radiant smile was infectious. "A city larger than ours? Just think of all the food!" She giggled, and I couldn't help it. I laughed, too.

We were free.

The softest tingling spread from my shoulders to my fingers, from my spine to my toes. I grinned to myself, laughter bubbling from my lips again.

There would be no loveless future bound to a man who paid to have me. I would choose my path, and I would choose my love.

Before me, clothed in fabric of the night sky and draped in the color of his ocean, was Saalim, my new king. He was not the man I knew, but I could not lose hope that somewhere within him was the man I loved.

Masira had not abandoned me. She had rid us of a vile King and, in doing so, had given me the world.

But I was greedy, and I wanted more.

I had promised Saalim I would fight for him, and I would not renege on a promise.

I had vowed that I would have a life that was whole, one that I chose for myself, and I would not break that vow.

I was done giving. It was my turn to take. And I would get what I wanted.

Following my sisters from the tent, I turned back once more to Saalim. He stood with his arms crossed, talking not to his guards, not to Nassar, not to the lingering women.

He was silent and still, his gaze clinging to me.

EPILOGUE

Saalim

S AND SWIRLED IN THE WINE DREGS at the bottom of my goblet, and it crunched between my teeth, too. The damn dirt was everywhere, and I was sick of it. Slamming the goblet down, I turned to Nassar.

He and Amir sat across from me in the throne room. I stifled a scoff. This tent, a throne room?

"Start over," I said, interrupting their discussion of the village and our departure.

Nassar glared at me, never shy about letting me know his displeasure. "I suggest you listen this time, my king."

I waved him off then turned to Amir.

Amir shifted on his stool and summarized what I had missed. "Our caravan will be ready to leave tomorrow at dusk. We need to determine who will stay behind and govern."

Looking at Nassar, I smirked. "Your chance is here, my old friend." I had been surprised by how quickly Nassar understood the motives and mores of these village people. It was almost as if he had once lived amongst them.

Nassar's eyes narrowed, and he brushed unseen sand from his sleeve. "I'd rather milk one hundred camels than stay in this Wahir-forsaken desert."

"Disgusting animals," I agreed, thinking of the journey back to Madinat Almulihi, during which I'd once again be surrounded by them. Flies flocked as though they were rotting fruit, and Sons, the smell.

Amir cleared his throat.

I looked away from a soot-blackened lantern. "We will settle this tonight. Tell the men to meet at dinner, and we can elect someone. Do you think Usman would be willing?"

Nassar and Amir guffawed and gave each other knowing looks.

"What is it?" Did I even want to know?

"Usman would be willing, I think," Amir said while trying to hold his grin at bay.

Nassar giggled. "More than willing! Just remind him that he'd be staying here with the daughters."

I had forgotten that Usman with women was a like a starved man for meat. "Fine, fine." I sighed, watching my men laugh like girls. The desert was driving them to madness, too. "Leave me. We will finish this tonight when everyone can have their say."

They left mumbling things I could not hear. I pressed my eyes closed when they had gone and leaned back in the ridiculous throne —gold and silver twisted into the hardest and most uncomfortable chair I'd ever sat upon. Again, I considered the man who sat here before me.

On our journey to the settlement we had encountered nomads who willingly shared with me rumors of Alfaar. The Salt King, they called him. They said he was the strongest king of the desert and that I would perish under his blade. They told me his village was built on salt bricks and his people were as loyal to him as worshippers of the Sons.

Alone in the room, I allowed myself to laugh aloud.

I studied the tent walls. Perhaps once they were white, but now they were a terrible yellow, filthy from the years of oil and dust that collected in the fibers. I looked at the ground, covered in derelict rugs, the threads of which had pulled loose at the edges. Some were even threadbare at the center. Would not a king of so much wealth be able to have new rugs woven upon request? Or could he not see the wear? I picked up the goblet—tarnished silver, its surface scratched from the sand and uncaring hands. Did they not even have someone to polish their silver? Alfaar's absurd throne, shining like a false sun, sat in the middle of it all.

It reeked of vulnerability—of a fragile mind and an even more frail rule of law.

I had not known the man, but from what I saw of him prior to his execution and in my days in his palace—tents, rather—I felt like I'd known him for years. Alfaar was no Salt King with his crown of stolen treasure. He was no god, even if he and his people fancied himself one.

He was vermin, and he deserved to die squealing as such.

It was coming again, the gnawing sense of isolation. Of being alone. It came in waves, at once suffocating, then suddenly gone again. I stood and paced around the room—empty save the throne and few stools. The salt had been locked away, Alfaar's guards long since sent home.

The first time I felt it was when one of Alfaar's sons had taken me through the palace. He had shown me where I could sleep, since I'd refused that vile man's quarters. The son had said it was a room used by the ahiran to court men.

The feeling had come then, swift and from unknown depths like a squall. It swept through me. Looking at the small room, garish with bright fabrics as worn as the rest of the palace, and knowing what Alfaar had forced his daughters to do, allowed his guests to do to his children, I felt nauseated. I thought of Edala and Nadia—Masira carry their souls—whom my mother and father taught to stand with faces turned up, the word "no" always falling from their tongues. My mother and father who protected us first. Sons, how I wished they would be sitting in the palace when I returned home.

Thinking of my own family, the nausea subsided, but still remaining was the sense that I was alone. It was not that I had my family no longer—that grief felt different. No, it was something else, and it was inscrutable.

It was as though I was missing something indispensable. Like the space left when the ocean's waves pulled back and no other waves replaced them.

It must be home. I had been away for too long. I needed to return to Almulihi. Tomorrow, I reminded myself. Tomorrow, we would leave, and surely being home would fill the void that seemed to have opened upon being here.

I tried to find my way back to my room. The assemblage of the palace tents so convoluted and careless, I was not surprised when I found myself in one of the passageways outside instead. A servant stood a ways down the lane, so I strode forward to ask her how to find my way back.

The servant saw me nearing and rushed into a tent with a squeak of alarm. I regretted sending so many of the guards home. They, at least, would have been willing to show me the way.

Sighing, I kept walking. Despite the heat, the air was preferable to the stuffy tents. As I rounded the corner, I saw two of Alfaar's guards ahead, their backs turned to me.

"Excuse me," I said. The men turned and separated.

I saw then that they spoke a woman. Her face was uncovered, scarf draped over her hair. I should not have recognized her, but the way she watched me was unforgettable. Her eyes were as black as her father's, yet unlike her father, she stared at me without flinching.

The guards bowed, and as though an afterthought, the woman bowed, too, barely taking her eyes from me.

And I could not look away from her.

"My king," one of the guards said. "Is there something you need?"

Still, I stared at the woman. She watched me like she knew me. Her black eyes liquid and shining—with what? Sadness? Did she see me as a murderer? No, that did not fit with the softness I saw there. What was she thinking? Suddenly, I was uneasy—not with fear, but rather, curiosity.

Her mouth parted as if to speak. *Her mouth.* I dropped my eyes to her lips, bowed like a soaring bird's wings. Something in me stirred, and then she spoke. "King Saalim."

The way she said my name. *Say it again.*

"Are you lost?" she asked.

No, not anymore.

Yes, help me.

I shook my head, casting off the traitorous thoughts. What was wrong with me? With the greatest effort, I tore my gaze from the woman and looked to one of the guards, explaining that I needed to find my room.

"I can take him," the woman said, stepping forward.

Too quickly, I replied, "Very well." She was closer now. If I reached out I could touch her. If I did, would I understand her—this feeling? With the thought of my fingers on her shoulder, the stirring returned.

One of the guards turned to the woman with shock and shook his head. "No, Emel. I will."

Emel. I wanted to taste the word as it passed through my lips, but my mouth remained sealed.

The guard was right. It would be highly improper. Without looking at her again—I did not dare lest I stay pinned forever to the sand by her gaze—I followed the man to my room.

Sitting at the edge of the mat, I thought of the woman and what Alfaar had forced upon her, upon all of his daughters. What had the woman been like as an ahira? Did she acquiesce? The idea was irreconcilable with what I saw after I became their king and what I saw today.

The ahiran had huddled together in the tent after their father had been slain. Not one had wept like some of his wives had. They simply watched us with wide eyes, nervously flicking away their gaze when I looked at them. They were diffident, wary—pathetic things shaped by their father's foul hands. Even I felt a twinge of sorrow when I saw them, knowing what their life had been. But not the woman. Not Emel. In the way she held her shoulders, her head, she allowed no room for pity.

"Emel," I said aloud. There it was—the stirring and longing and loneliness—humming there like a sitar long after the string had been plucked.

Nassar warned me that few of Alfaar's family would take the journey to Almulihi. It would be too much for them, he had said. Their lives were too sheltered. They would be scared to journey outside. I hoped he was wrong and that some would come. They had been gifted with an opportunity that would likely not present itself again. How else would they leave their settlement, if not with my caravan?

Would Emel join us? I lay back on the bed, thinking of her eyes.

It was like she knew something about me. Like she carried secrets that I should know.

I wanted to know those secrets.

"Emel," I said once more. The ache grew like a wave. I shook my head, pressing my fingers to my brow. This desert would propel me to madness. Praise Wahir, I would begin the journey home tomorrow. I could not spend more time thinking of Alfaar's broken family and crumbled home.

I would not waste time thinking of eyes that were dark as a moonless night, that stared with a terrifying intimacy, eyes that seemed to hollow me further and steer me toward what, I couldn't say.

Trails of destruction still remained in Madinat Alumulihi. The ashes of my dead family just barely lost to the sea.

I could not be distracted by vague feelings and a black-eyed woman when I had to find those who destroyed my family, tried to take from me my home.

The current of the sea was pulling me back. I could almost hear the wind whispering its plea. Home called with my people who waited for me.

Madinat Almulihi needed their king.

And I needed my revenge.

WATCH FOR THE SEQUEL IN 2022

Son of the Salt Chaser

Saalim, now a king, pursues revenge against the invaders who murdered his family while the forgotten Emel, her beloved's memory of her stolen by her own desert-transforming wish, travels to his kingdom by the sea to reclaim what was lost.

ACKNOWLEDGMENTS

Where do I even begin to show my gratitude for the people who allowed my dream to become a reality? Let me start right here and work backwards: thank you, reader, for picking up this book and making it all the way to the end. I can write as many stories as I want, but having you read it means more to me than I can say.

To the entire CamCat Books team who allowed my book to be more than pages of printer paper bound by my local copy store, thank you. In particular, an enormous thank you to Cassandra Farrin who was so delicate and dead-on in her edits and suggestions. This book would not be what it is if it weren't for you. Words do not suffice to thank you adequately. To Maryann Appel who did the most beautiful work designing this book. You were generous in your tolerance of my incessant and often unsolicited opinions of the design. Thank you. And finally, to Sue Arroyo. For calling me "honey" and "sweetie" and making me feel welcome from the very

beginning. I love being a part of your CamCat family, and I cannot thank you enough for having me.

Dayna Anderson is the reason this book is in your hands. Dayna, thank you for "liking" my Twitter pitch and seeing the potential in my unpolished manuscript. You were the original champion of this book, and I will never forget the gift you have given me. Thank you, thank you, thank you.

To the early readers of this novel that didn't shy away from providing me blunt and valuable feedback, thank you. Not only did you allow me to make this story better, you gave me so much of your time when you agreed to read my novel. Giving me your free time is a precious gift, and I want you to know it did not go unappreciated.

I would be remiss not to thank the people that inspired me to write—the online book community. Through my blog and social media, I connected with all of you and found a place that I didn't realize I needed to be until I was there. The bookish world is my second home, so thank you for inviting me in to share your favorite books, gush over the same book boyfriends and girlfriends, share your own writing experiences, and be my bookish besties. Internet friends are real friends, and I have found so many friends in you.

Lastly, an enormous thank you to my husband. For all the days that you did the housework so I could write. For reading my romantic fantasy more times that you can count, even though you don't enjoy romance. For encouraging me to keep going after every rejection, critique, and bad review. And finally, for being the Atlas of our world–your strength is enough for all of us.

ABOUT THE AUTHOR

Evolving from book blogger to author, A. S. Thornton has a particular fondness for writing forbidden love in ancient deserts.

She lives with her husband who deserves a trophy for the amount of gooey love scenes he's edited. After spending time in Chicago and Colorado, they decided the snow is wholly overrated, and settled in Northern California.

When not writing, she's taking care of dogs and cats as a veterinarian. You'll never find animals at the center of her writing, though. Those fictional worlds don't have veterinarians and her literal brain can't accept that the poor critters would be without parasite prevention.

www.asthornton.com
Instagram @as_thornton

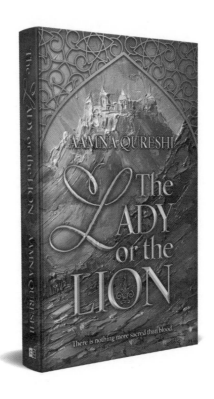

MORE FROM CAMCAT BOOKS

THE LADY OR THE LION
by Aamna Qureshi

A Pakistan-inspired fantasy, retelling the story of *The Lady or the Tiger?*, in which a fiercely loyal princess tries to prove her grandfather's innocence in an attack on neighboring leaders, while she navigates forbidden love and court intrigues alongside the handsome ambassador determined to prove her wrong.

THE TRIAL

T HE APPOINTED HOUR ARRIVED.

From across the mountain, the people gathered into the galleries of the arena. Though considered a barbaric custom in the nineteenth century, the trial by tribunal was tradition. It was with sick fascination that the villagers filled the seats, the overflowing crowds amassing themselves outside the amphitheater walls.

The sky was a murky grey above them; summer was over. A breeze travelled through the air, and the villagers shivered, clutching their shawls and their children close. The chatter and clamor ebbed to hushed whispers as the Badshah entered the arena at its height, where his ornate throne awaited him. His bearded face was stoic and severe: his lips pressed into a thin line, his eyes sharp. The onlookers lowered their heads in respect as he took his seat. His wife, the Wali, sat beside him. A low murmur pulsed through the crowd as one more took her seat beside the Badshah.

It was the Shehzadi.

The low chum-chum of chudiyan echoed through the arena as she moved toward her throne, her blood-red gharara trailing behind her. Her golden crown glistened, bright and shining as her blue-green eyes.

She held her chin high, proud as ever, as she took her seat. The villagers had not expected her to come. How she could stomach such an affair was beyond them! To see one's lover torn to shreds or thrust to another was no easy sight. Yet, there she sat, directly beside her grandfather. They sat directly opposite the two doors, those fateful portals, so hideous in their sameness.

All was ready. The signal was given.

At the base of the arena, a door opened to reveal the lover of the Shehzadi. Tall, beautiful, strong: his appearance elicited a low hum of admiration and anxiety from the audience.

The young man advanced into the arena, his back straight. As he approached the doors, the crowds silenced. A crow cried in the distance, and the lover turned. He bowed to the king, as was custom, but his gaze was fixed entirely upon the Shehzadi. The sight of him seared through her.

He reached for her, she reached for him, but their hands did not touch: they were tangled in the stars between them, destiny keeping them apart.

From the instant the decree had gone forth to seize her lover to trial, she hadn't spent a second thinking of anything else. And thus she had done what no other had done—she had possessed herself of the secret of the doors.

Now, the decision was hers to make. Should she send him to the lady? So that he may live his days with another, leaving the Shehzadi to her envy and her grief? Or should he be sent to the lion? Who would surely tear him to shreds before she had a moment to regret her decision?

Either way, they could never be together.

Then, his quick glance asked the question: *"Which?"*

There was not an instant to be lost. The question was asked in a flash; it had to be answered in another.

It was time to seal both his fate and hers.

1

DURKHANAI MIANGUL HEARD the bell echoing throughout the mountains. Her hand lay atop her grandmother's, the Wali of S'vat, whose hand lay atop her grandfather's, the Badshah of Marghazar. Together, they three had rung the bell to alert the tribespeople of foreign entrance into their land.

For the first time in centuries, the capital city of Safed-Mahal was opening its doors to foreigners, those from their neighboring districts.

Coming to harm her family.

The sound resonated through the mountains, in cacophony with crows crying. It was said that crows brought visitors with them, and as a child, Durkhanai was always excited to see who would visit her castle in the clouds.

But today, she knew the visitors would bring turmoil. While entrance throughout Marghazar was permissible, sparingly, for trade, entrance into the capital Safed-Mahal had been forbidden for centuries.

Until now.

"It is done," Agha-Jaan said, his old face flushed florid from the wind.

"Yes, jaanan," Dhadi said somberly. "Now we prepare."

Durkhanai was clad in a pistachio-green lengha choli, her ears and neck dripping emeralds and pearls encased in pure gold. The ensemble made her eyes more green than blue and her skin a soft brown. Beside her, her grandparents were dressed in bottle green: her grandfather in a sherwani, her grandmother in a silk sari.

Maroon red mehndi covered Durkhanai's hands in flowery details of blooming roses. Her curly hair was swept up in an updo with ringlets framing her face in front of her dupatta, which sat atop her head and fell down one shoulder.

She was the essence of a princess, but she would need to be more to protect her people. Wind slapped her cold on both cheeks, turning her nose numb: up in the bell tower, there was no spring. It was the beginning of April, when the world cracked open its shell to let greens and pinks begin to spool out. The weather was softer, warmer.

From here, she saw the great expanse of lands she was heir to, the jewels of the earth. The palace was on the side of the mountain, with views of both the empty valleys and the populated ones.

On one populated mountain, she saw two waterfalls, and while ordinarily the glittering water brought her peace, today the two holes punctured in the mountain flowed water like eyes flowing with tears. In the distance of the unpopulated lands, she could almost see the blue green S'vat river, which protected them in the north from the Kebzu Kingdom.

Now, for the first time, they would need protection from those within their lands.

Ya Khuda, protect us, she prayed.

They waited for the bell to quiet, the valley to turn silent. Then, hand in hand, her grandparents made their way to the door, to head back down to the palace below.

"Come," Agha-Jaan motioned for her to come.

"Just a moment longer," she responded. "I want to make dua."

Her grandfather nodded, allowing her solace, and she was alone.

"Ya Allah," she prayed. "You are the Protector of all people, so please, protect my people. Bless us, forgive us, let no harm come to us. Ameen."

She blew onto all her lands, the homes that dotted the mountains, praying her people and her country would stay safe from those who were coming.

"I will protect you," she promised her people. It was her sacred duty to protect this land. With a final glance, she went back down to her palace, to prepare.

A banquet had been arranged for the ambassadors, and Durkhanai had to change to get ready for it. The defenses were up, but their greatest defense was their behavior: they had to act absolutely unbothered by any of this and entirely innocent—which they were.

They were to be kind—but with an undercurrent of cruelty.

As Durkhanai walked to her rooms, she noticed a man walking alone in her hall, his fingers dancing along the windowsill. She paused, blinking.

Who was he? More importantly, what was he doing here?

Durkhanai approached until she stood beside him. Noting her presence, he turned and smiled at her, his black eyes molten and warm, hiding a thousand emotions and layers.

"And you are?" she prompted.

He smiled an easy smile.

"Ambassador Asfandyar of the Afridi tribe of Jardum," he said. His deep voice was stone: ragged and solid. "Pleased to meet you."

He lowered his head with respect, but a smirk tugged at his lips. Durkhanai frowned.

From what she knew, the Jardum people were courageous and rebellious. They were good fighters who were pragmatic in picking their battles and making alliances.

She didn't even know him, but she knew he would be trouble.

Sudden anger flashed through her: she had known the foreigners were coming, but now that they were here, in her home, the irritation was thrice folded. And in her halls!

This would not do.

"How pleasing indeed for you, ambassador," she said, voice clipped, "that such an egregious occasion has arisen to force Marghazar's hand into welcoming your sorry hides into our pure lands."

He met her glare with an easy half-smile, nearly laughing.

"Forced your hand?" he drawled. "And here we were under the assumption the mighty Marghazari couldn't be forced to anything."

Her breath caught. She had slipped.

She had let her temper get the better of her, when she knew she was supposed to be fawning over the ambassadors with sweetness to prove her grandfather's innocence.

Her cheeks burned.

Worse still, he had twisted her words and was looking at her like she was as non-threatening as a child. It tore at the insecurity deep within her that told her she would only be a pretty little fool: beloved, yet useless.

Decorum be damned. In that moment, she felt less the sweet rose petals, and more the deadly thorns.

"Haven't you any manners?" she asked, a bite to the words. She had never been anything but loved and adored, and the way he looked at her made her heart freeze over. "You will speak to your princess with respect, ambassador, lest I have to cut off your tongue."

"Princess?"

He raised a brow, mock surprised. He cocked his head to the side, looking at her intently. She wanted to point out that she was, in fact, dressed as one, and how daft he must truly be to not realize, but she refrained from doing so. Instead, she lifted her chin.

CamCat Books

VISIT US ONLINE FOR MORE BOOKS TO LIVE IN:
CAMCATBOOKS.COM

CamCatBooks   @CamCatBooks   @CamCat_Books   @CamCatBooks